SO GOOD TO SEE YOU

Also by Francesca Hornak

Seven Days of Us

History of the World in 100 Modern Objects

Worry with Mother

SO GOOD TO SEE YOU

a novel

FRANCESCA HORNAK

PEGASUS BOOKS
NEW YORK LONDON

SO GOOD TO SEE YOU

Pegasus Books, Ltd.
148 West 37th Street, 13th Floor
New York, NY 10018

Copyright © 2025 by Francesca Hornak

First Pegasus Books cloth edition July 2025

All rights reserved. No part of this book may be reproduced in whole or in part without written permission from the publisher, except by reviewers who may quote brief excerpts in connection with a review in a newspaper, magazine, or electronic publication; nor may any part of this book be reproduced, stored in a retrieval system, or transmitted in any form or by any means electronic, mechanical, photocopying, recording, or other, or used to train generative artificial intelligence (AI) technologies, without written permission from the publisher.

ISBN: 978-1-63936-911-9

10 9 8 7 6 5 4 3 2 1

Printed in the United States of America
Distributed by Simon & Schuster
www.pegasusbooks.com

For Luke

Oxford, June 2004

Three undergraduates are sitting in a beer garden, wearing black tie. On their table are tickets to St Arthur's College ball. The garden is full of other students due to attend the same event – young men interchangeable in their suits, girls' make-up too visible in the late afternoon light. The air is thick with aftershave and anticipation.

At the table, one of the three undergraduates is recounting an awkward moment with an American visiting student. The two men opposite her laugh, as her eyes squeeze shut with re-enacted embarrassment.

'Like, I've never even remotely flirted with him!' she says, one narrow palm on her sternum. Her voice is like a newsreader's on double speed, her hands fluttering everywhere like birds.

'Rosie, you flirt with everyone! Men, women, children. Cats,' says one of the men.

'Daniel Pyke! You literally flirt with mirrors.'

'Takes one to know one.'

The other man at the table, Caspar, says, 'How do I not know this American guy?'

'You do,' says Rosie. 'Nate. His room's on my landing. Curly hair. But he's never in college. He hangs out with the other international students.'

'What does he look like?' says Caspar. 'Besides hair? Is he fit?'

'He's, um, quite skinny.'

Daniel says: 'Nate Kennedy, yes sir,' in an East Coast accent, narrowing his eyes and grinning. The impression is uncanny rather than cruel, as though he has briefly become another person.

'Oh, *that* guy,' says Caspar. 'Gotcha.'

Another young man approaches the table, people greeting him or stepping aside so he can pass. He is very tall, and wearing Reebok Classics with his black tie. He has the same permanently surprised blue eyes as Caspar – his cousin.

Daniel opens his arms wide.

'Sergio! Last night in this dump, mate! We're going large.'

They greet one another with a mid-air arm-wrestle, clearly lifted from a film, revealing Serge's monogrammed cufflinks.

'Looking sharp, guys,' he says, surveying the table.

His gaze rests on Rosie. Her pupils dilate.

'Where's your sister, mate?' says Daniel, as Serge sits down. 'She's staying this weekend, right?'

'Still getting ready,' says Serge. 'Which could take hours. Told her to come and find us.'

He blurs some, but not all, of his private school consonants, inadvertently making them more conspicuous.

'Don't get any ideas,' he adds.

Daniel looks at him with mock affront.

Rosie pours Serge a glass of Pimm's, and tops up everyone else's drinks.

When Daniel puts his glass down only ice remains.

'Rosie just friend-zoned that American guy, Nate,' he says to Serge.

Serge raises his eyebrows at Rosie. Her face reddens.

'So then what? After he lunged?' says Caspar.

'We had tea. In my room.'

'Jesus! Now he'll think he's still in with a chance.'

'We always have tea. That's how we became friends.'

'Guess you'll never see him again, anyway,' says Caspar.

Rosie looks suddenly wistful, as if this finality had not occurred to her.

'But *can* a man and woman be friends?' says Daniel.

'Pikey's going deep,' says Serge, approvingly. '*When Harry Met Sally.*'

'Not if he went to a boys' school,' says Rosie. 'Which Nate didn't.'

'So you and I aren't friends?' says Serge, looking at her.

'Single-sex schools must be so fucked up,' says Daniel. 'I'd have gone mental without girls.'

'They are,' says Serge. 'You missed out, man. The masters would've loved you.'

'Piss off, Sergio,' says Daniel, jovially. 'So is this why *I'm* still in the friend zone?' he adds, looking at Rosie. 'Cos I went to a sink school in Essex?'

'You had your chance.'

Daniel winks at her, and she looks at him like a tiresome sibling.

'Wait, what?' says Serge, looking from Daniel to Rosie. 'When was *this*?'

He is smiling, but his eyes look rattled.

'Freshers' week,' says Caspar. 'At the school uniform bop. How did you not know that?'

'He wasn't there. Too cool for that shit,' says Daniel. 'Right, Sergio?'

Serge laughs and says, 'Can't believe I never knew you two got it on!'

'We didn't "get it on"! We got it out the way. It was literally a two minute snog,' says Rosie.

'I'm too common for her,' says Daniel, grinning. 'And too short.'

Rosie gives him the sibling look again.

'Genuinely,' says Daniel. 'I had to sit on a bar stool to reach her. I remember it well.'

Conversation moves on to the fact that freshers' week still feels recent, and the startling truth that their time at university is over. The sky flares shocking pink.

They all speak with the easy assumption they will remain in each other's lives.

PART ONE

NOVEMBER 2016
TWELVE YEARS AFTER GRADUATION

From: Caspar.Campbell@gmail.com
To: RosieLittleton81@gmail.com
Date: 13 November, 2016, 07.50
Subject: Serge

Hi hi, what's up with your phone? Can you call me? It's about Serge ... Bummer you can't join me and Daniel tonight. Sack off your folks!

Cx

Serge's Bedroom

10 Chiltern Mansions

8 a.m.

Rosie wrote three drafts, before she was satisfied. The final note said: 'Morning . . . Had to leave for my sister's thing, didn't want to wake you. Good luck with the new film x'.

She knew she could have sent these words as a text. But her phone was out of battery, and the situation – in daylight – had a sordid quality that she hoped a handwritten note would elevate. It was intentionally bland, anything more might have implied feelings or expectations.

She placed the note on Serge's bedside table, and studied his handsome face in the half-light. With his extravagant eyes closed he looked sterner than he did awake. The rim of his ear was fierily pink, like a conch shell. It still struck her as endearingly human.

The previous evening they had met at Serge's local pub. This was their first contact since he had abruptly ended their relationship, two months earlier. Rosie had broken this silence – which she had instigated – on the pretext of returning a bag of his things. It contained an A.P.C. jumper, a copy of *Why I'm No Longer Talking to White People About Race* and some Bose headphones. These were the only possessions of his she had acquired, after two years as a couple. It had been a running joke that Serge never stayed at her flat.

They had settled into their preferred sofa in the pub, where it was as velvety and low-lit as ever. After a bottle of red wine they had gone back to his flat, so that Serge could return items of hers, and started kissing in the customary spot in the kitchen. Then they had moved to his bed. Afterwards, she found that the toothbrush she used to keep in the bathroom was gone.

All of this now seemed like a memory of two different people. Looking at Serge, she knew that the evening had been a one-off. He had voiced no regrets about their break-up – not that they had discussed it. He would not want to resume their relationship, and he would assume Rosie felt the same. She had assured him, when he ended it, that she understood. The phrase 'last hurrah' floated incongruously through her mind, and she imagined couples shouting 'Hurrah!' as they orgasmed.

She looked around the bedroom, the shadows familiar from waking there as his girlfriend. The whole flat was familiar from parties she had attended, pre-dating their relationship. She remembered the heady anticipation of these evenings, when Serge was not her boyfriend but her longest-standing infatuation. A melancholy feeling rose, and she turned to leave. Passing the chest of drawers, she paused. Then she suddenly swept a pair of cufflinks off its surface and into her bag.

Outside in the sunshine, she felt appalled. Her cheeks burned, and her heart was beating too fast. She had never stolen anything before, if this was stealing. She stood still on the pavement, while couples walked around her with coffees and dogs, wondering what to do. She could ring Serge's doorbell, claiming to have forgotten something, and drop the cufflinks as she pretended to retrieve it. But it was so early. Ending the encounter this way felt unwise. She would be effusive and wretched and he would be too groggy to notice – making it worse. Her niece's christening was at one, she would miss the train if she deliberated any longer. As she walked away Rosie wondered how, at thirty-five, she could be in this kind of situation.

* * *

The christening was at the church in her parents' village. Eighteen months earlier her sister Kate had been married there – as if she were checking off adult milestones. Rosie's phone was now charged, disclosing Caspar's oddly urgent email, but she still hadn't called. She sensed the information he wanted to share would be unwelcome, and she couldn't face telling him she had slept with Serge.

She also knew Caspar would beg her to join his drink with Daniel Pyke. She thought of Daniel this way now, after so long, a first name and surname.

The godparents were summoned to the font, and stood in a row looking pious. Rosie thought of her own three godparents, and the ten-pound notes they sent every Christmas and birthday. Serge had seven godparents, all of them glamorous or distinguished. One was a national treasure. As she vowed to follow God she thought of the cufflinks, and felt unclean – as if her soul was itching. It was only when she held her niece that her heart rate slowed.

Afterwards, everyone walked to her parents' house for drinks. The rooms were even tidier than usual, cushions standing to attention and the carpets like creamy golf courses. She began handing round crisps, hoping nobody would be sympathetic about her break-up. This latest romantic disappointment had cemented her family role as maiden aunt, a failure her parents blamed on her career in 'the arts'. This was referred to with the same hushed dismay as if Rosie worked in pornography. She wished they understood that her job, selling foreign rights at a major publishing house, was often drearily corporate. But the combination of other languages and literary fiction still struck them as alarmingly exotic. Her father, a retired army officer, only read books about World War II.

She made an excuse to leave the conservatory, and retreated to her old bedroom. It had been redecorated, but the familiar space prompted a sense of life having stalled. She could hear Kate and her husband Matt changing the baby in the bathroom. A 'bad nappy' was still a family event.

'Kate?' she called, when the bathroom door opened. Her sister gave the baby to Matt, and lay on the bed. For a while they discussed how little sleep Kate was getting, and her daughter's various habits and difficulties. Rosie asked and listened, without giving advice. It was strange to be relegated this way, by her younger sibling. It had started with Kate's engagement, gathering pace with each stage she reached first.

'How are you?' said Kate, eventually.

'Fine. I saw Serge last night.'

'Serge? Why?'

'I had some of his stuff to give back.'

'Ah. That old line.'

'I know. But I didn't want to leave it on that note. That day on the heath.'

Serge had ended everything on a walk around Hampstead Heath, a week before her thirty-fifth birthday. She recalled sitting on a bench by the ponds while he talked about 'timing', and realising, through the wet heat of tears, that this was their first in-depth conversation about the relationship.

'Sure. I had that with James,' said Kate. 'Like, when I dumped him I was crying, I looked like shit. So we did the stuff handover, and it was kind of closure.'

Her sister always returned to her own experience, however tenuous the link or universal the situation. It was her way of showing interest.

'So how was it?' said Kate.

'Fine. I mean, a bit weird. Cos we hadn't spoken since that day. But loads to catch up on.'

'But did you talk about how he ended it? Or you two?'

They hadn't at all. Serge had behaved like an old friend meeting up to exchange news, and she had followed his lead. In his kitchen she had commented, playfully, on his enlarged biceps and then they had started kissing as if they were on romantic autopilot.

'It was more, like, a catch-up,' said Rosie.

She knew already that she could not confess to sleeping with him. Her sister had always been suspicious of Serge.

'So he didn't say sorry, or anything?'

'He kind of did all that at the time.'

Serge had apologised for dumping her – but Rosie had apologised more for crying.

'I still think he should have got his shit together sooner,' said Kate. 'Like, don't go out with someone you've known since uni, and give them this whole impression you're up for settling down, and *then* suddenly discover you're "not ready".'

'"Too busy" were his exact words.'

It was meant to sound wry, but it came out submissive. She wondered if Serge really had given her the impression he was 'up for settling down', or if Rosie had given this impression to everyone else. It had never felt wise to demand his long-term plans.

'Too busy's worse!' said Kate.

She began advising Rosie on dating apps, her arms behind her head and her eyes closed – as if she were basking in her married status.

While Kate talked, Rosie thought about the risk she had taken by sleeping with Serge. But there had been no obvious moment to explain she was no longer on the pill, or to demand he find a condom. Perhaps, she thought, she had not wanted him to. She checked her phone, knowing he would not have called. There was only a text from Caspar.

> Hey, sorry for stalker number of msgs! I just wanted you to hear this from me, not Facebook or wherever, but Serge is seeing someone. I'm sorry, I know it's the worst thing to hear. She's actually nice (they met at work), but it still pisses me off after his spiel to you about timing. You deserve better than my Peter Pan cousin. Call me Cx

For a second, she thought she might be sick.

White Cube Gallery

Bermondsey

3 p.m.

As soon as Serge saw Isla waiting for him outside the gallery, he knew he couldn't tell her about Rosie. There was something in the vulnerability of Isla glancing around for him that made him want to protect her from the truth. He also knew that if she were to find out she would not want to see him again. Serge had never felt on the back foot this way with any of his ex-girlfriends. Until now, this novelty had been exciting.

All morning, which he had spent in a nauseated fug of self-loathing, he had wondered how he and Rosie had ended up in bed. He had considered calling Rosie, to clarify the situation. But her note, he reminded himself, was a clear statement that she understood. He knew it was cowardly, as well as rude, not to even send a text. But a text would lead to further contact, and further complications. And he was so consumed with feeling guilty about Isla, and the risk of losing her, that he had no capacity for additional guilt about Rosie. She would be fine, he told himself. Rosie was the most competent person he knew. Perhaps, he wondered, worrying about Rosie was patronising – even vaguely misogynistic.

Serge had first seen Isla Malone on set. He was directing a short pro-bono film for a literacy charity, as part of a campaign to teach refugee children to read. The film's premise was the transportive power of books, and various celebrities were acting classic literary characters peopling a Syrian child's imagination.

Isla was part of the costume and make-up team. All week, Serge's eyes seemed to track her involuntarily. There was an ease and conviction in her movements that was mesmeric. He watched other people relax when she touched their faces. She didn't chat the way most make-up artists did, but there was something so assured and nurturing – goddess-like, he thought – about her presence that her subjects quietened too. He had watched a hyperactive child star fall asleep in the make-up chair, while Isla transformed her into Pippi Longstocking.

Serge liked Isla's face when she was concentrating, her eyes narrowed and lips pursed, and the way her hands worked with tiny, painterly strokes. There was a photo on her Instagram of a melting foot, created with prosthetics, that was so real it was uncomfortable to look at. Even this was somehow sexy. Serge found himself questioning whether his own talent was in the same league, and how far his success was luck.

Inevitably, this sudden fascination with a stranger made him reconsider his relationship. He now saw the compliments he paid Rosie, slightly compulsively, as an attempt to convince himself of something. The fact that Isla didn't look like Rosie, or any of his willowy ex-girlfriends, made her body more compelling. He started noticing other women with similar bodies, like discovering a new musical genre and listening to it obsessively. He realised that he had never wondered about Rosie. Even the things he did not know about her, he felt confident he could predict. Oddly, this did not equate to intimacy.

He and Isla had first kissed at the film's wrap party, during a heated discussion about whether books or nature were more crucial to child development. Serge knew he was right. He had trained as a teacher after Oxford, at his grandfather's insistence, though he had never worked as one. But Isla's arguments for nature, involving her own dyslexia and rural childhood, had been persuasive. He had lost his thread watching her talk, her eyes fervent and smoky, her faint Somerset accent riper now she was drunk. When she invoked hypothetical children of her own, he had shocked himself by imagining how a child of theirs might look.

They had ended the evening in her bed, where the way their bodies melded had made sex with every other girlfriend seemed inferior in retrospect. Sex with Rosie, in particular, had always involved a gear shift – as if they needed to segue from two friends laughing at a *New Yorker* cartoon into animals. It had been physically enjoyable, because Rosie put so much effort into anything she did. But the shift back to two friends was jarring.

With Isla the animal feeling was always there, even when they were just shopping or eating or falling asleep or talking – often half-arguing. There was even a thrill to these conflicts, in their novelty. All his past relationships had been marked by harmonious laughter, and had ended amicably. He had definitely never argued with Rosie – a hangover from their sunny friendship.

He also found himself asking Isla's advice about work, and then taking it, something he'd never done with other girlfriends. He loved her commitment to her craft. A large part of her job was re-creating wounds on actors, so whenever she or a friend had an injury she photographed it for reference. The first time she showed him all the close-ups of scabs and bruises on her phone, it felt like entering an inner sanctuary. He half hoped to fall off his bike, so he could send her a really impressive photo.

They had seen each other several times a week after the first night together, mostly in Isla's small, shared flat in Peckham. He wasn't sure what she knew about his family, if anything. He had already decided that he wanted her to know it all, at some point. But it was easier, for now, to withhold the details. She often called Serge posh, half boasting about her state education. He had joked that a comprehensive in Somerset was hardly 'street', but he envied her having nothing to hide. Isla had a natural, classless cachet that he had worked all his adult life to ape.

'I've missed you,' he said, into her scalp, after they had kissed for a long time in the street.

'I saw you forty-eight hours ago.'

He had told her he was meeting 'a friend', but had not explained that this friend was also his recent ex. It had not seemed necessary. Now he wished he had, as if this initial omission had led to greater dishonesty. They stood kissing for a while longer, leaning against each other like a trust exercise, until rain began spotting the pavement.

The exhibition, black and white photos of Mexican street life, was hung in a series of bare white rooms. The immaculate space was strangely oppressive. Isla stopped for ages at a close-up of a crucifix, and Serge stood just behind her, looking at the image without really seeing it. He felt clammily paranoid. Always, with Isla, he felt the need to be a better person than he feared he was, but now he had actually proved himself unworthy.

He had an urge to confess something else, anything, as if this might absolve him – and an even stronger urge to compensate Isla for his betrayal. He took her hand, and she looked up and smiled. This made him despise himself more.

Hugo's Wagyu

Peckham Rye

5 p.m.

After the exhibition Serge suggested they try his friend Hugo's new burger pop-up. Isla realised how accustomed she was, already, to Serge knowing where to go and having some connection to it. She liked the fact that he did not jump the queue, when she knew he could have.

Standing very close together in line, she felt – as she always did – that they emanated their own energetic field. She had never known a man who was as good at art exhibitions as sex. Serge had also shown himself to be good at protest marches, film premieres and parents – charming Isla's mother by washing up and playing with her cat. She looked at the tan line on Serge's neck now, and wanted to nibble it. Whenever she was with him she felt a need for contact, if only their toes in bed, all the time. That morning she had listened to the message he'd left her an embarrassing number of times. His voice could make her knees feel unstable.

Isla's first impression of Serge Campbell was that he was the product of moneyed, metropolitan parents. She had met men like this at art school, and learned to avoid dating them. But Serge had quickly proved her assessment inaccurate. He had an obsessive drive that she recognised in herself, and an ability to lead a whole film set without domineering. His charisma was striking, in the same way as his height and blue eyes, but it was the interest he took in other people – not the interest they took in him – that touched her. He knew the runners' names on the first day of shooting.

Once they were dating, it became clear how vastly different their lives had been. He had grown up in a huge house in London, she in a damp, rented bungalow near Frome. Serge had attended a famous boarding school and spent his holidays between his parents' homes in Tuscany and Dorset. She had gone to the local comprehensive and spent her summers drinking cider in stone circles. He was part of a sociable clan of cousins, with conventional hierarchies of adults and children intact. Growing up with her young, chaotic mother – whose work as a ceramicist barely covered bills – Isla had often felt like the adult.

But these contrasts only made their connection feel more fundamental, as if they had fallen in love across foreign borders. Even their four-year age difference sometimes felt vast, he having come of age without a mobile or the internet. She loved his weekend hedonism too, like a wholesome strain of her own occasional urge to self-destruct. When she was with him she had a sense of ceding – perhaps the need to protect, or annihilate, herself. And when she fell asleep beside him she felt safe, perhaps for the first time ever. Nobody else she had dated, either the cossetted art students or the boys from her hometown, had absorbed her this way. With them she always anticipated time apart.

Today, Serge was hungover and seemed distracted. After congratulating his friend, and asking the nervous waiter for recommendations, he was quiet. She had missed his heat in her bed the previous night.

'This is so lush,' she said, when their food appeared.

Serge agreed, praising Hugo again, but she knew he did not view £18 burgers as indulgent.

'Can I tell you something?' he said, abruptly.

She swallowed. She sensed he was about to reveal something personal, perhaps a diagnosis or misdemeanour.

'I mean, I hardly ever talk about this.' He started massaging his temples, almost aggressively. 'So, you know my surname? Have you heard of Campbell's? Like Sotheby's and Christie's?'

She confirmed that she had heard of Campbell's, the auction house.

'OK, so Rory Campbell, the founder, he was my great-grandpa.'

For a second, because Serge looked so ashamed, Isla wondered if Rory Campbell had been a notorious fascist, or con artist. Then she saw that Serge was confessing how rich he was. His forehead was shiny.

'OK. Wow. That's cool. Did you know him?'

'My great-grandfather? No. But I knew his son, my grandpa. Sterling Campbell. He was actually the one who made Campbell's so big. My great-grandpa was more, like, a patron than a dealer.'

'Is that where you get your entrepreneur spirit?'

She used a tongue-in-cheek voice, sensing that he needed her not to view him differently. She didn't, or not drastically. It was already obvious he had money, from his flat and production company. But she saw, now, that he did not realise it was obvious. He hoped his curated accent and careful omissions disguised it, or mitigated it. The naivety could have grated but she felt protective instead, the way she hated to hear her mother's dysfunctionality criticised.

'Ha,' he said. 'Perhaps. Must have skipped a generation. With my dad.'

He still looked pained, so she asked what was wrong.

'Nothing, just, it can complicate things. I've found.'

'Why? Cos you have, what it's called, a trust fund?'

It was meant as a joke, but she realised it was too direct.

'No! There are no gatekeepers. And obviously we don't get, like, an allowance or anything,' he said, as if this was an important distinction. 'I got my share outright, when I turned twenty-five. We all did. Me and my sister, and my cousin. It's really unusual. Hardly anyone does it that way.'

'Oh. OK. How come?'

She had not expected details, but now she was intrigued.

'My grandpa hated the idea of adults going to a trust. The whole begging bowl thing. He wanted us to be in control. Or to piss it away, and deal with the consequences.'

She wanted to know how much he had inherited, but she knew she couldn't request figures. Given the sums art dealers handled, his windfall must have been millions. Various things about Serge came into focus. His insistence on paying the bill with friends. An anxiety about being seen as posh, alongside a preference for organic groceries. The effusive sociability and curiosity, especially towards anyone serving him. His embarrassment about his Knightsbridge dentist.

'So, are you in line to take over Campbell's?'

'Me? No! My grandpa sold it. Years ago. So, yeah, that's where it's from. The money.'

His shoulders were hunched. He kept stirring his virgin cocktail, as though he couldn't look up. When he did, his oceanic eyes seemed to be pleading forgiveness.

'I'm not judging, Serge. It's not like it's blood diamonds.'

He laughed, his shoulders loosening.

'I know. Just, like I said, I don't talk about it. With most people. The whole, silver spoon, thing.'

She took one of his hands between hers in reply. It was very big, and made hers on either side look stubby. She had artificial blood under her fingernails, as usual.

'But you did your teacher training, right?' she said. This had always struck her as incongruous, but impressive.

'Right. Yeah. My grandpa had this thing about everyone needing a trade. We all trained in something.'

She knew she couldn't tease him about using the word 'trade'.

'That's cool,' she said. 'That it hasn't made you—'

She hesitated.

'Spoilt?' he said, smiling.

'Yeah, I guess. You work harder than anyone I know,' she said, truthfully.

Hugo was walking over to their table. He had Serge's self-assurance, but not his charm.

'So Pikey's back in town,' he said, to Serge. 'Caspar was down yesterday. He mentioned it.'

'Really?'

Serge frowned and shifted. Isla wondered if he was more hungover than he had admitted. He had eaten very little. She felt an almost maternal concern for his wellbeing.

'Yeah,' said Hugo, over Isla's head. 'Apparently he's been out of work for years. So wait, are you two not in touch?'

'Not regularly. Now he's in LA.'

Serge turned to include Isla.

'Just this guy we were at Oxford with,' he said. 'Actor. Daniel Pyke.'

'Daniel Pyke? In *Riptide*?'

'You've seen that?' said Serge.

She considered revealing that Daniel Pyke had been her first on-screen crush – expecting Serge to affect playful jealousy. But he looked vaguely impatient, so she didn't. Conversation turned to Hugo's artisan ketchup.

When Hugo had gone Serge reached for her hands again, enclosing them both between his. With anyone else she might have wanted to break free, but it felt nice, as if her hands were treasure.

'Anyway, look, there's something else I wanted to say,' he said. 'Can we – I guess – make this official? Us.'

His eyes were earnest, but she had assumed their relationship was already exclusive. There had been no time to date anyone else.

'We're having "the chat"?' she said. 'I haven't been shagging around. Have you?'

The teasing voice she often found herself using with Serge was back. The power she felt was intoxicating.

He blanched, and she realised she had undermined his sincerity.
'No!' he said. 'Of course not. I just, I don't want this to be casual.'
'Do I have to sign a prenup?'
He laughed, and said, 'Please?'
'Yes, then.'

He leaned forwards to hold her face in his hands and kissed her for ages – their tongues tangling, so that she began to think about sex. When he said, 'I love you,' onto her lips, she said, 'I love you too,' and it felt as if there were no longer any barriers between them, as if every possible channel were wide open.

The Ladbroke Arms

London

6 p.m.

Daniel was back from Los Angeles for a week, for his mother's sixtieth. He sat waiting for Caspar in the pub where they always met, poised to make life in Hollywood sound – if not dignified – at least funny. He had already drunk a large vodka tonic, and wanted a cigarette.

Caspar walked in and said, 'Here he is!' and they hugged for a long time. Halfway through, Daniel was shocked to find his eyes prickling. He clapped Caspar on the back, prolonging the embrace until he had regained control.

Daniel had moved to LA soon after Oxford, for a part in a sitcom pilot. The move was meant to be temporary, but twelve years later he was still there, still hoping for a life-changing role. There had been other reasons to leave the UK in 2004, besides the sitcom, but he tried to forget them.

With Caspar's Coutts card behind the bar, they covered the fundamentals of their lives in London and LA. Caspar talked about a house he was hoping to buy, and Daniel mentioned a call back for a new series called *The Runes Of Gorm*. He was not drunk enough to talk about how desperately he needed the work.

After the second glass of wine they were both giddy.

'OK, so I also have news,' said Caspar. 'D'you remember Nate

Kennedy at St Arthur's? American, visiting student. Huge crush on Rosie.'

Daniel immediately felt uneasy at Rosie's name, or perhaps at Caspar's determinedly casual tone. It signalled that the group's fracture was never to be discussed, even though Daniel had lived abroad too long for it to matter on a practical level. There was no chance of seeing Serge at a party. Or Rosie, though he would have liked to.

'Nathaniel Kennedy, yes!' he said. 'Nice bloke. Big hair. Really skinny?'

'I mean, I guess. He's pretty ripped now.'

Caspar poured more wine, affecting bashfulness.

'So he works for the *New York Times*, and he randomly got in touch with me for this piece he's writing about auction houses. Anyway, we'd been emailing loads, so when I was just in New York we met up—'

For a second Daniel feared that Nate Kennedy had come out, and that Daniel had implied he was unattractive.

'—and he introduces me to his friend, JP. His name's literally "John-Pencey Delahunt", amazing, and we all go on this ridiculous night out. It was Halloween so we're in fancy dress, properly raucous. And I go back to JP's . . .'

Daniel raised his eyebrows, and almost said 'Bunga bunga?' – in reference to an old in-joke.

But Caspar said, in an excited rush, 'And we basically spent the next twenty-four hours together and now he's coming to stay, next week. At mine!'

Daniel clinked his glass against Caspar's. Behind the triumph, he knew, was Caspar's yearning to be half of a couple. While he talked about JP's job at the Met Opera, Daniel wondered when he would come to crave monogamy himself. He always found the first stage of romance addictive, in a similar way to audience laughter. But as soon as things progressed, he fled.

Caspar enquired after Daniel's love life, and he told Caspar about a date with a barista and how they had gatecrashed an A-lister's pool party. The original anecdote had been hugely embellished, but he had told it so often it had come to feel like memory. He had never called the barista, and now had to patronise a different coffee shop. Los Angeles was full of bars he had to avoid for this reason. He imagined a mob of beautiful, wronged servers, coming for him. 'But you're still enjoying it? The American dream?' said Caspar, when they stopped laughing. He had always had an instinct for doubt behind bravado.

Daniel was about to protest, but seeing his old friend in a British pub made him candid.

'Mate, I dunno. It's been over a decade. Jesus.'

'But this *Runes* thing sounds like a big deal?'

'Maybe. Just, clock's ticking, y'know?'

'You're only thirty-four!'

'Geriatric, in LA.'

'It'll happen, buddy. Keep the faith.'

'How's Serge's sister?' said Daniel. 'She's still acting, right?'

He heard the same, forced casualness in his voice as Caspar had used about Rosie.

'I mean, there's a lot of resting. God, I don't know how you guys do it. I'd go insane.'

'We're already insane. It's an Equity prerequisite.'

'Did you hear about Serge and Rosie?'

'No – what, they broke up?'

It still felt odd to be asking about former friends' lives this way.

'Yeah. He dumped her, totally out the blue. Like, I had no idea he even had doubts. And she was completely blindsided. He just invited her to the heath for this walk. She thought he was going to propose!'

'Shit! Poor Rosie.'

'I know. She's gutted. I think the way everyone was so excited when they got together – this whole *One Day* idea – she was so caught up in that.'

Daniel had not felt excited when Rosie and Serge got together. Mostly, he remembered his shameful, spiteful hope it wouldn't last – as if the relationship had cemented his position as an outcast.

'What happened?'

'I mean, you never get the full story with Serge. He gave her the timing line, but he's already seeing someone else. Who's only twenty-eight.'

'How's Rosie doing?'

'Not great. Freaking out she'll never meet anyone. Planning to freeze her eggs.'

They both sipped their drinks, and Daniel thought how Serge must have derailed Rosie's plans. Once, during a student dinner party, he had found a comically precise To-Do list in her kitchen – working back from pudding like a countdown. He had teased her about it for months.

'But, were they solid, as a couple?' he said. 'Like, if they were so meant to be, what took them so long? I mean, clearly she was always obsessed. I just never fully got that vibe from him.'

'They were both always with other people,' said Caspar. 'Serge was, anyway.'

Daniel remembered the way Rosie used to morph around Serge, laughing excessively and suppressing any opinions. Daniel had pointed it out to her once, in what turned out to be their last ever conversation.

'Look, correct me if I'm wrong,' he said, 'but was it that Serge was in his thirties, he knew Rosie was holding a candle and suddenly she seemed, all, "good on paper". After that hot mess model.'

Before Rosie, Serge had dated a Burberry model called Olympia Harrod. The relationship had resulted in some blurry pap shots of Serge – envied by Daniel from LA.

Caspar looked doubtful.

'I'm just saying,' said Daniel. 'I don't reckon they'd nail a chemistry read.'

'OK, someone's been in Hollywood too long. Forget what I said, run away!'

At closing time, Daniel took the train back to his childhood home in Southend. He googled 'Nathaniel Kennedy', and found several widely shared pieces on US healthcare, focusing on addiction. A 'long read' about a famous dynasty profiting from ADHD medication had gone viral. Daniel thought he would need some amphetamines to read the whole thing.

He bought a G&T and bag of Twiglets and called his mother, knowing she would be waiting up. The terraces rattling past triggered a bleak, anticipatory homesickness. A part of him hoped he wouldn't get *The Runes Of Gorm*, so he could give up and come home.

Oxford, June 2004

Rosie, Serge, Caspar and Daniel are still waiting for Serge's sister to arrive so that they can go to the St Arthur's ball. It is dusk, and Daniel keeps flicking his lighter on and off. Rosie looks at Serge often, as if she needs to check he is still there.

A blonde girl walks into the beer garden, adopting a catwalk sashay when they see her.

'Here she is!' says Caspar.

'Cazzy Cuz!' says the girl, hugging her cousin Caspar from behind. Her fragrance announces itself.

Serge introduces his sister, Allegra, to Rosie and Daniel. She has the same long-haul tan and surprised eyes as Serge and Caspar, but a different, more theatrical manner. When she laughs she flings her whole head back, like a demonstration of whiplash.

Allegra opens a packet of Marlboro Lights and offers it to the group. Only Daniel takes one. She leans towards his lighter, her breasts brushing the table, and thanks him through her first inhale.

Rosie compliments her dress, and Allegra says it is 'just Portobello'.

'I actually *prefer* vintage,' she adds conspiratorially. Her bracelets clatter as she lifts and lowers the cigarette. 'It's the *story*. Like, who wore this? How did they *feel?*'

Rosie agrees animatedly, adjusting her pristine dress.

'You look really familiar,' says Allegra, turning her breathy focus to Daniel.

'Do I?' he says.

'Don't be coy,' says Caspar. 'Daniel's our resident act-or. Daniel Pyke. He was in that film, *Riptide*. He hates that I fancied him.'

'No way!' says Allegra. 'I fucking love that film! That's amazing. Serge! Why have you *literally* never told me this?'

She is staring at Daniel now, in open admiration. His whole face has lit up, though he dismisses the film as 'practically straight to DVD'.

Allegra begins to ask him about *Riptide*, a cult arthouse film in which Daniel played a troubled teenage surfer. Daniel answers by praising the director, the script and his fellow actors. Serge says, to his sister, 'There's literally nothing this guy doesn't know about cinema. Like, if you thought I was a film geek.'

'And Serge tells me you two are collaborating?' says Allegra, as if she is a mother cajoling children to disclose a secret.

'That's the plan,' says Serge.

'Don't get them started,' says Caspar. 'Please. I feel like I've already seen this bloody film.'

'Can I be in it?' says Allegra.

She blinks at Daniel, and he laughs appreciatively.

'It's about a guy,' says Serge. 'So no. Daniel's going to play the lead, anyway. Right, Danny?'

'Shotgun,' says Daniel, grinning at Allegra. 'We haven't written it yet, though. So we can write you in.'

Serge frowns.

'You two in one film – that'd be a nightmare,' he says. 'But yeah, no, we're going to bash out the script this summer, then we pitch it in September. Daniel's the lead, we both direct.'

'So you write, too?' says Allegra, looking at Daniel.

'Yup. But yeah, I want to direct, ultimately.'

'Same!' says Allegra. 'I would *love* to direct. And produce. Serge's godfather Miles is an incredible producer. Miles Whitehall. He owns Reel.'

'I'm aware,' says Daniel.

He half smirks, as if Serge's famous godfather is a source of amusement.

'Hey, you should come to Italy!' says Allegra. 'He's staying this summer. Miles.'

Daniel looks at Serge, as if for confirmation, or permission.

'Is he?' says Serge, casually. 'Then yeah, come stay, Pikey. Writers' room!'

'La dolce vita?' says Daniel.

'May your creative partnership be long and fruitful,' says Caspar, raising his glass.

PART TWO

JULY 2019
ONE MONTH BEFORE CASPAR'S WEDDING

From: campbell.delahunt.wedding@gmail.com
Bcc: campbell.delahunt.wedding@gmail.com
Date: 28 July, 2019, 10:00
Subject: one month!

Hey glorious guests!

A month to go ... we can't wait to see you in Provence. If anyone hasn't confirmed flights, accommodation or dietary requirements please let JP know asap, so he can add you to a colour-coded spreadsheet. Here's a quick recap of the itinerary (because JP ...).

Thursday 29 August ...
6pm Official US vs UK softball match (boules

outvoted by JP's fraternity), and picnic at
Parc de la Torse.

Friday 30 August . . .
3pm Rehearsal at Chateau de Beaupont, you know who you are! (Codeword: Madge)
7pm Drinks, dinner, opera recital at Chateau La Coste sculpture gardens

Saturday 31 August . . .
4pm Le Mariage!
We can't stress this enough: Chateau de Beaupont is remote. There is no Uber or Lyft, and Vauvenargues is not known for its Wi-Fi or cell signal. A shuttle bus will be running between the chateau and Aix, but if you need a taxi please pre-book (see travel info) or be fit to drive!

Sunday 1 September . . .
11am till late – brunch and pool party at Villa des Pavots, Caspar's parents' house.

For those staying the whole weekend we attach a list of things to do in Aix. If you only have Saturday, we urge you to catch the calissons at Maison Bremond!

Much love xxx

Ravenscourt Park

Hammersmith

11.30 A.M.

Caspar and JP had invited Rosie for a Sunday walk, to discuss 'wedmin and also something in person'. Immediately, she feared it might involve Serge. There had been no contact since the 'last hurrah', two-and-a-half years earlier. Whenever she thought of Caspar's wedding, and seeing Serge there with his fiancée and children, her stomach felt hollowed out.

She was so anxious about the whole thing she had booked a local yoga retreat, for afterwards.

Rosie had helped nearly all her friends to organise their weddings, and was now Caspar's Best Woman. Increasingly she felt these duties as an imposition, though she knew she was partly to blame. She was incapable of declining obligations – as if she was at a buffet piling more and more food onto a full plate. Serge was also Caspar's best man, although his only job was a speech. Horrifyingly, Caspar had requested that Serge and Rosie give this together. He was hopeful, he said, that the task would 'get them back on track'.

As Rosie approached the park she saw the grooms kissing on a bench – JP, clean cut as a '90s catalogue, Caspar, permanently, prettily rumpled. She caught her own reflection in a window, and suddenly feared her new beret was affected and made her look like an egg in a hat.

On her arrival at the bench there was a lot of joyful hugging and beret analysis. They began walking round the park, moving aside for straight couples and scooting toddlers. A woman passed with a newborn curled in a sling, and Rosie averted her eyes.

Two weeks after the 'last hurrah', Rosie's period had not come. Then, the day she bought a pregnancy test, she had begun to bleed much more than usual. The test was negative, but apparently this was inconclusive – the heavy bleeding could either be a late period or early miscarriage. The technical term was a 'chemical pregnancy'. For weeks, Rosie had wept whenever she was alone, even in the time it took to pee at work.

JP was talking about how Caspar's mother wanted to serve kedgeree the morning after the wedding. He kept saying: 'It's lit-er-ally like she's obsessed with haddock.'

Caspar was being unusually quiet.

'And you're sure you're OK to do your speech with Serge?' he said, turning. He had a refined intuition for people's anxieties. This was different – Rosie had found – to accommodating them.

'Of course! I'd actually prefer it,' she said.

'Really? Thanks, Ro. I just think it'll be more fun, y'know? I'd love for you two to be properly friends again. It's sad, inviting you to stuff separately. It's been like Serge and Daniel, all over again. It's like, none of you are on speaking terms!'

'Daniel and I are on speaking terms! He's in a different time zone.'

This was true, but Rosie and Daniel's lapsed contact was more than geography. Rosie had considered emailing him before the wedding, but then she had looked at his celebrity Instagram account and decided to wait for him to contact her.

'Wait – Serge and Daniel had a break-up too?' said JP.

Rosie was surprised that Caspar hadn't explained Serge and Daniel's falling-out to JP. But Caspar's approach to tension was always strenuously cheerful denial. Even at the time he had refused to take sides, despite clearly feeling for Daniel. There was a mafia quality to the way the Campbells closed ranks.

'More like a breakdown. In communication,' said Rosie airily.

In a sense this was true. The whole conflict had been conducted in silence, so that she had never fully understood Serge's grudge against Daniel. She had asked, as Serge's girlfriend. But he had been so defensive, almost denying that he and Daniel were ever friends, that she had not felt able to ask again.

'Over what?' said JP.

Caspar was now staring at the horizon, as if he wanted Rosie to explain.

'I mean, nothing major. It was timing, really. Cos they pissed each other off straight after Oxford, and then Daniel moved to LA, so they never sorted it out,' she said. It still struck her as sad, if unsurprising. She had never known a pair of apparent kindred spirits to be so competitive, constantly trying to outdo each other's knowledge of Fellini.

Caspar looked even more tense now, so she added, before JP could comment: 'And you've never had to invite *me* and Serge to stuff separately! Now he's basically married with kids.'

She had used this phrase before, and perfected a nonchalant delivery. The speed with which Serge had committed to someone else still stung.

'Those twins are ridiculous,' said JP, 'they should be on commercials or something.'

'And Nathaniel Kennedy's your best man?' said Rosie. She did not want to dwell on Serge's cherubic twins, a boy and girl. The way Serge had created an instant nuclear family was typically successful.

'Nate? He is, yeah. Remembers you.'

Rosie remembered Nate, too. He had studied at Oxford during her final year, his room opposite hers. She liked his ready laugh, and the fact that she had not found him physically attractive had been relaxing. They had established a ritual of drinking Earl Grey in her room. He seemed to find this exotic, just as she had been fascinated by his lived experience of junior high.

Nate turned out to be more analytical than the encouraging smile and interest in basketball suggested. She liked this too, the way he managed to combine scepticism with enthusiasm. She could tell he was besotted with her, but he was so easy to talk to – despite what she called their 'slanguage barrier' – that she had allowed another ritual to develop, of walking back to college after nights out. Often, he insisted she take his jacket. The bond was private – they went out in separate groups but returned together.

She still felt awful remembering the evening – just before they were both due to leave Oxford – when Nate asked to kiss her. He had given her a piggyback all the way back to their college, because her feet hurt. She had declined the kiss, and made it worse by saying he gave 'the best hugs'. It was true, but his smile had vanished.

'And Daniel's reading the vows,' said Caspar. 'You know he's in this massive new film, *Knifepoint*? About a chef going schizo? Reckon he'll get a BAFTA.'

Rosie did not say that it sounded alarmingly close to Daniel's own father. It seemed too personal, in front of JP. Instead she said, truthfully:

'I keep trying to watch him in his *Runes* thing, but I get distracted by the wig.'

'I know, right?' said JP. 'He's like, Viking Barbie. In a good way.'

'He can literally pick the parts he wants now,' said Caspar.

Rosie didn't point out that Caspar didn't need to work, either. She knew he needed to believe his job was necessary. The psychology of inherited wealth was exclusive and unspoken, just like the sums involved.

They passed a café, and JP suggested coffee. He glanced at Caspar, and she knew the 'in person' moment was coming.

'OK, so, listen – it wasn't just wedmin we wanted to chat about,' said Caspar, as they sat down. Nearby, a father implored his children to use indoor voices. Caspar and JP smiled at them, and then each other. Caspar kept rubbing his neck and moving his hair around, while JP looked from him to Rosie encouragingly.

'So, you know how we've been looking into adoption?' said Caspar.

'I mean, I knew you were open to it. Have you started—'

'Uh, no! Not yet. That's what we wanted to talk to you about. Basically, adoption turns out to be a bureaucratic nightmare. So we've actually been looking into egg donors. And surrogates.'

Rosie realised she needed to absorb a lot of information at speed. She had known Caspar wanted a family, but only abstractly. The visceral longing, the fear of a childless future, had been hers.

'And yeah, in a way, a donor's more straightforward. But it's also, just, so surreal. Like, I was thinking of when you looked into sperm donors, but you couldn't handle the idea of never meeting your child's father.'

He looked at JP, as if for support, and JP took his hand.

'And we basically came to that conclusion too. We want the mother to be part of the baby's life. Child's life. Ideally someone we know, and love already. So . . . listen, I know this is a massive thing to ask. Massive.'

He stopped and took a big, nervous breath. 'But we just wondered, how you'd feel about . . . '

He left the sentence hanging, biting down on his lower lip and smiling.

'Wait – *me*? Me be your egg donor?' It came out squeaky.

'Yeah! And surrogate.'

'Me? And you? Sorry, sorry, I'm just, uh, I wasn't expecting that!'

'We get it! This is, like, totally out of the blue,' said JP. 'You don't need to say anything now.'

'Of course,' said Caspar. 'I know it's so weird.' He half laughed. 'And I know it's not how you pictured having a baby. But we just wanted to put it out there.'

'Because, obviously, we're not going to action anything before the wedding,' said JP.

'No sex before marriage, right?' said Rosie, and then wondered if it was misjudged, because he seemed to recoil slightly. She wanted to exchange glances with Caspar about 'action', but she knew she couldn't. He was marrying JP. Perhaps that was love – tolerating action as a verb. Friends often told her she was too picky.

'Aren't I too old?' she said. 'I'm thirty-eight in September.'

She wondered if her potential miscarriage might be significant, but it demanded too much explanation. She had never told Caspar, or anyone connected to Serge, about the last hurrah.

'Nope, all good,' said JP. 'Thirty-five is the NHS cut off, but we'll go private. I mean, sure, we shouldn't wait a bunch of time. But look at you! Your eggs must be perky teenagers!'

She felt flattered, but also ambushed, and now recalled JP's awkward laughter at her saying she looked like an egg in a hat.

'OK, so, tell me more,' she said.

Caspar outlined their idea for one of Rosie's eggs to be fertilised by his sperm, and potentially for her to move into the self-contained basement flat under his house. JP explained how they would raise the child, with Rosie being 'very much a presence' in its life.

It was like listening to a manifesto, which made it hard to tell how she felt. But she must have looked encouraging because she could see the expectation in the men's faces. She had often told Caspar how badly she wanted a child. It had been easier to confide in him than her friends who were mothers. When her sister had announced her second pregnancy, Rosie had had to pretend her tears were joy. Caspar had understood.

'I know how tough it's been for you,' he said, as if her thoughts were on loudspeaker. 'And it's like, you of all people, deserve to be a mother. I mean, it would be such a loss to the world if you weren't. Like, we were reading the egg donor profiles and I kept thinking, they don't sound half as great as Rosie.'

His childish Campbell eyes were beseeching. She felt JP's adult presence, as he said:

'But please, take your time. We don't want to pressurise you.'

It seemed rude to leave after this proposal so Rosie suggested lunch, aware that her weekend was evaporating. At four Caspar said 'Shit, I'm meeting Serge at six,' and they hurried through goodbyes. The idea of Serge's life continuing somewhere still gave her an empty feeling.

She walked home down long residential streets, all the ground-floor bay windows flashing with cartoons. She wondered if her years in her small, silent flat might be ending, if she might have a baby with Campbell eyes after all. She still dreamed of Serge often. In the last dream she had watched him walk to his execution, weeping into a bean-shaped surgical bowl. In the morning she had felt repulsed by her own unconscious.

Once, her therapist had invited Rosie to address a cushion as Serge – saying it would help her to move on. Rosie had accused the cushion of squandering her final years of reliable fertility, and thus her last chance to date at leisure. It had seemed too dramatic to say, 'I will always love you,' to Ikea's Svartpoppel.

Century Club

Soho

7.30 P.M.

Serge had sensed he would win Best Director for *PLUR* – a Romeo and Juliet story set at an illegal rave – since his nomination. He always knew when he was going to win, even at prep school, just as he always knew when he would have to be a magnanimous loser.

He sat back down after accepting the statuette, aware of his pulse and people's glances. A Society of Film Award, known as a SOFA, was a notch below a BAFTA. He had directed and produced *PLUR* himself, starting his own production company, Vanguard Films, to ensure creative control. He ought to feel elated – the way Caspar looked now, as Serge's plus one. Still, he felt Isla's absence as a wrong note. He had mentioned her in his speech, but he knew she would not look it up. She used to accompany him to any industry event, even heavily pregnant.

He laughed as the next winner made a joke about the SOFA award's phallic shape, and thought how Isla no longer seemed to have time for anything beside the twins. Serge had thought, when a scan revealed two heartbeats, that he would be an involved father by default. But instead Isla used the anomaly of twins to shut him out. Everything was apparently twice as fraught, with double the opportunity for him to fail.

It hurt, both the demotion to support act and the twins' ensuing preference for Isla. But he knew he was also to blame. Vanguard Films was in debt – the kind that only independent film could engender – and Serge had been working incessantly to fix it. Isla had no idea. Whenever he was home, she accused him of shirking his paternal responsibilities.

It was a logical assumption, the debt having started the week the twins were born. An investor had abruptly pulled out of Serge's next film, *Beating Heart*. Not wanting to alarm Isla after the birth, he had said nothing about the investor – or the fact that he had already poured his entire inheritance into Vanguard Films, emptying every savings account. Instead, manic with sleep deprivation, he had taken out a huge mortgage on his flat – granted on his past income from ad campaigns. It hadn't even helped. He was struggling to make the payments, and now owed nearly a million pounds in tax and across the film industry.

He kept smiling and clapping, the SOFA statuette heavy on his thigh, trying to enjoy his success and the venue's glamour. Here *PLUR* could exist in his mind as an achievement and not a crippling debt. He cringed to think how much the crowd scenes alone had cost.

* * *

When he and Caspar left the after-party, they were both laughing in the breathless way they used to on childhood holidays, high on Orangina. They had drunk multiple Aperol spritzes while Serge was photographed and congratulated. The night air was sobering. Caspar was describing his stag, as they walked through Soho.

'So gutted I missed it,' said Serge. He had been in Tokyo, directing an ad for Reebok.

'No worries, buddy. Just a shame you couldn't see Rosie. Before the wedding. The whole ex thing. Never easy.'

'Man, no. It's all good. She's with someone now, right?'

He wasn't certain of this, but it seemed likely. Men often fell for

Rosie – in fact, she had always struck Serge as the perfect wife. It was one of the things, ultimately, that had made the relationship claustrophobic.

'Rosie? No. I mean, no shortage of offers. Obviously. But nothing serious since you guys.'

He suddenly remembered the odd night, soon after their break-up, when he and Rosie had slept together. He knew he had only wanted – in a drunk, stupid way – to make up for ending it, perhaps to convey that the relationship was not easily forgotten. In his defence, Serge thought now, he and Isla had not been exclusive. But his tacit silence with Rosie, ever since, only affirmed the sense of a guilty secret. The prospect of seeing her at the wedding was uncomfortable.

'Anyway, listen, Daniel didn't make the stag either,' said Caspar. 'New series of *TROG*.'

'Busy man, right? I'm actually trying to get him attached to *Beating Heart*. My next film.'

He had not voiced this plan to anyone, except Daniel's agent – who he had sent the script. It pained Serge to be capitalising on Daniel's fame this way, via an agent. But Daniel's name would secure financial backing, finally refilling Vanguard's accounts, and Caspar's wedding was the ideal opportunity to sell the project to him.

Caspar looked round, his expression like a child receiving a huge, unexpected present.

'Really? That would be so great. You two. Working together.'

He sounded cautious, as if he didn't want to sabotage anything with excitement. Serge knew that the fall-out with Daniel had saddened Caspar more than anyone. But this had never been reason enough for Serge to address it, or forget it. A million-pound debt was reason enough, though.

'Sure. I mean, if he's up for it. He'd definitely greenlight us.'

There was a pause.

'So how are the twins? How's dad-ing?' said Caspar.

'Amazing! They're like, proper people now.'

He opened the photos on his phone, and felt the familiar dissonance between the joy he took in his children's existence and the stress of their physical presence. Or perhaps it was the stress they caused between him and Isla. It still seemed surreal that they even had two children. He scrolled to a picture of the twins sucking each other's thumbs, and Caspar responded appropriately.

'JP and I are up for kids.'

'Do it! More cousins!'

There was no point saying anything else. It was impossible to convey either the love, or the way parenthood changed a couple.

'I mean, clearly, it's a bit more complicated, for us,' said Caspar.

'Right. But at least it'll be planned. And you'll only get one.'

'The twins weren't planned?'

'No, man! Of course not, we'd only been together six months.'

He remembered Isla's stunned phone call after the pregnancy test, and his own elated terror.

'Shocker! Seems weird I never knew that.'

Serge wondered why Caspar was surprised. He had assumed it must be obvious that the twins were unplanned, though he realised now none of his family had asked. He had proposed in Isla's second trimester, when everything seemed possible.

'It's all good,' he said. 'Wouldn't have it any other way.'

Neither of them spoke for a few seconds, the clamour of Soho at odds with the conversation.

'Hey, did you get the flash mob link? JP's got this whole idea that you guys storm the stage, halfway through our first dance.'

He began singing *Like a Prayer*, shimmying as he walked and doing dramatic arm gestures.

'Amazing,' said Serge, only half listening because people nearby were laughing. He turned to look. As he did so, the voices turned to jeers. They came from three men, a few metres behind him and Caspar. One of them, a short, stocky blond, was ahead of the others – holding his wrist out limply – a parody of a gay man.

The others were gasping with laughter. Serge noted their clothes, and saw that London was an occasion.

He and Caspar kept walking, though they were now both aware of the hooting.

'Nice dildo,' one of the men called, and Serge realised he meant the SOFA.

He stopped and turned, and all three men stopped too. The short one was older than Serge had expected. His skin was a jaundiced artificial tan.

'All right, faggots?' said the man, after a tense second.

'I'm sorry, *what?*' said Serge.

'Oooh. Boyfriend's getting involved,' he said. The others laughed again.

'Serge. Come on,' said Caspar. Serge could see that he was trying to disguise fear as impatience. The thought that a stranger could intimidate his cousin enraged him.

'Shut the fuck up,' said Serge, stepping towards the man.

For a second he looked surprised, then his face twisted into contempt.

'What did you say?'

'You heard me.'

The man looked at Serge's undone bow tie, level with his own face.

'Posh twat.'

'Prick.'

He took a second to impose his height over the man, then turned to walk away. A second later he felt a slamming force between his shoulder blades. He turned again to see the man rearing back, bottle in hand. Serge reacted without thinking – years of childhood judo in his reflexes. The man staggered, groaning. Serge was shocked to see blood, and realised he had caught the man's face with the statuette. The other men were around their friend now, shouting and swearing.

'Serge! What the hell?' said Caspar.

Two policemen were running towards them now. Serge registered people across the road, phones aloft. It was only once handcuffs were locking around his dress shirt, that he thought of Isla and the twins and remembered that he was meant to be flying to Vancouver for work the next day.

10 Chiltern Mansions

Marylebone

11.50 p.m.

The box room floor was littered with bottles and balled-up nappies and Calpol syringes, so that in the dimness it resembled a kind of infant crack den. Isla sat beside the twins' shared cot, her arms trapped between the bars, hands clamped on their backs. The air in the small room was thick with summer heat and milky breath, but she couldn't open the skylight – a siren would flail past, waking Juno and Huck. She thought of the feathery quietness around her own childhood home, miles from a main road.

The hours between seven and midnight had passed in an orgy of waking and shushing, both twins screaming like surround sound. Ewan the Dream Sheep – a monstrous lamb-shaped 'baby sleep aid' – was blaring white noise, like the static Glastonbury used to leave in her ears. Ewan also offered an ominous heartbeat and a mournful, dribbly lullaby. The melody always returned Isla to the weeks after the birth. She remembered staring into the crib, her chest bursting with love and milk, while part of her brain whined 'what about me?' like a jealous sibling.

She hadn't heard from Serge, though the award ceremony would have finished hours ago. Looking out towards the West End, she wondered if he resented her not accompanying him. But Serge never understood the effort of leaving the twins with a stranger. It was one of many reasons Isla felt ambivalent about Caspar's wedding. The whole occasion would only highlight their own lack of wedding plans. And Serge's ex – from Oxford – was going. This would not have troubled Isla, once, but motherhood seemed to have abducted whole swathes of her old self.

When Juno and Huck were asleep she tiptoed down the hall, like an intruder in her home. It had taken months to think of 10 Chiltern Mansions as home. Serge's grandfather had bought it when Marylebone was still bohemian, and his children and grandchildren and various cousins and friends had all lived in it at different times – like a very grand hostel. When Isla was pregnant, the deeds had been signed over to Serge. Isla was not consulted, though it would have been irrational, and rude, to reject the offer. Still, something about the way the process had happened over their heads unsettled her. Now, when she experienced even mild irritation with Serge's family, she saw herself re-cast as ungrateful – as if their generosity had gagged her. She knew Serge felt a version of this, all the time.

Ten Chiltern Mansions was beautiful, with views estate agents described as 'breathtaking', and had clearly been an ideal base for Serge in his twenties. But it was not suited to children. The tiny Edwardian lift was impossible with a double buggy, and the twins were always lunging from her arms at the Francis Bacon etchings or crawling into fireplaces. The room where they slept was still full of Serge's decks and vinyl, as if they were unexpected guests.

The block's other flats all seemed to be owned by rich European widows, who doted on Serge. No families appeared to live in the surrounding streets. Occasionally, she attempted a baby yoga class in Maida Vale, where everyone else cooed over one baby and she tried to corral two squirming, howling bodies. But mostly she did laps of Regent's Park, or stayed in the flat. The way she missed work felt like a stitch in her side.

Serge was still out – he never left parties before midnight. It was one of many ways his life hadn't changed, as hers had. He had not messaged either, but had already tweeted a photo of his SOFA statuette to hundreds of Likes. A seed of exclusion throbbed in her chest. Serge had been keeping his work separate for months, but had never shared a success with Twitter before her. She thought of all their conversations about *PLUR*, all the scenes she knew she had influenced.

Her phone announced a voice note, from an unsaved number.

'Ah, um, hey, Isla! It's Caspar. So, there's been a slight incident. Just, Serge's been, uh, arrested. He's fine, he's fine. Don't worry. But we got into a . . . situation . . . with this guy. Being really rude. Like, homophobic. Serge, uh . . . pushed him. In self-defence, like, defending me. And himself, obviously! But then, ummm, the police showed up. He'll be out soon. So, look, don't worry, OK? He's fine. Not a scratch. They've taken his phone, though. OK, so, uh, don't worry. Speak soon. Much love. Bye.'

Isla called Caspar, who did not pick up, and then Serge. His upbeat baritone promised to get back to her. She contemplated calling his parents, but it was past midnight – she would end up reassuring them, instead of being reassured. There was nobody else to call. Her mother was taking 'a life sabbatical' in Spain with a new boyfriend, and had deliberately chosen a house without Wi-Fi or phone signal.

Isla's old friends would only be impressed by the anarchy. Her friends from work might understand, but she had not seen them since giving birth. She had an abrupt sense of belonging nowhere, having always felt that she could be herself anywhere.

Saturday night was audible outside. She imagined Serge drunkenly inviting a fight with a stranger – behaving as though the twins didn't exist. Still, she wished she knew he was unhurt. She imagined a court case, perhaps prison, and her knees felt as if they were full of carbonated water. When the twins were born she was so anxious about everything that she used to assume Serge had been in a car accident whenever he was late. She had never worried this way, or not consciously, until motherhood. He had always come home, she reminded herself.

* * *

When Juno and Huck woke, at five, she had only slept an hour. By eight, she still hadn't heard from Serge. She considered a tour of London police stations, but the prospect was even worse than waiting in the flat. She wondered how it was possible to feel so lonely when she was never alone.

Instead, she made the twins more toast and rechecked Serge's social media. For a moment, she was disorientated – it seemed impossible that a blurry video of him was trending on Twitter. But Serge's arrest had somehow become public knowledge. The story had been reported on Vice and other news websites, with the same footage of Serge confronting a homophobic stranger and performing a judo punch. He appeared to have become a viral LGBTQ hero, overnight.

A right-wing columnist called Nigel Trott had commented:

Typical that the liberal elite is fawning over @SergeCampbell's affray as noble #whenABHgoeswoke.

But most people were saying it should be a GIF, and commenting on Serge's likeness to a young Damon Albarn.

He called when she was in the shower, the twins sliding around her feet, and she missed it. A text followed.

So sorry! Back soon. All fine.

Immediately afterwards, he tweeted:

Thanks for all the love everyone. I'm a free man!

Replies to his followers confirmed the other man was unhurt and had not pressed charges, video footage apparently having proved that Serge was acting in self-defence.

She stood in her towel, water dripping from her hair onto her phone, thanking the universe. But the gratitude was short-lived. Soon, a kind of righteous indignation seeped into the space that anxiety had vacated. She resented the way Serge and Caspar regressed to teenagers together. She was angry, now, that Serge had condemned her to a night of solitary panic. She hated that he had even had the opportunity to get arrested, that his old life was apparently still carrying on.

Serge continued to tweet chirpy messages to his followers. Resentment, fanned by fatigue and the twins' screaming, rose to fury. She had an urge to hurl Serge's laptop – or perhaps a priceless Campbell sculpture – down the mansion block stairs and watch it bounce and shatter. Instead, she kicked an Amazon box he had left by the bin – until the twins began laughing and copying her.

Leaning against the worktop, she let her thoughts go to the place where she and Serge broke up. She had been indulging this impulse often, lately. When she and Serge were first dating she used to contemplate commitment in the same way – examining it from all angles, like a risk assessment. It was pointless, looking back. She had been committed since their first kiss.

She was chiselling dried Weetabix off a highchair, when she heard the lift stop at their floor. The front door unlocked, and Serge called, 'Hello?'

'We're in here.'

She returned to the Weetabix so that she would be cleaning when he walked in, knowing this was obnoxious but unable to stop. He appeared in the doorway, tousled and contrite in his black tie, but a little triumphant too. The twins fell over each other to embrace his legs, like fans. He kissed their heads, and then came to hug Isla.

She smelled his stale sweat, and flinched. He looked at her, the victory deserting his face, and she knew they were going to fight.

Canal Studios

Hackney

10 a.m.

Daniel saw the email from his agent Camilla in a cab on his way to the interview. He was already feeling slightly deranged with jet lag, and the message – even just the name Serge Campbell – prompted a spike of adrenaline. Apparently, Serge had sent Camilla his latest script and was 'super keen' that Daniel read it, adding that they were attending the same three-day wedding in August. It was so characteristically entitled that Daniel wondered why he was shocked.

Daniel had flown straight into London from LA to do press for *Knifepoint*, with barely an hour to change. The film, which was set in a swaggering restaurant kitchen, starred Daniel as an unstable sous chef. His publicist had arranged a Monday morning photoshoot and interview, to appear in one of the *Telegraph*'s supplements.

'So good to meet you!' he said to the journalist as he walked in, wondering whether it was a double kiss moment. She stuck out her hand instead.

'Jessica, right?' he added, having consulted the call sheet as he ran up the stairs.

'We've met.'

He looked at her, still holding her hand, trying to quickly assimilate the shrewd eyes, large, freckled breasts and loud voice. They held no clues, though he felt sure the encounter could not have been sexual.

'Of course!' he said. 'Shit! Sorry! Knew I recognised you. Never forget a face. Where was it again?'

'St Arthur's. I was the year below you.'

He had expected her to mention a press junket, and this reference to Oxford was disorientating – doubly so after Camilla's email. But he acted a flash of recognition, cursing his own 'plane brain', and opened his arms. 'This is incredible! Woah! Small world, right?'

Jessica seemed satisfied, but he wished the interview had not begun on this note. Their common ground should have made the conversation feel less artificial, but he was now miserably conscious of his failure to place her. Daniel could imagine little worse than discovering he was forgettable.

They sat down on a sofa in a corner of the studio, and an intern appeared with coffee. He thanked her so effusively she looked startled, and he wondered if he would ever get used to people waiting on him and why it should be problematic. She offered him a muffin and he declined, thinking of a recent unflattering pap shot. For a second, he remembered being able to eat without thought.

'Did you see this?' said Jessica, handing Daniel her phone. It was open at the Mail Online, bearing a photo of Serge Campbell. It seemed implausible that Serge had already surfaced twice in Daniel's day, but there he was, SOFA award in hand, grinning. Daniel felt a kneejerk twist of resentment, until he realised the columnist, Nigel Trott, was condemning Serge for some kind of brawl. It didn't sound like Serge, who was famously unflappable.

'Amazing, that he used a statuette in self-defence!' said Jessica.

'Right! Classic Campbell. Defending one's kin with one's trophy!'

She giggled, gauchely feminine now.

'We actually just featured Serge,' she said. 'This piece on "Guys Doing Good". He started a whole scheme for low-income graduates.'

Daniel thought of Serge's constant efforts to atone for his heritage, with more irritation.

'You two were friends, right?' said Jessica.

'Sure, sure. I mean, yeah, I was always closer to Caspar than Serge. Because Cas and I did English. With Rosie Littleton? We were, like, these three thesps in this proper jock college. With all the rugby dickheads. And Serge was always hanging out in other colleges. Or pissing off back to London. So I definitely spent the most time with Caspar and Rosie.'

It was all true, but he knew he was jabbering. He was relieved when Jessica began talking about another St Arthur's student, now England rugby player, who she had recently interviewed – as if St Arthur's alumni were her speciality. Journalists were a much odder species, Daniel felt, than they appeared on their pages. Either there was a dogged, intrusive edge to their curiosity, or they were smiling in person but shockingly snide in print. Jessica pressed Record and launched into questions about *TROG*, and how his character Thane's wig had its own Instagram. She kept pushing her hair back, releasing wafts of deodorant, and smoothing her shirt as if they were on a strange date. He found himself flirting back, biting his lower lip and using her name a lot, both out of habit and to compensate for not recognising her.

He sat forwards now, in answer to a serious question about his father's sudden death when he was five. Journalists always raised it, because he had once – truthfully – attributed his instinct to entertain to this trauma. Part of him wished he had never mentioned it.

'The thing is, Jess, when we lost my dad, everyone was so sad, y'know? My mum, my nan, the whole community. Cos he was such a big personality. And I realised I could make them smile again by, just, showing off, really. Singing, dancing, little comedy sketches. I used to put on these shows, doing impressions of celebrities, or our regulars, just for my mum and my aunties. Classic only child. But I just wanted to make them forget for a while. Cos then I could, too.'

She nodded, expressing less sympathy than most female journalists. He was relieved – any compassion made him see his frantic childhood grief afresh. In hindsight, acting a mentally fragile chef had been a risk. There were too many parallels with his father.

Jessica moved on to Daniel's experience of Oxford. This was another theme in interviews, as if his degree was wildly incongruous. The subhead of his first big profile had been: 'From Deep Fat Fryer to Dreaming Spire', because his parents had run a fish and chip shop. Pyke's On The Pier was really an early gastro pub, serving beer-battered hake to five-star reviews. But even when Daniel clarified this – and the fact that he had been an outrageously precocious child to ambitious parents – the chip shop narrative prevailed. Often, it came with a fishy pun on Pyke. After a few interviews he found himself playing up to his new role – the pretty Essex boy with a brain.

'So Oxford was a culture shock?' Jessica asked, eagerly.

'Oh for sure. My first Formal Hall, I was like "What the—? Is this actual Hogwarts?" To be fair, though, I was usually too pissed to dwell on it.'

She smiled, and he immediately regretted this comment. Her memory seemed unnervingly accurate.

'Did that help with feeling like you fitted in? Drinking?'

'I mean, we were students! What else you gonna do?'

He needed a drink, now. Press was always easier slightly buzzed.

'Cos I was just wondering,' said Jessica, 'if you drew on your memories of St Arthur's, for *Knifepoint*? Like, if you saw a correlation between all that male bravado in college, and the macho culture in the kitchen? At what point "banter" tips into bullying?'

'Sorry?' said Daniel, playing for time. He understood, but had no neat answer.

'I mean, just personally, I remember a load of stuff at college that might seem dodgy now? All the nicknames?'

'I mean, I feel like that's standard, right? The stupid name from freshers' week that sticks?'

'But this was different. It was guys in older years literally naming – ranking – people as they came in, y'know? Like, Caspar Campbell was "The Camptown Lady"? Or "Woofy"? My friend Jen was "Tinky Winky", cos apparently she looked like a Tellytubby. That boy who was clearly autistic was "Rain Man".'

'He dropped out, didn't he?' said Daniel, thinking aloud.

'Exactly! And "Fittest Fresher Awards" – what was that?'

Daniel recalled his own pique at losing 'Fittest Male Fresher' to Jessica's other recent interviewee, the giant blond rugby player. He wondered if she had grilled this man on St Arthur's political correctness, too.

'I mean, it just used to seem so off – to me – that you were literally known as "Pikey",' she carried on. 'Given that, like you said, you were in a minority. Coming from a working class background.'

She stared, as if she was cross-examining him.

'Right. I mean, it is my name. But I hear you,' he said. 'Pikey. The bantz. It was what it was, right? Sink or swim. But yeah, no, I didn't base *Knifepoint* on that. Or any, like, personal experience.'

He had known, dimly, that Pikey was offensive. But mostly he remembered feeling grateful that his new peers felt he warranted a moniker at all.

* * *

Afterwards, in the make-up chair, he sat scrolling through accounts of Serge's arrest, and then reviews of Serge's latest award-winning movie. He found himself reliving a Sunday afternoon at the King's Arms, Oxford. Finals were approaching, but he and Serge had sat there long after Caspar and Rosie, having come up with the concept for a film. The idea was about a working class student at Cambridge, and they had written the whole treatment on Serge's laptop that day. It wasn't their first collaboration, but they had never achieved such momentum – each of them contributing their different perspectives, seeing their visions align. They had stayed until closing time, fuelled by peanuts and exhilaration. Daniel could never remember whose idea it was first, or whether it was even possible to say. Their working title was *Bursary Boy*.

When his make-up was done, he stood against a white backdrop, the lights and umbrellas returning him – as always – to childhood modelling. He had already provided almost his whole repertoire of expressions, lingering on the two Caspar called 'happy surprised' and 'annoyed surprised'. He was smouldering now, eyes suspicious, his thumb pressing his bottom lip as if he were trying to wipe away a sticky crumb.

'Amazing!' said the photographer. 'Now get mad! Be like, go fuck yourself!'

He hardened his brow and jaw – thinking of the rugby players who christened him Pikey, and joked that his dad was in prison. Some of them would be at Caspar's wedding.

'More!' said the photographer, laughing.

He saw Serge, now. He could already picture him at the wedding – innocently upbeat, entreating Daniel to be in his next film.

'Woah!' said the photographer. She was half laughing behind the explosive clicks. 'You're scaring me!'

Oxford, June 2004

Daniel and Allegra are at the St Arthur's College summer ball. It is nearly midnight. They are sitting on a bench in the quad, smoking and passing a bottle of wine back and forth. Music and shouting are audible from a marquee. Nobody else is around.

'It's literally everything for me,' says Allegra. 'Acting. Like, my earliest memories are me and Serge putting on shows in our parents' bed.'

'Their bed?'

'Yeah. It's this fucking four-poster, Moroccan tent thing. Ridiculous. But an insane proscenium arch.'

Daniel laughs. In the moonlight his face looks like a black and white headshot.

'And you were the star, right?'

'No!' she says, laughing and pushing briefly against him in flirtatious protest. 'I don't give a shit about attention. Fame, whatever. I just love being on stage.'

'Is that not a contradiction in terms?'

'What?'

'Isn't theatre just a microcosm of fame?' says Daniel. 'Like, there are hundreds of people in the audience, and only you on stage, and they're all looking your way?'

'But, you're *not* you on stage! You're someone else. That's what I love. Stepping into this whole other person.'

'Sure. I get that. But you're still there, somewhere, right? It's still you, hearing the laughs. The applause.'

'No! That's the thing. I genuinely feel like I'm not me any more. Afterwards, I'm literally like, "what just happened?"'

She sits back and stubs out her cigarette.

Daniel looks sideways, and smirks slightly.

'What?'

'Nothing.'

She sits forwards and looks at him now, more insistent, though her eyes are lax.

'What?' she says again. 'Say.'

'Just, wish I'd had your confidence. At your age.'

He announces this as if he is much older than twenty-one.

'You were working at my age!'

'Yeah, because someone cast me. I had no idea what I was doing, did I?'

'I bet you had some idea.'

He finishes his cigarette and leans back, propping his elbow up on the bench.

Allegra's head suddenly darts into his space. For a second their mouths are pressed together.

There is a frozen moment, like the time between a race-start beep and the runners leaving the blocks.

Then Daniel turns his head away and says, 'Woah, er, maybe we shouldn't?'

He looks nervous now, as if he is the younger of the two, and would no longer be able to drop the word 'microcosm' into conversation. Allegra is still leaning across him, her hands on his chest, so that he is trapped against the bench. She manoeuvres herself so that she is sitting in his lap. She is tall, and Daniel is slight – in this position they look the same size. She leans in and they are kissing, for longer this time, though Daniel has no other option.

'Sorry, just,' he says, his voice muffled.

'What?' she says. 'Oh, cos of Serge! I won't tell him. Seriously. Or I won't if you won't?'

It sounds like a dare.

A group of students pass, shouting and leering. Someone begins singing 'Uptown Girl'.

Allegra moves to kiss him again, more confidently, emboldened by the audience. Eventually Daniel moves his head, almost ducking.

'Hey, we're gonna see each other this summer, right?' he says. 'In Italy?'

She looks confused.

'But look, uh, let me take your number,' he says.

He puts his hands on her hips, as if to move her and begin the number exchanging process. She seems to interpret this as desire, and wraps her arms round his neck, giggling.

'Sorry, no, you're just – dead leg!' he says, managing to shunt her off his lap this time. Because of her height he can't manage this in one swift movement, and she lands awkwardly on the bench, her skirt riding up. She looks shocked for a second, then frowns.

'Listen, give me your number,' he says, quickly, as if in response to the frown. 'We'll go out! We should go to a play, I don't get to the theatre enough.'

He hands her his phone, and she enters her number, her expression coquettish again as she passes it back.

'Cheers, babe. I'll call you,' he says. 'Definitely.'

ABBA's 'Dancing Queen' floats across from the white peaks of the marquee.

'Go back in?' he says.

She stands up, unsteadily.

'Don't tell Serge, OK?' she says, again. 'He's really overprotective. My whole family's like that.'

Daniel smiles and says, 'Course not,' matching her tone. 'Nothing to see here!'

He picks up the bottle of wine, offering it to her first. Then he drinks from it himself, tipping his head right back as if he needs everything that is left inside.

PART THREE

AUGUST 2019
TWO DAYS BEFORE CASPAR'S WEDDING

From: campbell.delahunt.wedding@gmail.com
Bcc: campbell.delahunt.wedding@gmail.com
Date: 29 August, 2019, 05:00
Subject: Nearly there!

Hey Team!

We are so excited to see you soon in sunny Aix. It's currently 40 degrees (104 for our US guests) and the weekend looks set to be a scorcher. Please see attached list of everybody's flight times, for those of you meeting at JFK, Heathrow or Marseille.
 Please also see final dietary requirements and do let us know if we've missed any. JP is panicking about you celiacs accidentally ingesting a baguette. (Caspar's dad's view: 'Allergies? That's their problem.')

If you need anything on the day please speak to Rosie or Nate, our eminently capable best man and woman. Caspar's cousin Serge is also a best man, but as you may have gathered Serge is a little more handy with a SOFA statuette than a spreadsheet.

Over and out xx

Departures

Heathrow

9 A.M.

Rosie was paying for her porridge at EAT, when she heard a man say her name. She knew it was Serge before she turned round.

'Hey!' he said. He looked older, lines bracketing his smile, but it suited him. He leaned in to kiss her efficiently on both cheeks so that she said the word 'Hi!' on his nose. She had forgotten how his height made her feel.

'How are you?'

He looked delighted, his big eyes flicking across her face like searchlights. Time seemed to be speeding up and slowing down all at once.

'Fine!' she said. 'You?'

'Yeah, great! Wedding should be amazing!'

He rubbed his hands together like someone miming glee. She thought of how often she had watched his arrest online.

'We're over here,' he said. She saw his parents, a woman and two toddlers at a table and felt overwhelmingly caught off-guard. JP's spreadsheet had listed Serge as flying earlier than her. She had pictured their first meeting in Provençal sunlight, not Heathrow's ghoulish lighting. She wasn't wearing mascara, and it felt like a calamitous oversight.

'Hi!' she said, offering a little wave, and looking at Lucian

Campbell because it was easier than making eye contact with Serge's fiancée. She followed him to the table, even though the prospect of eating porridge with them was as surreal as one of her dreams.

Serge's father smiled in the vague, genial way he used to at the Campbells' house in Dorset, where he seemed to be permanently writing a biography of his grandfather. Marina started to stand, saying 'Rosie, *hello!*' the way she always had, somehow conveying sympathy, as if being Rosie must be an ordeal. She was wearing a Kantha jacket and pearls, her own uniform in the way that Serge's Reebok Classics were his.

'Don't stand up!' said Rosie, hearing an edge of panic in her voice.

'This is Isla. And the twins,' said Serge, as if this needed no explanation.

Isla looked up and smiled, briefly. She had the kind of deep, luminous tan Rosie periodically tried to fake, and a halo of wavy, dirty-looking blonde hair. Her eyes, lips and nose were all large and defined, like a lioness. Rosie felt her own features as faint and forgettable, her 'textured bob' dismally optimistic. Both toddlers had Isla's colouring, but Serge's galactic eyes. The boy was pulling at the mess of chains and pendants around Isla's throat, and she moved his hand without acknowledging him – like a part of herself. Her jewellery looked like an extension of her body too, an effect Rosie had always coveted.

'Hey,' said Isla.

There was a slight, incvitable rasp to her voice. Her tattoos, and the ennui she exuded, made Rosie feel middle-aged and also like a child meeting a laconic teenager.

'Hello!' said Rosie.

Her own voice appalled her with its jauntiness.

Isla took a sip of coffee. A smudge of foam remained on her cupid's bow, as if her mouth was so luscious it couldn't help catching things.

'You aren't delayed too, are you?' said Marina eagerly. 'BA's hopeless. We've been here for hours. We'll probably miss the baseball, or whatever it is, at this rate.'

She was almost laughing, and Rosie now remembered Marina's fetish for bathos and caveat – the delight she took in wet holidays, technological malfunctions, inaccurate period drama and impenetrable packaging. It had always been hard to match and mirror her peculiar strain of exuberant pessimism.

As his mother kept saying the wedding was likely to be 'very American', Rosie noticed Serge touch his mouth discreetly with his finger while staring at Isla. After a second she licked her lips and reached for a napkin. Something about the intimacy of the moment, of Serge protecting Isla from embarrassment, made Rosie want to flee.

'So we need to get on this speech, right?' he said, turning back to her. 'Rosie and I are giving a best man's speech together.'

'Are you? Honestly, all these speeches now,' said Marina. 'The trouble is they're too long.'

'We'll keep it short,' said Rosie.

'Will we?' said Serge. 'I've got a shedload on Cas. He's not getting off lightly.'

'Right!' said Rosie. 'He was an absolute reprobate at Oxford.'

Isla looked up at her. Rosie couldn't read her expression.

'Didn't Caspar give a rather embarrassing speech at your engagement party?' said Lucian affably, looking from Serge to Isla. The faux pas blossomed in the silence.

'Well done on the SOFA, by the way,' said Rosie, since nobody else seemed to feel responsible for moving the conversation forwards.

'Right, cheers!' said Serge, pulling a cutely contrite expression.

Isla was looking into the middle distance, as if she were studying a bin twenty feet away. Rosie wondered if she had resented his arrest, even though he had been hailed as a hero. It was typical of Serge to emerge from an assault charge apparently even more likeable than before.

'OK, so let's chat speeches tomorrow,' he said. 'You're at Georgette's, right?'

'Er, yup. Think so!'

She wondered why it was a reflex to sound incompetent.

'Awesome. Catch you there then, Rosie.'

He leaned in for another double kiss, and she realised she was dismissed as they all smiled.

For some reason she blew a kiss to the whole table, almost shuddering at this odd, uncharacteristic gesture as she walked away.

She stood in WH Smith, staring blindly at the newspapers, trying to absorb what had just happened. She imagined Serge and Isla acknowledging it later, quickly and unthinkingly. Rosie had been fixated on all Serge's exes since Oxford – particularly her predecessor, Olympia Harrod. She knew Isla would not feel threatened by Rosie in this way. It was crushing to realise you could not inspire even lukewarm jealousy.

The *Telegraph*'s masthead caught her attention. It featured Daniel's face – looking nothing like his real, funny self – alongside the words 'Vikings, Knife Skills, Toxic Masculinity: Daniel Pyke Feels the Heat'. She bought a copy, with a thrill of tangential pride and anticipation of seeing Daniel – perhaps teasing him about fame, the way she used to for borrowing her fake tan.

Marseille Airport

Provence

2 P.M.

The hire car, with its steering wheel on the left, felt appropriately abnormal. Serge looked at Isla as she took the driver's seat, but she was staring at her phone – resisting his eyes. It was an effort not to reach across and touch her. She looked disarmingly healthy, as if she hadn't suffered like he had. The twins had changed, too, and this was also painful. The words 'trial separation' still felt unreal.

Every day in Vancouver, Serge had re-lived their fight after his arrest. He had arrived home, expecting Isla to understand, perhaps even admire, his actions. He had thought she might find the attention on social media funny, as he had. Instead, Isla had accused him of behaving as if he had no responsibilities. He had argued he had a responsibility to his cousin. This had spiralled into both of them talking over one another, Serge trying to put the arrest in context, Isla repeatedly using the phrase 'on my own' – until they were almost having separate arguments. The twins had begun to scream, and she had shouted that she needed 'a break' and that they should view his month in Vancouver as a trial separation. Assuming she was using this threat as leverage, and furious that she would do so, he had agreed.

But it had not been an empty threat. She had finally emailed two days after his arrival in Canada, just as he was about to call to plead forgiveness. Her email had set out her terms, coldly, and said that she needed time to think, and that he must respect her wish for no contact. She promised to send photos of the twins, and to organise weekly FaceTimes, with minimal adult interaction.

He had spent the day in shock, directing a perky ad for Google. Later he had replied, acknowledging her need for space and accepting her diktats – on condition they tell nobody. He couldn't see what else to do. His request for secrecy restored some sense of control, but he knew it was an illusion.

Serge had kept telling himself that they would work it out in France. Sunshine always thawed Isla, the stress of daily life would lift, and they would have time to talk. Caspar's wedding had become a beacon during his nights in Vancouver. Until then, he told himself, Isla just needed to calm down. His mute obedience would make her think. She would realise she did not want to destroy everything to prove a point.

Still, it had been a struggle to honour her rules. He had nearly called many times – after a drink, panicking at dawn that she had met someone else, or torturing himself with photos of the twins. But he feared Isla would view a spontaneous call as arrogance, an entitled disregard for her wishes. So he had kept his promise, and made no contact. The three organised video calls were futile. He had mostly spoken to a blank square, unsure if his children could hear him.

Serge had not adhered to his own stipulation – he had ended up telling his sister. Allegra had been FaceTiming him, drunk, and had begged Serge to add Isla and the twins to the call. Ignoring his excuses, she then tried to add Isla herself, and Serge had blurted out about the separation to make her stop. Allegra expressed dismay, but he could see she was enjoying the crisis. She had always savoured Serge's failures. His C in GCSE French, among his A*s, had sustained her for years.

Isla was sitting up unnaturally straight and still hadn't looked over, as if she were daring him to speak. This was the first time they had been alone for weeks, Serge having returned from Vancouver the previous evening and spent the night at an airport hotel. His parents' presence all morning, and their indulgent view of his arrest, had only added to the tension. The night of the SOFA awards still seemed like a bizarre short film he might have made himself.

'OK?' he said, to Isla's profile.

She made a non-committal noise, and turned onto the wide European road. On one side was a pine-covered slope, on the other were low, putty-coloured buildings. He felt a reflexive lift at being abroad, taking in Cézanne's light and billboards for Badoit, aware that his eyes would soon adjust and it would all stop looking exotic. He and Isla had travelled frequently, right up until her third trimester. He had assumed it would continue with children.

'How's your mum?' he said, because it was the only neutral question he could think of.

'Fine. I think. Living her best life with Miguel.'

'Right. Any dramas with these guys? While I was away?'

She paused, and he knew she hated the way he was talking as if it had been a normal work trip.

'Not really. Huck lost Yaya,' she said, playing along. 'I made a new one.'

Yaya was a small, smelly square of orange crochet that Huck liked to suck. Isla's mother had made one for each twin, presenting them at birth like blessings. Huck was inconveniently attached to his, against Serge's advice.

'Shit. Did he accept it?'

'He's been holding it all morning,' said Isla, as if Serge should have noticed the imposter.

Neither of them said anything more, while Serge wondered how they could be so frosty and still speak in parental shorthand. Isla switched on the radio. Hectic, squiggly jazz invaded their air-conditioned silence.

'So. How've you been?' said Serge, eventually.

'All right.'

He felt slightly desperate.

'What are you going to do about the zombie job?'

Isla had been headhunted for a new TV drama, involving zombies. She had mentioned it over breakfast with his parents, and he had pretended he already knew.

'Nothing. I'd need full-time childcare. Even if I put them in nursery I'd need someone to pick them up.'

He wanted to ask her to stop talking about herself as if she were a single mother, but instead he said, 'A nanny? Au pair?'

Isla made a face. She often claimed that childcare under two 'damaged attachment'.

'I had nannies. I turned out OK,' he said.

In the past Isla might have smiled and said 'debateable', but now she just said, 'A nanny's worse. At least nursery staff are on view.'

He suspected her real objection to nannies was her relentless inverse snobbery – but this could never be raised. He couldn't afford another person on his payroll anyway.

They queued for a tollgate. Serge handed Isla his debit card, thinking of the sickening balance in his current account. He was now relying entirely on Daniel Pyke putting his name to Vanguard's next film. It had been fifteen years since the abrupt, silent end to their friendship. Long enough, Serge told himself, for them both to move on. His mother's motto, 'least said soonest mended', which usually struck him as un-evolved, now seemed eminently wise.

They emerged from the row of tollgates.

'So you've met Rosie,' he said, angling for some response. The neediness in his voice was alien.

'I've met Rosie.'

'Was that weird?'

'Not particularly.'

'Okaaay.'

'What?' said Isla, turning.

'Are we going to do this all weekend?'

Isla pouted slightly. Instantly he felt a shift, like a rollercoaster clanking into life. He remembered how bracing – alluring, even – he used to find her ease with conflict.

'I can't switch everything off because you don't tell your family anything, Serge!'

'I mean,' he breathed in and out through his nose, 'we're away. Can't we try to enjoy that?'

'Isn't it enough that we're pretending in public?'

He wanted to ask what she meant by 'pretending', but she was watching a moped alongside the car, her jaw clenched. The moped was trying to overtake. Isla sped up in response, and showed the other driver her middle finger. Serge looked away. People were always surprised to hear about Isla's road rage – how her languid, public demeanour masked a volatile impatience. He used to feel privileged to know this, as if he had been granted VIP access.

The moped overtook, revving in triumph.

'Fuck's sake,' she muttered.

He said nothing.

'What?'

'I didn't say anything.'

'That was really dangerous!'

'I can drive, Isla.'

He knew he sounded childish.

'Right. You just don't.'

This was true – Serge had sold his car to cover the secret mortgage, pleading concern about climate change, and had wondered if Isla would guess he was in debt. But she had just switched to driving her old Mini. It barely accommodated the twins' car seats, a point she raised frequently while Serge cycled to and from film sets.

They drove on without speaking. He changed the radio station, and French hip-hop replaced the jazz – the rapper's throaty indignation matching Isla's hostility. He remembered how determined he had been to repair relations in France, to show her that they just needed time together. The idea already seemed unrealistic, and they weren't even at the hotel.

Hotel Georgette

Aix-en-Provence

2.45 P.M.

Hotel Georgette was off Place Richelme, a shady square famous for its food market. It was the kind of hotel that appeared in discerning city guides, and Caspar and JP had reserved all thirty rooms. On Saturday, all the top table guests were to stay at the wedding venue Chateau de Beaupont. Isla and Serge were then returning to Hotel Georgette on Sunday, before leaving on Monday. Isla thought of the additional packing this would entail, and wondered how she had become so uptight.

Other guests were arriving at the same time, so that they had to keep stopping to greet people. In the past Isla knew she would have enjoyed the sense of tribal anticipation in taking over an entire hotel – so unlike her experience of family. But she already felt drained by one morning of acting as if everything was fine. It seemed to come easily to Serge.

They checked in, the twins asleep, and were shown across a courtyard full of olive and lemon trees to their ground floor suite. It was spartanly Mediterranean, with a honeycomb terracotta floor and immaculate white fabrics – primed for toddler handprints. Seeing the miniature toiletries and paper circles under the glasses, she remembered other hotels where she and Serge had stayed, finding ways to have sex around her pregnant stomach. It often seemed that they had leapfrogged from honeymoon couple to battered family in a day.

There was a travel cot in the suite's sitting room, and Isla decided to sleep on the sofa beside it. Serge kicked off his shoes and lay on the huge bed. She couldn't tell if it was a clumsy invitation to talk, or a signal to leave him alone. She went into the bathroom to put on a bikini. As she changed, she thought how she used to enjoy walking around naked in front of Serge, indulging his jokes about her hippie roots.

'I'm meeting Daniel tomorrow, for coffee,' he said, speaking to her from the bed. 'Pyke. Or I'm hoping to. Hasn't confirmed. Trying to get him attached to *Beating Heart*.'

'Daniel Pyke?'

She caught her own comically startled face in the mirror.

'Yeah. We were friends at Oxford, remember? Or, in the same group.'

Isla knew that Serge had been at university with Daniel Pyke, but not that they had been close. Any time his name came up, Serge had sounded uncharacteristically bored – dismissive, even. She was tempted to raise this point, but Serge's connections often dated from Oxford, or school, or even his Hampstead nursery. She was glad, now, that she had never mentioned her own one-sided history with Daniel Pyke. There was a curious power in withholding this information.

'Can't you meet in London?' she said.

'He's in LA. Plus this stuff's always easier off duty. More chilled.'

Isla didn't reply. Serge used his family so unthinkingly to his advantage that there was no point. His preference for networking on Campbell Champagne was hardly immoral, anyway.

'Fine. I'm going to swim,' she said, emerging from the bathroom. 'Get me if they wake up.'

His eyes opened. She felt his gaze on her body.

'I'll watch them,' he said. 'I haven't seen them for so long.'

'They'll be hungry,' she said, knowing this would require him to ask for assistance. 'Don't let them sleep past four.'

She wondered why she could not cede control, when she craved respite.

Outside it was brutally hot. She stood looking out across the city's rooftops, the light so bright that distant aerials were visible. She couldn't decide whether to swim or sunbathe, or try to do both. This choice — how best to use an infant nap — seemed to figure too often in her life.

In the end she swam, fast, to maximise the novelty of being in a pool without a toddler under each arm, like a three-headed monster. Flipping onto her back, water filling her ears as she squinted at the sky, she realised she would soon meet Daniel Pyke. At thirteen, Isla had been obsessed with his character in *Riptide*. She still remembered a scene where a teenage Daniel strode out of the Atlantic, wetsuit unzipped, eyes dark and soulful. She used to pause the DVD, repeatedly, at this moment.

Closing her eyes, she tried to order her thoughts. It felt strange, but also utterly natural, to be with Serge again. She had not anticipated his resolute cheerfulness, though it was typical of Serge — and all the Campbells. She had found herself being unduly cold in response, even antagonistic in the car, as if she needed to balance his false positivity. She knew it was not constructive, but she could not seem to find another mode. She thought back to the day when Serge had returned from the police station. Their row had escalated in minutes, as they always did. At some point Isla had heard herself yell that she needed 'a break', and waited for him to back-pedal. But, shockingly, he had said, 'OK. Fine. If that's what you want,' and left the room. She had heard him showering and then packing for Vancouver, yanking drawers open and shutting cupboard doors too hard, and had wanted to retract her words. But rage, or pride, had stopped her. He had left at dawn, with no goodbye.

She had expected him to call upon landing, grovelling. When he did not, she had sent him terms for a trial separation – certain he would cave. But again, he had agreed without resistance. His only condition was that they attend Caspar's wedding as a couple. His concern with saving face infuriated her.

Every day she felt even angrier, assuming he was calling her bluff in childish revenge. Then she wondered if his failure to protest was a silent judgement on her melodrama. After a while she began to panic that he actually no longer wanted her, but was too cowardly to end it. This thought, over the month, had cost her more sleep than the twins.

When her fury threatened to plummet into grief she had driven to her mother's empty bungalow in Somerset, where she could pretend Serge had never existed. The house was bordering on squalor, all the appliances malfunctioning as usual. Ever since her mother had bought it, charming the landlord into a vastly under-priced private sale, maintenance had slipped to student levels. But the air and grassy hills of her childhood were restorative, and she had acquired a deep tan.

Beyond this, it made shockingly little difference to live as a single parent. She spent the days watching the twins roam her mother's overgrown garden, and railing against Serge in her head. All night, she wondered why he did not call. She had often struggled to read him, but it used to be part of their charge. Now, the uncertainty was like stepping into mid-air.

After swimming she lay on a sun lounger. A minute later, unable to relax, she sent her mother a picture of the twins on the plane – knowing Saffron might reply instantly or not for several days.

Isla had managed to reach her mother on the phone, soon after Serge had left for Vancouver, and they had spoken for two hours. The call had resulted in Saffron offering Isla her empty house. Then, despite her insights on Serge being 'emotionally checked out', she had not called Isla for the rest of the month.

Her mother must have been in town, now, because she

immediately sent back five heart emojis, and then a selfie of her and Miguel drinking Sangria captioned 'Salute'.

Isla reacted with a thumbs up.

Saffron wrote:

> How is it seeing Serge?

> Weird. He's acting like everything's normal.

> Avoidance. Common maladaptive response.

Her mother was finally having therapy, and now applied its language with abandon.

Isla replied:

> One way of looking at it.

> Sounds like you're very angry with him.

> You could say that.

> Does he get why? Not showing up for the twins … Not holding space for you … putting work first?

> Yes / no. More avoidance.

Her mother replied with a Leo emoji, Serge's star sign, and wrote:

> Hugs to the babbers. Love you.

Isla knew Serge found her relationship with her mother disconcerting, but he could never have understood. Saffron Malone – beautiful and impulsive – had given birth to Isla at twenty-two, after a doomed affair with a married tutor at art college. Isla's father had joined a cult soon after her birth, and moved to Goa. She had written to him, once, when she was nine. His reply, months later, had been brief and generic. She had never tried again.

Saffron was estranged from her own parents, partly because of the ill-advised relationship, so she and Isla had effectively grown up alone, together. Saffron laughed and cried constantly, unlike Isla, alternately dispensing adult advice and allowing her daughter to clean up her excesses. Her interest in the twins had been similarly erratic, veering between doting enthusiasm and late cancellations. Isla had trained herself to expect nothing. More was a bonus.

Serge did not have an intimate bond with either his mother or father, but relations were warm and consistent. Marina and Lucian operated as a unit, and still referred to Serge and his sister Allegra as 'the children'. There were frequent convivial afternoons at their houses, and regular gifts of tasteful toys and classic picture books, but his parents never offered much practical help with the twins. Marina always expressed awe at Isla handling two babies, implying that she could not manage this herself. Isla had not wanted to test her.

Her eyes itched with sleep deprivation, as always. She lifted her head, straining to hear if the twins had woken, but the courtyard was quiet. Briefly, treacherously, she imagined a parallel world where her children did not exist. It was futile. She was cornered in a three-man cell of love and need – a cell that only the twins, one day, would be able to leave.

The Lobby

Hotel Georgette

3.30 p.m.

The moped ride from the airport had left Daniel teeming with adrenaline, as if he had just done live TV. He had not known, until he was wearing the helmet, how badly he was craving anonymity. Daniel used to doubt actors' reports that fame was oppressive. He still welcomed the gushing requests for selfies from *TROG* fans. It was the sense of silent surveillance he found difficult. At Stansted, he had felt strangers' eyes on him like CCTV. He was at the hotel's front desk, when Rosie walked in.

'Oh. My. God,' he said, so loudly that people looked up. 'Rosie bloody Littleton!'

He dropped the bags in both his hands simultaneously, as though he were acting a reunion scene, and stepped forwards to hug her. He had decided, weeks ago, that when he saw Rosie he would behave as if distance alone had separated them. He would not even refer to their years of silence, or the phone call that had effectively ended their friendship.

He went for a Hollywood hug, lifting her slightly off the ground. But when they parted she looked flustered.

'So great to see you!' he said, encouragingly.

'You too!' she said, though it sounded reserved. 'How are you, Mr A-list?'

She straightened her clothes, which his embrace had muddled.

'Meh, y'know. How about you? How *you* doin'?'

'Fine! All good. Nothing major.'

'You look amazing! Like, identical.'

It was true, Rosie's small, neat face seemed to be impervious to time.

'No, *you* do! I need your dermatologist,' she said, as if she had remembered how their repartee operated.

'I just stay hydrated,' he said, in a perfect Californian accent.

She laughed, but it was still restrained.

He offered to carry her bags, but she declined and promised to find him later.

He walked into his room and began to unpack, trying not to feel thrown by Rosie's cautious greeting. Even with all his clothes folded, thinking of his mother's mantra 'a tidy room is a tidy mind', he couldn't relax. He opened the balcony doors and stood in the small space, vaping. The month in England had been wildly pressurised, his publicist taking the opportunity to book daily interviews, premieres and appearances. He had hardly seen his mother – either leaving the house at 5 a.m. for morning TV and radio, or returning after midnight, high on attention and self-doubt and often cocaine. By the end of the month, he had gone from using at weekends to several times a week – at first to handle all the red carpet events, then just to feel normal. He had only spent one whole day at home, miserably hungover, prompting his mother to ask if he should 'take a break'. But he had reassured her that he was fine, because it was bliss to just sit with her watching *Gogglebox*.

From the balcony there was a vista across dense pine forests to a single, majestic mountain – cypress quills punctuating the horizontals. After a moment, the nicotine and view slowed his nerves. There was a woman in the courtyard below, on a sun lounger. He recognised her. She was noticeably attractive, and had sworn at him when he had overtaken her car on his moped. She turned onto her front, and his eyes tracked her buttocks and thighs. He wondered how she fitted into the wedding, and if he would meet her that evening.

His phone pinged with two texts, and he turned back to the room. The first was from his agent Camilla, asking him to call. The second was from Serge. It was a short, upbeat message suggesting they meet 'for coffee' to chat about Vanguard's next film. The only reference to their fifteen-year silence was the greeting: 'Hey Dan, long time!'

He sat down, his face warm, realising he had been braced for this contact. It should have been gratifying to have Serge chase him, after everything, but he felt more affronted than victorious. Serge's film, *Beating Heart*, was set on a council estate, and starred a charismatic drug dealer questioning his sexuality. It sounded original, but the idea that Serge associated all these concepts with Daniel was annoying too.

He called Camilla first.

'Darling! You've seen the *Telegraph*, have you?' she said. 'Gorgeous pics.'

Her voice had an enunciated quality that made him think about very cold white wine. He pretended he had read the interview. Often, he found, he put off looking at his own press. It was odd, given that his default insomnia tactic was finessing his Desert Island Discs choices.

'Sorry you had such a grotty time at Oxford,' she said. 'Look who's laughing now, though!'

Daniel's stomach performed some rapid origami. Ever since the interview he had been questioning his time at St Arthur's, but he hoped he hadn't said anything too damning on record. The timing, just before Caspar's wedding, would be painful.

'Now, speaking of Oxford, promise me you won't agree to anything with Serge Campbell, will you?' said Camilla. 'We can't have you doing independents as favours! Not when the studios want you!'

He promised, though he had no intention of accepting Serge's offer. The call ended, Camilla reminding him to get his beauty sleep, and he sat trying to compose a reply to Serge.

He would have to meet him, it was too awkward to refuse. He thought back to the interview, how he had talked about being closer to Rosie and Caspar than Serge. It was true – he used to see and speak to Rosie and Caspar during the holidays, and had met their families. But Serge and Daniel's term-time camaraderie had been unique. He vividly remembered their first evening one on one – his flattered surprise when Serge suggested they see *Mulholland Drive* at the Everyman. They had walked back through Oxford in nascent snow, Daniel trying to second-guess Serge's response to the film, and then realising Serge actually wanted his opinion. Their sparring had felt unnecessary without an audience. After that night, their cinema trips became a ritual, graduating to DVD screenings in Serge's room. Daniel had never met anyone his age eager to analyse Kubrick and Linklater.

He stood up, having sent a bland response agreeing to meet the next morning. The prospect of the softball match was suddenly exhausting. He made coffee using all the minibar's Nespresso pods, already craving the cocaine he had bought in Marseille. He had promised himself he would save it for Saturday. Locking it up in the safe, he remembered Rosie saying she sometimes wished she could send an understudy to parties, and thought how accurately this summed up his feelings about the weekend ahead. Until recently, he knew, he would have relished the chance to officiate a friend's marriage. Now it loomed, like a public audition to play himself.

Courtyard Suite

Hotel Georgette

4 p.m.

Serge leaned over the cot, watching the twins sleep. Their noses were an inch apart, like divers buddy breathing. Huck's hand moved to Juno's, and their fingers meshed. Their bond had always fascinated Serge – just as the merging of his genes and Isla's struck him as a miracle. He had hardly been able to stop touching them all day – even when they twisted back to Isla. Juno kept saying, 'No, Dada!' wagging her finger at him. It would have been funny, if it hadn't felt like a weight crushing his chest.

His phone rang, and he walked to the other room, hoping it was Daniel replying to his breezy message. He would see Daniel soon at the softball, he realised. Allegra would have to see him again, too.

It was not Daniel, though. It was Serge's assistant, Joel. For the past few months Joel had been in charge of Vanguard Films' latest initiative, hiring graduates from low-income backgrounds, in a scheme hashtagged #filmforall. It had got a lot of attention on social media, having been picked up by the *Telegraph* and the *Huffington Post*, but had not attracted any investment.

'Hey! Sorry to call when you're away,' he said. 'Just wanted your take. You know Erin?'

Erin was one of the graduates hired through the #filmforall scheme.

'She didn't get pissed again?'

At a recent premiere, Erin had got drunk and heckled the cast of *Nepo Babes*, a reality show about celebrities' daughters.

'No, mate. That would be easier. Basically, I asked her to open your post while you were away.'

Serge knew that Erin would have resented this menial task. She was bright and ambitious, but she had a curt manner that riled him. He knew his own expectation of gratitude did not reflect well on him, either.

'Obviously I told her to leave anything personal. But I found her, like, taking a photo of a letter.'

'What letter?'

'From Big World. Their lawyers. And it was very clearly, like, "private and confidential". I just thought it was sketchy.'

Joel was speaking too fast, trying to spare Serge embarrassment. Vanguard Films owed Big World studios thousands of pounds. He decided not to ask what the letter said. Joel was aware of budgets being tight, but not the extent of Serge's debt.

'Did she say anything?'

'She put her phone away really fast, so I couldn't call her on it. But I just feel like she's a loose cannon. And since her contract's up for renewal—'

'When?'

'Mid-September. So we'd need to give her notice, like, today. Otherwise she'll assume she's here till December.'

Juno woke up, shouting, 'Mama!'

'Look, do it,' said Serge. 'Don't mention what you saw. Just be, like, "Erin, been great to have you, thanks for everything, let us know if we can put a good word in anywhere." Give someone else a chance.'

The shouting doubled, as Juno woke Huck.

'I'd do it,' said Serge, 'but I think it needs to be face to face. Sorry, man, I know it's shit.'

He hung up and hurried to the twins, already questioning his decision. If he had liked Erin more he might have taken her aside and given her a chance to explain. But if Erin were likeable, she would not have been photographing his unpaid invoices.

Parc de la Torse

Aix-en-Provence

6 p.m.

The softball match was at a park on the edge of Aix. An acquaintance from St Arthur's, Hugo Ranger, had offered Rosie a lift with his wife and newborn son. Rosie was in the back with the baby. His eyes were still cloudy and remote, his head lolling like Christ's in a fresco. When he gripped her finger, she felt a spike of longing.

They drove through the city in the slanting afternoon light, past custard-coloured houses with blue shutters and scarlet geraniums framing each window. Rosie hoped she would get to speak to Daniel again. The interview in the *Telegraph* had shocked her. The journalist, who had gone to St Arthur's, had implied that he had felt so alienated at Oxford that he had drunk excessively to survive it. Rosie remembered the writer, Jessica Blackwell, as a slightly truculent girl in the year below her – privately known as 'Jess Porno Tits' by Serge's most obnoxious friends. Rosie hoped Daniel's words had been taken out of context, but she feared the fall-out with Serge – perhaps even her own silent parting with Daniel – had poisoned his whole memory of university.

Parc de la Torse was large and scenic. Rosie stood by the car and tried to check her reflection in the window, while Hugo and Bella grappled with the baby. She wasn't sure if her shorts and Breton top achieved the preppy look she assumed was correct for a softball game in Provence, or if – now they weren't part of a Gap window display – they were just dull. The prospect of seeing Serge made her feel as if she had drunk too much coffee.

A cream yurt, like a small circus, stood across the park. The wedding guests were around it, sitting on picnic rugs or playing softball. Caspar came jogging off the pitch shouting, 'Rosie!' She felt her bright, public self switch on as she held her arms out.

'Flight OK?' he said. His eyes were bloodshot. He had been texting her at 2 a.m. about the gluten-free option at the reception dinner.

'Fine! I saw Serge. And his parents.'

She smiled to indicate this wasn't a complaint, having relived her odd blown kiss all day.

'Great! JP, Rosie's here!' he said, leading her towards the pitch.

Her anxiety surged at the sight of two teams and a fast-moving ball. People often assumed Rosie was athletic because she was so slim and enthusiastic, and she minded that she wasn't. Her inability to catch was both a Littleton family joke and a disappointment.

'Can't believe how American this is,' whispered Caspar, as if this was something risqué. 'Look, he's gone full jock.'

JP was by the pitch drinking beer, and yelling through cupped hands.

He turned to greet Rosie with a big distracted smile, and she tried to ape his enthusiasm, while Caspar went to get her a drink. A thin, solemn child walked up to the batter's box. The bat was nearly as long as him. The British bowler threw gently but the child swung too hard, missed and almost fell over. His face flushed at the 'coo' of commiseration. A man bounced forwards from the batting queue. He was wearing glasses and a baseball cap, so it took Rosie a second to recognise Nate Kennedy.

'Hey, hold up!' he said to the bowler. 'Can we go again?'

He looked different, not just because of his glasses. He seemed more solid, or perhaps more at ease in his body, and less likely to bump into things. He crouched by the child, looking at him intently as he spoke. Then he mimed hitting a ball – turning his whole body like a golfer – patted the boy's shoulder, and moved aside.

There was a hush as the bowler pitched again, even more gently this time, and a snap as the bat made contact. The ball soared and the child looked round at Nate, as if for advice, who was now shouting, 'Run, run!'

'Is that Nate's son?' said Rosie to JP.

'Zach? No! He's our friend Audrey's.'

He pointed to a tiny blonde woman who was shouting, 'Go, baby!' and clasping her hands.

'We were all at college,' said JP. 'Her husband couldn't be here.'

The child was running now, his small face determined, a British fielder fumbling to give him time. When he reached the last base there was a generous cheer from both sides. Nate ran over to high five the boy, and then lifted him up above his head.

'He's hot now, right?' said JP, smiling at her watching the scene. 'He went on this whole health kick, a few years back.'

Rosie made an impressed sound at Nate's good health. It was easier than admitting that she found any man focusing on a child hypnotic.

'Kennedy!' JP shouted. 'Get your ass over here.'

Nate looked round and smiled. He walked towards them, taking off his cap and running his hand over the back of his head.

'Rosie!' he said. 'Wow! How've you been?'

She saw his face, now. It was squarer, and there was stubble where there hadn't been. His hair, which he used to moan was 'a bouffant', was very short. But his eyes looked the same, still disappearing into crescents when he smiled. She thought of her room at Oxford in her final year, and how he had usually been laughing. She wondered if she looked the same to him.

'Hi! I've been fine! Fine. You?'

She thought he was about to embrace her, but he just stood in front of her smiling a lot.

'I'm good,' he said. He was looking straight at her, as if he was remembering something, and she found herself smiling back.

'So you're, what, a "middle school" softball coach now?' she said.

'Ha. Maybe. One day.'

'Can you help me now? I'm a disastrous batter. Bats-woman? Bats-person?'

Her voice sounded unnecessarily chipper, playing the English Rose to Nate's accent. She thought she saw something quizzical in his expression, as if he had detected this.

'Bats-woman,' said JP. 'That sounds like a superhero.'

'Oh my God, sport is definitely not my superpower,' she said.

'Really? You look like you'd be good at hurdles or high jump, or something,' said JP, looking at her legs.

'It's false advertising!' she said, thinking of the egg donor proposal, which, mercifully, had not been mentioned again. 'The athletic gene bypassed me,' she added.

'So, big news, right? Co-parenting?' said Nate, looking from Rosie to JP, as if he could see Rosie's thoughts.

JP's eyebrows darted up. 'Oh – nothing's final,' he said. 'Ball's in Rosie's court.'

Rosie felt her cheeks warming, as she groped for another sporting idiom.

'I told Nate, I hope that's OK?' said JP, looking at her.

'Oh! Sorry! I thought it was all set,' said Nate.

Rosie wondered how the situation must have sounded. She hoped JP had not painted her as terminally single, or desperately broody, though she feared he might have.

'I mean, we're hoping,' said JP. 'Since Rosie's the female equivalent of the guy everyone wants at the sperm bank. Like, the six-foot Swedish engineer who happens to play grade eight cello.'

'Minus sporting prowess,' she said.

'Nobody's perfect,' said Nate.

A waiter appeared with a tray of tiny tacos. Nate and JP took one each, but Rosie refused. She was too anxious to register hunger, and they were the kind of canapé that might shatter at first bite, splurging salsa down her new top, or have to be stuffed in whole, rendering her temporarily mute. She wished she didn't still consider food in this way, a relic of being a teenager when she observed her own complex rules about which foods were acceptable to consume around boys (fruit, toast, ice cream) and which were 'unfanciable' (stew, egg sandwiches, certain crisp flavours).

Nate popped the whole canapé in his mouth and chewed, looking around the park contentedly. The waiter moved on, and she suddenly thought how Nate had been one of the few boys she had eaten with freely, often stopping for chips after nights out. She had eaten without inhibition around Daniel, too, but this was different. She used to see Daniel almost as another girl – just with secret access to the male brain. She remembered asking him if certain foods really were off-putting to men, and how Daniel had laughed and insisted she eat an egg sandwich in his presence, claiming it was immersion therapy.

Someone shouted, 'Nathaniel! You're up,' and Nate jogged to the batting square. She realised she had never seen him among his friends, having only known him as a visiting student. She found herself watching him – his eyes squinting into the sun, his body braced almost menacingly. His shoulder whipped round as the bat sliced the air. The ball flew. His legs began pumping, and as he reached the last base he raised his arms in victory. The American team ran towards him cheering, and somebody turned his cap back to front so that he looked like the teenager she remembered.

Beyond the softball pitch she saw Serge, walking towards the yurt. His silhouette set off a jolt in her body, as if it were branded on a fragile part of her psyche. He was carrying his daughter on his shoulders and holding his son's hand, while Isla pushed a vacant buggy behind them. Rosie turned away, quickly. She had expected to feel the same greedy curiosity she felt when she googled him, not the pain that was now spreading across her chest. An image of blood in the shower flooded her thoughts. She wondered if that baby, if it had been a baby, would have looked like the toddlers with Serge now.

Daniel's Room

Hotel Georgette

7 p.m.

The party had started an hour earlier, but Daniel couldn't seem to leave his room. He stood in the en suite examining his reflection – first full length, then magnified with the shaving mirror. He knew, rationally, that he was good-looking. But having heard photographers analyse his face, since childhood, he also had a rich understanding of his flaws. At seven, he knew his better side.

He tried a trick, now, that he'd developed for auditions. He made himself imagine – with Strasbergian intensity – that the mirror was a window, and that he was looking through it at another person. The effort always delivered solace. He would see, like a Magic Eye picture emerging, how he appeared to others – imperfections receding into a whole.

It worked, but seconds later he felt 'the nothingness'. Daniel had known 'the nothingness' since boyhood, when it used to ambush him on modelling shoots. It would begin with a sudden numb heaviness, even if he was beaming and bouncing on a trampoline. An acute sense of being confined to his own body followed, while somehow also seeing himself from outside.

'I am me. Daniel Pyke,' he would say in his head. 'That lady is photographing me for a poster.'

It was like becoming a stranger, who had got behind his face and was surveying his world with utter objectivity. Sometimes it was strangely enjoyable, like prodding a bruise, and he would invite it in – like an exit from normality. Other times the narrating would go on too long, scaring him, as if his mind were sucking itself into a vortex.

According to Caspar's therapist the nothingness was a type of 'intrusive thought' dealt by 'the tricky brain'. Daniel doubted other people's thoughts were as intrusive as his. He could be nodding in a meeting, and suddenly visualise peeing into someone's coffee or straddling the seventy-year-old studio executive. It wasn't that he feared he might do these things. The problem was that his brain seemed intent on proving he was depraved.

Even Caspar, whose brain had its tricks, had looked blank when Daniel tried to explain the nothingness. All he could offer was his therapist's number. Daniel had never called, knowing he would be told to stop drinking. Instead, he let his psychiatrist prescribe more and more pills – with the same zeal as someone perfecting a Negroni.

The only person who had ever appeared to relate was Rosie. Daniel remembered trying to explain the nothingness to a group of slumped, stoned girls at a student house party. One of them asked if it was like trying to imagine infinity, and Daniel had said it was weirder. Then Rosie had said, 'Is it like when you get … *she's my mum?*' It sounded close to Daniel's own existential vacuum. But instead of saying so, he had grabbed the comedic opportunity, repeating 'SHE'S … MY … MUM' in an awestruck voice, until everyone was slightly hysterical.

His phone pinged with a message from Caspar:

> Where are you Danny Boy?

He downed a tiny whisky from the minibar, and replied:

> So sorry mate! On my way, stuck on a call.

There were other spirits, beside the whisky. He drank the rum – hoping it might ignite the party mood he couldn't seem to access. It didn't, but he managed to leave the room.

Once in a cab, he opened Twitter on his phone. He checked that the app was set to the anonymous, alias account he used when he wanted to voice something 'dicey'. This was the term his US publicist used to cover anything remotely negative, ungrateful or controversial, after Daniel had briefly offended a lot of people with a flippant tweet about cocaine. The mass condemnation had been surprisingly disturbing, and he now reserved his @DanielPykeOfficial account strictly for plugging his work and carefully staged 'off duty' photos.

The alias account was called @Gareth32, a combination of his middle name and childhood door number, and he had come to rely on it as a kind of diary. Sometimes he wished he was Gareth, free to be as belligerent as he wished. He used it now to tweet, 'Why isn't organised fun more fun?' and felt a little rush as it appeared, somewhere, to Gareth's twelve mysterious followers.

He swapped to @DanielPykeOfficial and tweeted a selfie he'd taken on arrival in Marseille captioned 'Bonjour Provence'. Within seconds it had a hundred Likes. The switch between his two accounts always induced a bump of anxiety, but not enough to deter him.

The Softball Pitch

Parc de la Torse

8 p.m.

The sun was setting, but a hazy brightness hung in the air after the match. The caterers had recreated an American diner menu with sliders and fries, and were now serving miniature ice creams. Serge had drunk two beers, but he still felt tightly wound. He kept looking for Isla, but whenever his eyes found her, a relation or someone from Oxford would stop him to chat. She was wearing a flimsy white shirt and denim shorts, her jewellery shining against her skin. Serge knew he would be introducing himself if they were strangers.

Across the park Daniel was just arriving. It was startling to see him after so long. He and Caspar began jogging towards one another in exaggerated slow motion. Something in the moment recalled the first time Serge had ever seen Daniel – racing Hugo Ranger to down a pint, amid cheers. Serge had been surprised, perhaps having unconsciously expected Daniel to be like his shy, stoic character in *Riptide*. He had found the boisterousness grating, at first. It was only when Daniel relaxed at Oxford that their shared obsession with cinema had emerged, and with it a kind of mutual fascination. He could still remember his elation at finding someone else willing to recite reams of Scorsese dialogue.

He ended another conversation to find Isla, but when he turned around Rosie turned at the same moment, so that they were opposite one another. There was a second of slightly stunned surprise, before they both said, 'Hi again!' in unison. He moved to stand beside her, so that they were both looking out at the joyful, expensive scene. For a few minutes they discussed their flights and hotel and Aix. While they spoke she licked her doll-size ice cream, showing flashes of tongue. The bizarre nature of past intimacy struck him. It was even stranger with Rosie, after their three distinct chapters – a loaded friendship, a lightweight relationship, then silence.

His sister appeared. She looked even thinner than usual, her temples almost concave. It always made Serge feel helpless, like when he saw the twins suffer.

'*You* two! Déjà bloody vu!' she shouted. She pulled Rosie into an avid hug. 'We've missed you, sweet girl! How *are* you?'

'Good!' said Rosie, adopting Allegra's febrile energy. 'So good. How glorious is this park?'

'I know, right? And how fun was that game? I'm, like, fully living out my *Grease* fantasies.'

She mimed something that might have been softball or a cheerleading routine.

'So how are the foreign rights, Rosie?' said Serge, partly to make Allegra stop.

'OK. Full on. Keep meaning to find a little indie publisher instead.'

'God, you're brave,' said Allegra. 'I could never sit at a desk all day.'

Serge wondered if his sister realised work was not normally a choice. Ten years after leaving RADA she was still permanently auditioning, usually for parts as the lead's quirky sidekick. Despite barely requiring her to act, they still eluded her.

'Did you do fringe this year?' Rosie asked her.

'Yup! Fool's errand.'

Allegra's voice was bright, but her eyes had the blank look they got when she was low. Serge knew he should talk to her about it.

'So you well, Rosie?' she said suddenly, as if she had just woken from a micro nap. 'Got a gorgeous man?'

'Er, not right now!' said Rosie. 'You?'

'God, no. Stuck in apps hell. Last guy said I was "too much". It's like a running theme. I should put it on my profile.'

There was so little of his sister, but men had always complained she was excessive. It still made Serge sad. Rosie protested that these men were clearly insufficient themselves, and then diplomatically asked after the Campbell parents. They all glanced at Marina, who was watching Lucian eat a hot dog with amused horror.

'Yeah, all good,' said Serge. 'They just sold the place in Italy. Which is gutting.'

'Oh, shame. I guess it's a lot to manage from London?' said Rosie. 'With their place in Dorset.'

'Right. First-world problems!' he said. 'Still a bummer, though.'

'Ours not to question why,' said Allegra.

It was true, the sudden decision to sell had felt oddly sensitive, involving his parents' age and energy levels.

'Anyway, *so* heavenly to see you, Rosie,' said Allegra. 'I really want to hang out with you this weekend, OK? We've missed you! Ma was—'

Serge looked at her.

'Sorry! Sorry. Not helpful.'

'How are your folks?' he said, as his sister walked away.

'Fine, fine. Kate's pregnant, again. Dad's retired, under Mum's feet. Playing a lot of golf.'

Serge laughed, and sipped his beer. He had not thought of George Littleton, and his unspooling views on Brexit, for a long time. His own parents had been quietly aghast after one meeting. Isla's mother was different to them too, but somehow Saffron Malone escaped their labyrinthine snobberies – either because ceramics qualified as art, or because so many of Marina's titled relations were token hippies themselves.

'So this speech,' said Rosie. 'What've you got?'

'Sorry...'

'Serge!' she said, in playful reproach.

'Let's bash it out tomorrow? Coffee?'

'It's OK for you – you're giving acceptance speeches every week.'

'Hardly,' he said, but it was pleasant to have his success acknowledged. 'I'll carry it if you like.'

'Long as you don't upstage me.'

He looked at her, his face saying, 'How could I possibly?' and she laughed.

'So where shall we meet?' she said.

She was smoothing her hair, exposing a milky inner wrist. Their odd final night returned to him with a bolt of regret.

He suggested Aix's bookshop, where he was meeting Daniel, and sent her a dropped pin. His phone swooshed and hers pinged in receipt, as if the devices were making a date. Rosie said she ought to mingle and he watched her neat back view weave across the softball pitch. The conversation had been reassuringly normal. Rosie was too sweet, and too sane, to bear a grudge or be indiscreet.

He began moving towards the yurt, looking for Isla. On his way, he saw that Joel had called again, and sent a text.

> Hey, have you seen Twitter? Must be Erin, she went mad when I told her... Should we put something out before it gets worse? Can ask my dad?

Joel's father was a QC, specialising in libel. Serge checked his Twitter. He was shocked to see two hundred notifications.

The Yurt

Parc de la Torse

8.15 p.m.

Isla couldn't leave the yurt, because the twins were finally asleep in their buggy, parked behind the bar. All evening, after the softball game, she had felt harassed and invisible – a mother ghost tailing two small, barrelling bodies. Huck had an instinct for the most dangerous item in any vicinity, Juno was just shockingly loud. Isla had shushed her around the Campbells all evening, minding that she felt obliged to.

Now that they were asleep she should have been able to enjoy the party, but she could not. Earlier she had seen Serge talking to his ex-girlfriend, both of them laughing with his sister. Rosie's legs were very long with no discernible calves or thighs, like noodles. Isla's body had tensed as she watched them together, and remembered the easy greetings at Heathrow. Rosie had the same, chatty, private-school confidence as all Serge's Oxford friends.

Serge had once told her that he had ended the relationship abruptly, because it 'wasn't right'. But since he had never said anything else about Rosie, it was hard to know how it was wrong – or why they seemed so friendly now. Serge's sister Allegra had once described Rosie as 'pathologically appropriate', and referred to her 'obsession' with sending handwritten cards. They didn't sound like things Serge cared about. But they also sounded nothing like Isla herself. As far as Isla knew, they had not stayed in touch, although she wondered, suddenly, if Serge would tell her if they had.

He walked into the tent now.

'Hey! Sorry you've been doing everything,' he said. 'Shall I take over? Have you eaten?'

'They're asleep.'

She knew she sounded unduly sharp but she couldn't seem to change register.

Caspar walked up with two men, and introduced them as Hugo and Oscar.

'Hugo's just had a baby,' he said, as if Isla were a uterus, before insisting Serge meet JP's parents.

Isla was left with the two men.

'So you've got a sprog, dude! Congrats! You getting any sleep?' said Oscar.

'Mate, it's all Bella,' said Hugo. 'Breastfeeding's amazing! It's like, "Put him on the boob", he's out like that.' He clicked his fingers, delighted, as though he had invented breastfeeding.

Isla had not managed to breastfeed for long, and it felt like her second maternal failure after the C-section. She had pictured herself as a mother who breastfed toddlers. She recalled a health visitor who had demonstrated a method for breastfeeding twins simultaneously, using two pillows. Afterwards, Isla had screamed into one pillow and hammered the other.

Hugo took a happy swig of beer and swallowed a burp, squaring his shoulders when he saw Isla watching. She realised, now, that she had met him in a different, carefree era. She and Serge had eaten at his burger pop-up, the day Serge had asked to make their relationship official. She did not feel inclined to remind Hugo, or to mention the twins. She knew it would only prompt endless, awestruck questions about sleep routines.

Near the entrance to the yurt she noticed a woman who must be his wife. She was standing in a bouncy squat, moving a newborn between different positions and kissing its scalp in a desperate, submissive way Isla remembered doing herself. It suddenly let out a tortured bleat, and brought up milk down her back. Hugo leaped towards them to proffer a muslin. Isla watched the woman's face melt as he took the baby and gurned at it. She wondered why she could not feel glad for this couple. They had done nothing wrong.

The other man left, and she stood alone at the bar. She could feel a male presence beside her. She didn't look up. The man nudged in slightly closer, even though it wasn't crowded.

'All right?' he said. 'Good to see you. Again.'

She turned, and found that she was standing beside Daniel Pyke. Her brain seemed to buffer, as if it couldn't compute him in three dimensions. Immediately she thought of her thirteen-year-old self, repeatedly watching his topless scene in *Riptide*, and hoped her face didn't betray this.

He looked older, of course, and his smile had a polished, LA quality. But she found she recognised details of his face and expression, alternately sultry and boyish.

'You swore at me, earlier. In the car. I was on the moped.'

'Oh! Shit! Well, to be fair, you shouldn't be on the road.'

He smiled, looking down and nodding, affecting contrition. His driving seemed irrelevant now. She had actually been annoyed with Serge at the time.

'Daniel,' he said, looking up and offering his hand in greeting and apology.

'Isla.'

'As in La Bonita? Or the whisky?'

'God knows. My mum was probably on mushrooms when she picked it.'

He laughed and said, 'Good for her.'

His voice had an actor's weight and warmth, but there was a roughness to it. It was nothing like his character's in *Riptide* either, though she was shocked to realise how well she could remember his Cornish accent.

'What we drinking then, Isla?' he said. 'Champagne?'

She glanced at the buggy, willing neither twin to wake.

He leaned over the bar for an open bottle, and poured two flutes.

'So, we good?' he said.

'Long as I don't have to drive near you.'

He laughed again. He was shorter than he looked on screen, and there was an intensity to being face to face. She looked into his eyes for longer than necessary as she took the first acid sip.

'Deal. So what brings you here, Isla?'

'In-laws. Caspar's side.'

'You're married?'

He pulled a puppyish, crestfallen face. She felt slightly lightheaded.

'Engaged. In theory.'

He made his face into a question, one eyebrow up.

'Wedding's on hold. Life's pretty hectic.'

'Which Campbell?'

'Serge. Caspar's cousin.'

'No! No *way*! My boy Sergio! Seriously? You know we used to hang out, right? We were, like, proper film geeks. Literally, Caspar banned us from talking about the *Nouvelle Vague*. Such ponces.'

He chuckled, fondly. Isla stopped herself expressing surprise. She had assumed that Serge had been playing up the friendship, earlier, to justify the work meeting.

'We're chatting tomorrow, actually, cos . . . ' He looked down and up again. 'I'm an actor, and he's got this part in mind. For me. But he's probably told you that, right? That we're meeting?'

She couldn't tell if his modesty was genuine.

'Maybe,' she said, conscious of her own acting. 'Wait – didn't you see Serge with me, in the car?'

'I'll be honest. I was pretty distracted. By the rage.'

He made a show of suppressing a smile, his head tilted. Then he refilled her glass, sloppily, so that she had to duck and catch the froth with her lips.

'So you in the industry too?' he said. 'Actor, dancer?'

'Make-up artist. Special effects.'

'No! Seriously? You guys are geniuses. I'm in this show, in LA, and my character got mauled by werewolves – they made it like my guts were hanging out. My mum was literally like, "I cannot watch this".'

She laughed, in a husky, flirtatious way that she hadn't for ages. They both knew he was referring to *TROG*, but she was now stuck in the charade of pretending not to have recognised him.

'So how did you get into that? Make-up?'

She was taken aback, it was so long since anyone had taken an interest in her life beyond motherhood.

'I just always loved film. And art was the only subject at school I wasn't shit at, so I did my foundation course. But my mum's an artist, and I knew I didn't want that life. Plus make-up was kind of my only way in. I couldn't afford to intern for ages, or whatever.'

'Sure. Same. I actually wanted to direct, but acting was my foot in the door. So what you working on, at the minute?'

'Well, we have twins. They're one. So, I can't, really.'

'Wait, what? I knew Serge had a kid, but twins! That's another level, right? So boys, girls, identical?'

'One of each.'

'Wow. So you just went from no kids to a full-on family situation?'

'Pretty much.'

His incisiveness surprised her.

'That must be mental. Do you have help? Serge's on set a lot, I guess?'

The flirtatious note had shifted. He was looking at her very sincerely now, as if he was concerned about her wellbeing. She looked away because it was somehow overwhelming, even though she had spent enough time with actors to know how they operated. His chest was a forearm's length away. She could see it was hairless, as it had been in *Riptide*.

'He is away a lot, yeah,' she said.

Daniel looked at his drink and nodded, but she couldn't tell whether this was an unspoken comment on Serge's parenting. He said something she couldn't hear, and she leaned closer, tucking her hair behind her ear as she asked him to repeat it. Serge walked back in at the same moment. The way his face changed was so subtle that only Isla would have noticed.

'Pikeeeeey!' he called.

He walked over and put his arm around Daniel from above – a brief headlock. Daniel stood taller. Isla was surprised by 'Pikey'. Serge was usually excessively aware of offensive terms.

'Sergio!' said Daniel. 'Wow. Been so long. Just been hearing about your twins. Congrats, mate. You been busy.'

Serge stepped closer to Isla, putting his body almost between hers and Daniel's.

'Cheers, man. You too! And we're on for tomorrow!' he said. He seemed slightly manic, as if he were too close to laughter. 'So how've you been, Pikes?' he carried on. 'How are the vampires treating you?'

'Werewolves. World of difference to the kids, my friend,' said Daniel.

He was grinning, but Isla sensed impatience.

'Werewolves! Of course. My bad,' said Serge, his face twinkling. She felt defensive, suddenly, of Daniel. She had taken so many absurd jobs herself. You had to, unless you could fund your own projects – like Serge.

'The wolves are good, mate. The wolves are good. Gotta pay the bills,' said Daniel.

'I hear you, buddy. Been doing a shitload of commercial myself. Mouths to feed, these days.'

Isla looked away. She used to find Serge's posturing as breadwinner endearing, knowing that it sprang from insecurity. Now it struck her as tone-deaf.

Serge launched into a story about a seeing a wolf when he was snowboarding, and then another anecdote about a university ski trip. Daniel listened, and laughed, interjecting with shared memories. Isla still couldn't read their dynamic. She presumed they were both slightly drunk, overcompensating for having failed to keep in touch. Her mother often said men were unable to maintain any relationship unless the person was in front of them.

One of the twins began to cry. Isla waited for Serge to respond, but he was mid flow. She caught Daniel's eye as she moved to the buggy.

Rue Clemenceau

Aix-En-Provence

10 p.m.

Rosie had not spoken to Nate again after the softball match, but when they left the park at the same time it seemed natural to walk back to Hotel Georgette together. The night air was warm, and the back streets of Aix were still busy with people eating outside. She wondered if he was thinking of the times they had walked back from sticky nightclubs through Oxford. It was a relief to be out of Serge's presence. Her heart had kept double-time throughout their brief conversation, and the strain of appearing both friendly and dispassionate had left her with an insistent headache.

She and Nate began trying to summarise the past fifteen years, starting with their jobs and apartments. But the conversation kept narrowing to specific tangents and observations and memories, until it felt like a screen with too many tabs open. They were walking slowly but talking constantly, and when she stepped into a road without looking the right way Nate automatically put the flat of his hand on her arm to stop her.

'So your friend Daniel's a big deal now, right?' he said, as they crossed.

'I know! Though, we've kind of drifted.'

Rosie had not spoken to Daniel. He had arrived at the park late, and when she went to approach him he had been deep in conversation with Serge's fiancée – so Rosie had quickly turned. After that, she couldn't find him. Even seeing him, she could tell he had changed. He had always had a hammy ebullience, permanently putting on a show, but it was offset by an appealing frankness. Now his manner was even stagier, as if the other side had been pushed out. She doubted it would be possible to broach the *Telegraph* interview, after all.

'I thought you guys were all super close?'

She was briefly tempted to describe the entire fall-out, or what she knew of it, but it felt disloyal. She wasn't sure if Nate knew about her two-year relationship with Serge, either, though it was difficult to mention in passing.

'We were. But Dan moved to LA straight after Oxford. And Serge is so busy. So I really only see Caspar. Regularly.'

'Oh! OK,' said Nate. 'That's too bad. Sorry I mentioned the surrogacy, by the way.'

'God, don't worry. It wasn't your fault.'

'Do you know what you're going to do?'

'Not really. I need to make a pros and cons list or something,' she said, only half joking.

He looked round, smiling, clearly remembering her detailed lists.

'It's a huge thing to ask,' he said.

'I know. But it could be my only chance. Not to do it alone.'

She was surprised at how honestly she was talking.

'You'd do that? Alone?'

'I looked into it, a while ago. But more as an insurance thing. So I didn't leave it too late.'

He nodded, matching her practical tone, though she feared her womb's keening was audible. She imagined a flood-warning siren – desolate panic.

'That's why they asked me,' she added. 'Cos Caspar knows I'm open to, er, alternatives.'

'Well, it's not only that. They want your DNA, right?'

She was about to make a glib reply, but he said, 'Wait, that came out wrong. Like you're a thoroughbred or something.'

'I thought I was a Swedish engineer?'

'Right. The engineering part.'

They walked into the empty hotel foyer. A lamp revealed the damask wallpaper in flat, orange light. She almost jokingly suggested Earl Grey, anticipating a particular loneliness that struck her in hotel rooms. But she feared Nate would remember the last time they had drunk tea, after she rebuffed him, so she said goodnight instead. He walked to the lift. She watched his back as he waited for it, and the dip between his shoulder blades.

The hotel's door opened and Allegra came in, carrying her shoes. Her toes were dirty, in a way that might have looked free-spirited if she were younger.

'Rosie! Again!'

She leaned unsteadily on the reception desk.

'D'you think they'd do food now?' she said. 'I'm literally starving.'

Rosie noted the downy hair on Allegra's shoulders, and felt deeply uncomfortable. Serge had never wanted to discuss his sister's eating disorder, other than it had started at boarding school, gone away, and returned in Allegra's late teens. Rosie knew the Campbells had tried to help, but since nobody spoke about it, there was a sense of permanent, collective denial. Rosie had never seen Allegra at a normal weight, except at the St Arthur's summer ball.

'There might be room service,' she said. She moved towards the desk to try the phone, but Allegra assumed she was offering an embrace. She opened her arms, and wrapped them around Rosie's neck, squeezing her for a second and then hanging, limply, against her.

'Can't believe how long it's been, Ro-Ro.' She rested her head on Rosie's shoulder, her hair tickling Rosie's cheek.

'God, sorry I totally put my foot in it earlier,' she carried on. 'Just, seeing you, it's like – I mean, obviously I bloody adore those twins – but you and Serge—'

She could feel Allegra's ribs expand as she breathed, and thought of her childhood pet hamster.

'Like, you guys just had so much in common. *People* in common.' Rosie laughed. It sounded as stiff as her body felt against Allegra's. 'Cos with Isl— no, wait. Shit, I shouldn't be saying this.'

She pulled back and put both hands over her mouth, like a child.

'Saying what?'

It came out before Rosie could stop herself.

'Look, promise you won't say anything, OK?'

She paused, dramatically.

'They're on a "trial separation",' she said, making air quotes. 'Isla called it. Serge's obviously being a complete nightmare. But they're not telling anyone. Even Ma and Pa. So forget I said anything. Literally.'

Rosie promised, trying to sound neutral. She longed to know more, but Allegra was examining a bowl of glossy apples on the desk.

'D'you think these are real?' she said.

She took one before Rosie could comment, and bit into it noisily.

'So good!' she said, closing her eyes as if it were cake.

Rosie walked across the lantern-lit courtyard to her room, her mind firing. It was shocking to realise how little you knew about people's lives. Serge had cheered so loudly for Isla in the softball game that Rosie had found herself looking away. She wondered if Isla knew, or cared, that Serge and Rosie were to meet in the morning. Isla seemed so serene as to be indecipherable.

Her sheets had been turned down, the lamps dimmed and a bottle of water placed by the bed. Somehow these small, anonymous gestures of care made her feel even more alone. She thought of all the things she and Serge knew about one another – how he ate taramasalata on crumpets when he was hungover, and how she always had to get up to pee before falling asleep and still watched *Neighbours*. One Valentine's Day he had given her a *Neighbours* annual, and she had been dismayed at the lack of conventional romance. Now she wondered if this amassing of personal trivia, and the choosing of gifts around it, was not more romantic than roses. It was why the end of a relationship felt like bereavement. The consignment of all that working knowledge to memory seemed such a waste.

She lay in the dark, conscious of Serge's cufflinks tucked into a pocket in her suitcase. She had kept them at the back of her underwear drawer ever since taking them. Any time she saw them there she was flooded with a panicky guilt, disgusted that she had stolen something of sentimental value. Other times the theft would blast into her mind unbidden, like a hideous cuckoo clock. At these times she told herself that the cufflinks were not stolen, just waiting to be returned. This weekend was her opportunity. There was a satisfying symbolism to getting Serge's wrists out of her knickers.

Room 7

Hotel Georgette

11.15 P.M.

After speaking to Isla and Serge, Daniel had walked away from the yurt to fake a phone call – needing some respite from the party. He had intended to go back, but a group of students had recognised him from *TROG* and called out, 'Thane! *Venez ici!*' He had ended up smoking weed with them and answering their heavily accented questions, which had been far more enjoyable than the Campbell-Delahunt occasion.

Aside from his conversation with Isla, he had felt off-key all evening – as if everyone else was set to a different, lighter mode. It reminded him of the rare times he had stayed sober while people around him drank, although he had drunk plenty at the park. He could tell that many of the younger American guests recognised his face, although nobody actually acknowledged it. He would not have expected them to, at a party. Still, it was disconcerting to feel himself studiously ignored and to sense their preconceptions. Worse, at one moment in the yurt he was certain he had seen Rosie quickly pivot on seeing him.

He arrived back at Hotel Georgette, still buzzing with the French students' adulation, knowing he would need another drink to dilute the adrenaline. He walked into the lobby. At first he thought he was alone, but then he saw Allegra Campbell sitting on a sofa eating an apple. There was another apple core on the coffee table. She turned to look at him. She was much thinner than he remembered from the St Arthur's ball, the only other time they had met. Close up she looked ageless – like so many women in LA – her body pubescent, her face gaunt.

'Hey!' said Daniel. 'Wow! Allegra, right? We met, way back. At that ball thing. How you doing?'

She nodded, barely smiling. Her eyes were glassy.

'Oh yeah. Hey. How are you?'

'I'm good! I'm really good,' he said.

He sat down, thinking they would chat, poised to make a joke of his gauche student self if she mentioned their aborted kiss. But instead Allegra stood up, swiftly.

'Cool. OK, good to see you. Night,' she said, walking away.

Daniel stayed on the sofa, feeling small and snubbed – as if he was a teenager again. At seventeen, Allegra had radiated a kind of daring aplomb which he remembered finding sexy despite himself. She had struck him as being just like the girls Serge knew at other Oxford colleges. They all seemed to be friends already, from some impenetrable school network, crushingly certain of their beauty and power. Allegra's worldliness had been even more striking, because she had been so young.

He stood up and threw away the apple cores before going upstairs. In his room he opened the minibar and drank the last tiny bottle, without bothering to read the label. It was vodka. The sting of Allegra's disinterest morphed to indignation. He walked into the en suite, feeling sloppy and affronted, ready to fight an inanimate object that got in his way.

He felt sure, now, that Rosie had been avoiding him all evening – while laughing with Serge. He thought of the way Serge had addressed him as 'Pikey' in the yurt, and half laughed at *TROG*. It did not incline him to be in Serge's film.

After showering he lay on the bed, and googled 'Isla Serge

Campbell' on his phone. The search brought up various photos of Serge and Isla at screenings and parties, sometimes posing, sometimes just intoxicated with each other. In the most recent photo she was pregnant, Serge's arm tight around her. The images gave her surname, and he found her Instagram. He looked at her posts for a long time, then watched an old, sweetly hesitant video she had posted on YouTube about prosthetics. She did not look, or sound, like Serge's exes. When she had revealed she was his fiancée, Daniel had felt as if fate was laughing at him.

He leaned against the headboard and swiped back to his original search. Below the images of Serge and Isla, the search results were all about Serge only. One of them caught his attention. It was a tweet from an account called – thrillingly – @SergeCampBELLEND.

It had only been posted a few hours earlier, but already had 214 retweets. He opened the thread, and found a virtual mob of people condemning Serge. The stupor of drunk semi-arousal caused by Isla's photos lifted. He sat forwards and scrolled, almost too fast to read. The word 'privilege' kept coming up. He scrolled back to the original tweets by @SergeCampBELLEND. They referenced a piece in the *Huffington Post*, about Serge's 'activism'.

@SergeCampBELLEND
According to @HuffPost @SergeCampbell is some kind of woke trailblazer but I want to show a different side to the story. I'm done with people acting like the sun shines out of Campbell's ass.

@SergeCampBELLEND
Serge Campbell makes out he's this heroic employer by hiring graduates from low-income backgrounds to combat systemic privilege in the film industry. Then he drops them the second they've filled their brand-building purpose.

@SergeCampBELLEND
I was hired by Vanguard Films as part of #filmforall. But today I was told, with two weeks' notice, that I was 'no longer needed'. I have rent to pay. I don't have family in London. This isn't a hobby for me.

@SergeCampBELLEND
Serge Campbell is not who people think. He's a narcissist who deserves to be called out. Sadly being an obscenely privileged cis white male still equals a free pass to abuse power, and treat marginalised people as free PR. #SergeCampbell.

At first, reading the comments, Daniel felt sorry for Serge. He knew the singular anxiety that Twitter could induce. But as he contemplated the account of being hired for show, his sympathy waned. He recalled his shock, three years after Oxford, on reading about a new film called *Bursary* by 'hot young director Serge Campbell'. Their protagonist had morphed into a teenage boy from Sunderland, and Cambridge had become a boarding school in Sussex. But the essence and arc was the same. *Bursary* had won awards at Sundance, launching Serge's career, while Daniel sold popcorn at Disneyland. Naturally, none of the press around *Bursary* mentioned that Serge's godfather had produced the film. It had all revolved around Serge, and the young lead.

The whole thing had felt like the final act in a story that began in July 2004. The start of the story was Serge ignoring Daniel's messages. In retrospect, Daniel had taken embarrassingly long to take the hint. After weeks of silence he had concluded that the entire invitation to Italy, to write the script and pitch it to Miles Whitehall, had never been genuine. Daniel had already known that only people like Serge got to direct in their twenties. He had just imagined that Serge was willing to hold the door open for him.

He logged out of @DanielPykeOfficial, and into his alias account. Experimentally, he wrote a reply from @Gareth32 to @SergeCampBELLEND. He did not know whether he was intending to send it. There was a thrill just in seeing the words.

@Gareth32 Exactly this! So over rich kids running the arts, when people with more talent can't get a break.

He hovered over 'Tweet'. This, he told himself, was different to the trolls who mocked his acting. This was a deep-rooted societal problem, warranting attention.

Then, as if his thumb had a conscience, he turned off his phone.

La Brezza, Tuscany, July 2004

Serge is sitting at a table on a terrace at his parents' villa in Tuscany. It is mid-afternoon but the table is still cluttered with the ruins of lunch – bottles of Chianti, dregs of salads, focaccia, olives, salami and cheese sweating in the sun. He looks younger here, dunking cantuccini into a bowl of green ice cream.

Allegra comes out of the kitchen, with a small glass of sorbet. She begins to eat it, in tiny spoonfuls.

'Ma got stracciatella for you,' says Serge.

'Yeah, I saw. But I actually *prefer* this now? It's more refreshing?'

Her voice has taken on a new, tentative uptick – different to a month ago at the ball.

Serge looks at her, as if he is about to dispute this. Then he says nothing, and pushes the packet of cantuccini towards her.

'I'm sorting out a date with Daniel, to come and stay,' he says. 'Pyke. If you can remember anything from that night.'

His tone is jovial, but she looks up, shocked.

'Daniel Pyke?'

'Yeah. Is that a problem?'

'Yes! I thought you'd forgotten.'

'What? Why's it an issue?'

Allegra puts down her spoon and sighs dramatically.

'It's not, it's just ... It's complicated.'

'Complicated how?'

'OK, I wasn't going to tell you. But I may as well, now.' She sighs, again. 'We kissed, OK?'

'What? When?'

Serge is frowning.

'At the ball. Duh.'

'But – how did that even happen?'

'We were outside, smoking. And having this amazing conversation. Like, a proper DMC?'

Serge looks unconvinced.

'Genuinely! We have so much in common. Or it seemed like we did.'

'Right.'

'Then, yeah, it just happened. I can't even remember. He had his arm here,' she demonstrates a man putting his arm up along the back of a bench. 'So it was just this organic thing.'

'What? That actually really pisses me off. You don't try it on with your friend's sister. I think we even joked about it. Jesus.'

'It wasn't like that, though! We had this real connection. Like, we both felt it. Straight off.'

Seeing Serge's expression, Allegra looks exasperated.

'I knew you wouldn't get it,' she says. 'Just cos you never feel *anything*.'

He half laughs, as if this is a compliment.

'Anyway,' she continues, 'we were kissing and I was like "actually, maybe we shouldn't do this".'

'Good!'

'So he asked for my number.'

'Your number? Seriously? So what, you're seeing each other now?'

'Well. He was all like, "We should go out, let's go to the theatre, baby, I'm going to call you, I'll definitely see you in Italy, dadada-dada." Fully into it. But then I never heard from him. Nothing. I just—'

She stops, looking out wanly at the Tuscan hills.

'I know it's dumb cos he's, like, older and successful.'

'He's been in one film,' says Serge. 'And a Pringles ad.'

'But I really thought he felt it too, you know? Like, more than just a physical thing? But it's nearly been a month. Three-and-a-half weeks. So. Actions louder than words.'

Her voice is stable, but her eyes are now pink and filmy.

Serge stands up, muttering something about Daniel being a player. He sits beside Allegra, and hugs her, awkwardly. This seems to upset her more, she begins to weep quietly on his shoulder.

'Legs, why is this such a big deal?' says Serge. 'So you kissed, he never called. His loss. He probably knows he can't, like, he should never have—'

'I don't know. I just feel like I made an idiot of myself,' she interrupts.

'You? He's the idiot! He was the one—'

'No, but, I just keep thinking, how he said this thing.'

Her voice is hiccupy as she wipes her nose.

'What thing?'

'That I'm fat.'

'*Fat?* What the fuck?'

'He implied it. Like, I was sitting on his lap, OK?'

Serge looks slightly repulsed.

'And he made some joke about how I was crushing his leg. Or trapping him. By being so big.'

'Allegra – listen – you're not big. OK? Jesus!'

'I am, though! Now. Compared to before. So I just keep thinking, the mental spark was there for him. But maybe when he actually felt—'

She looks at her thighs despondently.

'No!' says Serge. 'I can't believe he said that. What a dick.'

She looks at him balefully.

'I thought you were friends?'

'Fuck that. You don't say that. To anyone. I'm going to have such a go at him.'

'No!' Allegra looks horrified. 'Don't, please! Seriously. That would be so embarrassing. Really. Please don't, OK? I don't want him to know all that. It's private.'

A middle-aged man is walking onto the terrace. He has wavy grey hair, tucked behind his ears, and is wearing a collarless white shirt.

'Shit – Miles,' says Allegra, wiping her face harshly. She stands and walks into the house. When Miles reaches the terrace Serge is back in his chair, equanimity restored.

'*Buon pomeriggio!*' says Miles. 'God, this place is heaven. All memories of easyJet erased.'

He sits down, and a woman Serge addresses as Lucia begins bustling in and out of the kitchen, clearing away lunch. Both men make Italian-sounding exclamations of pleasure when she returns with coffee.

'How is she?' says Miles, nodding at Allegra who is visible in the kitchen. 'She looks much better.'

'OK,' says Serge. 'It's an ongoing process. I guess.'

Miles nods and they both reach for their cups, to avoid further discussion.

They start talking about Serge's upcoming teacher-training course instead, which he will begin in September.

'I mean, it's a fallback,' says Serge. 'Just so I have a trade.'

Miles's mouth twitches almost imperceptibly at this phrasing, but he nods sincerely.

'Cos I'd love to go into film, ultimately,' says Serge.

He returns Miles's gaze as if there are two years between them – not thirty.

'Directing or producing?'

'Both,' says Serge.

Miles looks indulgent, but curious too.

'Any ideas to run by me?' he says. 'You wouldn't believe the dross we get sent.'

'Well, there's one I've been thinking about,' he says, after a moment. 'For a feature.'

He outlines an idea for a film about a working-class student's experience of a Cambridge college.

Miles looks thoughtful.

'There's definitely an appetite for that kind of thing,' he says. 'That kind of post-Thatcher, class commentary. But Waugh rather cornered the dreaming spires market.'

'Right,' says Serge, quickly. 'I mean, it wouldn't have to be Oxbridge, though?'

'Well, no, absolutely. A boarding school might actually make your point more clearly?'

'What, Eton or somewhere?'

'I think Eton's too obvious. I think you want a minor public school. So there's a bit of an inferiority complex. Lots of absurd rules.'

Serge half laughs, clearly understanding the reference.

'Maybe bring some north-south tension in?' says Miles. 'Have him hail from a really grim northern town. More salt of the earth, I think, than your Essex geezer. You want to properly root for him.'

'Right,' says Serge. 'Yeah, actually, that could work. And it would widen it, politically, right? It's like, a necessary story to tell?'

'Certainly more sympathetic,' says Miles. 'Probably more commercial. So did you come up with this? It's good. Real potential.'

Serge hesitates.

'Yeah. Yes. I did.'

PART FOUR

AUGUST 2019
THE DAY BEFORE THE WEDDING

From: campbell.delahunt.wedding@gmail.com
To: RosieLittleton81@gmail.com,
nathaniel.thomas.kennedy@newyorktimes.com,
Serge.Campbell@vanguardfilms.co.uk,
Daniel@Danielpyke.com
Date: 30 August, 2019, 06:05
Subject: wedmin

Hey team,

Hope you had fun last night ... So rehearsal is still set for 3pm at the chateau, inc flash mob, but we would massively appreciate eyes on the seating plan at 2pm ... Plus a few other minor dilemmas ... JP and I have basically lost our minds!

Cx

Courtyard Suite

Hotel Georgette

7 A.M.

Serge woke to Juno and Huck shouting. Isla was saying, over their noise: 'Huckleberry, it's OK to be angry, but it's *not OK* to hit.' He realised that he must have fallen asleep as soon as they got back from the park, jetlag overriding the drama unfolding on Twitter. Isla suddenly shouted over the twins, 'Just be quiet!' and there was a shocked pause before they began bellowing again.

He reached for his phone, remembering @SergeCampBELLEND. He knew he shouldn't read the condemnation that had sprouted overnight. But he did anyway – his eyes straining to read the tiny, scathing words – his mouth still gluey. Most people seemed to be debating 'systemic inequality' in the abstract, but a few tweets were addressed to Serge directly. A man with nineteen followers called @sudden_death_boy wrote:

You're an embarrassment you don't deserve to live.

It was clear that these people were disturbed, but he still felt violated. He couldn't say whether it was the shock of mass disapproval, after his recent Twitter glory, or the truth behind their rage. Worse, was the possibility that Erin might Tweet her photo of the letter. He pictured Isla and his parents finding out about his debts, the prospect like a wave rearing in front of him. He realised that the shouting from the other room had stopped, without him offering help.

Isla opened the door and said she was taking the twins to breakfast. He could tell she had not seen Twitter, and decided not to tell her. She was above caring about strangers' opinions, anyway. It was one of the things that had always impressed him about her.

The twins tumbled into the room. There was something pure and comforting about their creamy skin and robust bodies, even their high volume, after his phone's silent glare. He wished he could spend the day pressing his face against his children's cheeks.

'Wait, I'll come with you,' he said.

'They can't wait, they've been up since five,' said Isla.

'Five! You should have got me, I'm jetlagged anyway.'

'They're always up at five. When are you meeting Daniel?'

Now he remembered finding Isla with Daniel at the bar, leaning towards one another. It had set off a chain of memories – all the times Daniel had flirted with his girlfriends, or encroached on Serge's past or intended conquests. He had never understood why Daniel vied with him this way, or the constant jibes about Serge's background. But he found himself mocking Daniel's looks in retaliation, dragged into the pointless rivalry like an undertow.

'At ten. But I've got to write this speech after. With Rosie Littleton,' he said, as if using her full name made her sound less like his ex.

Isla looked up, her face brittle. He realised she might be jealous. It struck him as hopeful.

'Guess we'll stay here, then.'

'Where were you going to go?'

'Nowhere. It just would've been nice for them to see you. And to have a hand.'

He realised his mistake and considered offering to cancel – knowing Isla would insist he go, to highlight his error in judgement. Often, with Isla, he felt he was sitting a test rigged for failure.

'Can you take them swimming?'

'That's an hour, max.'

She was rubbing sun cream into her skin, and he thought how long it was since they'd had sex, and how he had never anticipated this change. Isla had wanted sex more, rather than less, when she was pregnant. He guessed she felt self-conscious about her postnatal body, and often tried to reassure her, but she still shunned him.

He stood up from the bed – aware of his own body, simultaneously skinnier and softer than he used to be.

'Do we need anything? While I'm out?' he called, from the bathroom.

'Nappies.'

'Size four?'

'Five.'

He had failed another test.

The Courtyard

Hotel Georgette

8 a.m.

Isla had given the twins breakfast outdoors, in the courtyard. The table and ground below were now covered in food, as if wild animals had eaten there. Her neck was tender from sleeping on the sofa. Serge had joined them briefly, rumpled and artificially upbeat, rushing to get the twins Nutella against Isla's wishes. He was now showering in their suite, ahead of his meeting. She used to admire his obsessive work ethic – the way money hadn't dulled his drive. Lately, work seemed more like an escape.

Rosie Littleton walked into the courtyard. She stopped to talk to Hugo and his wife, with their baby. Isla was sitting nearby but she knew she was hidden by olive trees, and found herself studying Rosie. She had the kind of fine, delicate features that confined certain actors to period drama, and was exhaustingly animated – her long limbs making her gestures even more excessive. Isla knew that all Serge's previous girlfriends had had Rosie's type of marionette body. It had never mattered to her, but now she shifted so that her thighs were no longer touching.

The idea of Serge sitting with Rosie in a French café, reminiscing about Oxford, or perhaps their relationship, created a tight feeling in her lungs. She wiped a blob of yoghurt out of Juno's hair, and then found some in her own. Huck poured a glass of juice ceremoniously into his lap.

Allegra walked into the courtyard next, clasping her forehead and miming a hangover. She and Rosie began mirroring one another's expressions of wild hilarity and disbelief, before Rosie and the couple left. Allegra looked around, bereft without an audience, until she saw Isla.

'There you are!' she said. 'Hiding! I barely saw you last night, bambinos. God, I feel like shit.'

She sat down as if she'd been dropped, then leaned forwards to drink from Isla's coffee. For a while they discussed Allegra's life, while the twins screeched over them.

'How are you, though?' said Allegra, switching to concern. She pushed her sunglasses up. Her eyes were very bloodshot. 'I FaceTimed Serge, when he was in Vancouver,' she said. 'He looked shattered.'

'Right. The job sounded full on.'

Even saying this Isla realised how much she disliked secrets – and the vigilance they demanded. She knew that Serge would not see their secret this way, having been trained to withhold all his life. He had once said, early in their relationship, that Isla was the only person he had ever opened up to.

'Is it awkward, with Rosie here?' said Allegra. She was whispering now, as if they were in a play and Rosie might reappear with disastrous timing.

'I mean, it is what it is. Everyone has exes.'

'God, I'd forgotten you're so bloody zen, babe. Anyway, for what it's worth, you've always been our favourite. Literally nobody cares about the whole Oxford thing. So boring.'

Isla laughed, though she felt unsettled. It was typical of Allegra to say something that sounded reassuring but induced paranoia.

She left and Isla sat finishing her coffee, trying to ignore Allegra's lipstick on the cup. It had never occurred to her to question the

Campbells' affections. She was not close to Marina or Lucian, but they had found a conversational groove that seemed to work – discussing exhibitions and old films, and Isla's own more outlandish credits. Now, the thought that Serge's family might actually have favoured Rosie – despite Allegra's assurance – suddenly seemed plausible. It was surprisingly hurtful. Isla thought of Marina's many arbitrary prejudices, from Pink Lady apples to sudoku, and wondered where she must have transgressed.

The Café

Hotel Georgette

8.30 a.m.

Rosie had dreamed that she was in a TV talent show and that the Campbell family were the judging panel. She had woken herself by singing, loudly, which seemed so silly that she half wished someone had witnessed it. Afterwards she had lain in bed for ages – the dream tangled with her real memories of speaking to Serge and Allegra the previous day.

She was now due to have breakfast with Imogen Martin, a close friend from St Arthur's. Imogen was already in the hotel's café when Rosie walked in. She was standing beside an institutional toaster, like the one in their college dining hall. It was dizzying to think those Oxford breakfasts were fifteen years ago. The pressure to live the *Brideshead* fantasy – with sufficient punting, and Pimm's and boys on bicycles – returned to Rosie for a second. Sometimes she feared she had never grown out of this mode, constantly assessing reality against a template. The way her relationship with Serge had never quite matched the daydream had been one of its many perplexities.

Imogen had left her husband and children in London. She and Rosie began walking round the buffet, selecting crescents of fruit and yoghurts in little jars, Imogen saying, 'Isn't this so civilised? I can't believe nobody's screaming!'

Her ecstasy highlighted the gulf between their lives.

'So how was it with The Ex?' she said, as they sat down. Imogen always referred to men this way, as if she were a dating columnist. 'You chatted last night, right?'

'Yeah. Just about work, family.'

'Ew,' said Imogen. 'Cordial.'

Imogen had always been suspicious of Serge's social ease, and often compared him to a chat-show host. Rosie did not necessarily see this as an insult.

'It was, just, like old friends. Which we are, I suppose.'

'I guess it was always a very *pleasant* relationship, though, right? Until he ended it. I'd really struggle to go back to being friends, after that.'

Imogen had always been prone to intense post-mortems over breakfast, frequently linking Rosie's military father to her preference for emotionally unavailable men.

'Well, it's nearly three years ago,' said Rosie.

'You're still allowed to have feelings.'

'Yeah, but, I can't do anything with them, can I?'

'You could tell him. That you were sad. Or pissed off. That dumping a broody woman just before her thirty-fifth birthday is unforgivable.'

'That's going to make me sound really cool.'

She saw she had confirmed Imogen's assessment that she was too proud, or somehow emotionally avoidant herself. She resisted mentioning Serge and Isla's alleged separation. It would only be interpreted as pathetically raised hopes.

'Not that I need to look cool,' she carried on. 'But what's that going to achieve? Now? And we have to give this best man's speech.'

'Oh shit, yeah. Hey, what about JP's best man? The Visiting Student. Wasn't he madly in love with you at Oxford?'

'Nate Kennedy? Yeah, he was there last night.'

'Was he? I didn't see him.'

'He's changed quite a lot.'

'Has he now?'

Imogen's smile was half smirk.

'He was really into the softball.'

'And that's a deal-breaker?'

'I'm just trying to identify him! It's not a deal-breaker situation, anyway.'

Imogen laughed as if Rosie were incorrigibly picky, and Rosie felt depressed that she was still in a position to entertain this way. Her friends followed a script too, but their parts had evolved. Their new role was to pose a rueful ennui with motherhood and marriage, and to ogle Rosie's freedom to pee alone and date strangers. Except, it was a tactful, token envy – the way her friends used to claim to covet Rosie's Celtic colouring, while comparing tans.

'Ooh, incoming!' said Imogen, looking at her plate with unnatural intensity.

Rosie turned – Nate was walking towards them.

'You're right, he looks completely different,' said Imogen, whispering now.

'Good morning,' he said. His smile made Rosie feel ashamed of talking about him, so recently.

'How did you guys sleep?' he said cheerfully.

Rosie described her unconscious singing, without mentioning the Campbells' part in the dream.

'What song?' said Nate. 'It was a power ballad, right?'

Rosie claimed to have forgotten, although she now recalled that the song had been 'Baby One More Time'. It seemed so mortifying as to be poignant.

'And is this a regular thing?' said Nate. 'You could start a YouTube channel.'

Rosie said it had never happened before, and he recounted a night when he had woken up eating cereal out of a cycling helmet. Imogen then told a long story about her son almost opening a stair gate in his sleep.

'Do you need a ride to the rehearsal?' said Nate to Rosie, when Imogen had finished.

She realised she could smell his shower gel, or cologne. The scent was ozone and male, and made her think of sex. It was disconcerting – as if her body were a rebellious teenager. She accepted the lift offer, and they exchanged numbers and arranged to meet in the lobby at one.

Rosie and Imogen kept chatting while he moved around the buffet, but she knew they were both conscious of his presence. As soon as he had taken his plate into the courtyard, Imogen said, 'What was that? The flirting!'

'I wasn't flirting! It was just funny. The cereal. And we need numbers, for wedding stuff.'

'He's actually quite hot now.'

Rosie felt defensive of Nate's younger self, even though she had rejected him at the time.

'Well, he's not, I mean . . . I'm not—'

Imogen raised her eyebrows. Rosie could tell she felt nineteen again, and that this was as thrilling for her as it was demoralising for Rosie. She kept looking at the café entrance, anticipating Serge's silhouette, the way it blocked out everything else. She didn't say that she was soon to meet him alone, and had tried on multiple outfits in preparation.

Café Mana

Rue Courteissade

9 A.M.

Aix was beautiful in the morning – the buildings painted ochre, salmon and mint, like bars of soap. Walking down the streets, the marzipan scent of patisseries mixing with diesel, Daniel felt his muscles loosen. Even Serge's Twitter disaster seemed less compelling. He found a table outside, took his Xanax, ordered a coffee and lit a cigarette – feeling it was justified in the setting. He was about to text Rosie when he heard a British voice say, loudly, 'Poor Virginia, with all the Americans staying. The trouble is they all expect their own bathroom!'

He looked up at 'Virginia' – knowing the voice must be referring to Caspar's mother.

Serge's parents were walking towards him. Caspar had introduced Daniel to them at the park the previous evening, as part of a large group. It was a re-introduction, really, though he had only met Marina and Lucian Campbell in passing at university. Marina was looking straight at him, so he smiled. Her face remained blank. He felt his smile falter. She kept staring, as if she were trying to place him, perhaps confused by having seen him on screen.

Daniel stood up slightly to greet them, certain she would recognise him close up from the previous evening. Her expression shifted to mild alarm and she sped up, pressing her handbag to her side.

Lucian hurried in response, and from further up the street they both turned to look back at him.

Daniel was torn between humiliation and incredulity, when he realised they were returning.

'I'm so sorry, I'm *completely* blind!' said Marina, smiling widely. 'You're Caspar's celebrant, aren't you?'

'That's me,' he said, quickly stubbing out his cigarette.

He smiled a cheesy, headshot smile, to show that he too was in on the joke about celebrants.

'And Virginia says you *know* Caspar?' said Marina.

He realised that she assumed he was some kind of professional, secular officiant. She probably presumed he was gay too. She was oblivious to his long friendship with Caspar – and also to his fame. He wondered if Serge had ever even mentioned him to his parents, or if he had been deleted from history.

Irritation made him effusively polite.

'I do,' he said. 'I do indeed. We both read English, at Arthur's.'

He knew that saying 'read' rather than 'studied' would grant him entry to the part of her subconscious that was resisting him.

'Oh!' Marina now looked shocked. 'So you must know Serge? And Rosie?'

Her face softened, as if Daniel were safe to speak to.

'Of course. Absolutely. Serge and I are meeting up, now.'

Marina looked alarmed again, and he saw he had exposed more gaps in her knowledge.

'He's got a work thing to chat about,' he said, quickly. 'I'm in the industry, too.'

'Right! Work. Well, hope that goes well,' she said brightly, as though he had referred to a minor operation.

'Presumably you've got to be at this "mob" rehearsal?' said Lucian. 'We're on grandparent duty. Keeping Serge's twins off the dance floor.'

'Ha. They should join, that would be amazing!' said Daniel. 'It's at two, right?'

'*Two?*' said Marina. 'I thought it was three? Have they changed everything at the last minute? The trouble is it's all emails!'

Her eyes lit up, apparently thrilled at this potential confusion.

'No, no, you're right. The dance rehearsal's at three.'

Even being corrected by Marina about the time felt damning. 'The thing at two is just, like, the "select few". Some seating plan drama.'

He said 'select few' in a precious voice, judging that Marina would register his tone as facetious. But she seemed to suppress amusement, as if she thought he was serious.

'Ah! *Select!*' she repeated. He imagined her asking Serge, later, about 'Caspar's funny little celebrant friend'.

'Long as we're not required,' said Lucian.

The sun was oppressively hot.

'And you're, what, getting brunch?' said Daniel.

Marina looked startled again, as if he had asked whether they were going to the loo.

'No, we're going to peer in at the cathedral,' she said.

'Ah! Enjoy,' said Daniel, immediately regretting the Americanism.

They bestowed broad smiles, and left.

Daniel drank all the coffee in his cup, wincing at the bitterness.

He watched them amble up the street, taking in their leisurely gait and linen clothes. He hated the way people like Marina Campbell could still make him feel craven and laughable, as if he had been rewound twenty years.

He took out his phone, and opened Twitter. It was still set to his @Gareth32 account.

He opened a reply to @SergeCampBELLEND and tweeted, without hesitation this time:

The irony is that Serge Campbell made *Bursary*, a condemnation of the British class system, with family money.

Rue Joseph Cabassol

Aix-en-Provence

9.50 a.m.

Walking through Aix to the English bookshop, Serge felt hot and troubled. Breakfast with Isla had been strained. He had resisted looking at Twitter after waking, but he was acutely conscious of the judgement roiling in his phone.

As he walked he tried to rehearse his pitch, but whenever he visualised saying 'it would be great to work together' he stalled. He was certain Daniel would not actually mention *Bursary* – the fact that he was keen to meet suggested it was long forgotten, in light of Daniel's success. But it still gave the meeting an uneasy backstory.

Book in Bar was at the end of a side street in central Aix. The back half of the shop was part café, so that the smell of paperbacks mingled with espresso, and the hissing and bangs of the coffee machine drowned out people's bookshop voices. Daniel was already at a table when Serge arrived. He glowed with new fame, simultaneously occupying extra space and shrinking under a cap.

'Campbell!' he said, too loudly. 'So good to see you, mate.'

Serge sensed people noticing Daniel, and was shocked to register something like jealousy. It was irrational – he needed Daniel to be famous. It was the reason for the meeting. He bought their drinks, wondering how much his compulsion to pay for other people had cost him over the years, and they sat talking about the film industry.

Periodically they both broke into laughter, almost competitively noisy.

It was different seeing Daniel one on one, to the previous evening in the yurt. Serge found himself struggling to keep up with the conversation, groping for specific things to praise in *Knifepoint*. As he said something about a scene in the film's Michelin-starred restaurant, he recalled another restaurant in Tuscany. He saw his mother imploring Allegra to order more than a salad, and his father looking away helplessly, while Serge railed against Daniel in his head.

He was almost relieved when Daniel's phone began ringing, and he stood up to take the call outside. His swagger was even more pronounced than it had been at twenty. Serge sat waiting for him. The call seemed to be taking a long time – almost insultingly long. His patience and resolution failed, he opened Twitter on his phone.

Immediately, he wished he hadn't. Just in the last hour a new tweet, crowing that *Bursary* had been made with family money, had been retweeted by a well-known comedian. As a result it had been retweeted hundreds of times, with the hashtags #ClassAppropriation #Trustafarian #CancelCampbell. It now had its own life and momentum, far beyond Erin's original thread.

Serge's face flooded with heat. The whole situation seemed to be sliding out of the internet's corners, and into reality. He sat staring at his phone, then – the handset slick in his palm – deleted the Twitter app. He put his phone face down on the table, and pushed his fingertips into his eyes.

Was it wrong, that he had told a working-class protagonist's story? He had assumed at the time – a time, admittedly, when people seemed less outraged about privilege or appropriation – that it was better than not telling the story at all. But now he wondered if he should have dared to tell any story that was not his own. Except, nobody wanted to hear Serge Campbell's story. Nobody cared about the burden of inherited wealth and unearned status. Perhaps this was Twitter's point. He had no right to make art at all.

Daniel returned, apologising and scanning his reflection in the window. Serge launched into his pitch, trying to collect himself as he did so. *Beating Heart*, he explained, would be a fresh take on hackneyed portrayals of council estates – exploring the way estate life might support, rather than stifle. The cinematography would be 'picturesque urban', the score would showcase young grime artists. Daniel was one of the few actors, Serge insisted, who could do justice to the lead. At one point he used the word 'trope', with reference to his own research into gangs, and wondered if Daniel might be silently cringing. It was an unfamiliar feeling.

But after a while Daniel's neutral expression shifted. He interrupted Serge to return to a point about the character's inner conflict, and Serge realised that Daniel wasn't cringing – he was genuinely engaged. They began discussing the protagonist, as if he were a person they both knew, his manner and his experience alive and accessible to them both. Serge found himself recalling their exhilaration over *Bursary Boy*, sitting in the pub, speaking over each other in their eagerness to contribute new ideas. The memory floored him, and he lost his train of thought.

'So where did this all stem from?' said Daniel, after a moment. 'Estate life?' His tone was direct, whereas at Oxford he might have made a joke about Serge's mockney accent.

'It was actually Isla. Just stuff she said, about the estates where she grew up. They got this bad rap, but there was actually this beautiful community.'

'Right. It's the same in Southend. Everyone's got each other's back.'

He waited a beat. Serge sensed he was making the same point as Twitter – that the only estates Serge had experienced were around country houses.

'And it sounds good, mate. Seriously,' he carried on. 'Great character. I'm just slammed right now. And all next year.'

He stopped, underlining his success.

'And, y'know, I wish I was in a place to do independents. Just, for the love. But I'm kind of focused on the studio jobs right now. Cos I'm still bloody renting! So, yeah, the pressure's on. To finally get a mortgage, all that shit.'

Serge murmured agreement. He had not anticipated Daniel mentioning money.

'You know what it's like,' said Daniel. His face broke into its big, mischievous grin.

'I mean, not personally, obviously. But you get it, this industry. Things are good now, but it can stop like that. Got to take care of future Daniel, y'know? Fucking make hay.'

Serge nodded. He had assumed Daniel would see an independent as a chance for artistic kudos.

'Sure, sure. I hear you. But listen, nothing's set in stone, man. Let me chat to finance. Be such a shame to miss you. We need that pretty face of yours!'

'Do that. It would be great to work together. Finally.'

There was a pause. Serge wished there was actually a finance department at Vanguard Films he could consult. He had made excuses not to see his parents' financial advisor for years.

'So where's Isla?' said Daniel.

It was unsettling to hear him say her name.

'Just chilling with the twins.'

'Must be full on for you guys.'

'We make it work.'

'How is it here with Rosie?' said Daniel, sipping his coffee. He sounded casual, but Serge recalled his girlish thirst for gossip. 'Blows my mind you guys ended up going out!'

He smiled frankly, but Serge felt a subtext. Daniel's dynamic with Rosie had always baffled him – the pantomime repartee like a dead end. Looking back, he suspected that Daniel had only flirted with Rosie to stake a claim, and that Rosie had only responded to make Serge jealous. The fact that Daniel and Rosie had not stayed in touch was confirmation.

'With Rosie?' he said. 'It's fine. We're meeting now, actually. Writing our best man speech.'

Rosie walked in as he said this. She had always arrived early, and he was usually late, so that his abiding memory of their relationship was hurrying across London.

There was a flurry of double kissing, and she sat at the table. They began talking about the wedding, all clearly conscious that they made an excruciating trio.

'Don't spare the Casman, will you?' said Daniel, as he stood up to leave. Several people looked over as he walked out, saying, 'I want that time he threw up on his tutor in the public domain,' loudly and without turning, as if he were exiting a set.

'So he's going to be in your film?' said Rosie.

'That's the plan.'

For a second, Serge wondered if Rosie would refer to *Bursary*, then remembered that she had barely ever mentioned the situation – even when they were a couple. They hardly used to discuss Daniel at all, in fact. If his name came up it was in the tone they might use for a distant, mutual acquaintance.

They established that Serge would open the speech, and began noting down anecdotes, sharing his laptop screen. Rosie was wearing a white strapless dress with a large ruffle across her chest, like a clown who'd just got out of the shower. It accentuated the small, pearly domes of her shoulders. Every time she laughed at one of Serge's suggestions her left shoulder moved closer to his arm. She kept tucking her hair behind her ears, and fiddling with her necklace. A shop assistant brought over her tea, and she said, '*Merci beaucoup*,' and straightened up demurely. Serge recollected how seductive he used to find Rosie's fluency in French, honed by a gap year as an au pair. He smelled her fragrance, and was transported to a weekend they had spent in Paris. It was only a few years ago, but it felt like a different time. Simpler, in many ways.

They began to write, most of the lines coming from Serge while Rosie laughed a lot. It was invigorating to be found funny. He reminded her of an evening when Caspar had tried to climb a Christmas tree in Bicester shopping outlet, and she began laughing so much her eyes started to water. She said something incoherent, and he remembered how quickly and endearingly Rosie could tip from polite laughter to hysteria. It had often seemed like the only time she let go. She had always laughed a lot, both as his platonic friend – when her laughter had a sweet nervousness – but also once they were a couple, as if she still felt nervous around him. Towards the end, it had put him on edge too.

When she surfaced, breathless, she said: 'What about when we went out after finals and he woke up on top of a bus stop? Why was he always climbing things?' Serge started to laugh now at this memory, and Rosie began giggling in response. She began half hiding her face, as she became flushed and grimaced. Pink patches appeared on her chest and neck too, like an atlas. It used to happen sometimes when they had sex.

A voice said, 'Going well?' and Serge looked up. Daniel was by the table, smiling slightly uncertainly. He picked up a pair of Ray-Bans, and said, 'Forgot these.'

Rosie sat straighter, as if to compose herself, but Serge could see her mouth still needed to laugh.

'Hey, sit down, man,' said Serge. 'Can we run this by you?'

'It might be too in-jokey,' said Rosie.

Daniel looked awkward now. Serge remembered the way his student bravado used to sometimes desert him, leaving a thin, lost-looking youth in its wake.

'Ah, listen, I should get back,' he said. 'Got a call. Send it to me.'

'OK, later, man. Cheers for today,' said Serge.

He left and they finished the speech, but on a more restrained note.

The Pool

Hotel Georgette

11.30 a.m.

Isla was near the pool with the twins, trying to distract them from the deep water with raisins. The effort of wrestling two sets of toddler swimming gear on and off their squirming bodies had outweighed the brief entertainment the swim had provided. Isla frequently found herself thinking this way about the twins' activities, analysing cost-benefit and breaking time into surmountable units. She remembered a poem from school about a life measured out in coffee spoons and thought how her life was measured out in episodes of *Peppa Pig*, and that coffee spoons sounded comparatively pleasant.

Serge would be with Rosie now. Isla pictured thin legs, and vivacious laughter. Juno burrowed her head into Isla's armpit, and Isla leaned down to press her face against her daughter's scalp. Huck tried to climb on top of Juno, so that they were like a three-person knot, and Isla pulled them both into her lap. She held one of their feet – she couldn't tell whose – in the palm of her hand, running her finger along the bead-size toes. Both twins were naked, like carved cherubs with their proud bellies.

'They're so darling,' said a creaky American voice.

She looked up. A woman she recognised from the softball was settling on a sun lounger, with a lurid cocktail. She looked like Meryl Streep. Isla wished she could have justified drinking now.

'Hard work too, I'll bet. I saw you chasing them around at the park.'

'Yeah. They're at the lemming stage.'

Isla looked at the tender groove at the nape of Juno's neck, and the swoop of Huck's eyelashes, and wondered how she could love them so much and also hanker after solitude.

'I used to say it's like dog years. One hour minding your kids, it's like seven regular hours. When they're little. It gets easier. Bitsy, by the way. JP's aunt Barbara.'

Isla explained her connection to the Campbells, and asked how many children Bitsy had.

'Five,' said the woman, casually. 'All grown. Plenty of time to myself now.'

Isla was about to express admiration, but Bitsy said:

'Though twins is something else, I'll bet. There was only ten months between our first two, and that nearly destroyed our marriage.' She laughed, sedately. 'So where's that handsome husband of yours?'

Isla didn't bother to correct 'husband'. Boyfriend sounded childless, but partner sounded joyless. She wondered what this meant for her and Serge.

'He had a work meeting. In town.'

'On vacation? What does he do?'

'He's in film. We both are.'

'But you don't get to escape for meetings?'

'I mean, not right now. It's not a great industry, with kids.'

'You miss it?'

The directness threw her. It felt risky to admit she missed work, as if this might topple something delicately balanced.

'Sometimes.'

Bitsy looked unconvinced. 'They don't have day care in London?'

'I mean, yeah. But the hours on set are mad. I'd never see them.'

She put more raisins into the twins' hot, grasping palms. She loved the way their hands looked screwed on to their wrists.

'What about your husband? Does he ever take them? Or is this typical?'

She gestured at the twins, clambering over Isla like animals.

'Umm. Pretty much.'

Bitsy nodded, her face was expensively immobile. It made her gaze feel more penetrating.

'But he can't, really,' Isla added. 'They're too used to me. We've got our routine. They won't go to anyone else, even my mum.'

She had said this before. It was simpler than dwelling on Saffron's smoking around the twins.

'You want to be the one, right? I used to feel that way. I wouldn't even get a sitter until we had our third. The thing is, you'll always be their number one. But you suffer. You go crazy if you won't let anyone help.'

Isla thought of the thrill of being on set, and creating something separate from her children. She imagined a space where nobody knew she was a mother. At the same time, she breathed in the pancakey smell of Huck's skin, as if she could inhale him back into her.

'And you girls are the lucky ones,' Bitsy carried on. 'I mean, none of the men did anything in our day. That was the deal. You could get a divorce, made no difference. I guess it was simpler, though. We had no expectations. Whereas my daughters – constantly disappointed.'

She harpooned the cherry in her drink with the stirrer, and popped it between inflated lips.

'But you must know all this,' she said, through the cherry. 'From your own parents? Your mom had to do it all, right? Work, kids, chores, parties, goddam PTA. While your dad came home and opened a beer. And we called ourselves feminists!'

Isla laughed, to imply recognition. She was not about to explain how her father had left while her mother was pregnant, and how Saffron had never fully recovered or matured, and certainly had not been on the PTA. Isla had learned to make a bowl of cereal at three, and to wash her school uniform at six. Somehow, this early domesticity had not prepared her for motherhood.

'Though I will say,' said Bitsy, 'my Carl did love to read to them. And the grandkids. Same books. Same silly voices.'

She drained her cocktail noisily, and said, 'He died last year. Cancer.'

'Oh! I'm so sorry.'

'Thank you, honey.'

Her face sagged where it could around the Botox.

'How have you been?' said Isla. 'Since?'

'Thank you for asking, dear. Most people don't.'

She became prim, in her new role as widow, and for a second Isla thought she wasn't going to elaborate.

'The thing is, you know,' she said, 'nobody gets it. Nobody! Because the only person who could get it, isn't damn well there. They're the one you want to call. The one you want to compare notes with. The only one. So that's what you're dealing with.'

'I can't imagine,' said Isla, lamely.

'Of course you can't. You're too young. And you don't even realise it, in a marriage. Every day, the two of you, you're building something. All the dumb jokes, the plans, the decisions. So many memories. The small stuff, and the showreel days. Even the fights. And you made these whole other people together! That always blew my mind.'

Serge used to say exactly this, as if the very concept of their genetic collaboration was phenomenal. She had found his awe touching. It was quintessentially Serge – both the marvelling at the commonplace, and the generosity. She wondered if he still felt awestruck.

'And then, out of nowhere, they're gone! Literally, nowhere. So all that stuff is gone too. I wish I'd known that. When the kids were little and we pretty much hated each—'

Someone said '*Bonjour*,' and Isla turned. Daniel was walking over, backlit by the sun. She had thought, after years of staring at actors, that she was immune to facial symmetry.

'How are we?' he said, adding 'Daniel' as he took Bitsy's hand.

'Well, hello, Daniel,' she said, her eyes travelling from his face to crotch and back. He grinned, graciously.

'Good meeting?' said Isla.

'Yeah! Quick! Serge's a busy man, right? I think I got, like, twenty minutes before Rosie.'

'Rosie?' said Bitsy.

'They've got to write a best man speech,' said Isla. It sounded unduly defensive.

Bitsy looked sceptical. Daniel's face was neutral. Isla realised he must know much more of Serge and Rosie's history than she did.

'Well, *mesdames*, I'll leave you to it,' he said, and she watched his back crossing the courtyard. At the door to the stairs, he glanced back. His smile – on being caught looking at her – was sweetly sheepish.

Room 7

Hotel Georgette

11.45 a.m.

In his room, Daniel went over to the window. He stood watching Isla through the shutter slats, studying her almost-naked body, knowing it was voyeuristic. The older woman waved 'bye-bye' to the toddlers. When Isla was alone she pulled both naked children onto her lap and kissed them voraciously, pretending to eat them, as they squealed. It felt wrong to keep looking, now, and he turned away.

Part of him wanted her to know what he had seen in the bookshop. The way Rosie had been giggling, and Serge's evident gratification, had bothered him. It had not felt flirtatious, exactly, but it had been intimate in a different way that was almost worse. Rosie's attempt to stop, in Daniel's presence, had been maddening. In Isla's place, he would have been hurt.

He thought over his own meeting with Serge. He had found himself drawn into the discussion – unable to resist a chance to analyse stakes and motivation, or to pin down a log line. He had recalled their lengthy dissections of films at Oxford, and the thrill of constructing *Bursary Boy* – as they'd called it. He'd never felt the same synergy with anyone else, before or since. Still, he knew he could never actually work with Serge. He wished he could say, in a *Sopranos* accent, 'Oh, so *now* you want me, huh? Huh?' Instead he had made a passive-aggressive point about needing to earn a living.

He took out his phone to see what new bile Twitter had produced for Serge. When the app loaded he was shocked. In a few hours, @Gareth32's tweet seemed to have assumed its own identity. Daniel's own posts often gathered thousands of likes, but this had a different, rampant quality. The hashtag #ClassAppropriation was multiplying like a virus.

He stood still, trying to disentangle the various retweets and replies. In among them all were various references to Vanguard's notoriously late payments, and he scrolled to find their source. He located it far down the thread. The creator of @SergeCampBELLEND had written, in response to Daniel's own alias tweet about *Bursary*:

Doubt there's much of that inheritance left, btw. Vanguard owes money left right centre.

It was conceivable that Serge's company owed money, he thought as he corrected the way Housekeeping had arranged his belongings. Production costs were exorbitant. But it was also a moot point. No Campbell could ever be in genuine financial trouble – the kind Daniel had known between jobs, or the kind that had contributed to his father's death. He remembered the way Serge had said 'let me chat to finance'. He wondered if 'finance' actually meant his father, or another millionaire godparent in the wings, poised to invest in *Beating Heart*.

He had not eaten all day and had planned to ask Rosie to meet for lunch, before the rehearsal. But it had felt impossible when he saw her in the bookshop – her eyes trained on Serge, clearly dressed up for the occasion. He decided to eat alone instead, perhaps to order a glass of red wine in the same Gallic spirit that he had lit a morning cigarette. He walked down the hotel stairs, wondering if he would see Isla in the courtyard, but she had gone.

Nate's Car

Vauvenargues

1.45 p.m.

The road towards the wedding venue looped around and up a steep hill, like a water slide. There was a sheer drop on one side of the car as it climbed to the village of Vauvenargues – Picasso's final home. Rosie was answering Nate's questions, but the time with Serge had left her disorientated. She couldn't say which was odder, being alone with Serge or the fact that they had not acknowledged the oddness. The same anecdotes would not have reduced her to convulsive giggles with anyone else – she generally found drinking stories tedious or alarming. But she had never graduated from laughter in response to nerves.

They passed a villa heaving with wisteria, and she recognised it as her yoga retreat. Nate asked if she did a lot of yoga. She was about to say that she tried to, but instead found herself admitting that she always felt excruciatingly impatient in yoga classes, and wasn't sure why she had booked a week of them.

Nate laughed and mentioned that he was taking the train from Marseille to Nice on Sunday, and would then be travelling by train to northern Italy. It sounded much more appealing than the retreat where, as she now told Nate, her phone would be confiscated. She resisted adding that it was all a private reward for enduring four days around Serge.

Nate mentioned an article he had written about screen addiction and mindfulness.

'You know how they say we're all wired to believe any threat – like, our phone dying – is a sabre-toothed tiger?' he said.

Rosie wondered why self-help invariably referenced a sabre-toothed tiger, but instead she said:

'Like fight or flight?'

'Right. And I'm like, always with the goddam sabre-toothed tiger!'

She turned, surprised at their synchronicity.

'I always think that!'

'I mean, how common were these tigers? If they died out.'

'Common enough to mess up humanity for ever.'

He laughed, a dimple in one cheek. She looked out at the Impressionist scenery. It was blissful to relinquish responsibility for her arrival somewhere.

'So we're gonna get a preview,' said Nate. 'What's your take on handwritten vows?'

'I haven't seen theirs,' she said, truthfully. She feared Caspar and JP's would be the usual clash of sentimentality and domestic diktats.

'But in general? Horribly American, right?'

She hesitated.

'It's OK, you can say. I've heard so many terrible ones,' he said. 'This one wedding, they vowed to take turns unclogging the toilet and his grandma stood up and told them to stop disrespecting Jesus.'

'I actually find it more uncomfortable when they're really gushing,' said Rosie. 'I'm obviously emotionally avoidant or something,' she said, remembering her conversation with Imogen.

'When they're ugly crying in the ceremony? No, I hear you. You're not emotionally avoidant. They should be more emotionally avoidant.'

She laughed.

'Plus, the old vows, they're pretty great,' he said. 'Just the words.

"Forsaking all others" and "till death us do part". I could never come up with that.'

'I always think "with my body, I thee worship" seems really inappropriate for church.'

'Right. How do you say that, with your mom there?'

'Most of my friends have just used this modern version. Without that part.'

'Worst of both worlds?' he said, cheerfully. 'No gravitas, still generic.'

'I mean, I wouldn't go that far,' she said, though she agreed.

'Plus, with handwritten vows, I always think one person winds up as primary writer. Like, no creative collaboration can be fully equal, right? Someone always dictates.'

She thought how Serge had dominated their speech writing, and then of his creative rift with Daniel. She was about to tell Nate about it, but he suddenly frowned at the satnav and shunted the steering wheel, briefly invading her space.

'Sorry!' he said. 'Re-routing.'

He pronounced it 'rowting' and she remembered how differences in American and British English used to be a mainstay of their jokes. 'Basil vs Bay-sil' had been an ongoing battleground, because pesto featured so heavily on noughties menus.

Even in the air-conditioned car the shimmering heat outside was palpable. She glanced at Nate's arms, the muscles twitching as he drove. He was wearing a sporty silver watch. It looked like it belonged there, as if it had sprouted on his wrist with a surge of late testosterone. She couldn't remember him seeming so physically male at Oxford. It struck her as a contrast with his chatty, inquisitive conversation. She knew if she had made this observation to Imogen, her friend would question why Rosie expected men to treat her like an audience.

Chateau de Beaupont, the wedding venue, was like an illustration from a fairy tale. The stone was a yellowish grey, turrets flanked the mansard roof and ivy grew around dozens of shuttered windows. A curving, double stone staircase led up to the front door.

As they approached she saw Serge, and wondered if he would notice Nate beside her. But he was laughing with Caspar, a huge, baroque fountain drowning out their words. There were both wearing pool slides and old T-shirts, as though palaces were their natural backdrop.

'Here she is!' said Caspar. 'So?'

'It's heaven!' said Rosie, knowing he needed her in giddy wedding mode.

'Come and meet Minnie. My godmother.'

They all walked up the stone stairs, and into an echoey hall. For a second she couldn't see after the sunlight, but she smelled the drapes and polish of the past. There was something forlorn about the place, which must once have been so busy, now hosting weddings and conferences.

Caspar and Serge stood near a suit of armour, reminiscing about childhood games of sardines in the house, while Rosie and Nate looked around in silence. After a moment Caspar led them through a boot room, the size of Rosie's own kitchen, and out onto a vast lawn.

The marquee was already set up for the wedding dinner, white tablecloths in pristine anticipation, and JP was frowning at a handwritten seating plan. Daniel arrived, apologising for being late, making it look even more like a film set. He kept his sunglasses on in the marquee, and Rosie wondered what she would think of him, if they met now.

'OK, so flowers are coming, flowers are coming,' said Caspar, walking around in small, jittery circles. 'And the favours. It's not going to look like this. Anyway, placement! Basically top table's here,' he pointed at a table near the marquee's dance floor, 'and then we kind of grouped people by, uh, theme. Do I mean theme? Like, "St Arthur's guests!" and "Yale guests!" and "showbiz guests!"

Anyway, could you guys just take a look and let us know if you think it all works? Like, Serge, d'you think Allegra's OK next to Val Harvey?'

'No, wait, remember they dated but he was sleeping with his intimacy co-ordinator?' said Rosie, before Serge could reply.

Everyone looked at her, quizzically. She knew the part of her brain that documented other people's lives was abnormally porous – in the same way she could not forget classmates' birthdays and landline numbers. She also knew – rationally – that this encyclopaedic knowledge was better concealed, or downplayed. Instead, she seemed compelled to display all the minutiae she retained.

'Shit, I forgot that,' said Caspar. 'Good one, Ro. So who've we got ... Ludo de Foye? Or Hamish Gordon Cole?'

Rosie stood by the place. 'Maybe Hamish? Weren't they at Bedales?'

She realised as Caspar called her a genius that she had revealed a freakish degree of knowledge, again. But it felt as if seating plans were in some way her calling, as if she owed it to Caspar to find the optimum configuration for his wedding. This was sobering itself, like seeing your mother's face in your own reflection.

They kept moving name cards while JP said, 'I'm into that,' or 'You got this,' and Daniel spoke loudly on the phone. Serge and Nate were standing back, discussing the Second Amendment. Both times that Rosie glanced over, it was Nate who looked up. When Caspar and JP were satisfied, they all walked to the lake for the rehearsal.

She realised Nate had hung back to walk beside her. It reminded her of how he used to wait for her on their landing at St Arthur's, so that they could leave college together.

'Your Campbell knowledge is pretty tight,' he said.

She hadn't realised he was listening in the marquee.

'I mean, I just remember that stuff. Female thing, maybe.'

She felt a blush rising.

'Also I used to go out with Serge. So I know his family from that, too.'

It was meant to sound casual.

'You and Serge?' Nate turned to look at her. 'What, after college?'

'Yeah. Ages after. Like, three years ago.'

'Oh! So, pretty recent?'

'Um, it doesn't feel recent. At all! Is that weird?'

'Guess it depends how long you dated. Or how serious it was.'

He was walking very slowly, as if they were on a private stroll far behind the others.

'Two years. But it wasn't that serious.'

'That's a long time not to be serious.'

The sun beat down on her parting.

'Maybe I'm not a very serious person,' she said weakly.

'Is that a thing? Isn't it more like, the right person makes you serious?'

He was looking out at the horizon, as if they were discussing this question in the abstract.

'I mean, that's the way I've always seen it,' he said. 'Not that I'm qualified to say.'

She wanted to ask why he was not qualified, but they were approaching the lake. Serge rehearsed his reading from Dr Seuss with undue fervour, clearly competing with Daniel's stage presence. While Rosie clapped she remembered how badly she had hoped Serge was serious about their relationship, because everything – except his seriousness – was in place. She had wanted him for years and finally, miraculously, they were a couple. He was so dynamic, and generous, and popular. Some people, she knew, thought he was arrogant. But this was thrilling in itself – to be an arrogant man's choice. They laughed at the same things. Even her parents approved, despite Serge's artistic career. And Rosie had believed, from the start, that their prior friendship endowed their relationship with more weight. But now she wondered, thinking of their laughter in the bookshop, if it had provided anything more than a canon of shared references.

After the rehearsal everyone walked back to the marquee, where about twenty other guests were standing near the dance floor, ready to practise the flash mob. Isla was there, shepherding her peachy toddlers out of the way. She looked like a natural dancer, Rosie thought, with a wash of dread. The flash mob, with its choreographed moves, would be awkward but probably manageable if she stayed at the back. It was the obligatory, spontaneous dancing afterwards that she feared, when all the social agility she had mastered over the years vanished. On dance floors she was exposed as the stiff beacon of self-consciousness she knew herself to be inside – a miserable flashback to towering over teenage boys. The notion that good dancers were good in bed had always alarmed her.

'OK, flash mob!' said JP.

Rosie stood at the back of the group, poised to rush onto the dance floor at the designated time. She realised Nate was beside her.

'Hiding?' he said.

'Letting the grooms shine.'

JP and Caspar began dancing slowly and dramatically to the opening of 'Like a Prayer'.

At the line 'When you call my name', everyone in front of Rosie surged into movement. Even though she had been counting herself in, it still came as a shock, so she was already behind. She forced her face into a fun smile and tried to keep up, even though she kept going to the wrong side or coming in late. Each time she made a mistake her body tightened. She could see Isla at the front, moving with a smooth, sexual fluidity, as if the music were powering her body – as if she were actually enjoying herself. Her hair bounced as she dipped forwards to execute a Charleston move. Rosie knew she was rushing the move herself, and that she looked like she was dusting her knees off after a fall. Serge was beside Isla, messing up frequently but cheerfully. Rosie remembered how her own wooden two-step used to jar with his abandon. He turned to Isla now for the partner move, grabbing her hands and laughing. They didn't look like a couple going through a separation.

Rosie was concentrating on them so much that she hadn't noticed Nate turning to her, and taking her hands in one movement. They were face to face, inches apart. He smiled. She sensed that he could see she was uncomfortable, but didn't want her to realise he had noticed. His hands felt big and warm, and one now moved to the middle of her back, so that they were in the classic ballroom hold. He felt very stable, like a wall or piece of furniture, and for a few seconds she felt pliant and floaty in response – as if she didn't have to do anything. A second later they were back in their places for the ending, and she fumbled through the last moves without thinking.

'OK, guys, that's a wrap! Amazing!' JP shouted over laughter and cheers.

'Can we hide here tomorrow?' said Nate.

'Sure,' said Rosie.

She hoped she sounded casually conspiratorial, like him, but she feared that gratitude was radiating off her.

The Garden

Chateau de Beaupont

3.45 P.M.

Daniel was standing away from everyone, speaking to his agent. Camilla had called, for the second time in an afternoon, and he was feigning enthusiasm about a forthcoming interview and promising not to party too hard. He wondered if she could tell that he had ordered a bottle of rosé with lunch, and inadvertently finished it. He had mispronounced a word in the rehearsal, and Caspar had joked about the vicar in *Four Weddings and a Funeral* saying 'the holy goat'. Daniel had pretended to laugh, with everyone else, smarting inside. He knew, already, he would not be able to save the cocaine in his room for Saturday.

Camilla hung up, after reminding him to read his *Telegraph* interview. Without the prop of the call Daniel felt even more apart from proceedings, or from himself. He opened the link to the interview. He didn't really want to know what he had said – or how Jessica Blackwell had interpreted it – but he also wanted an excuse to keep looking at his phone. Most of the profile was about *TROG*, as usual. But the standard paragraph about his time at Oxford read differently to other profiles, because Jessica Blackwell had told it through her own memory.

My recollection of Daniel Pyke at Oxford is of a classic class clown, albeit an unusually pretty one. Always last to leave the party, he was undoubtedly a 'player' in noughties parlance, but appealingly ready to laugh at his own expense. Which he had to, frequently, to gain his Etonian peers' acceptance.

The confidence of her prose threw him. She went on to give her own take on St Arthur's 'toxic banter', including a running joke that his mother was a corrupt college dinner lady who had pulled strings to get her son a place. Despite it all being Jessica's own memory, it read as Daniel's experience. He read on:

I ask Pyke whether his drinking – which, by his own admission, was heavy even by student standards – was linked to feeling othered. 'What are you going to do, Jess?' he replies, widening his Guinness-brown eyes. 'It was what it was. Sink or swim.'

Daniel didn't recollect saying this, but he had been so wired he might have said anything.

He kept reading, and by the end found his fear that it might offend his old peers had faded. If anything, a kind of defiance had replaced the anxiety. Perhaps it was time the people who had made St Arthur's so hierarchical heard the truth.

A table of tea things had been set up on the lawn, in view of the marquee. He walked over, just as Nate Kennedy approached at the same time. He no longer looked like a mop with an Adam's apple, as he had done at twenty.

'I don't think we ever actually hung out at Oxford?' said Daniel, after they had reintroduced themselves.

'Right? I think I only knew Rosie out of you guys. But I only studied there a year.'

He looked at Rosie, pretending to bow down to Caspar.

'How was that?' said Daniel. 'Must have been full-on culture shock? I mean, it was a pretty weird place. In hindsight.'

Jessica Blackwell's conversation style seemed to have infiltrated his own, he realised. Perhaps it was a better way to be – skipping the niceties.

'I actually loved it. But yeah, I could barely understand anyone the first month.'

Nate smiled, as if this was a fond memory.

'I hear you, geezer,' said Daniel. 'I mean, I'm only from Essex. And I had no clue what these kids were on about.'

'Oh sure. It was like this arcane frat house, right? Though I pretty much avoided that scene.'

'Good call. You know they literally called me "Pikey"?'

'Pikey? What is that?'

'Technically, Irish traveller. But these guys just used it to mean chav. White trash. I mean, they had shitty names for everyone. Especially the girls.'

'Really? What was Rosie's?'

'"Fit Rosie". Cos there was another girl they called "Fat Rosie". I mean, not to her face. Though she probably found out. They weren't big on discretion.'

Daniel suddenly recalled a distressing afternoon, when Rosie's friend Imogen had discovered she was known as "Horse Face". She had hidden in her room for two days, while Rosie brought her food and Daniel tried to make her laugh.

'Right. I guess that whole era was pretty shady,' said Nate. 'Mark Zuckerberg was right on the money.'

'That and the fact that posh kids have always been arseholes.'

He saw Nate look slightly taken aback.

'I mean, not all of them,' he added. 'Obviously this guy's a legend.'

He gestured at Caspar.

'Right. Like, he and Serge were clearly raised with all this,' Nate looked up at the chateau. 'But they'll talk to anyone.'

They both looked at Serge, now laughing with a man who appeared to be one of the chateau's gardeners. People always marvelled at Serge's ability to 'talk to anyone', not seeing that it was precisely Serge's upbringing that gave him the confidence to do so.

'Yup. The Campbells get schooled in charm,' said Daniel. 'Along with the tennis and piano.'

Nate smiled, but his eyes registered the cynical note.

'No, but seriously,' said Daniel. 'Serge's a great guy. I just fucking envy the way he never questions himself. I don't even think I'm the best at being Daniel Pyke!'

He had used this line before, both for the laugh it prompted and to ensure the other person knew who he was.

Courtyard Suite

Hotel Georgette

5 p.m.

Serge stood in the suite, ironing his shirt for the evening. The practical, mindless task was soothing. He felt almost optimistic, for the first time since winning his SOFA award. Dancing with Isla, even though the physical contact was enforced, had felt significant – like a return to something. They used to dance all the time, even just at home. And afterwards, in the chateau's garden, she had seemed lighter. He pushed the point of the iron into the cuff seams, wondering if a Madonna routine might have salvaged their relationship, and wanting to say this to Isla, but knowing she wouldn't appreciate a joke at their expense yet.

He hung up the shirt, thinking about Caspar and JP's vows, which he had heard at the rehearsal. They were cheesy, but he had grown more tolerant of cheesiness since meeting Isla, who was so much more earnest than his family. One of the vows had stuck in his head, like a song lyric:

'I promise to tell you when I have messed up, and when I am afraid. I will never move out of us, and into myself.'

Serge knew he used to voice his mistakes and fears, and that Isla had done too. He remembered long conversations in bed, two disembodied voices in the dark, confiding fears and regrets. He had said things, in those months, which he had never told anyone.

Most of it had revolved around his heritage, and its downsides. She had explained about her mother's chaos, including the many times during Isla's teens when Saffron had left their home – almost without warning – to stay with her latest boyfriend. There was more that Serge could have said, had the twins not blown everything apart.

But Isla had 'moved into herself' too, he thought, as he unplugged the iron. She used to rely on him, especially while she was pregnant. She had once said, jokingly, after asking him to open a jar, that she had never let anyone else look after her. It had stopped with parenthood though, as if she could not risk being dependent once she had dependents of her own. The only conversations they had in the dark, now, were about Calpol.

He went out onto the veranda, where Isla was drinking a particular brand of turmeric tea she took everywhere. The steam smelled of his flat, since her arrival. She was wearing a bikini, and he recalled their first holiday in Barcelona, feeling addicted to her skin. The twins were both in the cot, babbling in their secret language.

'Twig tea?' she said, using Serge's name for it.

He accepted – sensing an olive branch. It was the first time in weeks she had offered him anything, or used one of their private terms.

'I was thinking,' he said. 'Why don't I take the twins out tomorrow morning? So you can have some time? To yourself.'

'Oh. OK. Are you sure—'

She looked up and stopped, and he knew she had been about to question his competence.

'There's a carousel. They'd love that, right?'

'I guess,' she said, sounding unconvinced. 'If you went on with them.'

He took a sip of tea, searching for the right words.

'Just, I'd love to have some proper time with them,' he said. 'After being away. And to give you a break.'

'OK. Thanks. That would be nice.'

It felt like minute progress and he leaned forwards, his elbows on his knees, so he could look right into her eyes. He thought of the vows, and imagined confessing his debt.

'Can we—' he began, thinking they had to at least plan a time to talk.

He felt as if he could actually feel his secrets sticking in his throat, and thought of his childhood cat Tolstoy, who struggled with fur balls.

'Can we what?'

'Like, are we going to—'

There was a cry from the cot. Isla stood and hurried inside. After a second, Serge followed.

Courtyard Suite

Hotel Georgette

5.15 P.M.

Isla and Serge picked up a child each, and the twins looked up at their parents and then at each other – as if they were pleasantly surprised by this development. Huck began fidgeting first. Serge offered to take him swimming. Isla was about to say she would join them with Juno, and stopped. She thought of JP's aunt asking if Serge didn't help, or if Isla didn't let him. She took Juno out onto the veranda instead.

They sat watching Serge and Huck splashing in the pool, her daughter pulling apart a baguette. Isla's skin held the pleasurable, holiday tautness of bright sun and hotel showers. She tried to line up her thoughts, but Juno's warmth in her lap was fogging her brain. She remembered Bitsy's description of marriage as a world a couple built, destroyed by one party's death, and how she had pictured a wave engulfing an elaborate sandcastle. It was a sad image. She had never considered a relationship this way, as a joint construct – a separate entity, distinct from the two individuals.

'The others are swimming,' she said into Juno's hair, attempting a normal family observation. Serge kept ducking underwater and reappearing – Huck shrieking with suspense. Serge had lost weight. His trunks were slipping down, so that he had to hold them up with one hand. Isla had felt the difference in his body when he had pulled her close in the flash mob rehearsal, but she hadn't really seen it until now. It was painful to witness, as if their tension was consuming him.

Her mind returned to the dance. There had been one second, their faces inches apart, when she and Serge had both stopped laughing. The moment had passed, but it had felt like a fleeting truce. She thought now how she and Serge used to have sex almost daily before they were parents, despite long hours and punishing call times. She had never understood why women were supposed to see it as a chore, or faintly unfeminine. The notion that motherhood quashed desire did not resonate either. She used her vibrator as often as she always had done.

Serge still tried to initiate sex. He would nudge up to her in bed when he got back late, or start kissing her neck when she was washing up. She resented the way it had to fit around his schedule, as if their relationship came second to his career. But her skin still responded to his touch, and something in her still fluttered when she looked into his eyes. She resented this too, as if her senses were betraying her brain. So she forced herself to pull away – body thrumming, mind bristling. She would have preferred not to want him. Serge assumed she felt inhibited about her softer flesh, and kept telling her she was beautiful. She had not felt inhibited, until he said so.

He continued to plunge and emerge, and Isla found herself thinking of octopuses and how the females slowly died when their eggs hatched. A scuba-diving instructor had told her about this, when she was eighteen. At the time, she had only listened because she hoped to sleep with him after the dive. Now, she felt a sobering affinity with the octopus – this many-armed maternal martyr. Something had died in her when she gave birth. It wasn't sex, though. This was another thing Serge had not understood.

Chateau La Coste Vineyard and Sculpture Gardens

Le Puy-Sainte-Réparade

7 p.m.

The rehearsal dinner was at Chateau La Coste, a vineyard in the Luberon attached to a restaurant and sculpture park dotted with concrete nudes and abstract structures. The whole place reminded Rosie of the kind of subtitled films where families argued over photogenic salads. She was acutely conscious of the cufflinks in her bag.

Everyone was milling around a candlelit terrace, grapes dangling from the trellis overhead. The evening was still warm, the horizon mauve behind the vineyard. Waiters were passing round coupes of brassy, vintage Champagne. It was mustier than Rosie liked, but she kept agreeing with people that it was delicious.

Serge and Isla arrived late, with the twins in onesies, and were greeted with a lot of enchanted laughter. They looked more relaxed than at the softball, Serge moving Isla towards the bar with his hand on her hip. Rosie remembered Serge steering her out of a party this way before their first kiss, and how the gesture – in its promise of intimacy – had been more thrilling than the kiss that followed. She had not thought of their misaligned kisses for years, she realised, as if the pain of the break-up had filtered her memory.

At Caspar's request, Rosie began reminding everyone to take their bags and jackets to the cloakroom, so that the terrace would not 'look cluttered' in photographs. When Rosie told Serge, he said, 'Whatever the bride wants,' and picked up a baby-changing bag. Isla handed him a shawl, saying, 'Here, take my scarf.' Her west-country burr made her seem even more luscious, like an ambrosial milkmaid.

Serge returned in shirtsleeves, and Rosie wondered if she would be able to identify his jacket in the cloakroom and secretly return the cufflinks. She only realised Nate was nearby when he commented on the Louise Bourgeois spider sculpture, looming over the lake at the entrance to the park.

'How's your speech coming?' he said.

'Fine. But I'm giving it with Serge. And he basically learnt public speaking in the womb.'

Nate nodded, acknowledging this as fact.

'Hey, did Daniel have a hard time at St Arthur's?' he said, as if her comment had reminded him of something.

'Daniel? Not that I knew of. But he did this interview, just recently, about how toxic it was.'

'Right. He was kind of venting about it to me, earlier. I had no clue it was that bad. I was just in my ex-pat bubble.'

'I mean, he's right in a way. Looking back. Some of the guys really tried to force this caste system – like jocks and nerds, and ugly, clever girls and hot, dumb girls. But everyone was a geek, by definition. Just for being at Oxford. And Daniel always seemed like he was fine with it. Like he took 'Pikey' as a kind of backhanded compliment. He'd be the first to admit he's a massive show-off.'

'But you can't tell, can you? How a joke lands. Even if they're laughing. Didn't you go through something similar, at your fancy boarding school?'

She was surprised to hear that she had been so confessional with Nate – and that he had remembered her accounts of craving acceptance at an elite boarding school. The military had paid her fees, and although she had never been bullied she had been conscious of her modest background.

'Kind of. I figured it out pretty quickly, though,' she said.

'How to fit in?'

'Well. It doesn't sound great, like that.'

'We all need to fit in, right?' he said. 'At that age.'

'But fitting in, blending in . . . it's not the same as belonging, is it?'

She had heard this on a podcast, and felt foolish now for speaking in sound bites – even though Nate was nodding. Then he smiled and said, 'You planning a TED talk on that?'

She laughed, and finished her drink. It hit the back of her throat and she began to splutter. She tried to breathe, and the spluttering turned to choking.

'Are you OK?' said Nate, concerned. She tried to answer, but she couldn't. She wondered if it was possible to drown in vintage Champagne.

'Water?' said Nate, handing her his drink.

She gulped, and then coughed over his glass, feeling revolting. The choking had subsided, though.

'OK?'

'Yes. Thank you.'

She tried to smile, but another bark-cough burst out of her.

'Thought I might have to give you the Heimlich there.'

She asked a waiter for two glasses of water.

'Do I have mascara all down my face?'

He motioned at a place under his own eye, and she pushed her fingers across her cheekbone.

'Gone?'

'Nearly – just there.'

She tried again, but he said, 'Here,' and leaned forwards and moved his thumb over her face, his palm brushing her jaw as he did so.

'We're good,' he said, stepping back.

The waiter returned with their water.

'Driving?' she said.

'Yeah. One of the perks. I don't drink, though.'

'Since when?'

'Around ten years. I stopped counting the days.'

She turned, surprised. He used to drink at Oxford, but not so much that it seemed like a problem.

'You did AA?'

'Yup. The whole deal. You have to.'

'Oh. OK. When did it start? Because you never, I mean, I don't remember—'

'When you rejected me,' he cut in, looking out at the vineyard's tapering furrows.

Before she could respond, he looked round and said, 'Just kidding.'

She laughed, though she felt wrong-footed, and was about to acknowledge the teenage awkwardness of that evening. But Nate said:

'No, it started when a friend of mine died. Ten years ago. And there were things I wished I would've said. He was an addict, ironically.'

'I'm so sorry.'

He smiled, sadly.

'They called me a functioning alcoholic. I'd be that guy who was falling out of the bar, but fine at work the next day. It was my first job, at *GQ*. I was out every night, all these parties and premieres, and at first I kind of needed a drink to handle them. Then I got to rely on it, just to unwind. I'd be drinking at home, watching a movie. So it was this slow decline.'

'What stopped it?'

'My girlfriend gave me an ultimatum. And I couldn't quit, even for her. Or, I didn't. So we broke up, and that was the catalyst.'

She recalled him saying the right person made you serious and felt a twist of curiosity about this woman.

'Well – well done, then,' she said, clinking tumblers and then fearing it was tactless. In the coppery light he looked burnished with health.

They both turned back to the view across the lake.

'You know JP wanted the lake routine from *Dirty Dancing*, for the flash mob?' said Nate, nodding at the water.

'I do. I talked them out of it. You might've had to lift me above your head.'

'No sweat.'

'Have you actually seen it?'

'Of course! I have sisters. I think they were averaging daily screenings one summer.'

'Serge and Daniel hated that it was the only film I'd seen more than once. That and *Clueless*.'

'Hey, *Clueless* is a great film,' said Nate.

She could smell his cologne, the same one she'd noticed at breakfast.

The Restaurant

Chateau la Coste

9 P.M.

While the waiters cleared away plates of pavlova, people stood up to switch places. Isla stayed where she was – there was nobody she knew well enough to approach. Daniel had been sitting on the other side of the table during dinner, and their eyes had met several times through all the bottles and candelabras. He pulled out the seat beside her, now. She felt abruptly more awake.

'So. Isla. What's your deal? Where are you *really* from?' he said, with ironic emphasis.

'Near Glastonbury. My mum's a hippie. You?'

'Southend. Essex boy.'

'D'you get back there much?'

'Not much. I mean, I just spent a month at my mum's. But I barely saw her. Non-stop work.'

He drained the glass of Calvados in front of him, apparently forgetting it wasn't his.

'Me too. I mean, not the work. But I've just been at my mum's.'

'Your dad's not around?'

'Nope. Always just been me and her.'

She wondered for a second, how an absent father might affect Juno and Huck.

'Same here,' said Daniel. 'It's a funny one, right? Only child, single mum.'

'If she's anything like mine.'

Daniel laughed. They began talking about their mothers, and how Daniel's had always been ambivalent about him acting – and used to worry that he would fall behind academically. Their mothers were clearly different, but she recognised his description of a childhood spent alone or with adults.

They both looked around at staff flitting between tables, the rumble of conversation and braying laughter. There was camaraderie in watching this way, like spectators.

'So what's it like? Coming into all this craziness? Being on the inside?' said Daniel. He had lowered his voice, as if they had already acknowledged their mutual outsider status.

'Not sure you ever feel like you're on the inside. I mean, everyone's lovely. It's just so different. To how I grew up.'

A waiter stopped beside them, offering petits fours, illustrating her point.

'Sure. That's so cool you aren't fazed, though,' said Daniel. 'If I'm doing theatre and the cast's all ex-RADA, I still feel like someone's going to tell me to leave.'

She wondered, again, at how fast he had created a sense of confidences exchanged, and a united front of two.

'But that started at Oxford,' he added. 'Sticking out like a sore thumb.'

'Saint Martins was the same. I did my foundation there. Everyone used to get sushi for lunch, and I'd be there with my Greggs pasty.'

'Right! I feel seen! But you were too cool to care, right?'

'I mean if someone judged my pasty, I'd be like, "jog on".'

'See? You're cool. Me, that age, I was just gagging for approval. Typical actor.'

He refilled his adopted glass.

'Is that why you're in LA?' she said. 'To get away from that whole RADA thing?'

'Partly. That and the beach. Same thing, I guess.'

She thought of him surfing across the TV in her teenage bedroom, and her vivid yearning for his body.

'Nature's actually a huge deal, in LA. Everyone's always hiking, surfing,' he carried on. 'It's actually pretty grounded, in its own way. Shit! Did I just say "grounded"?'

'You're fine. We're all tree huggers where I'm from.'

'Do you miss it?'

'Yeah, actually. The other day I realised I talk about "clean air" like a luxury.'

'Could you go back?'

'I'd love to for the twins. But it'd be a nightmare with work.'

She realised, as she said this, how acutely she missed the West Country – how much she had supressed her feeling that London was the wrong place for children. The month in the fields and woods of her childhood had spot-lit her homesickness.

'So come to LA! You've got Hollywood, and the great outdoors. Two for one.'

Serge appeared behind Daniel.

'Hey, man,' he said. He smiled at them both. 'Think this opera thing's about to start.'

'I'm just telling your missus to move the fam out to California,' said Daniel.

'Really?' said Serge, looking from Daniel to Isla, bemused and uncertain. It was a novel expression on his face.

'Isla's after some tree hugging,' said Daniel.

'What's wrong with the heath?' said Serge.

'Serge feels grounded when he goes to watch Arsenal,' said Isla.

Daniel laughed.

Serge did too, but when his eyes met hers she thought she detected wounded pride.

The Cloakroom

Chateau la Coste

9.20 p.m.

The cloakroom was empty and unmanned, with a wall of white lockers and a poured concrete floor. Everybody was still having coffee and petits fours. The opera recital was due to begin in ten minutes, and later the cloakroom would be full of people gathering bags and jackets. Rosie took the cufflinks out of her bag and held them in her palm, a tiny, sharp bundle. Her armpits were prickling.

The wedding party's jackets and bags were all hanging on a rail along one wall. She scanned them, and saw Isla's green and gold shawl hanging beside the baby-changing bag. She examined the jackets beside them, trying to remember or guess which was Serge's, but neither looked familiar. She hung up her own pale grey scarf, as if to legitimise her presence in the cloakroom. Beside Isla's, it looked middle-aged. She touched Isla's shawl, and then smelled it, holding the fabric right against her face. The scent was more floral than she had expected. Then she sniffed the jackets near it, wondering if she could distinguish Serge's, like a police dog.

There was a flush, nearby. She had not seen a door off the cloakroom, labelled WC. Heat rushed to her face, right up to her scalp. The door opened, and Daniel emerged rubbing his nose.

'Daniel!'

'Rozzer!'

She was sure he hadn't seen her smelling jackets, but she still felt as if he had caught her burying a body. Daniel looked furtive himself.

'So how you doing?' he said, stepping closer.

'Great!'

She crunched the cufflinks together in her hand, now slick with sweat. His pupils were dilated, despite the bright overhead lighting. She thought of Nate, earlier, confessing his alcoholism, and wondered if Daniel's cocaine use was social or habitual. A drop of blood, rimming his right nostril, began to expand – threatening to fall.

'Oh, ah . . . are you OK?' she said.

'Me? Yeah. Why?'

There was a combative note to his voice that she had never heard before. Or perhaps only once, in their final phone conversation.

'I mean, I think you've got – er – a nosebleed.'

She felt sad and repulsed, all at once.

'Bollocks.' He wiped his nose on the back of his hand, and glanced at the smear. 'Flying. Always does this to me.'

He smiled, but his eyes were shinily alert.

It felt like a moment she could ignore or seize, even though they hadn't spoken properly since arriving in France. It would be easier to ignore it, she thought, but cowardly.

'But also, I mean, are you really OK?' she said.

'Sorry?' He frowned again, the fake puzzled expression he pulled in photo shoots.

'I mean, I just, I read your interview in the *Telegraph*.' Already, she realised her question had been too blunt, or mistimed. 'About Oxford. And, obviously, I know press is always butchered, but – well – I guess I hadn't realised—'

A drop of blood plopped between them, and he cupped his face and swore.

'I've got tissues,' she said, reaching into her bag.

Fumbling for the tissues, she dropped the cufflinks. They landed either side of the red spot on the floor.

Daniel crouched down to help her, his hand still clamped to his face. She tried to give him the tissues and grab the cufflinks at the same time, scraping her fingertips on the concrete. Her heart was beating so hard she feared he would hear it.

'They're Caspar's,' she said. 'Just putting them in here. Best Woman duties.'

Immediately she regretted lying. Her mission was just the kind of farcical situation Daniel would have appreciated, once. But they no longer seemed to have that kind of rapport, despite their ebullient greetings. The moment to ask him about his interview was gone – and with it any chance to ask after his state of mind.

'Best Woman,' he said. 'Course. You and Serge. Speech all sorted?'

He was now looking at her over the tissue, pressed to his face.

'Pretty much. No shortage of dirt on Cas. Well, you saw, we were pissing ourselves.'

She cringed at her uncharacteristic tone, an attempt to sound casual with Serge's cufflinks in her hand. Daniel nodded.

'Most of the Oxford stories aren't family friendly, though,' she added.

'Right,' he said, sniffing. 'But, maybe, just be careful? With Serge, y'know? And the lols.'

'Careful?'

'I mean—' He removed the tissue. 'God, Rosie. It just bothered me, to be honest, to see you *still* like this. About him. Now.'

Neither of them spoke, and she wondered if he was also thinking of their final phone call.

'Or, some idea of Serge,' he continued, with a flourishing gesture, as if he were painting a life-size portrait of Serge between them.

'I'm not "still like that" about Serge. Really!'

She attempted a laugh.

'Good. Isla's a sweet girl.'

There was a warning in his voice. It shocked her, both the sanctimony and the implied accusation – though she wasn't sure what he was accusing her of.

'You know Isla and Serge aren't even together?'

The words came out of nowhere, a little mutiny against her own character, like the cufflinks theft.

'What? They're engaged, mate.'

'They're not. They're having a trial separation. Allegra told me, but it's secret. Even his parents don't know, so please don't—'

Daniel's phone began buzzing, but he didn't seem to hear. He was staring at her, unblinking. Finally he took the call, saying 'Camilla!' with the same artificial enthusiasm he'd said 'Rozzer!'

He turned, and she watched his narrow back. She decided to wait for him to hang up, so she could reiterate that Serge's separation was confidential. She already regretted her indiscretion. But Daniel walked even further away, towards the door. Rosie remembered the cufflinks. He still wasn't facing her. She backed towards the rail, and pushed them deep into the twins' changing bag.

A bell rang for the opera. Daniel kept talking. She did not want to leave him here, in her crime scene, but she knew Caspar would mind if she was late. After a moment she walked to the door, and mouthed 'It's starting.' Daniel waved her on.

The Terrace

Chateau la Coste

9.28 p.m.

Daniel hurried towards the terrace, late for the opera recital, nostrils smarting. Either the cocaine was unusually pure, or he was high on indignation. There was no reason for Rosie to have Serge's cufflinks, or to pretend they were Caspar's. He wasn't sure which was more insulting – her lie, or her clumsy attempt at a mental health intervention. She, he felt, was the one who needed help.

He had seen the 'S.C.' and recognised the cufflinks instantly as the pair Serge used to wear at Oxford. They were inherited from his millionaire grandfather, improbably named Sterling Campbell. It pained Daniel that he retained these details. But monogrammed, heirloom cufflinks used to strike him as the epitome of all he was not. He felt an almost paternal pang for his younger self.

The recital was about to begin when he reached the terrace, where chairs had been set out in rows, and he had to squeeze past people to an empty seat. They should be happy, he reflected, to have Daniel Pyke's buttocks in their faces. He sat down and crossed and uncrossed his legs twice, so that the woman beside him inched away. His jaw was intolerably restless. He put four pieces of gum in his mouth at once, and chewed fast. The man on his right, who he recognised as a Booker-winning author, watched with disdain. Daniel discovered he didn't mind. Cocaine was a revelation, every time. It was like continuous, frenzied applause.

From his seat he could see Rosie, in the row in front of him. He thought about the way she had mentioned Serge and Isla's separation, in light of her lie about the cufflinks. All his recent encounters with Rosie now struck him as suspicious. Even her dress in the bookshop, and her interest in the seating plan, seemed dubious. He watched her craning to look at Serge, and realised – in a bright bolt of certainty – that they were sleeping together. He thought of Rosie's deep blush in the cloakroom, and wondered how he – a scholar of body language and facial expression – had not realised sooner. His mind felt like a circuit exploding with light. He saw himself now as a righteous Iago, poised to topple a nemesis with cufflinks instead of a handkerchief, and wished he could impress someone with this reference.

A tenor and soprano walked out onto the stage area, and stood in front of the small group of musicians. They bowed. Daniel whistled, and the Booker winner flinched. It amused Daniel that the man could not shush him here, 'among friends', the way he would have at the Royal Opera House. The audience quietened. It was very dark, the stage lit by oversize lanterns. There was the poised hush of anticipation as the first few bars breathed into the night air and the soprano closed her eyes and inhaled reverently.

The aria was 'O mio babbino caro'. Daniel knew it from countless films and car commercials, but the effect of her voice, just a few feet away, was visceral. The hairs on his neck stood up in one delicious shudder, like after a sneeze. At the first high note he had to fight the urge to jump up on his seat and stamp and roar with approval. The melody unfurled and cascaded, and Daniel vividly pictured a pure, clear draught of water. He felt as if he were surfing on the music, the vibrato and high notes lifting and piercing his soul, the swoops to the lower register soothing the storm inside him. Every moment in his life when he had felt moved, or ecstatic, or devastated, seemed to be reverberating through his body. Mute tears spilled down his cheeks.

As the aria ended he managed to regain control, and looked around the rest of the audience. Everyone was showing due rapture, the American guests with rictus grins. A few older men were nodding in stern appreciation, as if sniffing a rare Bordeaux. Civilised applause pattered out, alongside a few daring 'Bravo!'s

He saw Marina Campbell dab at her nose. It occurred to Daniel that opera was probably the sole emotional outlet she allowed herself, and this idea annoyed him even more than everybody else's numb composure.

As the clapping dissipated there was an audible sob. He turned and saw Isla in profile, wiping her face with her knuckles, her chest heaving the way Daniel's had been moments before. Her cheeks were flushed, and she was half laughing. Daniel felt something tip inside him – the same sensation he had experienced with every girlfriend, and two co-stars.

Serge glanced down at Isla and smiled awkwardly, as if he hadn't noticed her reaction until now. It seemed to encapsulate all that was wrong about them as a couple – a fake couple, as he now knew. Serge did not appreciate Isla, or even see her. He was oblivious to her beautiful, authentic responses to art – despite claiming to be an artist himself. There was something raw about Isla. Daniel had sensed it – from when she'd first sworn at him in the car – but it had become clear tonight, when it emerged they were both from such different worlds to the Campbells. Isla wanted something different, too, he thought. It was obvious.

Serge's shoulder moved, patting Isla's arm. Daniel wanted to stand up and announce what he had just seen, and heard, in the cloakroom. He wondered whether Serge had been sleeping with Rosie for months, or if he had defaulted to his ex when Isla had requested a separation. Either possibility enraged him.

The tenor launched into the drinking song from *La traviata*, prompting some merry foot-tapping from the Booker winner. Daniel let himself relax into the aria's major key, the male and female singers' answering calls transporting him again. As he listened to the swells of the music he found himself transfixed by the back of Isla's ear. She had multiple piercings all the way from the lobe to the top, a delicate chain looping between two of the studs. The aria built to its crescendo, both singers in unison, the soprano's voice rippling out above the tenor's. Daniel imagined holding Isla's whole head and face in his hands, taking fistfuls of her hair, his tongue swirling along her neck and into her ear. And then, as the two voices joined in one extended, climactic note – as if his brain was challenging him to come up with something disturbing – he imagined taking the chain between his teeth.

He shook his head slightly to exorcise the image, wondering why his mind worked against him this way, why it seemed determined to prove he was perverse. The crescendo ended and the applause started, much louder this time – the song having granted permission to be raucous. It sounded to Daniel like a flock of Hitchcockian birds. With each clap he felt their wings slapping closer and closer to his head, until it was an effort not to crawl under his chair. The woman beside him shifted, as if he might be contagious.

London, August 2004

Caspar, Rosie and Daniel are sitting in Caspar's local pub in west London. It is the first time they have met since their final day at Oxford, the day after the St Arthur's ball. They have graduated to mojitos, and are discussing Rosie's publishing internship and Daniel's audition for a sitcom pilot.

'What about the film, with Serge?' says Rosie, when Caspar goes to the bar. 'Aren't you meant to be going out to his place in Italy?'

'Yeah. Well. Clearly I'm persona non grata.'

'What d'you mean?'

'I'm NFI. Not fucking invited. Literally. Like, last time I saw Serge – the day after the ball – he was all, "Come to Italy! Writers' room! You have to meet Miles Whitehall, I'll message you," all this chat. Then we were texting, trying to get a date in. Then, suddenly, nothing.'

'Have you contacted him since?'

Rosie looks more concerned about Serge's wellbeing than his failure to reply to Daniel.

'Yeah. Like, I emailed him this little draft I wrote, couple of weeks ago. Kind of to see if the invite still stood. Nothing. So I text again, like five days ago now, to see if he got it. Still nothing.'

'Have you asked Caspar?'

'I don't wanna make it weird. Beg for an invite.'

'But I don't get it,' says Rosie. 'I thought Serge was so into it?'

'He was! But look. Might've been awkward out there, anyway. With his sister.'

'His sister?'

'Yeah. Like, if that came out—'

He stops, seeing her confusion, and says, 'Wait, did I not tell you this? How she jumped on me?'

'No! What happened? Tell me!'

'I'm clearly more of a gent than I give myself credit for.'

'Or more pissed.'

'Fair point. No, we were literally just chatting outside, having a fag. And she just goes for it. Like, full-on snog. No build-up, straight in with the tongue. She's basically straddling me in the quad.'

He looks half amused as he says: 'Posh birds are mental. Present company excepted.'

'Then what?' says Rosie.

'Nothing. I was like, "Maybe this isn't the best idea," and then she was like, "Oh yeah, promise you won't tell Serge." How he's really overprotective, all this. So then I took her number, and that was it. But yeah. Might be kind of weird, hanging out. By their pool.'

'You took her number? Why did you do that?'

Daniel looks uncomfortable now.

'Fuck, I dunno. I just, felt bad,' he half laughs, though he sounds embarrassed. 'Or, I didn't want her to feel bad. Same thing.'

Rosie juts her head forwards, eyes wide, a parody of exasperation.

'But if you agreed you weren't going to tell Serge, why did you take her number? Were you planning to have some secret rendez-vous or—'

'I wasn't planning anything! What else could I do?' says Dan, widening his own eyes. 'Push her off and be like, "Sorry, love, not tonight! But can I still crash your villa and meet Miles Whitehall?"'

'Yeah, but, taking her number. It just, it gives this whole other impression. Like you're serious.'

'You reckon? I bet she's giving her number, taking numbers, left, right and centre. Not like you can talk anyway. What about that Nate guy?'

'That's different!'

Daniel nods, mock-seriously.

'D'you think she told Serge?' she says, ignoring him. 'Is that why he's gone cold?'

'No. She was begging *me* not to tell him. And it was nothing. She probably can't even remember.'

PART FIVE

AUGUST 2019
THE WEDDING DAY

From: campbell.delahunt.wedding@gmail.com
To: Isla.Malone@hotmail.com
Date: 31 August, 2019, 05:00
Subject: La Maquillage

Hey Isla,

Just to confirm that you're still on for make-up at 2.30pm? JP is keen you bring that MAC primer . . . Not vain at all . . . xx

Rosie's Room

Hotel Georgette

9 A.M.

Rosie had slept badly, ruminating over her encounter with Daniel in the cloakroom. The relief she felt at the cufflinks' return was tempered by the memory of his pupils, and the way their first chance to talk had turned sour. He had left straight after the opera – announcing to nobody that he 'needed his beauty sleep', so that she had not been able to clarify her comments. It reminded her of the way their last real conversation, the summer after leaving Oxford, had gone awry. Irrevocably, it had turned out.

She checked her phone and found a message from Nate.

> Hey, I'm in Aix with Audrey and her son Zach – you free? We're heading to Le Grillon for coffee at 10.

Opening the shutters, to dazzling sunshine, she experienced a novel response – straightforward enthusiasm for an invitation.

* * *

Le Grillon was a crowded brasserie on the Cours Mirabeau, with green art nouveau ironwork and deep red awnings covering the seats outside. Rosie arrived early, and sat at a little marble table. She wondered how well Nate knew Audrey, and prepared herself to ask a lot of questions and to take an interest in Zach. But when Nate approached, he was alone.

'Sorry I'm late. Zach was having a meltdown. Wanted to go back to the hotel.'

He looked slightly embarrassed, as if he had engineered seeing Rosie alone, and she registered something like the tension of a date. All their other conversations had had an incidental quality.

They ordered drinks, and admired the architecture and people-watching opportunities.

'JP said you and Audrey were at college?' said Rosie.

'Yeah. We were part of a whole scene. Audrey and I dated too.'

He said this neutrally, as though he were alluding to their degree. She wondered suddenly if Audrey was the girlfriend who had issued the drinking ultimatum.

'Oh! Is that strange, seeing her now? Like, married with a child?'

'God no. This was way back. Freshman year. Plus we've all hung out together, ever since. Like, I was at her wedding,' he added. 'We basically grew up together.'

She noted that Audrey pre-dated her in his affections, and thought how her own friendship group had dissolved.

'I just always find it so disorientating,' she said. 'Seeing an ex, with someone else.'

'Like when you have to pick up your mail at your old apartment, and a stranger's there?'

'Yes! Like, that place was your domain, but now it's someone else's. And you might have left your hair there, or something.'

She stopped, wondering if this was off-putting, but he laughed.

'I find the reverse harder,' he said. 'When you find out your apartment had this whole life before you. Multiple lives. And you're basically a custodian – you might mean nothing to the apartment. There could have been another custodian who was way more significant.'

She told him about a time an old man had appeared at one of

the houses where the military had stationed her family, having lived there himself for forty years. Aged sixteen she had found it poignant, knowing the house meant so much to him and nothing to her parents. Her family had not understood, though Nate appeared to.

They continued with the extended analogy of homes and relationships, until the waiter brought over their coffees. They were in stubby white cups, with Speculoos biscuits. Nate leaned forwards to give her his biscuit without asking, and their knees brushed under the table. Neither of them acknowledged it.

His phone pinged, and he showed her the photo Audrey had WhatsApped of Zach eating an ice cream by the hotel pool and looking victorious, captioned 'Emperor child.'

'What are you thinking about the whole egg donor, surrogacy, thing?' he said.

'Uh, still thinking.'

She began stirring milk into her coffee.

'Have you talked to them about it? I think they assume you're into it.'

'Not since they asked me.' Her voice sounded strained. 'But yeah, I know they're expecting me to say yes. I'm just not sure three's ever an easy number.'

She realised she hadn't articulated this reservation, until now.

'Sure. I think a lot of people would have a hard time with that.'

'However much they tried to involve me, I feel like I'd always be—' She stopped. She was going to say 'left out' but it sounded juvenile.

'At one remove?' he said.

'Exactly. A bit sidelined.'

'Nobody puts Rosie in the corner,' he said, then quickly apologised – both for quoting *Dirty Dancing* and for sounding flippant about JP and Caspar's wish for a family.

They watched a couple walking past, a baby strapped to the man's chest.

'How about you?' she said. 'D'you want children?'

'Oh yeah. For sure. I mean, it would be a deal-breaker, for me, if someone didn't.'

She thought of Imogen asking if his playing softball was a deal-breaker and felt guilty, even though Imogen had introduced the concept. Rosie had actually liked his unabashed enthusiasm on the pitch.

'Also if they arranged their books by colour,' he said, as if to lighten something. 'Like crayons.'

'But so many people do that,' she said, relieved to be off fertility. 'You'd have to discount everyone on Instagram.'

'That's why it's effective. You immediately identify the sheep.'

'I don't mind the cliché. I just think it's impractical. If you need to find a book. How are you meant to remember spine colour?'

'Right! It's like saying you never intend to re-read anything.'

'What would you have done, just now, if I'd said I do that?'

'I knew you wouldn't.'

Her phone buzzed, with a message from Imogen. It said 'Serge's in the Daily Mail' with a blushing emoji and link. Rosie opened it without thinking, as if her fingers were compelled to track Serge's life. She scanned the text.

> Auction House heir Serge Campbell, 35, might appear to have it all. The great-grandson of art patron Rory Campbell, he is handsome, well connected, a successful film director and producer and counts the model Olympia Harrod among his ex-girlfriends. His famously 'woke' films have won him a slew of industry awards, and he found viral fame in July, after defending his cousin from homophobic abuse.
>
> But Campbell has now found himself the target of a smear campaign on Twitter. On Thursday an anonymous whistle-blower, claiming to be a former employee of Campbell's production company Vanguard Films, accused Campbell of

mistreating graduates from low-income backgrounds. Using the Twitter handle @SergeCampBELLEND, they tweeted:

Serge Campbell is not who people think. He's a narcissist who deserves to be called out. Sadly being an obscenely privileged cis white male still equals a free pass to abuse power, and treat marginalised people as free PR. #SergeCampbell

Yesterday, Twitter user @Gareth32 commented: The irony is that Serge Campbell made *Bursary*, a condemnation of the British class system, with family money.

The stand-up comedian Helen Murphy retweeted the comment, adding: 'The intern system in the arts is broken, perpetuated by millennial Marie-Antoinettes like Serge Campbell #LetThemEatPret.'

In a further blow, @SergeCampBELLEND accused Vanguard Films yesterday of 'owing money left right centre'. Companies House records confirm that Vanguard Films owes almost £1,000,000. Campbell has not commented on the allegations, or the Twitter furore.

Rosie scanned the comments – all of them vicious. She thought of Serge's laughter in the bookshop, wondering now if there had been something agitated in his eyes – something she had put down to his separation with Isla. He suddenly seemed like a very different, much less powerful, person.

'What's up?' said Nate.

'Serge's in the paper. Look.'

She handed him her phone, and he read it, frowning.

'Jesus. Poor guy. I mean, whether or not it's true.'

'I know! He'd never deliberately exploit people.'

Nate was looking at her, as he slid her phone back across the table. His face was pensive.

'Cancel culture's a bitch.'

'Plus the debt. A million! That's a lot, even for him.'

'It's wild, how much movies cost.'

The idea of getting into so much debt for films, with two young children, now struck her as selfish – or at best, foolish. She remembered how obsessively Serge used to work, so that she had come to regard his career like a jealous mistress. When she had finally watched *PLUR* she could not see Serge – or the Serge she knew – anywhere in it. The story of forbidden love bore no resemblance to their relationship, which had met such universal approval.

'Right. I guess inherited wealth can screw people up,' said Nate.

They left the café and began walking down the Cours Mirabeau, past Cartier and Lacoste boutiques in ancient-looking stone facades. Nate photographed a picturesque doorway, and they stopped to buy gifts in pastel boxes at the market. Still, she wanted to scroll through the tweets about Serge, like the awful impulse to look at a road accident.

Cours Mirabeau

Aix-en-Provence

11 A.M.

Serge had arranged to meet his mother at the carousel in Aix, to help him with the twins. He was late and the Cours Mirabeau was swarming with tourists, so that he had to use the buggy like a kind of plough to part them. Both toddlers kept up a stream of protest, Huck repeatedly straining forwards and then slamming his back hard against the buggy, impeding Serge's progress further. Breakfast had been overshadowed by Isla's litany of instructions, as if Serge could not be trusted. He had managed not to reinstall Twitter on his phone, and this felt like the only thing he was doing right.

Admittedly, the last time he had been in sole charge of his children, they had been more portable and less opinionated. He had already used up all Isla's allotted snacks, the twins ramming biscuits into their mouths and yelling 'More!' before they had even swallowed, coughing crumbs over each other. The thought that this was her daily existence was uncomfortable. He reached into the changing bag for wipes, and instead found a pair of his own cufflinks. He had thought they were lost, and wondered if Isla had packed them for him for the weekend. He often felt as if she oversaw too many practicalities, and that it did not suit either of them.

He and Isla still had not slept in the same bed. Serge had been disappointed – he had assumed, after the dance rehearsal and their conversation on the veranda, that they were making progress. But she had been distant after the opera recital, in the taxi and back at the hotel, as if something had shifted back during the evening. Having settled the twins she had lain on the sofa, and switched out the light. He thought of her jokey aside to Daniel, about Serge supporting Arsenal. He wouldn't have cared if she had said it to anyone else.

'Nearly there, guys! We're seeing Granny!' he shouted into the air above the buggy, mostly for his own morale. A pulse beat in his temples – punishment for the Calvados. His sister kept calling, but he hadn't picked up. The prospect of either Allegra's wild enthusiasm or flat-line despair – her only two modes – did not appeal.

They came to the worst section of the street, full of stalls selling Provençal souvenirs, and had to stop behind a British couple browsing lace tablecloths. Juno began yelling 'Unnee!' pointing at a pyramid of honey jars at the next stall. His sister was calling him, again. He wrestled an urge to prod the man's meaty calves with the buggy.

Across the street he noticed Rosie, looking at a stall with Nate Kennedy. He stared straight ahead, keen not to intrude, and swerved to overtake the British couple. Seeing Rosie in the bookshop had been a welcome distraction, but he feared he had embraced the laughter too readily. His whole relationship with Rosie had been that way, he thought with hungover clarity.

He recalled giving her a *Neighbours* annual for Valentine's Day, and cringed. For his first Valentine's Day with Isla he had spent ages in Le Labo, concocting her a bespoke scent. It was much harder to make Isla laugh hysterically than Rosie, and this gave their jokes a special currency. He couldn't recall making Isla really laugh, for months.

The carousel was charmingly kitsch. Two tiers of circus horses, miniature planes with propellers and swan-shaped carriages processed below the tent-shaped roof. Serge wedged the twins into a plane, remembering Isla's instruction to stay on with them. He saw his mother hurrying towards the carousel, craning to see him, like a meerkat. He was surprised to see his father, behind.

'Bambinos!' she shouted from the pavement, when she saw them. The fraught expression on her face didn't fade, as she came closer.

'Isn't this pretty?' she said. 'Such a shame it's all awful theme parks now. And children actually like good design if they're exposed to it.'

She was gabbling. Serge sensed something was wrong. His phone began vibrating, and he declined Joel's call as a siren loomed from the carousel, signalling the start of the ride.

Marina and Lucian were staring at him, and he realised they expected him to get off.

'I'm staying on,' he said.

'Wouldn't it be more fun for them to wave at you?' said Marina. 'Like you used to, in Siena?'

'La Vie en Rose' started creaking out of the carousel. All the other parents were standing on the pavement, taking pictures on their phones.

'Isla wanted—'

'Come on, Serge, they're fine!' said Lucian, unusually impatient.

The twins were cackling. Serge stepped off the carousel.

'See! Much more fun for them,' said Marina, as the plane twirled out of sight.

He stood between his parents, feeling like a child himself. The twins processed back into view, shrieking and waving, and he felt fleeting reassurance before they vanished again.

'So are you . . . are you all right?' said his mother.

Lucian looked away. He realised they must know about Twitter, though he would not have expected them to care. They had shown no interest in the online attention after the SOFAs, beyond indignation at his arrest.

'You mean, the stuff on Twitter?' he said.

'Well, yes, the Twits,' said Marina. 'But the paper. Is it accurate?'

'Paper?'

'In, you know, the *Mail*,' she said, sounding pained. 'Serge? You have seen it, haven't you?'

She took a bent newspaper out of her bag.

'I don't read that,' he said, knowing it sounded childish.

'Nor do we,' said Lucian. 'Allegra saw it. In the hotel.'

His sister's repeated calls now made sense. Marina flicked to a page near the back. He saw the photo of himself first, then the byline. The same columnist had ranted about his arrest, and 'liberal elite' posturing.

The heat bore down on his scalp as he read about himself like another person. He reached the details of Vanguard's debt, and all his internal organs dropped. His parents were staring at him. The carousel was now playing sinister fairground music.

'So? Is it true?' said his mother. 'You're in debt?'

'No! I mean, partly. But can we discuss it later?'

'It can't really wait, Serge,' said his father. 'Are you or aren't you?'

'It's not, like, an either-or thing. I mean, technically, yeah, we owe people money. But it's about to get sorted. When we get some investment in *Beating Heart*.'

'When or if?' said Lucian.

'So who's this "whistle-blower"?' said Marina, at the same time.

It was easier to answer his mother.

'This intern. We had to let her go.'

'But why? Why be so unpleasant? These "trolls". One can't help thinking of the Billy Goats Gruff!' She gave a short, inhaled laugh. Finding absurdity in any situation was a family coping mechanism.

'I don't know, Ma. She's angry.'

'But Serge, your finances,' said Lucian. 'What have—'

There was a loud thump from the carousel. Serge turned towards the sound. Only one twin was in the plane. At the same moment he saw Huck on the ground, face down like a dropped object. He heard his own shout, as several mothers around him shrieked.

He grabbed his son from the pavement, and pulled him to his chest. Huck was conscious but his face was contorted in shock. There was blood and dirt around his open mouth and flaring nostrils. He managed to breathe in and then to scream, the same hoarse, agonised cry over and over. A large, red lump was already showing on his forehead.

Serge felt nauseous, his heart pumping like a separate being. His mother was saying something he couldn't hear over Huck, and he shouted at her to stop the ride and get Juno. He had never seen either of the twins hurt like this. He kept rocking Huck, repeating 'I'm so sorry, I'm so sorry,' into his white curls. He thought of all the priceless cells in his son's skull, and fresh panic sheeted through him.

The carousel and gaudy music stopped, to a murmur from the children riding. After a moment his father walked over holding Juno, who was now crying too and struggling against her grandfather.

'Brave boy! It's just the shock. Just the shock,' Marina began cooing.

Serge wanted to yell at his parents for making him leave the twins on the carousel, and for choosing this moment to interrogate him.

'I knew I should have stayed on with them,' he snapped.

He hoped his parents understood this was partly their fault. He had a pointless urge to hurt himself – perhaps punching a wall or smashing his own skull against the pavement.

'Darling, he's fine! They have bumps all the time at this stage, don't you, my sweet? Gosh, I remember Allegra falling all the way down the stairs at Chiltern Mansions—'

'It's not a bump, OK? Look!' said Serge, over Huck's crying. It had started up again with new reproachful force, his face red as he shouted: 'Mama! Mama, come!'

'I'm here, Huck,' he said, hopelessly. 'Dada's here.'

'Long as he's crying, that's the main thing,' said Lucian jovially.

'Wowee, Huckleberry, look at that egg!' said his mother. Serge touched the tumour-like bulge on his son's forehead, his fingers tracing it like braille. He had never wished so much to rewind five minutes.

'How far d'you think he fell?' he said, to nobody. He sounded breathless. The man who ran the carousel was coming over now, looking apologetic.

'Oh, come on, Serge, look – it's barely a foot off the ground,' said Lucian.

'Where's the nearest hospital? I have to call Isla!'

'Hospital?' said Marina. 'Honestly, Serge, he's fine! He's stopped crying. Don't bother Isla. Let's get him a croissant.'

Huck's wailing had subsided to bereft hiccupping sobs. Serge felt his own heart slowing at the realisation that Huck probably wasn't brain damaged. The worst part, the fuel for future nightmares, was what else could have happened while he was distracted. He saw Huck, now, tumbling from one of the rising horses, Juno crushed under the carousel's wheels, Stephen King music drowning out their screams while Serge talked about Twitter. He knew he should call Isla. But he couldn't remember, or rationalise, why he had let the twins ride alone.

Across the street he saw Nate and Rosie. She saw Serge at the same moment, and must have seen Huck's bleeding face, because she started hurrying.

'Hi! What happened?' she said, putting her hand on the back of Huck's head.

'He fell off,' said Serge, nodding at the carousel.

'No! Oh God, that's awful! Poor little thing! And poor you!'

It was comforting to have his panic legitimised.

'Ooh! That looks bad, buddy,' said Nate, looking at Huck. He turned to Serge and said, 'There's a pharmacy right there – maybe they can check him over?'

They all turned towards a green cross sticking out of a sand-coloured wall.

'I can translate?' said Rosie.

'Yeah, actually,' said Serge. 'Good idea. Thanks.'

He felt vindicated, but also oddly emasculated by Nate taking charge – as if his fiscal incompetence was spreading to every area of his life.

They all walked towards the chemist, Serge holding Huck while his mother pushed Juno in the buggy, walking beside Rosie. He heard his father say something about 'elf an' safety' in a wry Estuary accent – undoubtedly lost on Nate.

The frigid air of the shop, with its familiar scent of shampoo and supplements, was soothing. His parents waited outside, the whole exercise proof of millennial overreaction.

Rosie explained the accident to the pharmacist, and asked if they needed a doctor. She looked very appealing, conveying concern with her frown and fluttering hand gestures and rapid French.

The man kept using the word *hématome*, and Rosie saw Serge's alarm and quickly explained it meant 'bruise'. Apparently hospital was unnecessary, unless Huck vomited or became confused. The pharmacist gave both twins lollipops, before saying to Serge and Rosie, in English:

'You 'ave beautiful children.'

Neither of them corrected the mistake.

Courtyard Suite

Hotel Georgette

11.30 a.m.

Isla lay alone in the suite's enormous bed, feeling slightly delirious with solitude. She stretched one arm and leg out across the bed, until she was almost in an F shape, relishing the space after two nights on a sofa. For a second, a voice in her head suggested she message Serge to remind him to reapply the twins' sun cream, and she reached for her phone. Then she let it fall back onto the mattress. The mental surrender was almost sensuous.

At some point, with motherhood, she had become someone who fussed about protocol. It felt alien, the way her pregnant body had done. She had assumed she would be relaxed about childcare rules, the way she was about her own life, and the way her own mother had been. Excessively, perhaps. She decided to thank Bitsy, later, for encouraging her to let Serge help – or to stop thinking of it as help.

Still, something was snagging her thoughts. She trawled her memories of the previous evening, and recalled the conversation with Daniel. It had seemed innocuous, at the time. But it had left her feeling as if she and Serge were more incompatible than she had ever acknowledged. She had woken up at 3 a.m., fretting about air pollution and whether Oxford Circus really was the right place for children to grow up, thinking of Daniel urging her to move to LA. Her sense, after the dance rehearsal, that she and Serge might find their way back to each other now seemed questionable. She reached for her phone, and found the meditation app that invariably sent her to sleep.

Almost an hour later she woke abruptly – the room now too hot as the sun pushed through the shutters. She reached out for a different pillow, wanting to feel the coolness against her face. It smelled of Serge. She closed her eyes again, still only half awake, and breathed in deeply. Hundreds of past embraces returned to her. She felt a flicker between her legs, like nerve memory. She put her hand between her thighs, experimentally almost, and breathed in the pillow again, thinking of Serge out of habit. Not the real Serge – but Serge as if he were a stranger. The Serge she had first met, on set, or at the wrap party. Her hand moved higher. At some point she became aware that the stranger in her mind had morphed into Daniel Pyke.

The Café

Hotel Georgette

12.30 p.m.

Daniel walked into the hotel café, hoping he wouldn't see anyone he knew. He had spent a restless night, flipping from side to side, feeling alternately outraged with Rosie and then strangely rejected. The idea that they might have rekindled their friendship, after so long, now seemed inconceivable. He had woken at eleven, groggy but also paranoid, thinking of Rosie's revelation that Serge and Isla were separated. It cast his own conversation with Isla, and his sense that they spoke a common language, in a new light. The café was empty besides two middle-aged women. As he passed their table, he heard one of them say:

'Well, it's got a terrific love story, and it shows the triumph of the human spirit.'

The line began echoing in his head, as if he was trying to learn it for a scene. He wondered how the Campbells and their friends spoke in such absolutes, until the repetition engulfed the meaning anyway. He kept half listening, and realised they were discussing *PLUR*. Serge, and his many achievements, seemed inescapable.

At the juice dispenser he filled a glass, his hands shaky. The nothingness was circling, and he submitted. It was preferable to repeating 'the triumph of the human spirit' like an incantation. His internal narrator began: 'I am in a hotel. Those are my hands. They are pouring a glass of orange juice. I am Dan. Daniel Pyke. @Gareth32. Pikey.'

Some juice dripped onto his shoe, and he remembered his blood plopping to the cloakroom floor and Rosie's evident shock. He sat down, took his Xanax, drank the whole glass of orange juice and released a quiet citrusy burp – half relishing, half loathing, his own disgustingness. There was a pop-art clock on the wall, its hands creeping around Marilyn Monroe's face. The ticking was unbearably loud, like a time bomb. He started wondering, and then actually calculating, how many more breakfasts likely remained in his lifetime. He had thought the answer would be sobering – galvanising, even – but the total sounded interminable. The narration resumed.

'I have just ingested the orange juice. My kidneys will convert it to urine, because I am a mammal. I am a bag of blood and tubes and slime and shit and every time my heart contracts I am another pulse closer to my death, when I won't exist at all. I will stop. I will just end and the world will carry on, while my bag of slime rots or smoulders in a giant oven.'

The woman who had been talking about Serge's film turned round. He recognised her now – she had been sitting beside him at the opera, and had shifted away from him, as if she had seen his thoughts. Daniel wanted to explain that he feared his mind himself.

He went over to the rack of newspapers, and picked up the *Mail*. Back at his table he read some upsetting headlines and then all the celebrity gossip, mostly about actors who were more famous than he was. Then he turned to the diary section, a strange throwback to 'society gossip' about minor royals and their friends. For a second, he thought Serge's photo was a hallucination – mortifying proof of Daniel's unconscious obsession. But it was Serge on the page, as though the whole world was obsessed with Serge Campbell.

Daniel began to read. His throat tightened with each paragraph. Seeing Serge shamed this way, in newsprint, was somehow more real than on Twitter. Guilt, clammy as nausea, flushed through him.

He had not intended for Serge to be humiliated on this scale, he reminded himself. It was not his fault that the truth had resonated with so many people.

He came to the part about Serge owing a million pounds and stopped. The sum, and the unequivocal tone, was startling. He had assumed all the tweets about late payments exposed Serge's arrogance, not real financial trouble. He remembered Serge blithely promising more money in the bookshop, as if Daniel were a dumb face-for-hire, ripe for dragging into his problems.

He couldn't face food, so he drank two coffees and left the café, knowing and regretting that the only way to feel more human for the wedding would be to do a line of cocaine in his room. After the weekend, he promised himself, he would cut down.

In the courtyard the sun was glaringly bright, like on stage. Isla was walking towards him. He put on sunglasses, and squared his shoulders.

'Hey,' she said. She was carrying bags and looked radiantly cheerful, different to the previous days.

'Child free?'

'They're with Serge.'

She smiled widely, so he knew that she hadn't seen the *Mail*. He wondered if she and Serge were actually back together – if opera and Champagne and a nice hotel had addled her judgement. He wanted to warn her. Or perhaps rescue her.

She explained she was going to the chateau to do the grooms' make-up. He moved aside to let her pass. She moved the same way. He moved in the other direction just as she did too, so that they were right opposite each other, too close now, apologising and half laughing. He almost made a reference to romantic comedy, but there was no way to without sounding sleazy.

Chateau de Beaupont

Vauvenargues

2.15 P.M.

As Isla was parking at the chateau Serge sent a message, saying:

> Nothing major but call when you get a sec.

She decided to reply after she had found Caspar and JP. Part of her relished the idea of him having to work something out, a tiny revenge for the way he always asked her where things were kept in his flat.

The grooms were in one of three bedrooms off the first floor landing, with walnut doors and gilt handles. At the rehearsal Caspar had explained that she and Serge were to stay in one of these rooms, with the twins. They would finally have to share a bed. It did not feel straightforward – when once sleeping apart had felt wrong.

She knew that Rosie and Nate were both in turret rooms, having overheard Nate mention Rapunzel, and Rosie lamenting her 'drowned cat' hair. Daniel was in the third room on the landing. Isla thought of the moment, in the courtyard, when they had stepped back and forth like a stilted mating dance. She had been glad he was wearing sunglasses, so that she hadn't had to meet his eyes so soon after fantasising about him.

JP opened the door, wearing a bathrobe monogrammed with

GROOM 1, and handed her a flute of Champagne. He began singing 'Chapel of Love', dancing backwards into the palatial room. It was full of Louis XV furniture, with heavy mustard curtains around huge windows, opening on to stone balconies. She had seen photos of brides posing by these windows on the chateau's website. She wondered if she and Serge would ever have a wedding.

Caspar was lying on the bed in his boxers, an eye pack on his face. He jerked up and hurried to hug her, apparently much more anxious than JP.

'You're here! Yay! I wasn't sure ... All OK? You're fine?'

His expression, as he released her, was slightly frenzied. She realised that the part of her job that involved quelling actors' nerves would be required.

There were baskets of fruit and pastries on the ottoman, and a bottle of Champagne in an ice bucket. JP's playlist was alternating blaring opera and hip-hop into the room. Isla began to unpack, the brushes and palettes transporting her to work and film sets. She remembered the job offer for the zombie series, and wondered if she should follow Bitsy's advice on work, as well as marriage.

JP was talking about the seating plan, and how Isla was on a 'showbiz table' with Allegra, Daniel and various other guests who worked in entertainment.

Caspar pushed up his eye mask and said: 'So how's Serge doing? Will he be, like, OK?'

'OK?' she said.

'After this morning. To do everything later?'

'Of course. He's only got them for a few hours.'

She looked up from her products and saw the grooms glance at each other.

'They are his kids,' she added, pointedly.

Her phone began ringing, with a call from Serge. She steeled herself to answer something he ought to know. But instead, he launched into a gabbled account of an accident. All she heard was 'Huck' and 'head'.

'Just bring him here,' she interrupted, when Serge said, again, that Huck seemed fine.

She could hear in his voice that he felt terrible. But all she could think of was her baby in pain, and that Serge was not qualified to judge his injuries. Anything involving heads had always spooked her, disproportionately.

'What's up?' said JP. Both grooms looked alarmed.

'Huck fell off a carousel. On his head. Serge was meant to stay on with them.'

She heard the rage in her voice, managing to check herself in front of Serge's cousin just in time.

'Sorry, I just need a second,' she said.

'Oh no, Isla, it's OK!'

Caspar moved to hug her, but she had already seen a wary look pass between the two men – presumably at the thought that Huck might derail their make-up. It made her even angrier, childless people never understood.

They had a strained conversation about flower arrangements, Isla barely listening while she styled hair and prepped skin. As soon as she heard Serge's voice outside she hurried out to the landing, the grooms following. Huck almost fell out of Serge's arms, reaching for her. His lip was split and there was a large red bulge on his forehead. It always shocked her how she could work with fake blood all day, but when she saw the twins hurt she felt faint. She began checking him all over, lifting up his T-shirt to inspect his small, square back, and pushing his socks down his sturdy calves.

'I told you to stay on with them!'

She didn't care that Caspar and JP could hear.

'Serge? Why did you let them go on their own?'

Juno was holding on to her legs now, both twins almost mauling her, their faces covered in something sticky – probably bought as distraction. She could see Huck was not seriously injured, but she couldn't stop.

'Isla, please! I'm sorry, OK?' said Serge. 'Don't make me feel even worse than I already do.'

'It's not about you! You should feel bad, he could've broken something! Fractured his skull!'

'I know, but he's OK. That's the main thing, right? Look, I'm sorry, I don't know what else to say. He's been fine ever since. Really.'

Huck was burrowing into her chest, as if he might find milk there again.

'I knew something like this would happen!' she snapped. All three men seemed to recoil. It reminded her of a day when she had shouted at a child in a sandpit for pushing Juno, and the whole playground had quietened.

Serge stood looking at her, his face helpless.

The chateau's front door opened, and two voices floated up the stairs. Rosie appeared, wearing khaki shorts and brand new Birkenstocks. Nate was just behind her.

'How's he doing?' said Rosie limply, looking at Huck. 'It was such a horrid thing to happen. I can't believe those things are so dangerous!'

'Rosie translated for me, at the pharmacy,' said Serge, stiffly. 'She speaks French.'

He hadn't mentioned Rosie's presence, on the phone. Isla looked at Rosie, prettily flushed, and her fluent French felt like an affront. She could see, now, what Serge and his ex had had in common. They were both accomplished in a singular, private-school way Isla was not.

'They were really confident he was fine. Honestly,' said Rosie. 'They said it looks worse than it is, because the mouth bleeds so easily. But it must be so stressful, I know.'

'*You* were there?' said Isla. It came out sharply, but she didn't care. Seeing Huck hurt had unleashed something primal.

Rosie looked stricken, her blush concentrating.

'We were just passing,' said Nate. He stepped towards Rosie, as if shielding her from a banshee.

Isla could picture the moment. Serge, distracted by Rosie on her date, not wanting to lose face or miss an adult conversation, leaving the twins to ride alone.

'Guys, can we chill?' said Caspar, in the doorway. 'Huck's OK, it's all good. These things happen. It's not like Serge—'

'It's just basic safety! They're one!' said Isla.

The Campbells always united when one of them was under attack. It was the same code that had resulted in Serge's arrest.

'Right, but, no wonder Serge isn't thinking straight,' said Caspar. 'Maybe it wasn't the best—'

'What?' said Isla.

She saw Serge look at his cousin, wide eyed, trying to silently communicate. His face was grey.

Serge cleared his throat. 'Can I chat to Isla, for a sec?' he said to the grooms.

'Go for it,' said Caspar, gesturing at a door across the landing.

Isla followed Serge, Huck clinging to her neck, Juno pulling at her shorts.

Their room was similar to the grooms', but there was a roll-top bath by the fireplace. The twins found this hilarious, and started pounding its sides.

'What did he mean?' she said. 'Why wouldn't you be thinking straight?'

Serge was sitting on a chaise longue, not looking at her. He covered his face with his hands, like a toddler trying to hide. After a moment she thought he was crying.

'Look, I need to tell you something,' he said, through his palms. 'I've really fucked up.' He wasn't crying, but his voice was hoarse. 'I should have told you ages ago. I just couldn't, I didn't know how. And the longer I didn't tell you . . . anyway look, it's out now. Everyone knows.'

Her breath seemed to suspend itself. She couldn't imagine what was out, what 'everyone knew'.

'The reason I was so distracted . . .' He emerged from his hands. 'OK – basically I'm in, I'm in debt. A lot. And, it is going to be OK. It is, I promise. But it was in the *Mail* this morning, and my parents found out so—'

'Stop – in debt?'

'I know, I know. I've fucked up. Massively. Like I said.'

'How much?'

She thought of the buffer of Campbell money she counted on. Even when she danced with the idea of splitting up, she had assumed Serge would support the twins – that she would never struggle the way her mother had.

'A million,' he said, quietly. 'Just under.'

Her mouth was dry.

'A *million*? What, you, personally? Or Vanguard?'

'Both. Me, really.'

'How, Serge?' The twins looked round, at her raised voice. 'You have so much!'

'I don't know, Isla! Just, one thing led to another.'

'That's what you say when you're cheating! Why didn't you tell me?'

He explained how an investor had pulled out of *Beating Heart* the week the twins were born, and that this had been the start – both of his debts, and his secrecy. He had thought, at the time, it was kinder not to tell her. Then he began recounting one terrible decision after another, from overpaying the Film For All graduates to insisting on his preferred unknown actors in *PLUR* – so that the film never made its extortionate production costs back. He kept stressing that he had wanted to maintain creative control, rather than deferring to his godfather as he had done with *Bursary* – as if this justified his spending. And then, despite its critical acclaim, *PLUR* had not met any of *Bursary*'s commercial success. Isla realised she had never thought to ask. It had received glowing reviews.

She looked out at the lawn rolling down to the marquee while he spoke, thinking how she had trusted that his having money meant he could handle it. She never enquired, because he was so self-conscious about his inheritance. She had assumed that someone advised him. She sat on the floor because standing up induced a feeling like vertigo, then wondered why she still thought of Serge's life as her own, and whether she wanted it to be.

She found herself almost tuning out, while he explained that he should never have started his own production company, but that the lure of autonomy had been irresistible. Then she heard him admit that he had secretly taken out a mortgage. He was looking at her, waiting for her to tell him it was OK, but she was too stunned to speak.

'I didn't want to freak you out,' he said, when she didn't answer. 'You'd just given birth.'

'But you took out a mortgage, without telling me!'

She thought he was about to argue that it was his flat, but he didn't.

'I know. I'm so sorry,' he said. 'It wasn't meant to get like this. It was just meant to tide me over. So I could fix everything.'

'Exactly! You're so arrogant! You just assume everything will be fine. For you.'

He said nothing.

'So you'll sell the flat?'

He looked up, as if she had suggested selling the twins.

'I can't – I mean, I don't want to uproot you guys. But if I can get Daniel attached—'

'It's just a flat, Serge! You love it. Your parents love it. But it's just property. It's like you don't even realise how lucky you are to have the option.'

He looked away.

'It's worth two million, right?' she said. She vaguely remembered an agent valuing the flat while she tried to breastfeed, and Serge's evasiveness about why the man was there.

He nodded.

'So how much is the mortgage?'

'Um. One point two. Million,' he said, indistinctly.

'One point two? So, if you sold, you'd get eight hundred grand but you'd still need—'

'Two hundred grand. To pay everything off. So we'd be left with, um, nothing.'

She attempted some feverish arithmetic, and gave up.

'Can't you declare, what's it called, insolvency?'

'I've looked into it. I'd still need to sell the flat. To pay everyone properly. Liquidation barely covers anything. Just, like, my tax and pay-roll. Everyone's payouts, at Vanguard. None of the other debts.'

She registered his desperation and felt momentary pity, despite herself. She wondered if his parents would help, or whether they already had.

'There's this whole thread on Twitter about it,' he said. 'Me. And in the *Mail*.'

'Surely that's the least of your worries?'

'I'm just trying to give you the full picture.'

'I couldn't care less about Twitter, Serge,' she said, anger replacing sympathy. 'Or the papers.'

He sat staring at the twins, who were trying to slide down the inside of the bath. Huck's scabs reminded her of work. She thought of Bitsy, and wondered why she had taken advice from a stranger who drank all morning.

There was a tentative knock. 'Sorry, guys, we need to keep moving,' said Caspar.

She hauled the twins out of the bath, and took them into the grooms' room – not caring that they wouldn't be welcome.

The Chapel

Chateau de Beaupont

4 p.m.

Rosie was seated between Serge and Nate, on a platform in front of the chateau's chapel. They were overlooking the other two hundred guests, who were seated in rows down to the lake. People kept batting at insects with their orders of service, as they waited for Caspar and JP. The air felt dense with heat and lavender.

She had got ready in her turret bedroom, at the top of a spiral staircase. The room was impossibly romantic – round, with three windows and a wrought iron bed – but its charm felt sadly redundant. Nate had the room directly below hers, and they had both remarked on the dovecote outside their tower – but this was not the same. She would have liked to share the delight with someone who was sharing the room.

Everybody turned as the band began to play 'To Know Him Is to Love Him', and the grooms walked up the makeshift aisle. At a distance they looked sweetly smart and cheerful, but up close she saw they were gripping one another's hands. She thought of all the other friends' weddings she had helped to orchestrate, one long procession of peonies and organ chords, but how the moment when you first saw the couple was always touching.

During the vows Serge kept crossing and uncrossing his legs, finally settling with one ankle resting on his knee. His expression was rapt, but his foot was jiggling so frantically Rosie feared he might kick her. She thought again of the damning report in the *Mail*, and his helplessness in the pharmacy. Nate was also watching Serge's long hyperactive foot. Their eyes met, as Caspar solemnly vowed not to abandon mugs of cold tea around the house.

The grooms exchanged rings, and Rosie relived the mortifying confrontation on the landing – the way Isla had been so flagrantly, publicly angry. Rosie could see her in the back row, her face impassive while everyone else laughed and sang. She was wearing a coral-coloured dress that would have made Rosie look like a corpse, and a flower garland on her head, at odds with her morose expression.

The vows came to an end and everyone stood up to sing 'Your Love Keeps Lifting Me Higher and Higher'. Rosie tried to enjoy the moment, even when everyone began clapping in unison – something she dreaded. She listened to Nate and Serge beside her, relieved that their voices were drowning out her own reedy attempt at the soulful lyrics.

Daniel was bellowing into his microphone, clapping above his head as if he were on stage at a festival. She tried to concentrate on Caspar and JP pledging their love, instead of thinking – again – about her odd encounter with Daniel over the cufflinks.

At the end of the song, the grooms jogged down to the lake, where JP pulled a rowing boat out of the reeds. He stepped in, and held out his hand for Caspar. They rowed out into the middle of the lake, where Caspar opened the bottle of Champagne that Rosie had put in the hull earlier, along with a 'Just Married' buoy, a basket of strawberries and a card where she had written 'WELL DONE, GUYS!'

Everybody cheered and took photos on their phones. While Rosie clapped she wondered, as she always did at weddings, whether anybody would ever love her this way.

The Lake

Chateau de Beaupont

5 p.m.

Isla stayed alone by the lake after everyone else had gone, watching the wind hurry its surface. Across the water Montagne Sainte-Victoire was glazed in golden light. She tried to find reassurance in its solidity, but it was like staring at a postcard. Juno and Huck were with a babysitter, though it didn't feel like respite. If anything, the twins would have provided welcome distraction.

Serge had kept looking at her during the ceremony. Listening to Caspar and JP's promises to respect and confide in one another had been almost intolerable. She had always associated Amy Winehouse's cover of 'To Know Him Is to Love Him' with Serge, and knew that he knew this. When the band had played the song she had bitten her lip, and glared at a Philip Treacy hat, to stop herself from collapsing.

Everyone was drinking Kir Royales in the gardens, but the idea of chatting and laughing was impossible. She could see Serge's mother, studying her phone at arm's length, and wondered what it would be like to detach from the Campbells and their many quail egg-fuelled occasions. Marina looked up, and began to walk over to where Isla was standing. For a second, she considered jumping into the lake.

'Isla!' said Marina, sounding brightly surprised – as she always did in greeting. Close up she looked frayed and overheated. She was wearing a green jacket, like minty foil, that Isla had seen before. It was undoubtedly designer, but somehow also terminally unfashionable.

'Lovely view,' said Marina. 'I keep thinking of Babar!'

Isla waited for the inevitable caveat, but Serge's mother just stood staring at a weeping willow, her thin neck taut.

'How's poor Huckleberry?' she added after a moment, as if she had overlooked a formality. She always used his full name because she thought Huck sounded like 'fuck'. It had created much appalled hilarity, after the birth.

'OK, now. The bump's gone down.'

'I think Serge got more of a fright than he did!'

Marina laughed, but the tension in her face remained.

'My brother Dominic was terribly accident prone,' she added. 'Some children just *are*. I mean, it can't have been more than a second and,' she mimed a toppling action, 'whuuump!'

'Yup! Can't take your eyes off them!'

Marina looked pensive, not having felt the rebuke.

'I suppose Serge wasn't concentrating,' she said, to the lake. She took a sharp intake of breath, like a sigh in reverse. 'I should have realised, that night, with those thugs in the street. How long has he been in all this—'

She stopped, searching for an acceptable word. 'This muddle?'

Isla registered another surprise. Serge had not told his parents about his debts, despite the Campbell money seeming so entwined.

'I don't know,' said Isla. 'I didn't even know he was in debt until today.'

'*Today?*'

'He just told me, earlier. Because it was in the paper.'

'So he really is in debt?' said Marina, as if this mattered more than Serge's secretiveness.

'Did you not know?'

'No! We've never interfered with his work.'

Her face was composed, but there was a nervous rise in her voice.

'I said Lucian should have put it in trust,' she said. 'Madness! Giving a twenty-five-year-old millions of pounds! And sweet Miles warned me it was rash, for Serge to start his own company. He'd have happily carried on producing Serge's films.'

'Right,' said Isla. She did not want to discuss inheritance conventions.

'You know it's all because Lucian's father was intent on everyone having "a trade". Honestly! My parents couldn't understand it. I was baffled, to be quite honest. It's unheard of.'

'You know he's mortgaged the flat?' said Isla. 'He just told me that, too.'

'What? A mortgage?' Marina looked aghast now, as if Isla had disclosed a terminal illness.

'Oh, Serge. Good God. Oh Christ! But surely you had a ... a sense. Of all this? Living with him?'

Marina was looking at her directly now.

'We aren't, really. We're having a trial separation.'

She watched Marina's powdery face absorb another shock.

'He didn't want to tell anyone,' Isla added.

His mother opened her mouth, but for once she did not seem to have a wry comment.

'Serge can explain,' said Isla. 'I need to check the twins.'

She knew she was being rude, cruel even, but she was too angry to care.

She turned to leave and saw Lucian, coming down the grassy slope.

'Isla, hel-*lo*!' he said, as they drew near each other.

His voice held its usual bonhomie, but he looked weary. Isla smiled tightly, without stopping. She was sure Marina would tell him about the mortgage and the separation, and that Lucian would be furious. It was satisfying to punish Serge's silence.

As she walked towards the chateau she saw Daniel, sitting alone in the chapel porch – fifty feet away. He was smoking, and looking down at his phone. His face shone bronze in the afternoon sun, and he had loosened his tie. She didn't speak or attract his attention, and in this way she was able to study him until she had passed.

The Portaloos

Chateau de Beaupont

5.40 p.m.

The Portaloos were spacious and tasteful, with orchids and hand cream and stacks of white flannels. By the end of the night the floor would be muddy and the cubicles would smell of asparagus pee, but for now they were neatly fragrant. It was pleasant to lock a door, and sit alone and unseen. Rosie let her face sag. Her cheeks ached with small talk and posing for photographs.

She heard two people come in. Allegra's drawl was distinctive, as she said, 'Oh my God, how fucking adorable were those vows?'

Rosie knew she should leave the cubicle but the idea of raving about the wedding and each other's dresses was draining.

'I know, right?' said another throaty female voice. 'So fucking sweet. I was properly weeping back there. Hey, isn't your brother getting married soon?'

'In theory. But he's basically bankrupted himself. Turns out. So Isla's pretty pissed off. Understandably.'

Two doors banged and locked.

'Yeah, I heard,' said the throaty voice, unconcerned. 'What's she like anyway? Isla?'

There was the gush of concurrent pees. It always took Rosie ages to start peeing when someone was in the next-door cubicle, even her sister.

'Isla? She's like, total free spirit. Doesn't just suck it up, when he's a dick. Like all his exes.'

There were flushes, and the doors banged open.

'Didn't he go out with Caspar's maid of honour?'

'Rosie? Yup. Must be so bloody hard for her,' said Allegra. 'Seeing him.'

Rosie's face burned, unseen. She heard the dainty zips and clatter of make-up application.

'Why? What happened with them?'

'Nothing, just Serge dumped her really abruptly.'

'How come?'

Rosie's whole body braced.

'Just, being a typical guy – pissing around. Like, in theory they were perfect. But there was always something missing, y'know? I mean, I feel like she was more in love with this *idea* of him? Properly had him on a pedestal. Like, I'm not sure they were fully vulnerable with each other?'

Allegra was speaking in a particular, faux contemplative tone Rosie recognised.

'And her parents were awful,' she added, in her normal voice. 'I think they actually voted Leave? So he dodged a bullet there. Anyway, she was desperate to get married, have babies, the whole deal. And he just wasn't up for it. With her. It's actually quite sad cos she's clearly still obsessed.'

'How long were they together?'

'Two years? Basically he broke up with Olympia, and Rosie seemed like the sensible option. Cos they were in the same group, at Oxford. And she'd been in love with him the entire time.'

Rosie had the sensation that she might never breathe again.

'Wait, Olympia *Harrod*?'

'Yeah. Lucky bastard.'

'What was she like?'

'I mean, feral. Obviously. But so fit. She was, like, twenty-one.

Ma couldn't stand her. She was at school with Olympia's aunt and she hated her, too. Anyway, they'll sort it out. Serge and Isla. She's chill. I mean, it's not like we're the easiest family to come into,' said Allegra proudly.

They laughed, and Allegra started talking about her efforts to avoid Valentine Harvey – the man Rosie had moved away from Allegra on the seating plan.

She stayed in the cubicle for a long time, sitting on the seat because her legs felt too weak to stand. Several people came and went. Allegra's assessment of her as 'the sensible option' and 'clearly still obsessed' seemed even more damning on reflection – like a welt rising from a slap.

The prospect of eating and giving a speech with Serge was almost unbearable. She remembered the afternoon when they had introduced their parents, full of forced laughter and her father's right-wing views. A sob loomed in her chest, threatening to destroy her make-up.

She wondered if she could stay in the cubicle all night, claiming food poisoning, but the prospect of Caspar's reproach stopped her. Her phone beeped, it was a message from Nate.

> Overheard . . . Booker winner ending conversation with white lady in Salwar Kameez: Sorry, I've just seen someone interesting.

She almost smiled.

After a while she stood up, her legs still soft, and left the cubicle. As she rubbed some fake colour into her cheeks, she remembered Isla berating everyone on the landing. She imagined how Isla would have reacted, on overhearing Allegra talking about her. She could picture her striding out of the cubicle, furious, and how Allegra would kowtow and back-pedal. She wondered how it would feel to do the same, or be the same. And gradually a new feeling gathered force – the brittle, alien energy of defiance.

The Fountain

Chateau de Beaupont

6.45 p.m.

A gong reverberated round the gardens, and people started drifting towards the marquee. Serge called Isla again. She had looked through him during the ceremony, and he hadn't seen her since. He kept hearing her voice say 'a *million*?' He closed his eyes for refuge, and saw Huck's face, bloody and screaming.

All afternoon he had felt people avoiding him, or glancing over curiously. The piece in the *Mail* seemed to be garnering @SergeCampBELLEND more and more attention online. He had now reinstalled Twitter on his phone, and found himself checking it constantly – as if virtual hatred were preferable to real life alienation. The gong sounded again, and Serge thought of his speech. The dread was novel – he prided himself on public speaking with ease.

'Serge,' said his father, walking towards the fountain. He was wearing a favourite Ikat waistcoat and had combed his hair, for once, but still looked scattered. 'Is this true? You and Isla?'

'Me and Isla?'

'She's just told Marina! She said you're separated and you've mortgaged the flat?'

Serge tried to absorb this news. He pictured Isla telling his mother everything, her eyes daring Marina to lose composure. He wondered how someone he loved could be so spiteful.

'It's not like that. It was just a trial separation. While I was away. So we could figure things out.'

'And have you?'

'I mean, we're getting there. Look, Pa, please! Not now.'

'Come on, Serge. First everything this morning – now this? Why didn't you say?'

'It's not that simple.'

'So you keep saying, but the point is—'

The gong rang again.

'Pa, I can't. I've got to make this best man's speech,' said Serge, walking away.

Daniel's voice, amplified by the microphone, boomed out of the marquee.

'Ladies and gentlemen, please be upstanding for Mr and Mr ... Campbell-Delahunt.'

Serge used the applause to ignore his father calling after him. When he reached the marquee he looked back, to see if Lucian was following. But he was looking into the fountain, as if the algae might have parenting advice.

Serge was seated on the top table, called *The Marriage Of Figaro*, between JP's sister and mother. Making conversation was painful. Across the marquee he could just see Isla, on a table called *Cyrano de Bergerac*. She was sitting beside Daniel, laughing. He remembered finding them alone before the opera recital, and his sense that they had uncovered some kind of common ground – probably their normality in his family's outlandishness. It was a galling thought.

A waiter cleared the scallop starters and brought round plates of confit duck and dauphinoise potatoes, and he forced himself to eat. He tried to catch Rosie's eye across the table, hoping she might sense his need for a fortifying smile, but she was deep in conversation with Nate.

He turned to look at Isla again, and a mouthful of creamy potato seemed to block his throat. Daniel had her hand in his, and was moving her fingers across the bridge of his nose. Serge knew why: Daniel had broken his nose during a charity boxing match at Oxford. The kink had just taken the edge off his prettiness, winning him even more female attention.

After a moment Isla moved Daniel's fingertips to her elbow. Again, Serge knew the story she was recounting – a teenage windsurfing accident, in Newquay. He wanted to push through all the sedate tables and yank their hands apart, before breaking Daniel's nose himself.

Cyrano de Bergerac Table

The Marquee

7.30 p.m.

Daniel never would have thought that guiding a woman's fingertips over the bridge of his nose could be erotic. But it had been, and now that Isla was describing a windsurfing accident, he found himself thinking about her naked in the sea.

'Here,' she was saying, sticking out her elbow. 'Feel – there's a lump. Where it healed.'

He touched her elbow, his fingers on the two bones, his thumb pressing the inside of her forearm. He wondered if she felt the contact the way he did.

'That's not a lump, mate,' he said, keeping hold of her arm. 'That's your elbow. It's the bone.'

She protested, grinning, and he rolled up his shirt-sleeve to compare. They spent a few enjoyable moments feeling each other's elbows, until he had to concede that Isla's did have a lump.

She smiled, in flirtatious triumph. He refilled their glasses, and they both drank. The wine tasted of raspberries. She began telling a story about how she had once accidentally opened a £400 bottle of Burgundy at the Campbells' house, and how everyone had pretended they were delighted. She was speaking more, and faster, than the previous evening.

'You know you have a great voice,' said Daniel. 'Seriously. You should meet my voiceover agent.'

'People think I'm a man on the phone. They call me "Sir".'

'That's good! That's resonance. People pay vocal coaches thousands to get that. You could sell, I dunno, M&S food or whatever.'

'That's your big dream?' said Isla.

'That and Hamlet.'

'I never get the appeal of theatre. All those lines. And doing it every single night, even when you feel crap.'

'Is that not what you do with the kids?'

She looked disorientated, as if she had forgotten her children.

'But I don't have hundreds of people watching me,' she said.

'That's the whole point. The buzz. Otherwise it would just be like any other job.'

'You really are a typical actor, aren't you?'

He smiled a 'you got me' grin, gratified by the reference to their previous conversation.

'I don't think I'm actually meant to be sitting here,' she said. 'Caspar said I was beside some theatre director. I think he's there.'

She leaned closer, right into Daniel's space, indicating a man in a Nehru collar shirt, across the table. Daniel could smell her shampoo or fragrance.

'Can I make a confession?' he said.

He paused, prolonging the suspense.

'I switched your name card. Before I called everyone in.'

She laughed.

'Couldn't miss our nightly chat,' he said.

THE MARRIAGE OF FIGARO TABLE

THE MARQUEE

8.55 P.M.

Salads, cheeses and a trio of Provençal-themed puddings had come and gone. Serge felt each course like a countdown to the guillotine. Finally, as the macarons were cleared, Daniel strode to the front of the tent. He ignored the microphone, his auditorium voice quietening the chatter.

'Ladies and gentlemen, guys and gals. I ask you all to charge your glasses, as I present my dear friend, our first groom, the brilliant and beloved Caspar Campbell.'

Serge sat, trying to listen to Caspar and then JP, wondering how many people had seen the *Mail*. He looked over at Isla's table – her seat was empty. The air in the tent was heavy with two hundred humans breathing and radiating in one place. Everyone stood to applaud JP, and Rosie turned to look at Serge. Half of his brain seemed to be accelerating, while the rest lagged behind, fuzzy with Sauternes.

He followed the sway of Rosie's lean body to the microphone. The lights seemed unnaturally bright, revealing a blob of duck confit on his shirt. His wish to evaporate intensified.

'Hel-lo,' said Rosie, the microphone rounding her voice to a syrupy alto.

'Hey,' said Serge. It came out tightly, as if even his vocal cords were betraying him.

Rosie looked at him, waiting for him to open the speech as planned.

'Right – Caspar Campbell!' he said. 'No, stop – fuck! We've got thank-yous!'

He felt people stiffen, the Americans at his swearing and the British at his stumbling.

'Thank you, Virginia and Toby, and JP's parents, er . . . '

He groped for their names, despite sitting beside JP's mother at dinner.

'Charlotte and Austin,' said Rosie, leaning into his space to reach the microphone. There was sprinkled laughter, from the younger tables.

'Yeah, uh, Charlotte and Austin, for this incredible day.'

He sounded as if he was reading aloud, though he was not, having believed a full script was unnecessary. His forehead was damp, and as he brushed it he found his hand was trembling – something he had thought only happened on screen.

'So, Caspar. My cousin, and one of the best men I know. Even though, technically, I am the best man today.'

He hadn't planned this terrible aside, it had just emerged – nerves hijacking his judgement. There was a surprised silence, as if he had just confessed something revolting. An American female voice said loudly, 'The dumbass who was in the paper?'

He leaned closer to the microphone and there was a burst of feedback, making people jump.

'Shit, sorry!' he said. 'So, my first memory of Caspar is a very tall four-year-old, playing *RoboCop* in his much loved Rainbow Brite costume.'

This provoked some titters, but not enough to fortify him. He lurched through the rest of his first section, rushing the anecdotes so that all the punchlines were lost. The fond insults, which had seemed so funny in the bookshop, either sounded inappropriate or inaccurate – a Caspar nobody recognised. He couldn't bear to look at his parents. Halfway through there was a smash, as a Campbell family friend fell asleep and dropped his glass.

After the section on Caspar's childhood and teens he stood back to let Rosie take the microphone, feeling relieved, at first, and then mortified as the guests responded better to her. He had expected her to be nervous, but she seemed to be enjoying herself – waiting for laughs and speaking with a slick but spontaneous-sounding assurance.

She delivered the story about Caspar sleeping on a bus stop, smiled as everyone laughed, and stepped aside to let Serge resume. In the final section Serge was to talk about JP and Caspar as a couple, and to offer some wry advice on marriage. In one of the marquee entrances, he saw Isla. She stared at him as if they were strangers.

'So, just to wrap up,' he said, 'a few words on marriage, for you two, from me.'

He realised he had omitted the whole section about JP and Caspar as a couple.

'Oh yeah?' said the American voice that had spoken before. 'When you treat your own wife like the goddam help?'

Serge glanced over. The woman looked like a very drunk Meryl Streep. Other people were turning, and wincing. She stood up unsteadily – either to deliver her own speech, or to walk out.

The silence seemed infinite.

He knew he needed to speak because it was his muteness – not the heckle – that was creating the tension. But there seemed to be a void in his skull. Someone began ushering the woman out of the marquee. As she passed Isla, she said, audibly, 'Get out while you can, honey!'

Serge said, 'I'm going to—' for no reason other than it seemed like a promising start. But he didn't know what he was going to do, or what he was going to say. Hundreds of eyes looked back at him.

'Well, this isn't at all awkward!' said Rosie. 'OK, Caspar, I've got some marital advice – bearing in mind I've never been married.'

She looked at Serge, as if with comic timing.

Generous laughter rolled around the tent.

'Apparently, you can be married,' she paused, her hair catching the light. 'Or, you can be right. Am I right?' She waited for more laughter, which came.

'Thought so. Must be why I'm still single.'

She stepped back smiling, and a female voice shouted, 'I would!'

Isla walked out of the marquee.

Serge let Rosie wrap up their speech, as he stood back – trying to hide the duck confit stain with his hand.

Nate walked across from the top table to the microphone, and Serge saw the way he looked at Rosie. Nate launched into a confident speech about JP's years at Yale. After some well-judged comedy he gave a touching account of JP's coming out, and the support JP had offered Nate during his own 'rough times'. He said he had known – when he first introduced Caspar and JP in Halloween costume – that they had 'something special'.

Rosie was staring at Nate as he spoke, in the same way Nate had looked at her. Serge walked out in the cheers that followed the toast, half tripping as he fumbled for an opening in the tent.

The Dance Floor

The Marquee

10 p.m.

At ten, a semi-famous DJ took over from the band and the dance floor became sweaty and euphoric. Isla was in the middle of a group of JP's female cousins, jumping around to a remix of 'Single Ladies'. Earlier in the day, they had all been politely discussing the weather. She hadn't danced like this, mindlessly with strangers, for a long time. She felt drunk in a different, joyful way to at home – where she drank to make bedtime less arduous. It was a nostalgic, communal kind of obliteration that would warrant the hangover.

The opening of 'You Can Call Me Al' started to merge with the end of the song. She took off her shoes and was transported to her eighteenth summer, when she had danced in a field for three days – ecstatic with independence and MDMA and feeling part of something. The music and place and people were different, but the elation was the same. JP's cousins began shouting the chorus at Isla and each other, their feet fixed, their hips and hair swinging. She suddenly recalled exactly how it felt to see men's brains slow down, as she and her friends passed. She hadn't realised, until now, that she missed it.

She had no idea where Serge was. Daniel had taken his place for the flash mob, executing the routine opposite Isla with a trained dancer's precision. He came jogging onto the dance floor now, holding two amber shots – one for her. She tipped the liquid down her throat, letting the burn suspend everything. It was cognac, and the Christmassy aftertaste woke hundreds of dormant memories of other parties and dance floors and appealing strangers.

He began to dance in front of her. At first he was mirroring her, but at a professional distance, like in the flash mob. People made space around them, half watching and copying them. She could feel Daniel enjoying the attention, and the sense that they were leading the crowd. He began to move more showily, still keeping their connection. For a second he was looking straight into her eyes, like in the final frame of *Riptide*. She was transported further back now, to being thirteen or fourteen. She was just making sense of the adult world, newly aware of herself and her body, dancing with her friends in front of older boys, all of them skipping classes and smoking weed in the woods outside her village. She remembered feeling, after years of struggling at school, that she had finally found the things she was good at.

Around her everyone was chanting the opening to 'Gold Digger' – ironically, but Isla didn't feel ironic. The bass came in, juddering through her legs and chest like a second pulse. Money and mortgages and Serge and even her children dissolved, so that the past was more vivid than the moment. Her hands floated up over her head. She felt as if she was meeting herself after a long separation.

The Bacon Butty Van

Chateau de Beaupont

10.15 P.M.

Rosie was explaining the necessity of bacon sandwiches at British weddings to Nate's friends – all of whom he had introduced her to after dinner. She had barely eaten before the speech, and was now celebrating her success with a bacon bap. There was ketchup on her dress, and she found she didn't care. Many people had congratulated her on coming to Serge's rescue with 'married or right' – one of her father's favourite clichés. Each time Rosie thought of Allegra saying, 'her parents were awful,' she felt more defiant. The flash mob had passed in a state of dizzy relief. She had drunk an espresso martini in three sips afterwards.

Serge appeared now, behind Nate. The atmosphere shifted, slightly, as everyone recognised the drunk best man. Rosie knew she would normally have felt sorry for him, but it did not come.

'Rosie!' he said. 'You seen Isla? I can't find her.'

'Isla? No.'

He stood looking back at her.

'Can I ask you something?' he said, as if Nate and his friends weren't there, or didn't matter.

He turned and walked ahead, confident Rosie would follow. She did, but not before she had finished the sandwich. It was satisfying to see him waiting for her, where he had stopped, away from everyone else. The air still felt baked, different to the dewy chill of British weddings. Across the grass she could make out Nate's white shirt in the dark.

'Thanks for carrying the speech,' said Serge. 'Drank too much. Sorry.'

'No problem.'

'Look, sorry to drag you away. From Nate. Just, um, has Caspar said anything? About this shit show in the paper, this morning?'

She baulked, inwardly, at "drag you away."

'Caspar? Not to me. He's pretty busy, today.'

Serge did not seem to register her sarcasm.

'And Isla's still pissed off about Huck,' he said. 'Jesus, this day! How's your night?'

She paused for a second, then said, calmly:

'Not great, actually. I overheard your sister, talking about me. And my "awful" family.'

It was exhilarating to be so confrontational – like striking a match. She wondered, as if she were watching herself, how far she could subvert her own character.

'What? Why would she say that?'

'Cos that's what she thinks? Even though she acts like we're best friends.'

'God, she's so full of shit. Look, whatever my sister said, I'm really sorry. I don't in any way share her opinions. You do know that, right?'

He leaned towards her unsteadily, and said, 'Honestly. I'm so sorry. Allegra's not in a good place. If she ever was.'

Rosie stepped back.

'It's not even Allegra I'm pissed off with.'

'Huh? Who are you pissed off with?'

The moment felt pivotal.

'You.'

He reeled back, exaggerating a frown.

'I actually can't believe I'm only realising it now. I told myself I was sad, but I wasn't. I was angry.'

'Angry? Why?'

'Serge! The fact that you're even asking, it just ... it says everything.'

'Says what? What are we talking about?'

He looked slow and unfocused, nothing like the image of Serge she treasured.

'For God's sake,' she said. 'Do I have to spell it out?'

He stared at her, still lost, inviting her to explain.

'How you let me think we were going to do all this,' she gestured at the marquee, 'have kids, grow old, and then out of nowhere you were like, "sorry, not ready"! But then, two months later, you're very much ready. It wasn't timing. It was you not being straight with me. For two years.'

'Are we seriously getting into this, now?'

'Why shouldn't we? I don't think you've ever said sorry. "Sorry for dumping you, Rosie," but not "sorry for taking your last years of guaranteed fertility".'

She expected him to look contrite – as he had in her mind when she said this to his cushion understudy – but he didn't.

'Are you serious? Rosie, you're only, what, thirty-six?'

'Nearly thirty-eight! I took a gap year!'

She could hear how absurd this sounded, and pulled her voice down.

'But that's my whole point, Serge. You have no idea about any of this, do you? Fertility.'

'Right. I watched my kids being born and I have no idea about fertility?'

'Oh my God! You're bringing up the birth of your children, when I'm trying to explain that stringing along a woman in her mid-thirties – who wants kids – is fucking selfish. And then silence. Ever since. We were *friends*!'

'Rosie, look. I'm sorry you wanted us to have kids and it wasn't right.'

'You think I'm upset because I wanted your kids specifically,' she said, realising that there was some truth to this.

Neither of them spoke. Serge breathed in and out impatiently, like a teenager being told off.

'I might have had your baby anyway,' she added. 'I had a miscarriage. Possibly. Probably.'

It came out suddenly, the way she'd told Daniel about Isla and Serge in the cloakroom.

'What? Probably?'

'I mean, they couldn't say for certain. I could have just been late. But it seemed like—'

'When was this?'

'After we broke up. That one night.'

'Why didn't you say?'

He was paying attention now, but he looked curious as well as concerned. It had taken this to interest him.

She made a noise like 'Uuurrrrrgh', and he stepped back again in the dark.

'You'd just dumped me! I didn't want to scare you. Or put pressure on you. Because God forbid a woman should be scary. Or needy. No, no, we have no needs. Like Barbie, with no pubic hair.'

It occurred to her that she actually had not had any pubic hair to speak of while she and Serge were together, though she had been the one to remove it.

'Rosie, look, I'm so sorry about the miscarriage. Or, the not knowing. Genuinely. But I don't get what you're blaming me for. No one forced you to be with me. You never said you wanted kids that badly.'

'Is that how you rationalise it? I was just waiting around, like a dog?'

'Oh Christ, Rosie! Please! Look, this has been a really shit day,

OK? And you think now, here, is the perfect time to dump all your issues on me. Like, years after the event. I've said sorry, OK?'

She could see Nate, looking over. The tenor must be obvious, even at a distance.

'OK, then,' she said.

Serge was still staring at her, incredulous and offended, so she said, 'Enjoy your night,' and walked away towards the marquee. She could not return to Nate and his friends, now. The glamour of being angry, of expressing herself like Isla, had been a chimera. All she had achieved was losing the grace and dignity she had worked so hard to preserve. She was not like Isla. She could not navigate conflict. And she wished she had not used pubic hair to make a point.

Behind the Marquee

Chateau de Beaupont

10.30 p.m.

Daniel had enjoyed dancing with Isla more than he knew was advisable. She moved with the same assurance as the professional dancers he had dated, without their mechanical quality. He could tell she was enjoying dancing with him too, and had assumed she would follow him to the bar. When she hadn't, he had realised how much he wanted her to – and how drunk he was. He had gone to his room for a quick line, to sober up. When he returned to the garden he had seen Rosie and Serge, standing away from the party.

Serge had been standing back, his arms folded, while Rosie became shrill. Daniel could not distinguish words but they were clearly arguing. It seemed unequivocal now that they were sleeping together. He felt newly enraged on Isla's behalf. Serge was unworthy of her, the way Serge was unworthy of his success. The argument appeared to end but Daniel stayed where he was, near the marquee's generator.

He took out his phone, and checked the @SergeCampBELLEND thread – as if he had acquired another addiction. He skimmed the latest tweets, impulsively liking a comment that said:

Is this the joker that lamped someone with his BAFTA?

He felt someone's presence, and looked up. It was Allegra, her dress a pearlescent column in the dark. He quickly put his phone away.

'Hey!' he said.

'Daniel! We need to stop meeting like this.'

'Like what?'

He felt flustered, having so recently contributed to the viral hate against her brother.

'This! You. Me. A marquee.'

It took him a second to realise she was referring to the St Arthur's ball. Her arch tone was such a contrast to her coldness on Thursday evening.

'Right! God, that ball. Feels like centuries ago, yeah?'

'To you, maybe.'

There was a faintly accusing note now, though he wasn't sure why. He was amazed she could remember the night at all. She had seemed so drunk, albeit in a cool, unravelled way.

'I mean, I was just in awe of you,' he said, truthfully.

He smiled his most winning grin.

She took out a cigarette, like a direction to find a lighter. He did so. Her face, revealed by the flame, had a distressing, sunken quality.

'In awe?' she said, on an outbreath.

'Yeah! You were so sure of yourself. Like, you really knew what you wanted.'

'And look how that turned out.'

'You used the words "proscenium arch"!' he said, having retrieved this detail and hoping it would prompt a laugh. 'I was just, like, I am *way* out of my depth here. Properly punching!'

She blew out another curl of smoke, looking past him.

'I was seventeen,' she said.

She met his eyes now, as if these words held a code. Then she walked off.

He stayed by the generator, watching her walk away. Nothing

messed people up, he thought, like a failed acting career. He had been the same, once, although fame had only delivered a new nightmare. He returned to his phone, and tweeted a picture of himself between Caspar and JP, in front of the chateau. He captioned it: 'My new gaff ... Just kidding, honoured to be joining these two exceptional humans in holy matrimony.'

He hoped this would satisfy Camilla, who had sent him 'a little reminder' that holiday photos made excellent posts and to ensure that he looked sober in any off-duty shot. She would never appreciate the tyranny of these requests, or the irony of being instructed to work harder on holiday. That was the price of success.

He thought again of Allegra's skeletal face, and his conversation with Isla about doing theatre, and wondered – as he posted the selfie on Instagram – whether fame was actually worth it. He put his phone in his pocket and went back into the marquee.

The Dance Floor

The Marquee

10.40 P.M.

Isla had noted the disappointment on Daniel's face when she hadn't followed him to the bar. It had been enjoyable to wield this power – and to know he would come back. He had been so attentive during dinner she had felt sorry for the woman on his other side – their conversation cycling from silly to sincere to flirtatious and back round, frequently returning to the experience of being an only child to a single mother. At one point, when they were discussing child actors, he had confessed that he felt parts of his early career had been exploitative. Then he had said, looking at her, 'God, I've never actually said that to anyone.'

The dance floor was over-full now, so that nobody was exactly dancing alone or with anyone else. Nobody she even recognised was nearby, and she could feel herself entering the same timeless, trance-like state as before – despite the increasingly cheesy music. She felt somebody taking both her hands from behind. This person turned out to be Daniel. He was shouting to her over Shakira, and she turned and leaned closer to hear.

'I can't dance to this,' he said. 'Cigarette?'

He was speaking right into her ear, so that she could feel his breath on her neck. She thought how jubilant her younger self would be to know that Daniel Pyke kept seeking her out.

Something bold, perhaps this younger self, made her put her hands on his shoulders.

'Come on! You know you love this song!' she shouted, knowing she sounded drunk.

Daniel seemed to relent, and twirled her under his arms. It was a chaste kind of dancing, the way someone might indulge an excitable child. A group of JP's friends crowded onto the dance floor as 'Despacito' replaced Shakira, all the new bodies forcing them even closer to one another. In the throng she felt Daniel's kneecap nudge between hers, jostling at first, then in sync with her legs. His thigh felt hot and solid. He was smiling as he moved away and took both her hands, then dipped her in the tiny space around them, as if they were dancing the tango.

She stumbled, and he said, 'You need air.'

Outside, away from the music, her adolescence retreated slightly. The darkness felt warm and kinetic with crickets. They stood beside a plane tree, the patches of naked trunk shining in the moonlight, and she accepted a cigarette. She had not smoked since finding out she was pregnant, afraid she wouldn't be able to give up again. The familiar acridity in her mouth and throat was bliss.

She leaned back against the tree, numbly lightheaded, feeling the breeze on her face and bare arms. For a second, as if her thirteen-year-old self was steering her thoughts again, she pictured Daniel putting one hand against the tree, just above her shoulder, and his other around her waist as he kissed her – slowly at first then more forcefully. She imagined pressing her body back against his, making him want her so much he couldn't think straight.

'Good move, missing the speeches,' said Daniel, interrupting her thoughts.

She had timed a visit to the twins deliberately, knowing it would be impossible to laugh gamely through Serge and Rosie's double act.

'I saw the end. When Rosie had to take over. Looked like she was loving it.'

'Doubt that. Knowing her.'

'What d'you mean?'

'She'd hate seeing Serge screw up. Though she'd hate giving a speech, full stop.'

'Didn't look that way.'

'Yeah. Well. Rosie's the queen of "fake it till you make it". Or she used to be.'

'She does seem quite fake, to be fair.'

Daniel's eyes narrowed, apparently considering whether this was fair or not. She took in his chiselled profile, as he dragged on the cigarette.

'Listen, I probably shouldn't tell you this,' he said. 'But I saw them – Serge and Rosie – out here, just now. Having this heated chat. Like she was having a go at him.'

Isla's chest tightened again. There was something so intimate, so very un-fake, about arguing.

'About what?' she said. Today, of all days, was Isla's to argue with Serge – not Rosie's.

'Couldn't hear. But not like Rosie to confront him. Or anyone, actually.'

'There was a weird situation, earlier, with the twins. I was kind of rude to her. Unintentionally.'

'I don't reckon she'd have a go at Serge about that. It looked pretty intense. Like, more than that.'

Her phone rang. She saw Daniel see Serge's name on the screen, as she pressed Decline.

'Is this cos of that thing in the *Mail*?' said Daniel.

'Kind of. More the fact that he never told me. Any of it. But we've been living apart. So . . . '

Her voice shrank, surprising her. Daniel stepped forwards. The embrace was brotherly – only their shoulders pressed together – though she was conscious of their ears against one another, where Serge would have rested his chin on her head. Daniel smelled different too – like fruity grooming products over cigarettes. She thought, incongruously, of air freshened Ubers.

'OK?' he said, the embrace coming to a natural release.

'Yup,' she said, because she feared she might fall apart otherwise.

'Good. You deserve to be,' said Daniel. It didn't really mean anything, but his expression was sincere. They stubbed out their cigarettes. Cher's voice blasted out of the marquee.

'Bloody hell,' said Daniel. 'Spliff? I bought weed in Marseille.'

Isla had not smoked cannabis for years but it used to feature frequently in her life. Serge disapproved of it on principle, saying it destroyed ambition. She knew he included Isla's mother in this theory.

'Why not?' she said.

'All right. After party.'

He smiled, and as they walked up the drive his side kept lightly bumping against hers.

The Marquee

Chateau de Beaupont

10.50 p.m.

After Rosie's tirade Serge had walked into the chateau and had lain down in a ground floor sitting room. He remembered playing UNO with Caspar there, as a child, though the door now bore a 'Private' sign. He was too drunk and annoyed by Rosie's timing to contemplate her accusations. She was supposed to be reliably restrained.

Eventually he got up and walked back to the marquee, looking for Isla – who wasn't answering her phone. She wasn't there. His sister was beside the DJ, trying to take his headphones. Serge couldn't face confronting her about Rosie. He started dancing with Caspar's colleagues instead, hoping to feel normal. The grooms appeared, and everyone cheered. Serge embraced his cousin even though Caspar was trying to dance.

'Sorry the speech wasn't great,' he shouted.

'Don't worry about it.'

Caspar looked like he wanted to get away.

'You seen Isla?' said Serge. He had to repeat the question three times, yelling into Caspar's ear, so that he started to feel more and more irritating.

'She was just here with Dan a minute ago,' said Caspar, at last. 'Think they went outside.'

His colleagues shouted 'Banger!' and began jumping in a tight circle to a Madness song. Serge stood right behind a man's pogo-ing back for a second, feeling profoundly excluded and unlike himself. He turned and left the marquee. The idea of Isla and Daniel dancing together – even Caspar talking about them as a pair – was painful.

Outside, he couldn't see them anywhere. He took out his phone to call Isla, again, and saw more notifications on Twitter. He swiped to read them as he listened to Isla's voicemail greeting – almost welcoming more abuse. The most recent was from Helen Murphy, the comedian whose retweet had catalysed his public shame. It said:

@Gareth32 – you're the spit of Daniel Pyke off TROG! But who's the dude who looks like @SergeCampbell????

He swiped to look at the Twitter account she was referring to, the same man with twelve followers called @Gareth32 who had commented on *Bursary*. He saw the photo Helen Murphy was questioning – a selfie of Daniel, standing between Caspar and JP.

At first, Serge thought he must be drunk, and confused. Then he assumed the photo was a retweet, that @Gareth32 must be a crazed fan of Daniel's. But the original selfie of Daniel had been posted by @Gareth32 – there was no retweeting. He scrolled back through @Gareth32's old tweets. That morning the man had tweeted 'FFS. Sometimes I kind of hate weddings'. On Thursday, around the time of the softball, he had written: 'Why isn't organised fun more fun?' Further back, @Gareth32 had mentioned *Knifepoint*, and *TROG*. Serge checked Daniel's official Instagram. Daniel had posted the same selfie, there, a minute after @Gareth32 tweeted it.

People kept walking between the marquee and the sandwich van. Serge stood looking at Daniel's feline face, glowing on his phone. He thought of Daniel choosing to shame him online from behind an alias, and his hands on Isla at dinner, and how he had found them talking after the softball and before the opera – how they had apparently been dancing and then left the dance floor together.

The tension of the past month seemed to converge. He ran into the marquee asking people if they had seen Daniel, and then hurried round the garden asking the same question, not caring how eccentric he looked.

Daniel's Room

Chateau de Beaupont

11 p.m.

Daniel's room was immaculate. The surfaces were all clear, the grooming products in height order. The only other possession was a Mulberry holdall in the corner. Isla thought, wistfully, of the time when she could pack her life into one bag.

They were both holding fresh drinks, having encountered JP's father on the drive holding a bottle of Vermouth. Austin Delahunt had refilled their glasses, explaining at length how he had come to accept JP's sexuality.

She hovered in the doorway, aware – on some level – that entering Daniel's room would signify something. The rug felt intimate under her bare feet. Daniel reached across her to dim the top light, and went over to the holdall.

'Shall we?' he said, showing her a little bag and a packet of Rizlas.

'Here?'

She had assumed they would smoke outside, far from the marquee. He looked around the bedroom.

'Yeah, maybe not. Can't be hot-boxing the boudoir. Shall we have a gander downstairs? Must be some mental rooms in this place.'

He looked at her, like a dare. She had the feeling, again, that she and Daniel were united as interlopers. Her teenage nostalgia returned for a second, as she recalled trespassing on a farm with her first boyfriend.

At the bottom of the stairs, Daniel gestured at the rooms leading off the entrance hall – all of which were marked 'Private'. The first seemed to be a cloakroom, full of coats and boots.

'Fuck that,' was his verdict. 'Not wasting this on the welly cupboard.'

The next door they tried was a very formal dining room, chandeliers like storm clouds and family portraits in heavy gilt frames.

'That kid, in that picture. He's looking at me,' she said.

'Why are you whispering?' said Daniel, now whispering himself.

They were standing too close together in the doorway.

The third room was a casual drawing room with a stone fireplace, chesterfield sofas and tables crowded with photos or board games. It smelled of wood smoke. Several large Chinese lamps cast pools of low light. Isla thought of the twins' fairy tale audiobook, where the third choice was always just right.

'Yeah, baby!' said Daniel. He bounced onto the sofa, and lounged back in the cushions. Then he bent forwards to roll a joint, on a 2004 copy of *World of Interiors*. Isla went over to a record player. The records were all jazz or Motown, and she chose 'I Heard It Through The Grapevine'. The initial crackle charged the air. Daniel looked up and said, 'Tune!'

He lit the joint, and passed it to her. She took a deep drag, the bonfire taste completing her rebellion. Their knuckles brushed one another as she returned it. Outside, a firework whistled and boomed. From the sofa they could half see the display through the French windows. Daniel cheered as more rockets burst into momentary galaxies.

He turned and smiled. His face, even lit up blue and green by the fireworks, was compulsive to look at. She wanted to call her younger self to say that Daniel Pyke had chosen her, out of everyone. She took another drag. The room seemed to tip, marginally. As she passed the joint back, she heard herself say, 'I really shouldn't tell you this.'

'Go on.'

He propped his elbow on the back of the sofa. The leather creaked. 'I had a massive crush on you when I was thirteen. In *Riptide*.'

'You did? That's cute.'

'I had to pretend I didn't recognise you, at the softball.'

'That's cute, too.'

He was grinning at her. He tilted his head and leaned forwards, fractionally, as if they were on camera.

His eyes were inches from hers now – and for a second they merged into one, like a beautiful Cyclops.

'You look like you've got one eye,' she said, quickly.

'I have,' he said, deadpan.

'What's it called, a skyclop?'

His face was still in her breathing space. Her tongue felt slow, like a dream.

'Y'what?' he said.

'A skyclop? Isn't that, like, the beast with one eye? You know this!'

'What are you talking about?'

'Skyclops! Don't they have them in your show?'

He leaned back against the sofa, and began sniggering and then laughing. At first she was saying, 'Stop! What's funny?' but then, when he squeaked something about *TROG* being Viking, not Greek, she began laughing too – even though she couldn't understand what he was saying or if it was even funny.

She kept saying, 'What? Tell me!', swatting his arm, but after a while she was also laughing too much to speak – and this was funnier than getting the joke. The laughter rinsed through her, and she felt something loosen that had been knotted for months.

The Hall

Chateau de Beaupont

11.10 p.m.

The hall was empty, besides a sea of wedding presents. Serge was planning to run upstairs and stride into Daniel's room to confront him, when he heard Isla's voice – and laughter. It was coming from the sitting room where he had lain down, where he used to play UNO with Caspar. He stopped, one foot on the stairs, and heard a man's laughter in response.

He walked over to the door and stood right beside it, listening. He could hear his own ragged breaths, and music playing in the room and more giggling. Then he opened the door so hard that the handle crashed against the wall inside.

Isla and Daniel were together on the sofa, both gasping with laughter – their heads ominously close – the way he and Isla never laughed now. Serge knew he would never forget this image. All the oxygen seemed to have been abruptly removed from the room.

They both turned towards the door, and stopped. Isla stared at him. One strap of her dress had fallen down. As she pulled it up, time seemed to restart. He registered the sour, leafy smell of cannabis, and saw Isla hand something to Daniel as she stood, smoothing her clothes.

'We're just— it's not,' she said.

It seemed possible that he might kill Daniel, and he knew that he had to leave. He turned and ran out through the front door and down the stone staircase, then on down the drive. He heard Isla calling his name, but he kept running. In his peripheral vision he registered people moving aside, shocked at his speed.

The drive was long – his chest was burning by the end. There was an old-fashioned bicycle leaning against one of the gateposts. A sign that said 'Welcome to Caspar & JP's wedding' in loopy cursive was tied to the handlebars. He stopped, panting, his sweat cold in the night air.

The bike, when he tugged it, was not chained up. He hesitated. He was far from sober, but the roads to Aix would be empty and he cycled daily at home. He could easily restore the bike to the chateau. The tyres were firm. He knew the way back to the hotel. Half his stuff was there, they would have a room somewhere. For a few hours, at least, he could escape.

He put one leg over the saddle, his foot finding the higher pedal. For a second he stopped again, thinking of how much he had drunk and the road's bends.

His phone began to buzz – Isla was calling. He pushed down on the pedal.

The Marquee

Chateau de Beaupont

11.15 P.M.

Rosie had spent the past hour making circuits of the party, chatting as if on autocue, and trying to forget the conversation with Serge. She walked into the marquee, hoping to find Nate, or Imogen. Allegra Campbell was behind the decks with the DJ, waving her frond-like arms to 'Karma Chameleon'. Even the Campbells, she thought, could not escape the universal naffness of a wedding dance floor.

She found Imogen at a table with Hugo and his wife. The baby was asleep on Hugo's chest, with giant ear defenders over its grapefruit-size head. Rosie sat down and began picking at a slice of wedding cake, though she wasn't hungry.

'Rosumundo! We're just having an incredibly middle-aged conversation about primary schools,' Imogen shouted over Pharrell Williams.

'I just had an incredibly juvenile conversation with Serge about what a dick he is.'

'Wait, what? What did he say? What did you say?'

Imogen had lipstick on her teeth, and was too drunk to hide her excitement. Rosie was glad it was too loud for Hugo to hear. She had always found Hugo Ranger objectionable, she realised. She wondered why she only felt able to admit this, to herself, now. Was it because he was Serge's friend?

'I told him,' she said. 'Like you said. How he messed me around for two years.'

'No way! What did he say?'

'Nothing. Threw it back in my face. Like, "Nobody forced you to be with me."'

Serge's face – slack and uncomprehending – returned to her. His features had not changed, but their entirety was no longer mesmeric.

'No! And you saved the speech! So he wasn't even, like, "Sorry you feel that way"?'

'Kind of. Maybe wasn't the best timing.'

She couldn't face repeating Allegra's comments.

'He had to hear it at some point,' said Imogen. 'Well done you.'

She leaned over to hug her, and Rosie felt a potent sense of anticlimax. The baby began screaming over 50 Cent, its head poking out of the sling like an angry tortoise. Hugo hurried outside, while Imogen started reminiscing about a terrible club in Oxford.

While she spoke, Rosie looked over at the dance floor. She could see Nate's head, bobbing in the crowd. He was in a group of JP's friends, including Audrey. After a moment Rosie realised that Audrey and Nate were dancing together. He was moving with the same easy, solid rhythm he had done in the flash mob – his collar undone. Audrey was so small, like a doll or blonde elf, that Nate looked imposing beside her. He was smiling widely at Audrey, and Rosie felt a flare of emotion – if not jealousy, something like it.

At the chorus they began doing jokey hip-hop moves to each other, Audrey leaning back like a rapper with her hand near her crotch, which somehow had the effect of making her look even more feminine. Rosie watched them both laugh, and registered that Nate must be completely sober. The opening of Prince's 'Kiss' filtered through the end of 'In da Club', and Nate and Audrey cheered at each other, as if the song held private significance. Rosie found she couldn't watch, and turned back to the cake.

Daniel's Room

Chateau de Beaupont

11.20 P.M.

Daniel had stayed on the sofa, after Isla had gone. She had not even looked at him as she bolted after Serge. He thought how he could not imagine anyone running after him calling his name, unless he was on a red carpet and they were a photographer.

The record ended. Outside he could hear people enjoying themselves. He stood and walked up the stairs to his bedroom, where he lay, fully clothed on the bed. He wondered how a connection could switch, so fast, from vital to hollow. Isla's admission of her teenage crush – which had briefly warmed his ego – now felt eviscerating. She had not wanted him. It had nothing to do with him. She had just wanted to link her own past and present.

His phone rang, just reaching for it took an enormous effort. It was his mother requesting a WhatsApp video call. He stalled. It was the second time she had called that evening. He wanted to see her face, but he did not want her to see him. He kept looking at the word 'Mum' and the little round profile picture in the middle of the screen, the two of them at Cannes, and let it ring out. It was late for Cheryl to call. He wondered if she had forgotten he was in France, not LA. She was getting older. It was an uncomfortable thought.

He listened for Isla and Serge returning to their room across the landing. He imagined the inevitable row – whether Isla's smoking weed with Daniel constituted infidelity, perhaps the way Serge was surely betraying Isla, himself, with Rosie. He wondered, numbly, if they might split permanently. When he pictured Serge's face, in the doorway, it seemed doubtful.

Nobody came up the stairs. He could still hear the bass outside, overlaid with shouts and laughter. He knew he could not return to the marquee. He considered missing the pool party the next day, to avoid seeing Serge and Isla, but he knew Caspar would hold this against him for years. Serge would never confront him, in public, anyway. He would just walk around Daniel, like sick on a pavement. In its way, this would be worse.

He picked up his phone again, to check how many Likes his selfie had garnered. There were thousands on Instagram, but when he moved to Twitter he was confused – his account only had one new notification. It was from Helen Murphy, the comedian. For a moment Daniel was confused. Then his mistake was abruptly, disastrously clear. He had tweeted a photo of himself, between Caspar and JP, from @Gareth32. Worse, Helen Murphy had included Serge in her reply. Serge might now see, or have seen, Daniel's tweet about *Bursary*. He sat up, sweating, rushing to delete the selfie from his alias account, his heart a pair of castanets.

He tried to take a full breath, then – on impulse – he erased his entire @Gareth32 account. At each 'Are You Sure?' question from Twitter, he pressed down harder on the screen, muttering, 'Yes, yes, fuck's sake, YES,' as though his phone might appreciate the emergency.

He wondered if he should contact Helen Murphy directly, or if it was safer to do nothing. He considered confessing to Camilla, and immediately discounted the idea. He sensed his agent already saw him as a loose cannon. He would have to wait – the prospect was agony – to see what Helen Murphy did next. He longed to tell his mother, but she would worry, like when he had confided that his classmates kept mocking his pose in an M&S school uniform ad.

There was nobody else he could confide in, nobody even halfway close enough. He could hardly tell Caspar.

Already he could see himself going viral, the unbalanced actor who had set up an anonymous hate account and trolled his own friend. His cheeky image would be destroyed, he would have to make tearful Instagram apologies, blaming his drug habit. He strode around the room, his skin at once clammy and full of heat, tugging his hair to distract himself with pain. He could not retrace his thought processes, the idiocy, the vanity, the risk – how he would look if the fake account emerged.

He located the sleeping pills that his doctor had prescribed, to be taken 'as required'. There was only one left, and he wondered – almost savouring the thought, but not quite – what he would do if there had been more. Then he lay down with his eyes squeezed shut, praying that nobody else had seen the selfie, and waited for the pill to take effect.

He should not have deleted the whole account! The thought came to him with a jerk of consciousness. He should have just deleted the selfie, and left the account alone. He had panicked, and made it all worse. He turned over and shouted 'Arrrrh', pressing his face into the mattress, wishing he could tunnel through it into oblivion.

He realised how badly he lacked somebody in his life who he could ask, 'What should I do?' Someone who would say, 'Breathe, calm down, stop – it's not such a big deal.' He recalled Rosie's question in the cloakroom, for a second, and the way she had looked genuinely – if clumsily – concerned. But the memory was oddly painful. He did not want to consider that Rosie might still be a friend. Their whole relationship had always been skewed by Serge.

He turned onto his side, his eyes shut, dreading the moment when he would wake up and remember everything.

The Drive

Chateau de Beaupont

11.30 p.m.

Isla returned to the chateau's gates, having looked for Serge everywhere in the woods flanking the drive – shouting his name, barefoot and ridiculous in her floral crown. When she had first run after him she had expected him to stop, to turn and face her. But by the time she reached the fountain he had already been a silhouette jogging down the drive. Daniel had not followed them and she had noted, dimly, that she didn't care.

The clamour of the cicadas felt urgent, now. She stood in the long grass by the gateposts, trying to imagine what Serge must have seen when he opened the door. He had looked appalled, even though she and Daniel had not been touching. The only other time she had seen Serge look that way was on the labour ward, when her heart rate had plummeted. Doctors had run in, and he had stood – frozen – his hands either side of his head like someone over acting horror.

She wondered how the scene in the private room would have looked a few moments earlier, before she and Daniel had started laughing, or seconds later. She feared that they might have kissed, had their laughter not interrupted the tension. She hoped she had created the interruption, subconsciously, the same way she had suggested they leave Daniel's bedroom. It was hard to say for certain, though.

Her palms were damp. She wiped them on her dress and called Serge, again. It rang to voicemail, and she thought of the day he had endured, and his recent recklessness after the SOFAs. She feared he might do something stupid, though what, exactly, she wasn't sure. There was no way for him to leave the chateau's grounds.

She instructed herself not to be paranoid – that he just needed to calm down, that she could explain. She began walking back up the drive, hoping he had returned to the party or their room while she was looking for him in the trees.

As she reached the fountain her phone rang, showing Serge's name. Her first feeling was relief. Arguing would be better than uncertainty, or the gnawing sense of guilt. She swiped Accept – primed to return accusations. But when she said, 'Serge?' he didn't answer.

All she could hear was laboured breathing, as if he had called by mistake.

'Where are you?' she said.

'The road.'

The signal was bad, but she could hear his voice was strained.

'What? Are you OK?'

He said something about falling off a bike on the way to Aix, and her pulse revved horribly. The road back to the city was treacherous even in daylight.

'But is it bad? Can you walk? Can you come back?'

He said something slurred. She wondered if he was in shock or delirious, if the accident was more or less serious than it sounded.

'Serge, listen!' she said. 'You need to get out of the road.'

'You'd be all over this,' he said, his words disintegrating to giggles, so that he sounded unhinged. 'The blood.'

'Blood?'

He began mumbling about Tarantino and then swore and said, 'It's going in my eye!'

'Your head's bleeding? Serge, listen to me, where are you? Do you need an ambulance?'

The line cut out. She called him back over and over, each time it went to voicemail. While she called, she ran up the drive towards the marquee.

'I need a doctor!' she shouted into the tent. 'Help! Please, help!'

People turned. Rosie stood up from a table and came hurrying over.

'What's happened?' she said. 'Is it Huck? Is he OK? Where's Serge?'

Isla tried to explain what had happened, or what she knew, but it sounded incoherent. Rosie kept asking for details and clarification, while Isla pictured Serge bleeding, prone on the ground – invisible to passing cars. JP's best man Nate was beside them now. His shirtsleeves were rolled up, he looked very adult and capable. Rosie said something into his ear, and he nodded.

'I can drive,' he said, turning to Isla. 'No sweat. Just a sec.'

He jogged over to the DJ booth, and spoke to the DJ. The music stopped, abruptly. Nate leaned into the microphone and called out, 'Do we have a doctor here?'

The silence yawned, as everyone looked at everyone else, disorientated.

Nate added, 'A nurse? Any medics?'

After a painful silence, he said, 'OK, don't worry, we're good.'

The song surged into life again, and he came back.

'Listen, if he called you, he's probably OK – right? I have first aid—'

'Can we just get to him,' Isla interrupted.

Rosie was standing back now.

'You're coming, right?' said Nate, looking at her.

'I mean,' said Rosie. 'I can't just— It's Caspar's, y'know.'

'But I can't speak French,' said Nate. 'We might need help. At the hospital.'

He was staring at her slightly desperately, as if he didn't want to be alone with Isla.

'Come on, please, let's go,' said Isla.

The three of them hurried to Nate's car. Rosie sat beside Nate in the front, Isla in the back.

For a second, despite her panic, Isla recalled Daniel's account of seeing Serge arguing with Rosie. It felt remote, now, possibly exaggerated and certainly not a priority.

'Was he heading to Aix?' said Nate, as the car started.

'I don't know!' said Isla. 'Probably.'

She imagined the twins, bereaved before they could remember their father.

'We'll find him,' said Rosie, turning back. 'It's one road, for ages. He won't be far.'

Nate's Car

Rue de Saint André

11.35 p.m.

Nobody spoke as they drove downhill. She could hear Isla calling Serge behind her in the back seat, and his voicemail greeting. It was surreal to hear him say, 'Hey, this is Serge! I'm not here right now,' in the middle of the crisis he had created. A part of Rosie longed for more details. The idea of pushing a man to such a dramatic gesture was compelling. She thought of her own attempt to provoke an emotional response in Serge, and how his dumb impatience had been strangely off-putting – repellent, even.

She looked at Nate, almost professionally calm as he drove. Isla suddenly shouted, 'There!' and he braked. Rosie saw the bike on its side, and a body nearby, at the same time as Isla screamed. She and Nate ran over, but Rosie stood back. There was something lifeless about Serge's silhouette. She made herself look at him, ready to swiftly shut her eyes, as if she were watching a violent film. Serge's head and body were whole, but he had a shocking amount of blood down his face. One trouser leg was ripped at the thigh.

She could hear Isla whimpering, 'Oh my God, fuck, you're alive,' crouching beside him. Nate was covering him with his jacket, and speaking in a reassuring voice. Serge began groaning and coughing. She heard Nate say, 'How many fingers am I holding up?'

'Should I call an ambulance?' Rosie called, trying to sound helpful. She did not want to be any nearer Serge. The blood was making her feel weak.

'No, I'll drive – it'll be faster,' said Nate. 'There's an ER in Aix.'

'But doesn't he need—?'

'We're OK. He's alert, the bleeding's stopped. I have no clue how long it would take. Or the DUI laws, for bikes. It's better we take him.'

Serge's face was white, his long body curled up in the foetal position, apart from his injured leg.

Nate walked back over to the car, wiping his forehead. As he passed he said, 'You OK?' and put his hand on Rosie's arm for a second. He opened the boot and located a first-aid kit, muttering, 'Jesus Christ,' as he returned to Serge. She watched Nate wiping Serge's temple, and Serge wincing like a small boy, while Isla held his hand.

Les Urgences

Centre Hospitalier du Pays d'Aix

11.55 P.M.

The waiting area for *Urgences* felt miserably real. When Isla had appeared – backlit by headlights – Serge had wondered if he was having some kind of near-death experience. But then he had seen Nate Kennedy, and concluded that his action hero competence was too plausible to be a mirage. Nate had covered him with his own jacket, and Serge had vomited over it – apologising profusely as he did so, as if to seal his shame completely.

Rosie had approached next, holding tissues at arm's length, while Nate adjusted the passenger seat for Serge. By this point everything felt too mundane and undignified to be a near-death experience. Nate had helped him to the car, almost carrying him, and into the front seat. As they drove, Nate said things like, 'You OK, my friend? Let me know if you need to throw up,' so that Serge felt even more pathetic. Rosie and Isla had sat in the back, saying nothing. Serge was in too much pain to dwell on this.

Now the four of them were sitting in a row of plastic chairs in the emergency department, waiting to be seen. A slow-moving nurse with a strong Marseille accent summoned him to triage. Isla asked Rosie to translate, in an awkward replay of Huck's accident. The three of them followed the nurse through double doors, Serge leaning on Isla. Each step sent a jolt through his body.

They all walked into a tiny, antiseptic-smelling room, and the nurse looked briefly at his injuries. Serge explained the accident to Rosie, while she translated his account into French. The nurse listened, without judgement or apparent interest. Rosie was behaving as though their strange argument by the marquee had never happened. For all these things, Serge was grateful.

His blood pressure was taken, and during the moment of squeezing, inescapable compression he relived the panic of the crash. How, as he cruised down the winding road to Aix, he had noticed the sign on the handlebars coming untied and getting caught in the front wheel, and had tried to stop but then realised – with mounting panic – that the brakes weren't working properly, that the bike was little more than an ornament. He remembered the shocking turbulence when he tried to stop with his feet, and then the chaos of skidding and the force of the impact. For a while he had lain by the road, winded, the bike wheels still spinning in the stillness. He had only realised the warmth on his face was blood when he touched it, finding there was enough to coat his fingers. He did not know if he had called Isla to punish her, or because she was the only person he wanted. Perhaps both.

After the phone cut out he had tried to stand, limped a few steps and then lain back down dizzily, wondering if Isla would come or if he might die as a result of a remote wedding venue. While he lay in the road, he thought of the day the twins were born, and how astonishingly perfect their miniature, greyish faces had looked. That was the last time he had seen so much blood.

Having taken his vital signs and examined his injuries more closely, the nurse said that Serge warranted a doctor's assessment. She sent them back to the waiting room, and Rosie and Nate went to the hospital café, poised to return if further translation were needed. He and Isla were alone now. The pain in his knee had dulled to a throb.

An old woman in a lilac dressing gown walked in and began shrieking that she had the right to '*fumer*'. Serge knew that he and

Isla could have laughed at this, once, and that Isla would have said the woman was her spirit animal. But Isla was on the phone to the babysitter, giving a sanitised account of events.

He saw Isla and Daniel in the private room, again, convulsed with laughter the way he never made her laugh any more. She had looked relaxed – like herself, like she used to before motherhood. He hoped the image of her righting her strap was not going to haunt him for ever. It was terrifying, how one tiny gesture could wreck something sacred. He hated that she and Daniel had sneaked into a room where he had happy childhood memories, too. She hung up, and they sat both looking straight ahead at a water cooler.

'Where were you even going?' she said, after a while.

Serge didn't answer. He wanted to make it hard for her.

'Serge? Please, Serge. Talk to me. Why did you do it? Was it everything today? The thing in the paper? Your parents?'

He couldn't tell if she was playing dumb, or really didn't understand how it had felt to find her alone with Daniel. Eventually, sounding desperate, she said, 'Because of us? Daniel?'

'What d'you think? You went off with him. Alone. After you'd been flirting with him all weekend.'

'He had weed! That's all we were doing. I mean, yeah, OK, I was angry with you. I'm still angry. Obviously. But he and I, we were just smoking.'

'Oh great. So you were just getting high together? That's nice.'

A disconcertingly young doctor appeared, clearly understanding this comment.

'Er, Serge Camp-bell? Please, come through,' she said, in an impressive English accent.

They both stood up, and he told Isla not to come but she followed anyway. He was relieved not to need Rosie's translation again.

They were shown to a curtained bay, and the doctor asked Serge to lie on the high hospital bed. It was difficult to accomplish this with dignity, because his body felt so battered. Isla sat in a chair beside the bed, twisting a tissue like a rosary.

The doctor began inspecting his wounds, and asking questions. Serge felt repellent, aware that his breath smelled of sick as he attempted to say occasional words in French, with self-deprecating laughter, and the doctor answered in fluent English. Her white smile and crisp parting made him feel even worse, so that when she washed her hands after touching him he felt it was more than protocol.

She recommended Serge remain in the bay for observation, as was standard for all head injuries, and left. She drew the paper curtain after her, as if concealing Serge from view, her feet tapping smartly down the corridor. He stared at a sharps bucket to avoid looking at Isla.

'You don't have to stay,' he said, after a while. It sounded surly, but he meant it. Sitting in silence was worse than solitude.

He glanced over, and saw her face was about to collapse into crying. It tugged something inside him, and he hated that she still had this effect.

'I'm not leaving you,' she said. 'You shouldn't be by yourself.'

'It's fine. Really.'

Forming words felt exhausting. He shunted himself onto his less bruised side, his back to her, and his body screamed in protest at the motion. She didn't reply, but after a moment he realised that this was because she was weeping. He considered turning back to her, but his left side hurt too much.

'When I saw you in the road, I thought I'd lost you,' she said. 'I actually thought you were dead.'

Her voice cracked on 'lost', like a pubescent boy's. He used to think of her sudden emotional displays as passionate, like August thunder, but now it seemed histrionic.

'Isla, I'm sorry, OK,' he said. His voice sounded flat. 'I wasn't thinking. It was really stupid. But I can't talk now. Go back to the twins. I'll get a cab later.'

'No, Serge! The twins are fine,' she said. 'I'll wait outside, if you prefer. But I'm not leaving you here. I can't leave you.'

He didn't have the energy to reply. Pain clamped his forehead. He closed his eyes against the neon lights. The wipe-clean mattress reminded him of the sanatorium at his school, and begged him to rest. After an expectant pause he heard Isla sigh and stand up, and the curtain's rattle. Then there was only the quietness of her absence, and the noises of the hospital.

Surrey, August 2004

Rosie is lying on a lawn with her sister Kate, at their parents' house. They are flicking through copies of *Heat* magazine. Bumblebees lurch around the hollyhocks. Rosie's phone buzzes and she sits up.

'What?' says Kate.

'It's Serge.'

'Oh yeah? What's he saying?'

'"Hey Rosie, how's it going?" Kiss.'

Kate raises her eyebrows twice, in quick succession.

'It's not like that,' says Rosie, beginning to type.

'It is. Hanging out the whole time doesn't magically make it platonic. What are you replying?'

'Nothing, just, "Hey Serge, all's well, busy-busy interning! How's Italia? Have a gelato for me!"'

'Gelato? Random.'

'He's in Italy. They've got a house there. Caspar's going out next week.'

'Why hasn't he invited you to his palazzo?'

Rosie ignores her sister, and stares at her phone like a crystal ball. It pings again, and she reads out Serge's message.

'"Italia's all good, thanks. Just a quick one, has Daniel mentioned my sister? She says he was all over her at the ball, took her number, etc, but never got in touch. She's gutted. And I'm pretty pissed off." Knew this would happen,' says Rosie, more to herself than Kate.

'Wait, Daniel Pyke?' says Kate. 'Lucky bitch. I still don't get why you don't fancy him?'

'Because. I mean, obviously I love him as a friend. But he's like a girl.'

'Did you know about him and Serge's sister?' says Kate.

'Yeah, but he said she made the first move.'

'So who d'you believe?'

'I mean, Daniel wouldn't lie. To me. But he's such a flirt. Like, even more than he realises. So she probably got completely the wrong idea.'

'Why's it all this big secret, though?'

'Daniel said Allegra made him swear not to tell anyone. Especially Serge. How the Campbells are really overprotective. So it's weird that she told Serge herself.'

'Don't get involved, then,' says Kate. 'Just say you have no idea. Otherwise you'll get drawn in and it'll be massively awkward cos you're friends with them both. Serge and Daniel.'

'What, just lie? Pretend I know nothing?'

'It's not lying. Daniel wasn't meant to tell you. So he's not going to tell Serge that he told you, right?'

Rosie is looking at her, almost in confusion.

'How about this,' she says, typing. '"Oh no! Maybe speak to Daniel? Have a great rest of holiday."'

'Perfect,' says Kate. 'They'll sort it out. They're adults.'

PART SIX

AUGUST 2019
THE DAY AFTER THE WEDDING

From: Camilla@maxwelltalent.com
To: Daniel@Danielpyke.com
Date: 1 September, 2019, 00:30
Subject: Please give me a call – urgent

Hi darling,

Been trying to get through, could you give me a call when you're up?

Camilla x

Hospital Forecourt

Centre Hospitalier du Pays d'Aix

12.30 A.M.

Isla walked outside and stood in the hospital forecourt. It was muggy with heat and exhaust, lit by tall white streetlights and bordered with spiky, cactus-like plants. After a while she tried her mother, without really knowing why or whether she wanted Saffron's counsel. She paced the tarmac, picturing midnight somewhere in Spain, a swell of tears gathering as she heard her mother's 'Hello?' over the noise of music and voices, perhaps a bar.

For a while Isla stood weeping into the phone, aware of strangers' stares, clearly assuming that she was relaying tragic news. Her mother began saying 'Babe? Isla? Babe, what's happened?' and she forced herself to stop crying and explain.

Saffron kept saying 'Go on', and 'Say more', even when Isla described Serge's debts. She knew her mother had acquired this new manner from therapy, but she was grateful not to be interrupted. She came to the end, and sat on a dirty white wall.

'Woah,' said Saffron. She exhaled audibly – probably a roll-up. 'You had me worried there. Thought it might be one of the babbers.'

'But he could have died! I thought he had, when I saw him.'

'I know, gorge, I know.'

'What d'you think I should do?'

'Do you need to do anything?'

'But I mean, when I saw him like that – bleeding – it was like none of the rest of it mattered. Even the money, whatever. I just wanted him to be OK. That was all I was thinking.'

'Of course. Of course, mate! You were in shock.'

Her mother's serenity was intolerable. Isla thought of all the times Saffron had talked herself into a hysterical spiral, while Isla tried to calm her.

'But when he walked in, when he saw me with Daniel. His face. He just looked so hurt.'

Her voice peaked and shrank with tears. There was a long pause, and more exhaling.

'Babe, can we just reality-check this?' said her mother. 'You were pissed. A gorgeous man's all over you. Actual bloody sex god. And you walked out of his bedroom, and didn't even snog him.'

She almost laughed at how selective her mother's new emotional intelligence seemed to be.

'That's not the point! I went off, on my own, with him.'

She thought, again, of what more might have happened if Serge hadn't opened the door.

'So? You're on a break! You could have shagged him senseless, you still wouldn't be in the wrong. Men are so possessive.'

'But I don't even want to be on this break! I just want us to be like we were. Before the twins.'

She had not known this was how she felt, until she heard herself say it.

'But they're here now,' said Saffron. 'That's the thing, with kids. No going back.'

Isla said nothing. She watched a father struggling to carry a girl in Snoopy pyjamas towards A&E. He was holding his daughter like a baby, even though she looked at least ten. She was moaning, and he was reassuring her in Arabic. She imagined a fatherless life for the twins.

'And these debts,' said Saffron. 'A million quid! What's that all about?'

'It's film. Production costs are nuts. People let him down. It snowballs.'

She didn't know why she was excusing Serge. She had said the same as Saffron herself, but now, hearing Serge criticised, she felt oddly protective.

'Yeah, but, why didn't he tell you?' said Saffron. 'That's the point. He lied.'

Isla was about to say, 'I'd just given birth. He didn't want to worry me,' but she knew her mother would judge this. She had judged it, herself.

'Like, why's his money so private?' said Saffron, because Isla still hadn't replied.

'It's different for him. For his family. They never talk about money. With me, anyway.'

'You *are* family. You should be involved.'

She knew her mother was right. But money, above a certain level, was a language Saffron didn't speak. Isla hadn't mastered it either. Perhaps Serge should have taught her, though his fluency now seemed doubtful.

'It's just money,' she said. It sounded stupid out loud. What she meant was that Serge's wealth had never mattered to her. In many ways it had only complicated things.

'What, cos his parents will cough up?'

She didn't answer. She had wondered this, of course.

'And what else is going to come out?' said Saffron. 'Bottom line, do you trust him?'

Isla thought, suddenly, of Daniel's account of Serge arguing with Rosie. She realised how badly she wanted Daniel to be mistaken.

'Or, put it another way,' said her mother. 'Does he make you happy?'

'It's not that simple, though. It's so intense with twins—'

'But it should be simple, Isla. That's the whole point. It shouldn't be all drama.'

She started explaining how she and Miguel had no secrets. Isla said she should go.

'OK, night, babe. Go and chill, smoke some more weed,' said Saffron.

Isla stayed sitting in the forecourt, eyes stinging, her chest feeling bruised with emotion.

She had not expected her mother – who was never out of debt – to judge Serge so harshly. It made her feel defensive again, as if she now understood Serge's irrational logic. His manic working, since the twin's birth, had been an effort to spare her anxiety – but she had read it as an attempt to escape. If his debts had not started the week they had become parents, he would have told her. She would not have interpreted his absence as evasion and abandonment. It would all have been different.

She thought about how close she had come to kissing someone else, perhaps more. It made her want to crawl out of her skin, and leave it on the dirty wall.

Le Café

Centre Hospitalier du Pays d'Aix

3 a.m.

Rosie and Nate had been sitting in the hospital's café for nearly three hours. Staff in scrubs came and went, chatting or taking pensive breaks alone. The hours had passed naturally, as if the crisis had accelerated them through years of familiarity. Nate was at the counter ordering more tea. She noticed the dip between his shoulder blades again, as he picked up the cups.

They had been talking so much that she missed Isla's text, sent several hours earlier.

> Serge is OK, just has to stay for obs, so you guys should go. We'll get a cab back. Thank you both so much.

She showed Nate, but neither of them stood or moved.

'What's going on with those two, anyway?' he said.

'They're on a trial separation. His sister told me, but nobody's meant to know.'

'Oh, they're that couple? The ones who get off on fighting and making up?'

'Guess so.'

'I wasn't sure if this was a one-off, or their whole deal.'

At one time, she thought, this statement would have maddened her. She would have taken it as a reflection on her own relationship with Serge, and how she had been too compliant – or reserved – for him. But she now felt more sorry for Isla than envious.

'Were you guys like that?' said Nate. 'When you were together?'

'No! The opposite. I don't think we ever had a fight. In two years.'

'But you and Serge, it seems like it was a big thing, right?'

She hesitated.

'Sorry,' he said, 'if I'm speaking out of turn. Just, your reaction when he was in the paper, yesterday. I got the feeling you still cared for him.'

She remembered her greedy curiosity at Le Grillon, and felt ashamed. Seeing Serge humiliated in the paper she had felt horrified pity – the opposite of attraction.

'I mean, I'd care about anyone in that situation. Being trashed in the press,' she said. 'But if anything, it just made me think I didn't know him. I'd always thought he was so together, that he had this really sound judgement. But it turned out he didn't.'

'Sure,' said Nate. 'But when you were helping out, with his little boy.'

She saw, now, that Nate had been watching her around Serge ever since she had told him about the relationship. But Serge's hysteria by the carousel had only invoked her sympathy, just like the trolling and his debts. A part of her, she knew, had enjoyed the pharmacist's assumption that she was Huckleberry's mother. But she enjoyed being taken for any child's mother.

'And when you guys were speaking, near the sandwich truck,' Nate continued. 'It seemed kind of intense. Like you still had feelings—'

'I overheard his sister,' she interrupted. She found she very much wanted to correct Nate's impression. 'She was being rude about my family. And me.'

'Oh no! That's awful. Did you tell him?'

'Yeah. Which was actually really unlike me. And stupid. Because then it became this whole other conversation.'

'Unfinished business?'

'In a way. Basically his sister was saying how he messed me around. And I guess I realised how annoyed I was, mostly with myself, for never demanding an apology. So it kind of became that conversation. But, it's weird. It was only a few hours ago, but . . .'

She stopped, thinking of Serge curled up by the road like a giant child, and thought how drastically her impression of him had changed over the weekend.

'But now he's dead to you, after that speech?' said Nate. 'Or was it the dancing?'

He was smiling. Even in the fluorescent light, his skin appeared to be made of superior material to other people's.

'Something like that.'

'Sometimes that's all it takes.'

She laughed, but she was thinking how – if that was all it took – there could not have been as much there as she had believed. Allegra was right. She had clung to an idea of Serge – formed when she was nineteen, stunned by his self-assurance, and cosmic eyes. But his eyes were inherited, like so much else about him. And now she was tired of talking about him, or even thinking about him.

They began walking down long grey corridors, Rosie letting Nate find their route out. They passed signs to a cancer ward, intensive care, the birth centre and the chapel. It didn't feel strange to be somewhere as intimate as a hospital. They passed a man pushing a pale child in Snoopy pyjamas in a wheelchair, a nurse walking briskly alongside. The man looked tearful, and Rosie felt emotional herself. Nate put his arm around her, briefly, as if he had seen too. It was friendly, the way Imogen or Caspar might have comforted her, but when Nate withdrew his arm she wanted it back.

They passed *Les Urgences*, and she said:

'It was so typical that Caspar and JP didn't have a single doctor friend when you asked.'

'I know. If we'd been, like, "Is there a minor royal in the building?"'

'Or a Pulitzer.'

'Right. We'd have been fine. Just no medics. Way too sensible.'

They were ejected through automatic doors, back into the world. Outside the stars and clouds were both visible, the air cool.

'Sorry I don't have my jacket,' said Nate. 'Serge threw up on it, remember?'

She made a joke about the cleaning bill, but she was thinking of all the times she and Nate had walked through Oxford at 3 a.m., Rosie wearing his sweaters. They had barely been adults. She wondered if he was thinking the same. She recalled his dancing with Audrey, and how much she hoped it was platonic.

'Not quite the night I had in mind,' he said, as they came to his car.

'I know. It was like a weird double date.'

He looked round, and she saw his dimple. 'That's your idea of a date?'

'No, I just, I mean— they were there, a couple. We were—'

She felt her cheeks flare, but he was smiling.

'You really need to raise your standards, Rosie.'

They got into the car, and she was conscious of being in a cocooned space. She fastened her seat belt, and when she looked up he was watching her and quickly looked away. He took the satnav out of the compartment between their seats, his elbow very close to her leg. Then he began typing the chateau's address, frowning in the silvery light. She noticed how the back of his head was a nice shape, and how his tanned hands moved over the screen.

'Back to the party?' he said, looking up, and she realised how much she liked the way his eyes became crescents when he smiled, too. He started to reverse out of the space with one hand on the wheel, and his other arm over the back of her seat, so that she was almost in his embrace.

They drove through Aix and then passed under a mossy stone archway out of the city, and on to smaller, winding roads. They didn't speak, but the silence was easy. The shoes Caspar had bought her lay in the footwell covered in mud. They were a size too small, though she had not told him. Her toes ached.

'We must have looked insane in A&E. All dressed up,' she said, glancing at Nate's shirt. There was a smear of Serge's blood on it.

'Not as insane as those two.'

'Isn't everyone insane in some way? Even the sanest-seeming people?'

'Like you?' he said.

'Hey! How am I meant to take that?'

'There is no how. Just take it.'

'Don't I have a right to know why you think I'm secretly crazy?'

'There's your insanity. Caring what I think. What anyone thinks.'

She recalled Allegra's comments, and imagined not caring.

'I mean, don't get me wrong, I'm the same,' said Nate.

'You don't seem like that.'

'Of course. Isn't everyone? That was why I drank. I cared too much. I was always trying to figure out who people wanted me to be.'

'I sometimes feel that way,' she said. She remembered the way she used to pretend to have seen certain films when Serge was talking, before and even during their relationship. It was just another version of the way she used to fake orgasms. She could hardly blame Serge for misreading her.

'Like, there are so many versions of myself I don't know which one is really me,' she carried on. 'Or if any of them are.'

They turned onto a tiny road, overhung by trees.

'Do you feel like you now?' he said, slowing down.

'Yes.'

She didn't hesitate, despite what she'd just said. He pulled over and stopped the car, the engine still buzzing. He unclicked his seat belt and leaned towards her. She turned to look at him. He put his hand around the back of her neck, his fingers at the base of her skull, and pulled her face closer to his. For a moment just their foreheads were touching, as if they were transferring thoughts. There was a second of anticipation, before she felt his lips.

Avenue des Tamaris

Aix-en-Provence

5 a.m.

It was light when Isla helped Serge into a taxi outside the hospital. He settled into the seat, avoiding her eyes. The streets were empty, apart from a few unsteady students and shop owners cranking up metal shutters – the end of one day colliding with the next.

Van Morrison's 'Into the Mystic' was warbling out of the radio. Isla recalled it playing in another taxi, on holiday in Barcelona, and Serge singing the lyrics with exaggerated passion and then kissing her for the rest of the journey. She remembered how they were always touching, at that time, their hands knotted on back seats and across tables and arm rests. His hands were far from hers now, and his eyes were closed. The song ended, and she leaned her head on the window, not bothering to wipe away the small tears rolling down her temples.

The cab left Aix, and climbed to Vauvenargues. They drove through the village, passed the crashed bike and turned into the chateau's drive – the gravel crunching in the silence. The marquee looked ghostly in the dawn. Inside the chateau there was the hot heaviness of lots of people sleeping. They walked up to their room without talking and Isla paid the babysitter, thanking her profusely for staying late. When she turned back to the room Serge was lying on the bed – as if he did not want to be under the covers with her.

She thought he might already be asleep, but he said, 'Twins OK?' without opening his eyes.

'They're fine.'

She lay down on the bed, carefully, knowing movement might hurt him.

'We don't have to go to the thing tomorrow?' she said, after a moment. 'If you aren't up for it.'

'I can't. My parents will freak out if I don't.'

It struck her as their first ordinary exchange, all evening.

'I'm sorry,' she said, after a long pause. 'That I upset you. We really were just smoking.'

He opened his eyes now, but spoke to the ceiling.

'But do you not get how hard that was to see? You two. Laughing.' He turned his head to her. 'I don't want someone else to make you happy like that.'

'He doesn't. Didn't. I was just high.'

It sounded feeble. Daniel had made her happy, briefly. But she knew she would never have ended up in the room if she hadn't been furious with Serge.

'You know Daniel was tweeting about me on that thread,' he said. 'From a fake account. It was his tweet that snowballed everything.'

'What? How d'you know?'

'He messed up and tweeted as himself last night. Like, as Daniel Pyke the celebrity, but from this fake account.'

'What was he saying?'

'Just adding to all the privilege stuff. He's always had this class warrior thing.'

She thought of her conversation with Daniel about Oxford and Saint Martins. She had the feeling, again, that she was missing information about Serge and Daniel's past.

'But he's always been really competitive with me,' said Serge. 'Needlessly. Like – I know this is weird for you to hear – but whenever I was seeing anyone at Oxford, or if I liked anyone, he'd try to get there first. It was a bit *Single White Female*.'

She felt foolish now at the thought that Daniel's attention might have been an act of rivalry. She wondered if this was Serge's intention, to make her feel small. It made her want to retaliate. 'He said he saw you and Rosie arguing last night.'

Serge turned his head to look up at the ceiling again.

'Did he? Why does that not surprise me?'

He closed his eyes again, as though the thought of Daniel bored him.

'What, it's not true?'

She turned onto her side, trying to get him to look at her.

'No. It's true. I mean, Rosie came and had a go at me. But why tell you that? What's he trying to achieve?'

'Why was she having a go at you?'

Serge turned now, so that they were both lying on their sides, facing one another.

'She overheard my sister talking about her. Classic Allegra.'

'Oh. Shit. But how was that an argument? Weren't you just grovelling?'

'Yeah, but Rosie started bringing up all this old stuff.'

'What stuff?'

'OK, listen.' He levered himself up on his elbow. 'She had a miscarriage when we were together. It turns out. And she told me yesterday.'

'What? Why didn't she say at the time?'

'Cos, well, obviously it wasn't planned or anything.'

'But you must have known she was pregnant?'

'No. We weren't in touch.'

'Wait – so when was this? After you broke up? Or she got pregnant your last night?'

He looked flustered now.

'It was really soon after we broke up.'

'After? What, you got back with her?'

'No! It was literally, like, a one-off random thing. Nothing. It never happened again.'

She saw him blanch as he realised his mistake – the implication of his tone.

'Hold on, you and I were together?' she said. 'This random one-off time?'

The twins' synchronised breathing was audible in the quiet.

'We were, weren't we?' she said again, her voice rising.

'Just. Not officially. I know I should have told you. I'm sorry. I felt so awful afterwards. That was the thing, it just made me realise how much I didn't want to lose you.'

'When? When was it?'

'Early on. Really early. We'd only been dating a few weeks.'

'But, how did it even happen?'

She wanted and also didn't want to hear his answer.

'I don't even know. It feels like such a different time. Like a different me. Before I knew you. Before the twins.'

She said nothing. He was looking over her shoulder, at the wall behind her.

'I guess I just felt bad,' he said. 'That I'd moved on so fast. Like, she'd realise the whole relationship had been a mistake. For me. I know that sounds shit.'

'It doesn't sound great.'

'And then I felt so guilty, with you. That was the thing – it was like a catalyst. I ended up asking you if we could make things exclusive the day after.'

She remembered his mini proposal, over burgers. He had told her about his money the same day, like a confession. Perhaps, looking back, it had been.

'I'm so sorry,' he said. 'It was so insignificant. It was almost, like, an extension of the break-up. I never contacted her after. That was another thing she brought up last night.'

Isla thought of the argument Daniel had described seeing. It made sense now.

They lay staring at one another, two feet apart on the lace bedspread. She felt shocked, but it was an odd kind of shock – closer to surprise than genuine horror. And it was tempered by something – clarity and relief. They had each wronged the other. Her own transgression, with Daniel, was both more and less of a betrayal than his own with Rosie.

'I don't know what else to say,' said Serge. 'I should've told you. But I felt like I'd just be hurting you to clear my conscience. And you'd never want to see me again. It was you I wanted.'

He lowered his elbow, so that their heads were level on the pillows, still staring at her.

He reached for her hand across the bed. His fingers and thumb and palm were so familiar. They seemed to be asking if she could forgive him.

'You were the only one,' he said.

After a second she weaved her fingers between his and squeezed – the way she used to when he reached for her hand in the street.

Daniel's Room

Chateau de Beaupont

9.30 a.m.

Daniel's ringtone jolted him awake. Camilla was calling. He let it ring, knowing it would be about his Twitter disaster. Even his agent would not call on a Sunday morning, unless it was a crisis. He imagined trying to justify @Gareth32, and longed to hide.

Sunlight was filtering through the curtains, and twice he heard voices outside, but he could not face getting up. He took his Xanax with the inch of tepid water by his bed. He was still sickeningly thirsty and desperate to pee, but his limbs felt paralysed. The room, with its thick drapes and murky palette, was like the bottom of a pond.

Eventually, he managed to shower and pack. He checked Twitter for the fifth time since waking. Nobody seemed to have noted his mistake. Helen Murphy appeared to have lost interest in @Gareth32's likeness to @DanielPykeOfficial. She was now asking her followers for their 'most perverted snacks'. Hundreds of people had responded. Daniel realised that @Gareth32 had probably escaped further questioning. He allowed himself a tentative sense of relief, just enough to get him through the pool party.

It was nearly ten, but when he opened his bedroom door the house around him felt still. The landing was very quiet, dust glittering in a shaft of light. He was halfway down the stairs when he heard someone enter the hall below. It was too late to retreat, and he froze, fearing Serge or Isla.

Nate Kennedy appeared, holding a tray of breakfast things and a bouquet of flowers from the marquee. Daniel nodded at him, without speaking.

'Hey! I feel like you look,' said Nate. 'I mean, no offence. You're up – that's impressive. Have fun?'

'Yeah, yeah. Great party. Yourself?'

'It was eventful.'

'Huh?'

'You didn't hear about Serge?'

'Serge? No. What happened?'

'He and Isla had some biblical fight. And then he went nuts and crashed a bike. He's fine. But I think he's still in the hospital.'

Daniel's stomach lurched.

'Hospital? Fuck! Was it bad?'

'No no, it's all good. Just routine observation. I drove them to the ER. It was a whole drama.'

'Bloody hell. So you'll be, like, hero of the hour at brunch?'

'I'm actually not going. Gotta catch a train. JP's pissed at me, but, hey. We get no vacation in the States. Have to grab every chance.'

He was exhaustingly talkative.

'You get lucky?' said Daniel, nodding at the breakfast and bouquet.

Nate smiled, half sheepish.

'I won't keep you then, sir,' said Daniel, stepping aside.

* * *

Outside, the clean blue sky was jarring. Nate's uncomplicated cheer, bounding upstairs to a naked woman, had induced a melancholy feeling. Daniel wondered why he could not achieve the same easy enjoyment, why he had fixated on Isla, over all the single women at the wedding. He could have slept with any of them – he knew this as an objective truth. Perhaps this was why he did not want them.

It was some consolation, at least, to know that Isla and Serge would not be at the pool party. Daniel decided he would put in a brief appearance, after breakfast in Vauvenargues. He needed something to shake off his hangover and the fug of sleeping tablets. Even as he thought this, he knew he was lying to himself. Just the short exchange with Nate had been taxing. He would need the rest of his cocaine to face a garden full of people. He hoped he and Rosie could continue to ignore one another.

At the bottom of the drive he decided to tweet something innocuous from @DanielPykeOfficial, as if this might bury his other mistake further. There was no point attempting a selfie now when he looked so rough. He found a photo he had taken outside Marseille airport on Thursday, and captioned it 'Au Revoir Provence', suggesting he were about to fly.

It felt briefly reassuring – a tether to his public, presentable life. But as he revved the moped and flew down the road, the mountain up ahead, he wondered if it was a life he wanted any part of.

Nate's Room

Chateau de Beaupont

10.15 a.m.

When Rosie woke, in Nate's turret room, he wasn't in the bed but the shower was running in his en suite. She lay listening to the sound of the water, thinking how long it had been since she had shared anyone's private space.

Her lips felt swollen with kissing, and she was very aware of the crisp sheets around her legs and the sun's warmth already penetrating the room. She thought of Nate's assured kissing – how it had been gentle at first, his hands in her hair and round her shoulders. Then it had become more urgent, his hands moving to her waist and hips. For a second – because he was American and they were kissing in a car – she had thought of the phrase 'making out', and wanted to laugh. But then his tongue had been fluttering against the place below her ear, his palms on her thighs, and she had stopped thinking completely.

She sat up on her elbows, and saw a bouquet of wedding flowers on the windowsill and breakfast things on the dressing table. There was something endearing about the way Nate had arranged the food on the tray and thought of everything she might need. She wished the weekend were not ending.

While the shower was running she got out of his bed and hurried up the spiral staircase, to her own room and bathroom above. When she had brushed her teeth she began to apply some natural-looking blusher – as she always did when she woke up beside someone new. But when she met her own eyes in the mirror, it seemed mad. Kissing Nate was new, but he was not.

The shower was still running when she walked back into Nate's room. She now noticed a packed suitcase that she hadn't seen before. She had hoped that they might have the morning together – perhaps leave the pool party early. She realised, now, how much she would have liked to spend the whole day with him. Or even to go with him to Nice, and then to Italy. She got back into bed, disappointment rising.

The shower stopped, and he came into the room in a towel. She wanted to stare at his body, and wished he had not already seen she was awake so that she could have studied his back and shoulders through half-closed eyes.

'Morning. I found the Earl Grey,' he said, glancing at the breakfast tray.

He was wearing boxers now, his skin still shining from the shower. He sat on the bed, and reached out a hand to her hip. His palm felt very warm through the sheet.

'I wish we would've done this sooner,' he said.

She thought of their walk through Aix to the hotel, on Thursday evening, and the way he had rescued her in the dance rehearsal and touched her face after she choked on Campbell Champagne, and all the other times they had ended up alone, or finding each other in a crowd. It seemed obvious, looking back, that she had wanted Nate – from when she first saw him helping Zach at the softball. She remembered the pang of watching him dance with Audrey, and the date-like feeling of their coffee on the Cours Mirabeau, and his pensive expression when she told him Serge was in the paper. She could blame Serge for her blindness, but it was her own fault.

Nate picked up her hand and stroked her palm with his thumb. She felt an ache of wanting him as he leaned over to kiss her. The kiss was tender, his lips parting hers, but when she reached up to his warm, damp neck he began to sink down onto her – like he had done when they had first lain on his bed in the dawn light. They had ended up undressed but had not had sex, preserving the sweet, almost teenage mood of the kiss in the car. Now she wished they had slept together. Kissing was too sweet. And it was too throwaway, too one-off, too easily left at 'this was fun'.

He smelled of the shower, and she wrapped her legs around him through the sheets. Their tongues seemed to be having a private conversation, as their hips pushed against each other. But after a moment she became aware that the rest of his body was pulling back, and that the kiss was ending.

'It's too bad we live in different continents,' he said. He was looking at her intently, their faces very close. The words sounded final, but she sensed he was asking something. She felt as if she could say: 'Change your ticket, don't go today,' or 'Take me with you!' or even 'Why don't I quit my job and come to New York?' but she didn't.

'I know,' she said.

'We should—'

'Emigrate?' she interrupted.

It was supposed to sound playful, a little test of his interest without losing face. But it came out almost sarcastic, as though his earnestness amused her.

Nate laughed, but she saw his expression shift – taking his cue from her tone.

He leaned forwards and kissed her again, as if he couldn't help himself, but it was a regretful, goodbye kiss, not the start of anything.

He stood up, and began to dress. Once he had started, he seemed to move rapidly. She sat marooned in the bed, holding the sheet against her chest. She wanted to tell him to stop, not to go, that she had not meant to say 'Emigrate?' in the superior, cynical tone. But she seemed to be mute. The closer he came to being ready – T-shirt, watch, shoes, running something through his hair – the less possible it felt to speak.

She wondered if he would suggest they keep in touch, though she could not imagine how this would work. She didn't want to become pen pals. But she didn't know how to suggest the alternative, that one of them fly to stay with the other. Perhaps the night was better left as a perfect memory.

When he was dressed he came back over to the bed, and hugged her for one warm second.

'OK, bye then, Rosie,' he said. 'So good to see you. You know where I am.'

She listened to him walking down the spiral staircase, his suitcase thumping on each stone step – until she couldn't hear anything.

Villa des Pavots

Le Tholonet

12 p.m.

Daniel arrived late at the pool party, having stopped for three coffees and several cigarettes to offset his hangover, and then all his remaining cocaine in the café's bathroom. Camilla had sent another message saying, 'Darling, please call, it's important,' but he still had not replied. He could not face trying to explain his mistake, and hearing her plans for damage limitation.

He stood outside Caspar's parents' house alone, sweating, aware that he needed to emerge from his helmet. When he did, the roar of over-lapping conversations assaulted his ears. He tried to breathe, taking in the Campbell villa, but his lungs refused to fill – as if it were a bitterly cold day.

Someone directed him through the house, full of kilim rugs and abstract art and antique furniture, to the orchard. Brunch was laid on a long table near the swimming pool. Everyone was sitting on blankets and deckchairs under cherry trees, looking like rubbed-out versions of themselves. Caterers offered cocktails nobody wanted, while wasps crowded the platters of fruit and untouched kedgeree.

He took a Bloody Mary from a tray and drank it too fast, appreciating the vodka and trying not to gag on the ketchupy juice. The sun was very bright, despite a boisterous wind. He gave his empty glass to a waiter and took another, gulping it as he walked towards Caspar by the pool. He heard a familiar laugh above the barrage of voices, and looked for it in the crowd. Serge was standing near the brunch table, with Isla, facing away from Daniel. His breath quickened. He knew he should leave, now, but Serge turned. Their eyes met over Isla's head – like in the private room. Serge looked shocked, and then irritated. Daniel realised he was walking over to him, near the pool but away from the rest of the party.

'Hey man. Thought you'd gone?' he said. The tone was too aloof to qualify as angry. His chin was raised, as if to reassert whatever he'd lost when he fled the chateau. Isla glanced at Daniel, and then down at her drink. The change in her floored him, almost more than Serge's hostility.

'Sergio,' said Daniel. He made himself smile. 'Likewise. Nate said you were in ER? You good?'

'And you're at the airport? According to one of your Twitter accounts.'

Daniel immediately regretted the pint of tomato juice in his stomach. Serge was looking straight at him. Daniel wondered how his eyes could be so infantile and so powerful all at once.

'Yeah, well. PR, mate,' said Daniel. 'Morning flight, afternoon, same difference.'

'Great PR move. Tweeting from the wrong account.'

Serge had dropped his voice to scathing, and Daniel lowered his own in response.

'Let's not do this now,' he said. He nodded over at the grooms, though it was his own dignity he feared for.

'No, let's do this,' said Serge. 'You were trolling me, literally just before we met up!'

A fleck of Campbell saliva landed on Daniel's cheek. He had a bizarre sensation of something inside him bending and straining, approaching fracture.

'Look, man,' Serge was saying, 'if you're still pissed off about *Bursary*, or whatever –'

'*Bursary*, or *whatever*? You serious?'

He felt a release as he spoke, as if all the stimulants in his body had broken a dam and were now free to gush through his veins.

'You claimed our idea!' he carried on. 'No apology, no reason, just cut me out. After you'd been all "Come to Italy, come meet Miles Whitehall!" And you still aren't acknowledging it, even now. It was off, mate. Really off.'

He expected Serge to cave, but he looked annoyed instead. Daniel fought an urge to shove him into the swimming pool. He could picture Serge's long arms windmilling, his Disney eyes wide open as he hit the blue water.

'Listen, I'm sorry if you were pissed off,' said Serge. 'But you know it wasn't that simple. It's not like you haven't done well for yourself. And if we're talking about not acknowledging—'

'You still don't get it, do you?' said Daniel, interrupting again. 'You never will. That's the thing that pisses me off. Guys like you getting the breaks, while people with genuine stories – actual, lived experience – don't stand a chance. Because they can't live rent free, and they don't have famous godparents. And then acting so woke. "Film For All"! The depressing thing is I think you believe your own hype.'

The Pool

Villa des Pavots

12.10 P.M.

Serge could feel the argument sliding out of his control. He had been about to confront Daniel about Allegra, but now – as always – he was forced to apologise for his DNA.

'Don't make this about that,' he said. He meant it as a warning, but it sounded weak.

'It is about that, though!' said Daniel. 'That's the point! I never had the luxury of saying, "Don't make this about that." I actually had to work to get where I am. And now you're back, begging me to be in your next film cos you maxed out your trust fund.'

He was ranting, but photogenically, as if he had rehearsed these lines. Serge knew it was not the moment to clarify that he did not technically have a trust fund.

'Cos, *now* you need me,' Daniel continued. 'Now you *want* someone like me in your gritty film. But back then I was just some chav from uni. No place for me in your script. Or your real life. Just good material.'

For a second Serge was so surprised, and then insulted, he couldn't answer.

'You think I went ahead with *Bursary* because I'm a snob?' he said. 'Why would you even think that? It literally never occurred to you I didn't want you around my sister?'

'Your sister? What are you talking about?'

'You know what I'm talking about! You screwed her over, and then you expect me to be like "Come to Italy, let's make sweet music". I was pissed off. I didn't want you around her.'

Daniel looked baffled for a second, and then incredulous.

'We even talking about the same night?' he said. 'That was nothing!'

Serge dropped his voice. 'It wasn't nothing for her.'

'Mate, give me a break! Are you joking?'

Daniel laughed – a hollow, stage laugh. Isla stepped closer to Serge. It was helpful, in its show of silent solidarity.

'You can dismiss it, Dan, OK?' he said. 'But Allegra relapsed because of you. Stopped eating. She'd been better for a year. Then you made her feel like shit, and, yeah, that was it. She's still sick now.'

For a second Daniel looked shocked, then bewildered.

'Listen, I'm sorry she's not well,' he said. 'Genuinely. The industry's a bitch. But that's insane to blame me. And look, you could've come and talked to me, sorted it out. Don't just give me the silent treatment. We were friends!'

Rosie walked up to them, looking concerned. Serge remembered, now, her accusations about silence, and past friendship.

'Look, forget it,' said Daniel. 'I don't even know why I was surprised about *Bursary*. Doesn't even matter, now. I don't need your—'

'Dan, maybe this isn't the time—' said Rosie.

Daniel turned to her.

'Oh, right. Take his side. As usual.'

'What?' Rosie half laughed, but it sounded nervous. 'I'm not taking sides!'

'Not taking *sides*? Do me a favour!'

He laughed, not the actorly chuckle, but a mad sounding squawk.

'Don't have a go at Rosie!' said Serge.

'Oh, here we go. Be her knight in armour,' said Daniel. 'You two have always been like this.'

Two spots of pink coloured Rosie's cheeks.

'Like what?' said Serge.

'You and Rosie. Something's going on. Hundred per cent.'

Rosie opened her mouth to speak but Serge said, 'Is this the bullshit you were giving Isla? You're paranoid, man. You shouldn't smoke so much weed.'

The Pool

Villa des Pavots

12.13 P.M.

Conversations were faltering around them, so that Serge's words rang out around the orchard. Isla looked at Daniel. A vein was protruding from his temple, looking soft and alive. She wondered how she could have wanted to kiss him.

'*Paranoid?*' he said. 'Doesn't take a genius to see what's going on.'

'Dan, stop! Please!' said Rosie. 'Why are you doing this?'

'Why am I doing this? Why were you acting so weird in the cloakroom? That's the question! Why did you lie about Serge's cufflinks?'

He crossed his arms, as if he was acting a triumphant attorney. Rosie was staring at him. There was no eager curiosity, or rapt concern. Her face and body were still. It was the first time Isla had seen her dynamic femininity drop.

'Cufflinks?' said Serge. He stepped closer to Isla, so that they were touching.

'Yup. I found Rosie literally holding your cufflinks, in the cloakroom at the sculpture place,' said Daniel. 'Trying to, I dunno, sneak them back into your stuff. Or something. She said they were Caspar's. Like I'm a moron. Like I can't see your initials, right in front of me.'

Isla's insides plummeted. She had found a pair of cufflinks in the changing bag, when she had packed it for Serge on Saturday morning. It had seemed unremarkable – Serge was always blasé about valuables.

'Come on! Just admit it!' said Daniel, his voice rising. 'Why else does Rosie have your lame little monogrammed cufflinks? Why is she lying about it? It's ludicrous! Be honest, for Isla's sake!'

He was shouting now, his face fixed in a crazed smile. Cutlery and crockery stopped moving, as people stared. Juno and Huck looked up at Isla in alarm. She realised how desperately she wanted Daniel to be mistaken.

Rosie stepped towards them. When she first opened her mouth there was just a small phlegmy noise, like when the twins spoke after milk.

'I, I was returning them,' she said. 'The cufflinks. In the cloakroom. I put them in the changing bag so you'd get them back. I didn't want it to be a big deal.'

'Not a big deal!' said Daniel. 'They have kids together!'

'No, no! Dan, stop!' said Rosie. She was almost laughing, but her face and neck were now crimson. 'The cufflinks, I've had them for years.'

'Why didn't you just give them back to me?' said Serge.

Rosie looked at him.

'I took them from your flat,' she said. 'When we broke up. I mean, God, this is so mortifying. I just wanted to get them back to you, not discuss it. I'm sorry. That's all it was.'

Nobody said anything. Isla knew it was too humiliating to be a lie. She suddenly liked Rosie more, despite Serge's confession to sleeping with her.

'Look, this is mad, can we please stop talking about these cufflinks?' she said.

Daniel was staring at Rosie, as if Serge and Isla were not there.

'But why did you lie?' he said to her. 'To me? Why didn't you just say that, in the cloakroom? You could have told me. You would have. Once.'

Rosie looked away, without replying.

'Right. Push me out,' said Daniel. 'Again. NFI.'

Caspar and JP walked over, their Hawaiian shirts at odds with the tension.

'What's up?' said JP.

'Nothing,' said Serge. 'Dan, let's talk later? Properly. Not here.'

'No, Serge. Let's not. I don't want to talk to you. I'm done with you lording it over me.'

'*Lording* it?'

'You literally called me "Pikey" yesterday. So, yeah. Go fuck yourself, mate.'

He turned to leave, and slammed straight into a waiter carrying a platter of kedgeree. He swore, as half of it spilled down his white T-shirt. There was some nervous laughter in the hush, as the waiter began apologising in French.

'Actually, d'you know what?' said Daniel, turning to the laughter, as if he was taking a curtain call. 'You can ALL go fuck yourselves!'

He grabbed the platter out of the waiter's hands, and flung it into the swimming pool. He was already striding out of the garden before Isla had registered what had happened.

'Uh-oh!' said Huck, in the silence that followed the huge splash.

An explosion of rice and haddock bobbed on the surface, while the platter made its descent. A moped revved as catering staff surrounded the pool, scooping hard-boiled eggs out of the water with long nets.

The Orchard

Villa des Pavots

1 p.m.

The pool was covered, and still unusable. Everybody was chatting and laughing as before, but the spectacle of the row lingered. Rosie was lying on an antique campaign bed in a corner of the orchard. It was sunny but blustery, and barbecue smoke was now blowing around the party. She closed her eyes and listened to fragments of conversation, as patches of light chased across her eyelids.

She noticed that she didn't feel self-conscious, sitting alone this way, as she once would have. Her confession to theft – which should have been mortifying – had been strangely cathartic, like shedding her old self.

Still, there was sadness under the release. It was clear that her friendship with Daniel could not be salvaged. He was too damaged, she could see, for her to truly resent his wild accusations – or even his attempt to humiliate her in public. She felt foolish now for having hoped they might retrieve their bond after fifteen years. He was a completely different man to the funny, striking, precocious boy she remembered.

She found she wanted to tell Nate about the row, though she had only really heard its dramatic ending. But she and Nate had already exchanged two rounds of finalities – more would be excessive. He had sent her a WhatsApp message after he left, saying:

> One more goodbye, from Marseille x

Rosie had replied:

> Au revoir. Have a great trip x

Now she wished she said something more personal, or had added a question, or photo, to prolong the exchange. She kept reliving a particular moment, when they were deep into their kiss in his car and he had pulled her onto his lap. She had to stop, she thought. He was going back to New York.

She opened her eyes, for distraction. On the other side of the pool Serge and Isla were sitting with the twins, who were naked and eating burgers the size of their faces. Isla looked exhausted. Serge was chatting and laughing with JP's friends, as if he hadn't disrupted another day of the wedding. After a moment, Isla walked over to the brunch table. On her way back, their eyes met. Isla seemed to hesitate for a second. There was a diffidence in her posture that made her seem younger than before. Rosie wondered if she was going to say something. But she just smiled, and nodded slightly. Then she walked past to where Serge was laughing with a ninety-year-old Campbell aunt, as if he was giving a masterclass in social ease.

Caspar approached Rosie now, so she sat up.

'Hi mister,' she said.

'Hey,' he said on an outbreath. He sat on the end of her campaign bed.

'This is all lovely,' she said, knowing it sounded half-hearted.

'Right. Shame there had to be so much drama. Again. Bloody actors!'

It was an old phrase that Caspar and Serge used to level at Daniel, and other thespians, whenever they were particularly emotional.

Rosie leaned forwards to hug him. He received it limply, then sat looking at a mossy urn.

She considered distracting him with an account of her kiss with Nate, but she didn't want it reduced to gossip.

'Have you thought about the surrogacy?'

The question caught her off guard. His eyes were pleading. She knew that if she just said yes, now, she could rewrite his wedding weekend that had veered off course.

She was about to say, 'I need longer to decide.' But she stopped, aware that this was dishonest. She did not need more time. She would have to disappoint him.

'I mean, I'm so sorry, Cas. I can't. I know it's not what you wanted to hear.'

'You can't?'

'No. It doesn't feel like the right thing, for me.'

She thought of what Nate had said about being a mother at one remove.

'What? Oh. OK. But... you seemed so into it?'

He was trying to keep his face neutral, but she could see he was bewildered.

'I know. I'm really sorry. I shouldn't have given you that impression.'

'Oh, OK,' he said again. 'I just, I guess I thought you wanted kids, a baby, so much?'

'I do. That's why I can't do it this way. I don't want to be a third party. I know you said I'd be involved. I'm sure it works for some people. But I'd just always feel like I was at one remove.'

Caspar looked down, but didn't protest.

'I'm sorry you were expecting me to say yes,' she said. 'I'd love for you guys to have a family. I'm here to help in any other way. When you do.'

'No worries. I get it. Thanks, anyway.'

He tried to smile, but he looked defeated. She waited to feel panic at disappointing him, but all she felt was relief that it was done. He said he ought to go and mingle, and stood up. His posture was stiff as he walked away.

Across the pool Allegra began shouting, 'Pa, could you be any more Chekhovian?' and Rosie thought of the energy she had expended trying to decipher the Campbells. She could never have spent Christmases and school holidays in their daunting houses as a third parent, or a semi-in-law. Even the thought – all the priceless clutter and obscure references to the Bloomsbury Group – put her on edge. The strange thing was that she had entertained it at all.

She took out her phone and wrote another message to Nate, almost without thinking.

> Ps I told Caspar I couldn't be their donor/surrogate/co-parent. Didn't go down well.

A double reply flashed up before the screen had time to lock itself.

> Nobody puts Rosie in the corner.

> But also, will speak to JP. They'll understand, it's all good x

Grande Roue de Marseille Ferris Wheel

Marseille Harbour

1.15 p.m.

Daniel's body was still pumping with adrenaline when he screeched into Marseille harbour on the moped. He had maintained the same level of righteous, almost delirious, rage all the way from Villa des Pavots, arriving in the city hours before his flight. There was a huge Ferris wheel on the quayside. On impulse, he decided to try it.

He held the steward's eyes as he requested fifteen tickets for himself alone, daring the man to comment. Already, he was shaping the moment into an anecdote: 'My flight wasn't for hours. So I was like, sod it, I'm gonna chill on a Ferris wheel.'

His carriage was little more than a giant basket, with no cover, or even a safety harness. It swung, gently, in the wind as it began to climb. There were families and couples in some of the other baskets, but they seemed remote, as if Daniel was alone on the wheel. The whole structure was even taller than it appeared from below. The ground was soon dizzyingly far away, the sea in the harbour a flat, plasticky blue, the tugboats returning him to childhood bath times. It was colder up here, and quiet. The only sounds were distant traffic and the mechanism's sudden disconcerting clanks.

He reached the crest of the wheel and his carriage stopped

completely, as if demanding reflection. With his new perspective, an unease began to replace the vindication. The details were blurry, though he remembered everyone arguing about the cufflinks. Gradually, more of the preceding conversation came back to him. The words he had been waiting to say to Serge started to replay in his head, but he recalled them now with a kind of dread. It seemed unfathomable that he had behaved this way, in public.

He saw himself the way the other guests must have seen him – ranting, intimidating, out of control. He had been high at midday, around children. He had thrown a plate of food into his host's swimming pool. He felt incredulous now, as if he was thinking back over someone else's actions. He had disgraced himself more thoroughly, and more ostentatiously, than ever before. Worse, he had ruined Caspar's wedding. Caspar Campbell, his only friend from university – perhaps his only real friend, anywhere. He could not bear to think about Rosie, and the things he had said to her.

His carriage sank until it reached the pavement, which already felt unnaturally low, as if the sky was his new element. After a moment's changeover, it began another circuit. This time he was braced for the vertigo. Shame was churning through him; worse than shame – despair. Serge knew about @Gareth32. Even with the account deleted, he would find a way to expose Daniel. That was inevitable. He peered further over the side, daring himself to lean too far, thinking of his father. A seagull wheeled close to his head, and he ducked with a stupid shout of fear.

He would never jump, he knew. He could not do it to his mother. He was too cowardly anyway – scared of a bird. But he would welcome a sudden, horrific malfunction from the wheel. The plunge would be quick. And a tragic death would absolve him of his final, disgraceful morning and his pathetic troll account. The Campbells were probably still discussing him, 'the mad little actor'. He could see Marina's amused disbelief. He was the most absurd and laughable kind of man. He felt deeply homesick, a yearning like grief.

His phone began vibrating. It was Camilla, again.

'Mills!' he said, trying to summon the bold, sociable voice he used with her. 'How's tricks?'

'Fine, fine, darling. And you? Sound a bit worse for wear?'

It was coming, he thought. Her disappointed rebuke, a lecture about tweeting while drunk.

'Now, gorgeous, I've been trying to get hold of you,' she said. 'It's your mother.'

He was at the apex of the wheel again, the carriage lurching lightly.

'Mum?'

'Yes. Your mother. She was trying to reach you yesterday.'

'Is she OK?'

His mother was in trouble, and he was marooned on a Ferris wheel in another country.

'Ah, well, not quite. She had a break-in yesterday. While she was at home. So she was very shaken. Understandably!'

He remembered ignoring Cheryl's calls now. One had come before the wedding ceremony, when he was doing a quick line in the chapel – the Virgin Mary watching sadly from the wall. The second call had been near midnight, when he was panicking about Twitter. He wondered if the first call had been during the break-in, if she had been cowering in the bathroom while thieves ransacked their home. The world swung below him. A vision of masked men smashing windows crossed his mind, and blood swooshed in his ears.

'Well, she wisely ran out to the garden and fortunately this sweet neighbour was hanging out the laundry, and helped her over the wall.'

Camilla sounded almost tickled, as if she were picturing a scene in *Coronation Street*.

'What did they nick? Did the police come?'

'Some jewellery, I'm afraid. So violating! But she was fine, the police arrived. It was the shock more than anything. She still sounded quite rattled when she rang last night. Being back in the house, on her own. Lucky I was in the office. On a Saturday night! *Plus ça change.*'

It was touching to think of his mother knowing his agent's number, the way she used to chaperone him to auditions. Then it struck him as a miserable indictment. If he were a normal person, with friends, she could have called someone at the wedding.

'God, I'm so sorry. I saw Mum's calls, I just didn't think—'

'I know, I know. You're away. But look, d'you think you might call her, darling? I'm sure she'd love to hear from you. I didn't want to panic you last night. We know what you're like!'

She didn't elaborate on his mental instability, so he thanked her and hung up. His carriage descended and he sat looking at the view without seeing it, remembering how he had half wanted the wheel to malfunction. He imagined his mother getting that call, and felt a new wave of self-loathing.

At the bottom he gave his remaining tickets to a large family at the front of the queue, and dialled his childhood landline. When his mother recited the number, the way she always answered the phone, his voice disintegrated.

'Mum, it's me. I'm sorry.'

He began sobbing on the quayside, in front of the people he had just given his tickets to. They looked worried, as if perhaps they should not have taken them.

'Daniel, love, don't cry. I'm fine. Could've been so much worse. It's only stuff! And they didn't get my wedding jewellery. Dad must've been up there, looking down. And Denise next door was brilliant.'

She stopped, waiting for a reply. Then, when none came, she said: 'It was a job getting me over the wall! We both needed a brandy!'

He was crying too hard to speak.

'Sweetheart, stop it! You weren't to know! You couldn't have done anything, anyway.'

'But, Mum, I didn't even call back. I was so wrapped up in all this stuff.'

His nose was running. He was beyond caring if anyone recognised him. They wouldn't, anyway. He was an adult sobbing, 'Mum,' with snot everywhere.

'What stuff?'

He tried to answer but it was a gasp – as if he was drowning.

'Come home, Danny,' she said. 'Just come home.'

Lucian & Marina's Car

Route Cézanne

5 p.m.

Serge's parents had asked to drive him back to Hotel Georgette, while Isla followed with the twins. Earlier, he had attributed his accident to 'everything with Isla', and sensed that his vagueness had alarmed them more than details.

He was now sitting in his old position in the back of the car, behind his mother, so that all he could see around the headrest were the pearls tugging her earlobes. His father's hair was whiter and sparser than it used to be. He realised how rarely he was physically close to his parents. The fact of their mortality came over him, for a second.

They established whether or not one of them had the other's glasses, and as they drove past a modern villa his mother said, 'What a hideous building.' After that, nobody spoke.

Eventually his father said, 'What was the kerfuffle about? Earlier?'

'We just saw the celebrant throwing the kedgeree,' said his mother. 'Too revolting!'

'Daniel. He's still bitter about Oxford,' said Serge.

'Oxford?' said Marina. 'Honestly! Why must people be so touchy?'

Being 'touchy' was high on Marina's list of things people shouldn't be. Once, Serge had tried to point out that it was easy not to take offence when your life was charmed. But his mother had found his earnest talk of privilege comic, and he had given up.

'The trouble is the internet's made it normal to take offence,' she added. 'Years later!'

'God awful business,' said Lucian.

'Can't anyone let bygones be bygones?' said Marina. 'I suppose they're all having therapy.'

He thought of Rosie's attempt to express her grievances the previous evening, and how she used to be incapable of conflict. He had been surprised, just as he had been by her standing up to Daniel, and confessing to theft – though he found that he liked the idea of Rosie doing something unpredictable. He wondered if he owed her some kind of formal thanks, for getting him to hospital so soon after their argument by the bacon sandwich van. Almost at the same time he registered that what he really owed Rosie – and had done for years – was an apology.

'But you and Isla?' said his mother, cutting into his thoughts. 'That's all that matters.'

'We're fine now,' he said, briskly. 'Just need to figure stuff out.'

It was not the whole truth, but it didn't feel like a lie, either. He and Isla had fallen asleep half holding hands on top of the bedspread – as if the worst had passed – and all day they had been careful and courteous around each other. Still, he knew they needed to talk, alone.

'Of course. But you shouldn't be at odds over money,' said Marina. She said 'money' the way other people might refer to 'the dishwasher'.

'It isn't just money. Wasn't.'

He felt inept and adolescent, as if his mouth were full of wool, addressing the backs of their heads.

'Well, no. Of course. It's never just one thing. So do say if we can help you. Why not come and stay for a while?'

'We really had no idea you were so up against it,' said Lucian.

'Hopeless of us!' said Marina. 'Do let us help you, Serge.'

They always offered financial aid in this implicit way, never naming specific arrangements or figures at first. It had happened often before his inheritance at twenty-five, and occasionally since. A nominal loan morphed into a gift. Interest might be mentioned, in a lawyer's presence, and then forgotten. At some point his father might hand him a letter about this loan or gift, vaguely embarrassed, signed 'with love and affection'. Or he might not. Either way, the money would appear in Serge's account and Serge would try not to think about how much he had already received.

He felt their generosity calling now, promising to ease his dawn panics, letting him keep making films. All he had to do was thank his father profusely, and buy him a bottle of Dom Pérignon. He was aware of his parents waiting for him to answer. He remembered Daniel saying, 'I had to work, to get where I am.'

'Look, that's so kind,' he said. 'And I know this sounds extreme, but I've actually been looking into insolvency. Just, wiping the slate clean.'

He had not planned to say this, today, even though he had been googling 'company insolvency' for months.

His mother's elegant profile whipped round.

'Liquidation?' said his father.

'Serge?' said Marina, her voice rising. 'You don't mean it? You can't just wash your hands and carry on, you know. It counts against people for years!'

Serge knew she was thinking of her cousin Perry, whose gambling habit had rendered him bankrupt in a decrepit stately home.

'Look, I know it's not good,' said Serge.

His father made a characteristic noise between 'Ha!' and 'Oink'.

'But I need to fix this myself,' said Serge. 'It's actually not as extreme as it sounds. I wouldn't be able to start another company for five years. But once we sell assets—'

'What, Chiltern Mansions?' said Marina.

'No, Vanguard's assets.'

He paused, then made himself add: 'But obviously, I'd need to sell the flat.'

'Need to?' said Lucian. 'Surely that only applies to personal bankruptcy? Individuals?'

'No, they were wonderful about that with poor Perry,' said his mother. 'The revenue, or the bailiffs or whoever it is. They let him keep Felhurst, though I believe he had to sell Beaufort Square. I suppose it was actually *more* valuable!'

She laughed slightly wildly, as if the idea of a Chelsea town house costing more than a castle was hilarious.

'Right, no, I'm not legally obliged to sell,' said Serge. 'The flat. But the mortgage, and everything, it's not sustainable.'

He stopped, hearing the weakness in his voice. He did not want to explain how he had emptied his personal accounts, or how liquidation would only cover his tax bill and Vanguard's payroll. He would need the full £800,000 from the sale of the flat – after paying off the mortgage – to pay his other debts across the industry. His parents would never understand how badly he wanted it all paid, in full. They would never accept that he could not happily sit in a Marylebone mansion block while people went unpaid, and his team lost their jobs. They would say it was life – or 'the film business' – that it was not dishonourable.

'The flat's not ideal,' he carried on. 'For us. The twins. All the stairs. No outdoor space.'

He realised that he had used 'us' automatically, planning out loud for a future with Isla.

'Well. Now. Hold on. Isn't the flat in both our names?' said his father cautiously.

'It's in my name,' said Serge. 'We changed it on the land register. When Isla was pregnant.'

It had felt like a step towards full independence at the time. He cringed at his own naivety.

'Yes, but, darling,' said Marina. 'It's still the family flat. It's not just yours to jack in.'

'Where would you move, anyway?' said his father.

'The property market's hopeless,' said Marina, as if they were having their own conversation in the front. 'When Virginia was looking for Caspar it was a nightmare, just all these ghastly new blocks. The trouble is it's all oligarchs buying up the middle of London and nobody else can afford even the rather poky houses.'

Serge forced himself not to react. His mother had no idea how she sounded, and though this was a fault itself, there was no point in saying so. Particularly when she had just offered to pay off his debts. The way money kept the family hierarchy intact was his own peculiar burden.

'I don't know where yet,' he said. 'I, we, haven't started looking.'

'But, Serge, I don't think you understand,' said his mother. 'We're offering to help! And if you stay with us you can have lodgers in the flat – you wouldn't even have to sell! Or declare insolvency, for Christ's sake.'

She sounded exasperated. It was unsettling for the three of them to be in such explicit disagreement. There was no point explaining that tenants would not solve his problems. Rent and mortgages were unknowns to his parents. Her notion of 'lodgers' was so theoretical as to be romantic.

'I do understand,' he said. 'I've had this on my mind for ages. But it's my problem. And this is my only option at this point.'

The weakness in his voice had tipped into churlishness. He hated himself for even having this conversation with his parents, from the back seat, as an adult. He would have cancelled himself, if he could have.

'Serge, come on. Don't be obtuse,' said his father. 'You've made enough rash decisions. Have you even had any decent advice on this?'

Lucian only threw out 'obtuse' in extremis. Serge hadn't heard it for years, though it had frequently been levied at him as a teenager when he had tried to defend Marxism.

'I'm not being obtuse. I want to help myself.'

'You're declaring bankruptcy to make a point,' said his mother. Her voice was shrill.

'Please stop talking to me like a child!' said Serge, knowing he was proving her right.

'Just stop the car, OK? I'll get an Uber,' he added.

Lucian braked, without looking round, and Serge got out. He had known any reference to an app would free him.

'Don't slam the door!' shouted his father, as if they had all been transported back to 1999 when Serge was cautioned for having MDMA in his Aquascutum coat. He remembered Marina saying, 'I thought *Allegra* was the difficult one!'

He stared at the Uber app failing to load, to avoid looking at his parents. He could hear them talking sharply to each other in the car before driving off, stirring up the chalky ground. He stood at the side of the road as the dust dissipated, staring at the blue sky.

Another car was approaching. He stood back, and then saw Isla through the windscreen. He waved, and she stopped. One of JP's cousins was in the passenger seat. Isla opened the window.

'What are you doing?' she said. 'Where are your parents?'

'They had to go on ahead. Can I get in?'

He wedged himself between the twins, his elbows encroaching on their laps. The car smelled of bananas and wet nappies. It was deeply comforting.

Isla explained she was giving JP's cousin a lift to Aix, and Serge used the woman's presence to avoid explaining his own. He wondered what she must think of his appearance, like a hitchhiker in his own family.

As they drove, he realised that he had never thought of Isla and the twins as his family before. The word had always meant his place in relation to Lucian, Marina and Allegra – at the bottom of a Campbell family tree.

Des Beaux Jardins Yoga Retreat

Vauvenargues

5.30 p.m.

The reception desk at the yoga retreat smelled of aromatherapy and rattan. Candles were burning, even though sunlight poured through the patina doors. A small, wiry woman behind the desk smiled beatifically, and handed Rosie a long disclaimer about injuries. Then she explained that the retreat recommended guests hand in any screens on arrival, still smiling, even though it sounded like an order not a suggestion.

On her home screen was a new message from Imogen, who had missed the brunch to fly home – bemoaning her domestic obligations. The message said:

> Hugo just sent me this!!! Can't believe I missed!

Below, was a video captioned 'I'm a celebrity, get me out of here.' At first, it appeared to be of Hugo's baby on a mat at the pool party. But behind, Daniel Pyke could be seen, shouting, 'Go fuck yourself!' The camera moved upwards sharply to capture him hurling kedgeree into the pool. She saw, now, that Hugo had sent her exactly the same message, accompanied by multiple spiral-eyed emojis. She wondered how many other people he had forwarded the footage to.

Rosie could still feel the woman at the desk, waiting. She felt even more reluctant to relinquish her phone now, as if it contained something urgent and dangerous. But she couldn't find the words to refuse. After a second she handed it over, and watched the woman lock it up with other hostage devices.

She walked into her room's drab silence, trying to feel peaceful and yogic. It was an odd combination of puritanical and luxurious, with a rigid, orthopaedic pillow on an emperor-size bed. She lay down. The sadness that had overcome her, at the barbecue, had settled into a leaden feeling of regret. Of what, though, she could not say.

She was still glad that she had explained about the cufflinks. She was even proud that she had confronted Serge at the wedding – despite his response. And she knew she had been right to reject the surrogacy. But she couldn't shake the uneasy sense that she had recently made a terrible mistake.

A bell rang outside – dinner was early at the retreat, to aid digestion. She braced herself to go and eat plant-based food with other women who were also trying to convince themselves they were happy.

The meal was served outdoors, under a canopy of wisteria. The woman from the front desk was bringing out a huge tagine. She was followed by a sinewy man with a top knot, bearing salads. He introduced himself as Hendrik, and set out the expectations of the retreat in a strong Dutch accent. All along the table, women nodded dutifully and laughed at a token joke.

It occurred to Rosie that she was not even considering whether she met Hendrik's approval. Nor was she experiencing the fraught imperative to charm her fellow guests, that she usually felt around strangers. Instead, she felt bored and vaguely rebellious.

When the welcome stopped, Hendrik sat opposite her with a mound of chickpeas and began speaking to a puppyish woman on her right. Rosie noticed how often the woman dismissed herself, with whinnies of laughter, while Hendrik treated her to his Mona Lisa smile. Eventually the woman seemed to run out of things to deplore in herself, and enquired how he had become a yoga teacher.

'I was an addict,' he said, simply. 'Am, an addict.'

'Addict?' said the puppyish woman, in alarm.

'Yes. And, indeed, this is now my drug. Yo-ga.'

'Oh! That's so interesting! How did you, er, make the switch?'

'Over dose.'

He pronounced it like two words, looking up at the woman, daring her to be shocked.

'Hit rock bottom, I think they call it,' he carried on. 'Pissed off my friends, my family, everyone. I was a mess.'

The chickpeas in Rosie's mouth became even mealier.

'But then,' he gestured at the female instructor, 'I met Francine, found yoga. And I got hooked on that, instead of cocaine. So, long story short, here we all are.'

The puppyish woman made a delighted noise, as if he had described meeting at a garden party. Rosie excused herself, and left the table.

* * *

In her room, alone, she felt agitated. The idea of Hugo Ranger forwarding the clip of Daniel's 'diva moment', indiscriminately, disturbed her. If Serge could go viral, Daniel's ridicule might be global. And, unlike Serge, Rosie wasn't sure Daniel could survive it.

She washed her face, thinking of his bloody nose in the cloakroom and his pulsing veins as he ranted by the pool. He had appeared deranged, right up until he said to Rosie, 'You would have told me, once.' She had looked away because he had suddenly seemed lucid, and this was harder to stomach than his delusions about her and Serge.

But hadn't Daniel always been insatiable – addicted to something? Wasn't he always searching, or running from something? She brushed her teeth, thinking how he was invariably the first to finish his drink, and the last to stagger home. He had once described a feeling he called 'The Nothingness' that sounded, in retrospect, like disassociation. He had always been trying to fill a void, and she had always looked away.

Looking out at the apricot sky, the panicked feeling grew – as if she were wearing a very tight bra. She thought back to an evening during their first term at Oxford. She and Daniel had been sitting in his too-tidy room, eating the Jaffa Cakes his mother liked to send, when he had explained about his father's suicide. His eyes had filled as he spoke – as they often did – his emotions always so near the surface. It was the reason he was a good actor. But it had unnerved her. She feared she had upset him, and had shied away from asking again.

Rosie thought now of the yoga instructor referring to an overdose. She imagined hearing that Daniel had done the same – intentionally or accidentally. It did not seem impossible. She knew exactly how she would feel, for the rest of her life, if the next time she encountered Daniel was his funeral. She had a cold feeling that she was not catastrophising.

She had abandoned him once. She had chosen Serge, in the *Bursary* fall-out, when she should have defended Daniel's right to be annoyed. She had known it at the time, but she could not bear to align herself against Serge – to risk Serge's rejection. This time, she would not look away.

But there was only one person who would know what to do, or how to help, and Nate was far away. And she had no phone.

The Courtyard

Hotel Georgette

8 p.m.

The night sky was vast and glittering. Isla was sitting beside Serge at the hotel's courtyard bar. All day she had kept silently returning to his confession, wondering whether she might have some kind of delayed reaction to the news that he had slept with Rosie. But she had not, and she felt – now – that she would not. It was, as Serge had said, a different time. Juno and Huck were asleep in their cot, the baby monitor propped up on the bar.

'Can you not just accept this help as an early inheritance?' she said now, having listened to Serge's account of declining his parents' offer. 'And have your dad write it off his will? It's going to be yours one day, anyway.'

He was picking at the label on his Coke. She noted automatically that the cut on his temple had scabbed, as if she were checking continuity on set. Her refusal to take the zombie job now seemed stupid and entitled.

'But that's basically still a handout,' he said. 'Like, exactly what my grandpa didn't want. The safety net.'

'What, so you have to teach your way out of it?'

It was meant as a joke, a reference to Sterling Campbell's insistence on 'a trade', but Serge looked deflated. For a moment she considered how and where they could live, he teaching, she doing the zombie series or whatever work she could get. At the same time, she realised she was thinking of them as a unit.

'Teaching would actually be all right,' said Serge. 'At least I'd be contributing something. Not stuck in development hell. Or making bloody content. It's my mess to fix.'

His jaw was stubborn now, like Huck's when he was determined to play with the bread knife.

'Yeah, but it doesn't just affect you. Your mess. What if you accept it for the twins? Can you look at it that way?'

'But I don't want them to grow up like me. Always counting on my parents to bail me out.'

She thought of her mother's erratic love – affection undercut by demands, or forgotten plans.

'That sounds pretty great, to me.'

'I know, silver spoon.'

'I didn't mean that. I just think if you can give the twins stability, you should. We should.'

Serge looked round at 'we'. She remembered the way they had edged closer to one another, when Daniel was yelling by the pool. Daniel's scorn had shocked her. He hadn't seemed vindictive, until then, but the way he had interrogated Rosie had been cruel – or perhaps just insane.

'Is all this because of what Daniel was saying?' she added. 'The privilege stuff?'

'No! Maybe. Partly.'

'What actually happened with you two?' she said. 'All that about *Bursary* and Allegra?'

Serge slumped forwards.

'OK. Basically, we came up with a really early prototype of *Bursary*, together. Before finals. And yeah, we had these big plans to make it together. But then he screwed my sister over.'

'Screwed her over how?'

'She came to this ball at Oxford, just before we left, and they kissed. Which should never have happened! Like, you don't go after your friend's younger sister.'

Isla thought of her conversations with Daniel about being an only child. It had taken her years to understand sibling dynamics.

'Then he took her number – so she thought this cool, older guy was interested – but he just ghosted her,' said Serge. 'And her eating issues started up again that summer, in Italy. She'd pretty much recovered, and then she had this massive relapse.'

'How d'you know it was cos of that?'

'Cos she was crying on me, about him. All summer. She was convinced it had something to do with her weight. And food was such a big thing in Italy, so it was really obvious when she stopped eating. Like, she and I, we'd always go to the same places, order the same thing. My parents were freaking out. They tried to get help when we got back, but it was too late. So I always felt like, if Daniel hadn't messed her around, at this critical time, she might not have relapsed.'

He swallowed.

'Shit. That must have been so hard to watch,' she said.

'Yeah. It was. It still is. And he never even acknowledged it – that they kissed. He was just messaging me, like normal, inviting himself to Italy, angling to meet Miles. When obviously Daniel was the last person I wanted at our house – around her.'

He was speaking more quickly now, as though he could still access his young indignation.

'So what, then you made *Bursary* without him? With your godfather?'

'Kind of. I ended up telling Miles about the idea, in Italy. It was just this organic conversation. And the thing was, Miles wasn't even that into it. He was telling me all these things I should change.'

'But you never told Daniel? About this conversation?'

'No. Cos I was so pissed off about Allegra. And by the time I was back from Italy he'd moved to LA anyway.'

'Go on.'

'So, then I pretty much took it on myself. The next two years, while I was doing my teacher training. Made all Miles's suggestions, wrote the script, went back to him. And by then, it was this completely different film. The lead was fifteen – Daniel was too old to play it. And it was much more about private education, this whole British north-south divide. And at that point, Miles really went for it.'

She could see it all now. How Daniel must have resented the way doors opened so easily for Serge, or perhaps the way Serge had shut a door in Daniel's face. But she felt for Serge too. She had never realised how protective he felt towards his sister – how anxious Allegra's issues made him. He looked tired and unsure, his back still hunched in a c-shape.

'Maybe it wasn't fair. To blame Daniel,' he said. 'Maybe she was more fragile than I wanted to think. Like it was waiting to happen.'

'Well, you only had her word against his. But yeah, it sounded like it was all news to him.'

'I know. Should have talked to him, I guess. Instead of just cutting contact.'

He tailed off. She wondered if he, like her, was thinking how this point could apply to the two of them and their impulsive split.

'Yeah, well, look. He went way too far today, anyway.'

'He's clearly ill, though. That's the thing. He's messed up too. I had no idea he felt that way about Oxford.'

'What, the Pikey thing?'

Serge tipped his head back and exhaled.

'Yeah. It was pretty off, looking back. All these public school idiots taking the piss out of his accent, his clothes. Obviously I wasn't part of that. I just used this stupid nickname. But I didn't stop it, when I could've. I think that was actually why I lost it with that guy, after the SOFAs. Cos I never really stuck up for Caspar at Oxford, either. Not properly. They were dicks to him, too.'

It was strange to hear Serge refer to the man he had hit in the street. Isla had only ever seen the incident as an act of drunk machismo, a final straw between Serge and herself. She leaned sideways into him, her head on his shoulder, trying to show she didn't blame his twenty-one-year-old self for anything.

They sat this way for a while, feeling the unsaid warmth of all their other reconciliations, the roundabout way they always made up – Isla slowly conceding, Serge gradually opening. The trial separation felt notional, after the maelstrom of the weekend. She had never really detached from Serge.

Her phone pinged several times, with three messages from her mother.

> Babe! You OK? And Serge? Make sure you hold space to talk. Sending metta.

> Also, a favour, could you get down to mine asap and forward the post? Think the bastards at HMRC are after me. No plans to come home tho, so they can piss right off! Big love xx

> Also when your there can you check gutters? Bloody neighbours sending daily updates. Ta

She felt the push–pull that her mother's communication always provoked, and replied:

> Will do x.

She knew brevity would rile Saffron, just as the clash of concern and demands had riled her.

'What's she saying?' asked Serge, glancing at Isla's phone.

'Basically asking me to be her PA. Because she's not planning to come back for ages. But now I'm thinking,' she paused, remembering her conversation with Daniel about the West Country and how much she missed it.

'Maybe I should just take the zombie job, and stay on at hers? With the twins.'

Out loud, the plan already sounded formed.

'At your mum's?' he said.

'Yeah. They're filming in Devon, so it actually makes sense. Or more sense than commuting from London. I mean, the house is a dump but it's free. And there's a childminder in the village. I chatted to her a few times, in the playground. She was really good with the twins. And they love it there, running around outside.'

The plans seemed to be pouring out of her – Serge's crisis and quandary forcing decisiveness.

'I've been feeling like this isn't working for a while,' she said.

'What's not working?'

He looked round, alarmed, as if they might be going backwards.

'Everything. London. The flat. Me, still at home full-time with the twins. I'll be better when I'm with them if I can get some time to myself.'

'I thought you didn't want them in childcare?'

'They've got each other. That's the handy thing with twins.'

'When were you going to tell me all this?'

'I just thought of it now! And we haven't been talking, remember?'

'You know I never wanted that.'

'Why didn't you call, then?'

'Isla, you asked me not to!' said Serge, though he sounded more fondly exasperated than angry.

A waiter switched on a string of fairy lights, giving the bar a festive air, and set a bowl of olives between them. Isla popped one into her mouth, answering his protest with innocent eyes.

'So this plan to move into your mum's,' said Serge. 'I'd come too?'

He turned on his stool to face her fully, his expression hopeful. She remembered feeling drunk on kissing him.

'Yes. Of course.'

He was about to say something – perhaps 'Zummerzet?' in the comedy Somerset accent she had once banned, but a wail erupted from the baby monitor. Serge said 'Juno,' and stood up. She had not realised he knew the twins' subtly different cries. He walked over to their suite, and Isla heard him open the door and then his voice through the monitor. She knew he would have forgotten she could hear him.

He started saying, 'It's OK, Juno. You're OK. Dada's here.'

Each time he spoke the arc of light on the monitor flashed green.

After a minute, Juno stopped crying.

Courtyard Suite

Hotel Georgette

11 p.m.

Serge sat on the sofa, listening to the twins' steady breathing. He had been up with them alternately since Juno's first cry, both of them unsettled by the heat and party food. He had now sung 'You Are My Sunshine' so many times it had begun to sound like a torture technique. Both twins were now asleep, but his mind was sharp and industrious and he knew he would not be able to himself.

He walked past Isla, pausing to look at her in the bed. She slept in the same position as Huck – on her side with her hands clasped, as if she were praying. They had not been able to resume their conversation at the bar. But Isla choosing the bed, over the sofa, said enough.

Outside, on the veranda, the moon was very round and bright. Sitting in a deckchair, he thought about Isla urging him to accept his parents' help, for the twins. He wondered now if he had ever truly believed in the liquidation fantasy. He feared it had been another juvenile attempt, like fleeing the wedding, to manufacture a hero's journey.

He took his phone and opened a text to his mother, hoping she was awake and knowing he was already forgiven. He wrote:

> Ma, I'm really sorry about earlier. Wasn't thinking straight, had a weird day ... Could we meet tomorrow? Would be good to chat. Sx

Almost instantly, she replied:

> Dearest Serge, don't worry. Understood. Do come to our Air B and B, ten-ish? Pa will send u the address as a text message. Xxx.

He sat back in the chair. A fondness for her formal texts, and for both his parents, welled in him. He thought of Isla describing his sense of a safety net as 'pretty great'. He had always seen his privilege as material, but he wondered now if his real fortune was his parents' constancy. The twins' childhood would never be as gilded as his own, even if he accepted an early inheritance. But he hoped he could provide the same steadfast presence in their lives.

He opened his email. It was time to write to Rosie, to acknowledge everything she had said at the wedding. For a while he tried to recollect her exact words, but then he realised he knew it himself. The relationship had always been at arm's length. He had never let her in, knowing he was not committed. From the first kiss he had felt something was off, but everyone had seemed so happy for them, that he had ignored his instinct. Once, he had expressed doubts to Caspar, but his cousin had implored him to 'give it a chance', protesting that 'slow burn beat fireworks'. It wasn't Rosie's fault. Serge had never stopped enjoying her company. But the relationship had always been an imitation of a couple, just as their friendship had never been truly platonic.

And yet, he thought, his Gmail account predicting her email address, there was something to salvage. It had been wrong to cut all contact. He felt so warmly towards Rosie – the way he knew his parents felt for their old friends. They were both approaching forty. The idea that they had history was no longer a childish attempt to sound adult. They did have history. They knew things that nobody else did.

He remembered their nostalgic laughter over the speech, the first time he had really laughed in weeks. Almost at the same time, he thought of Daniel and Isla giggling together on the sofa – how the image had crushed him, the way Isla might have been crushed to see him and Rosie in the bookshop. Perhaps nothing was clear-cut. All he knew was that, beneath all the upheaval of the past eighteen months, he was still certain that he and Isla were meant for each other – and that she felt the same.

He returned to the email, and the saddest part of Rosie's confrontation. The idea of her mourning something that might or might not have been a miscarriage, alone, was painful. There was something so characteristically Rosie about it – the uncertainty, the internal panic, the reluctance to cause a scene. Or perhaps, typical of a younger Rosie. She seemed able to speak up now. He could not deny his relief that she had not been pregnant, but he felt for her still.

He started to write. Several times he caught himself veering into platitudes. At one point he wondered if he should arrange to meet her in London, so that he could say sorry in person. But then he realised he was imagining what he would want, in her place. Rosie would prefer a written apology, to be analysed in private, without pressure to be gracious. He re-read it a few times, and pressed Send. The lightness this produced was fortifying.

He began drafting another email, almost on impulse, as if he needed to finish what he had begun. This time he did not enter a recipient, for fear the message might somehow send itself prematurely. At first he couldn't get beyond 'Hi Daniel', because every time he started a sentence he deleted it. He tried writing the middle, first, and then went back to the opening. He kept thinking of his conversation with Isla in the courtyard about 'Pikey', and remembering the way Daniel had echoed Rosie – accusing him of silently aborting their friendship. After nearly an hour, his draft read:

Daniel,

I've been thinking about the things you brought up today, and I'd like to apologise. First, I'm sorry about the way *Bursary* happened.

Like I said today, I was furious with you about my sister. Whatever happened between you guys really got to her, and her eating disorder came back that summer. I appreciate that it was probably not fair to blame you. I only ever heard her account, and she was so young at the time. We all were.

When things actually began moving with **Bursary** you and I had not spoken for over two years. You were in LA, working. It felt weird to get in touch after not speaking for so long, and with my sister still struggling. I get why you were pissed off, though.

The fact that Reel wanted a major rethink made it complicated too. Perhaps I was loath to share that with you, in case you disagreed with their ideas, because I was willing to do whatever they asked just to get it made. If you've seen the film you'll know it's pretty different to what we came up with. I hope in view of your success, since then, you can let it go.

Lastly, I'm sorry if I caused you any pain at Oxford. You have every right to be pissed off about the way certain people treated you in college. And I can see, in hindsight, that what I dismissed as a joke – calling you Pikey – was tin-eared at best. I was old enough to know that. I should never have used it this weekend. All I can say, now, is that I get it and I'm sorry.

For what it's worth, I have great memories of hanging out together at St Arthur's. Going to the Everyman, coming up with terrible sitcom ideas, annoying everyone with our Danny Boyle references and conducting entire conversations in *Top Gun* quotes. We had some good times.

Still, I'm not going to pretend I can understand or forget the way you've acted this weekend. I really think you need help, and I don't think I'd be doing you a favour by pretending otherwise.

I hope you can find peace.

Serge

He knew it sounded clunky. But however much he moved the words around, the man-to-man tone clashed with the self-help jargon. He could not face acknowledging Daniel's flirtation with Isla. Perhaps his mother was right – some things were better left unsaid.

It was odd to feel so unsure of something he'd created. He entered Daniel's name experimentally in the To box. The wind kept bothering the shutters behind him. He pressed Send, and then immediately hit Undo. Then he pressed Send again. This time, instead of hitting Undo, he re-read it in his Sent folder, as if the words might have changed in the process of leaving his drafts.

He sat on the veranda for a while longer. It had become clear, in composing the email, that he used to envy Daniel himself. At eighteen, Daniel's evident talent and his lived experience of film sets – and of a notional 'real world' – had threatened something in Serge. Even Daniel's knowledge of cinema had felt undermining, for being self-taught. He wondered if he had been unconsciously looking for an excuse to cut Daniel out of *Bursary*, the same way he had never allowed their friendship to graduate from term-time contact. But he meant what he had said about their good times. He had missed Daniel, at times, over the years. He had never met anyone since who watched films with the same fanatical attention to detail, or was so willing to discuss these details for hours.

He went inside, and got into bed beside Isla. She was on her back now, snoring lightly, under just a sheet. He lay very close to her, thinking how they always used to fall asleep with her leg over his thigh and her head on his chest, until pregnancy made this impossible. He used to feel as if everything inside them, all the heat and blood and oxygen, was pumping around and through them both like one circuit.

After a moment she turned and shifted herself into this position in her sleep. He moved his arm so that it was around her, and felt her body pressed along his. Her hair was tickling his mouth, and he whispered 'I love you' into her scalp. She muttered something incomprehensible and moved her cheek so that it was directly above his heart.

Surrey / Southend-on-Sea, August 2004

Rosie and Daniel are speaking on the phone, from their respective teenage bedrooms. It is midnight, but still warm outside. They are both alone in their houses. Daniel drains a bottle of Carlsberg.

'This always feels so retro,' he says. 'The home phone. Thought I'd have to ask your dad's permission to talk to you, or something.'

'Is it?' says Rosie. 'I don't find it weird. I like the landline.'

'Don't pretend. You've blatantly got a list of conversation topics there.'

'You called me!'

'True. Where are you, then?'

'My room. Which my mother's just gutted. Army wives are ruthless.'

'Listen, I need your mum. I'm sitting in a bloody museum of childhood here.'

'That's nice! I'm going to keep all my children's drawings and reports and stuff.'

'Who said we're having kids?'

Rosie laughs.

'They'd be pretty cute, though, you gotta admit,' says Daniel. He walks downstairs to a neat kitchen.

'Anyway, can I get your take on something?'

'Sure. Is it Serge?' Rosie's tone has quickened. 'Still no reply?'

'It's kind of past that. I just spoke to Caspar,' he says. 'He was out there, in Italy. He heard Serge chatting about *Bursary Boy* with Miles Whitehall. Like it's all his idea.'

'Oh,' says Rosie, after another pause. 'That's a bit tricky.'

'A bit tricky? I'm fucking livid.'

'But, what was the context? What did Caspar actually say?'

'Just that he'd heard them talking about it. Our film. In detail.'

'That doesn't mean it's all over, does it?'

Rosie is standing very still, looking at a mirror but through her reflection.

'Yeah, it does. I mean, Caspar was backtracking like, "Oh, he'll be in touch, it wasn't official, blah blah." But he won't. I guarantee it.'

'He might?' says Rosie, weakly.

Daniel is leaning against the kitchen counter, kicking at a crack in the vinyl floor. He takes another beer out of the fridge and opens it with his teeth.

'Nah.' He takes a long, frothy gulp. 'I've sent him all these bloody emails, texts, whatever. Like, "Hey mate!" "Still up for it!" And he's just blanked me. So, yeah. Dead to him.'

Rosie doesn't reply. She is casting around her room now, as if she is torn about whose side to take. Daniel waits, watching his reflection in the window. When she does not speak, he begins to talk again.

'God, it sucks being back here. I always think, it must be so weird for Serge and Caspar not to have that thing of going home, and finding nobody gets them.'

'How d'you mean?'

Rosie sounds guarded.

'It just seems against the natural order,' he says. 'Like, the universal expectation is that you go off to uni, then you come back and it all looks small and shit and provincial. And your friends from school say you're a ponce, and you feel like you can't relate to your family any more, and they say you've changed. Right? But the Campbells, they don't get that. The disconnect. I don't think Caspar even had to stress about coming out. His parents were just cool with it.'

Rosie says, 'OK,' non-committally.

'I mean, obviously, it's not the same for you,' says Daniel. 'Not like you lost all your old friends, just by going to uni.'

'Did you? Lose all your old friends?'

'I mean, up to a point, yeah. But that's a whole other thing. What I'm trying to say is, us two, we both want more – or something else – to what we grew up with. Right? You've always felt different to your family. Your mum and dad. Kate. You don't want to be an army wife, do you? Whereas Serge and Caspar, they aren't trying to branch out, or forge their own path, or whatever. It's just all there, ready. The arts. Media. Music industry, film. I'm not saying it's good or bad. Just weird.'

Despite his assertion that this is not 'good or bad' there is a new bitterness to his voice.

'They still have to work, though. Serge works really hard.'

'Right. At his connections.'

Again, Rosie takes too long to answer.

'You're allowed to exercise critical judgement, y'know,' says Daniel. 'On Sergio.'

He has switched to a teasing tone, but Rosie's reply is sharp.

'I do.'

'Right. That's why you still lose the power of speech around him.'

'I don't—'

She is blushing, even though she is alone in the room.

'Look, I'm only saying this as a friend,' says Daniel. His tempo has increased, as if he has wanted to say this for a long time.

'It really bugs me to see you change – or, like, hold back – around him. You don't need to do that. For anyone.'

There is a silence.

'You change around him, too.'

Daniel looks surprised at the petulance in her voice. Then, in his usual jovial tone he says, 'So you're saying I'm gay? Seriously, I'd go for Caspar over—'

'No, the whole court jester thing,' she interrupts. 'You don't need to put yourself down, or point out the – I don't know – the differences. It's like you need to show you're in on this joke, but he's not making it. None of us are.'

Daniel doesn't reply. Rosie adds, as if on impulse: 'It's awkward.'

'For who?'

'Well, Serge mostly. Cos he's the one you do it to.'

'This is what I'm talking about! God forbid Serge should feel uncomfortable.'

Daniel sounds petulant now, wrestling with the door onto a small back garden. It opens, and he swears as beer slops on his wrist.

'Look, it's irrelevant anyway. It's not like we're all hanging out every day any more,' he says. 'I mean, Serge is clearly done with me. So, whatever. End of an era. Party's over.'

There is another pause.

'Well, I'm actually moving in with Cas,' says Rosie. 'He's got a room, in his flat. My commute's a nightmare. And expensive,' she adds, unconvincingly. 'So it made sense.'

'Oh. OK, I didn't know. I mean, he didn't mention it. But that's cool. Mates rates, is it?'

'I guess. We haven't discussed … We only just decided. But you're off to LA, soon, right?'

'If this part comes through.'

'Of course it will!'

They continue talking about the sitcom pilot, but something has changed. Their bright, conversational balloon – the one they have batted back and forth since freshers' week – has popped.

PART SEVEN

AUGUST 2019
TWO DAYS AFTER THE WEDDING

From: Caspar.Campbell@gmail.com
To: RosieLittleton81@gmail.com
Date: 2 September, 2019, 00:01
Subject: sorry / thank you

Hey dearest Rosie,

Hope you got to your yoga place OK. Just wanted to say sorry for putting you on the spot at the bbq and in case I made you feel bad, in any way. I guess we just thought you were going to say yes, and that it would end the weekend on a high. But obviously it only makes sense if you were into it. And I get what you said about three being a crowd. Don't think you'll get away without being a godmother, though!

Thank you so much for being an amazing Best Woman on Saturday, and jumping in to make the dramas slightly less dramatic. You're a wonderful friend, and I love you dearly.

Caspar X

Rosie's Room

Des Beaux Jardins Yoga Retreat

9.30 a.m.

Rosie had agreed to an early call to join sun salutations, but when the respectful knock came she had ignored it. She had slept badly, waking often in the sterile room, worrying about Daniel and wishing for Nate. She kept replaying his exit from the turret room, fearing he had been thinking of her rejection fifteen years earlier, and had left in a spirit of self-preservation. The thought was wretched.

Now she stood up, and opened the shutters and window just enough to look out. Women in expensive yoga clothes were having breakfast outside, saying 'thank you' and 'sorry' to each other, compulsively. She went into her bathroom and stood under the rainforest shower, so loud she could have screamed without anyone knowing, trying to disentangle the clump of emotion in her chest.

Ten minutes later she was at the reception desk. She felt a fake flustered apology forming, and an excuse for needing her phone. Then she stopped. She had paid. She did not owe the woman at the desk an excuse, or even a reason.

The woman smiled in a way that was both warm and artificial and said:

'*Bonjour! Ça va?*'

'*Oui, très bien merci,*' said Rosie. '*J'ai besoin de mon téléphone. Je peux le prendre?*'

The instructor's face fell, minutely. Rosie held her eyes.

After a moment, the instructor turned and opened the safe behind her.

Rosie directed her to the right phone in the nest of confiscated screens.

'*Voilà*,' said the instructor, grimly.

Rosie went out to the garden, walking far away from a row of obedient female buttocks in downward dog. She sat in an egg-shaped wicker chair, hanging from a tree, wondering why these adult swings seemed to be obligatory in places that claimed Wellness. The homogeneity was enough to induce mental health problems.

She checked all her messages, but she only had two new emails – one from Caspar and one from Serge. She registered that the name 'Campbell, Serge' in her inbox did not induce the palpitations it would have a few days ago. Instead, she felt crushed to find nothing from Nate.

She read Caspar's first, a sweet message about the surrogacy idea. She replied quickly, without too much thought, and opened Serge's email.

> Rosie,
>
> This is long overdue, but I wanted to say sorry – both for hurting you in the past, and the way I reacted to you on Saturday night. I also can't apologise enough for whatever you heard my sister say. The fact that you helped me and Isla, after that, shows how special you are.
>   When we broke up, it was never my intention to cause you pain. I ended our relationship because I knew that we weren't right for each other, and because you of all people deserve to be in the right relationship. I assumed you sensed it too, but I can

see now that I was wrong. I remember feeling like it would be so easy to stay together, and to avoid hurting you, because we had a lot of fun and you're so great. But it would have been weak too, because neither of us would ever have got the chance to be genuinely happy.

I hope you can see it from my point of view now. If I gave you the impression that I saw us having children I'm truly sorry. I was so focused on my career, at that time, that I honestly had no plans to start a family. I'm glad you told me about the miscarriage – or the uncertainty over it. I'm so sorry you went through that alone.

I was thinking about what you said about how we haven't been in touch, and I'd really like to change that. It's been so good to see you again this weekend.

I have always hoped that you are happy, and that you find someone worthy of you.

Serge x

She sat curled up in the egg, re-reading. There was satisfaction in hearing him acknowledge his selfishness, at last. She could not be sure if he really understood the pain he had caused her. Serge Campbell would never be able to relate to the agony of rejection, the way ordinary people could. But this only confirmed what he had said – and what she already knew – they weren't right for each other.

One day, she thought, they might find a way to be in one another's lives. Long before their failed relationship, she and Serge had come of age together. They still had all their noughties memories of *Neighbours* and taramasalata and Diesel jeans, and all the printed photographs – their faces luminously young. Perhaps that connection could live on, in a small way.

A class was happening on the villa's roof. She could hear an instructor's sibilant murmuring, telling the group to 'really feel your feet rooted to the earth'. She wondered whether she would do any yoga this week, or if she would keep hiding.

Rosie had asked for her phone to call Nate. She had no plan, no script, beyond telling him to turn around and come back. But now that she was able to call him, it seemed absurd – as if she were trying to live in a film. She sat staring into the middle distance, attempting to compose a message, watching cars pass at the bottom of the drive. Part of her wanted to run down to the road and beg someone to drive her to Nice where she might still find Nate.

After a while one of the cars turned into the drive instead of rushing past. It paused, apparently checking the address or location. Then it continued up the drive towards her until it slowed to a stop near the other parked cars. She expected to see another woman get out, with a yoga mat and a giant water bottle, and an armful of coloured bracelets like a teenager. But when the door opened she saw a man's foot and calf. Then she saw that the man was Nate, getting out of the car and staring up at the building.

He looked serious and purposeful. And then, just as she was about to call out in delighted surprise, he saw her and began smiling so much he was almost laughing.

She scrambled to get out of the swinging egg, laughing herself.

'What are you doing?' she called, when he was close enough to hear.

'I thought you might need company.'

They were facing each other now, and he held both her wrists in his hands and began kissing her as if it was normal. She dropped her phone on the grass, so that she could reach her arms up around his neck.

After a while she said, into his mouth, 'What about your trip?'

'I got to Nice, realised I made a mistake, and hired another car to come back. I wasn't even sure this was the place you said. If I'd known I could've just called you . . .'

He looked down at her phone.

'I'm not meant to have it. I asked for it back, to call you. I acted like it was an emergency.'

'It was.'

'So, wait, are you joining me? Here?'

'Would you like me to?'

'No! I mean, I hate it here. You'd hate it. I want to leave.'

He laughed.

'What, I'm just your getaway car?'

'No, I want to come with you,' she said.

'Let's go, then.'

32 East Street

Southend-on-Sea

9 a.m. UK time (10 a.m. French time)

'Look at me, Daniel,' said Cheryl. 'Love, look at me.'

They were sitting at the kitchen table, drinking strong, sweet tea. Daniel had arrived in Southend at midnight but had hardly slept – his mind cannibalising itself with regret. At seven, he had found his mother in the kitchen, unable to sleep herself, and had told her everything. It was the first time he had ever confessed his sudden ostracism in 2004, or the despair that routinely pinned him to his bed, or the way his drinking – and other habits – had spiralled with fame.

He looked at her, as directed. She was not wearing her usual earrings, which had been stolen, and kept saying that the burglary 'could have been so much worse'. He found this possibility terrifying, not comforting.

'Mum, I should be the one looking after you. This is all wrong.'

She was staring at him, as if the answer to a puzzle might be in his eyes. She wasn't thinking about the break-in, she was too worried about him, and this was worse.

'You're not well, Dan. We're going to get you help, love. Whatever you did at this party, whatever happened with your friends. I don't care. I love you no matter.'

'Caspar's going to hate me. Everybody will.'

'Danny, listen. We can sort this out. There are places that can help. You need a rest.'

'I can't. I'm booked all next year.'

The prospect felt like a cage descending around him.

'Camilla can deal with that. You've got a diamond, with her.'

'I can't tell her! About this.'

'Listen, you're not going to be the first person in showbiz she's seen like this. Or the last.'

He thought of his gushing conversations with Camilla, twinkling with gossip.

'Let me, then,' said his mother, in response to his silence. 'I've got her number!'

She said it like a joke, but he could feel himself succumbing. The idea of stopping work, disappearing from view – like a temporary, harmless death – was so appealing he could have wept.

* * *

Upstairs his bedroom smelled the way it always did – a ghost of Lynx, and something unnameable but almost painfully familiar. He opened the curtains, his Mulberry holdall full of expensive clothes at odds with the teenage surroundings. Cheryl had turned his old desk into a kind of shrine to his career. There were framed photos on red carpets dating back to *Riptide*, and a ring binder of magazine cuttings – as if Google did not exist.

The *Telegraph* profile was still waiting to be filed. He stood staring it, wondering how the wedding might have unfolded if he had never heard Jessica Blackwell's take on St Arthur's, and then at all the evidence of his success on the desk, pressure building in his chest.

On impulse, he opened the wardrobe and took a large storage box from the upper shelf. It was labelled 'Oxford work'. He opened it and started throwing wads of typed paper in the bin, barely looking at them. As he did so, he remembered the gulf between English at school and St Arthur's – the shock of discovering he was not exceptional, that a love of Shakespeare only marked him out as green. A page of his handwriting, alongside someone else's, caught his eye. He recognised it now as a sitcom that he and Serge had attempted to write, called *Freshers*. He recalled, at the time, thinking his bubbly letters looked gauche alongside Serge's italics.

He threw it in the bin, almost viciously, with the rest of his degree. Then he cleared all the photos and magazine cuttings into the box, and shut it back in the wardrobe.

The only thing left on the desk was a family photograph of his fifth birthday – Daniel centre stage, blowing out candles. His parents were behind him, beaming and applauding, radiating youth and good looks. A week later, his father had drunk a bottle of vodka and jumped. Gareth Pyke had been thirty-six, Daniel's age now. He wondered, looking at the photo, why he had even auditioned for *Knifepoint*.

He sat down and rested his head on the desk's MDF surface, blocking out his dad's smile. It was the same desk where he had practised his autograph, long before selfies, and revised for A-levels. Cheryl had thrown a party at Pyke's On The Pier when he got into Oxford. She had always maintained his father's IQ was genius level. The nothingness was circling, begging Daniel to detach from everything.

He checked his phone for distraction, and his guts contracted at Serge's name in his inbox. He opened the email, braced to hear that he was irredeemable – for Serge to claim the last word. But the message was uncharacteristically humble. Daniel read it twice, surprised by the sincerity and the remorse. He returned to the paragraph about Allegra. There was some comfort in finally understanding Serge's abrupt coldness in 2004. Daniel knew he should feel wrongfully blamed, but he felt more shocked – and sad – at the full story of Allegra's relapse and ongoing pain.

He thought of his short conversation with her on Saturday, behind the marquee. He remembered her saying, pointedly, "I was seventeen," before she walked off. He saw, now, how drastically he had misjudged her in 2004. He had noted her worldly manner and womanly body and assumed she was invulnerable, infinitely more sophisticated than him. But it had all been a mask. It was ironic, given how well she played the femme fatale, that she had failed as an actor.

He sat back, wondering what might have happened if he had given Serge his own account of the kiss, at the time. It was impossible to say whether Serge would have believed him. They might still have parted ways, with Miles Whitehall writing Daniel's character out of *Bursary*. Daniel might still have chosen LA, over a hypothetical British film. And Allegra had begged him to say nothing. He had thought he was respecting her wishes. The idea that he might scar her would have been inconceivable.

He re-read the rest of the email, squirming slightly at Serge's guilt over 'Pikey'. Again, he thought of Jessica Blackwell, and how she had warped his memories along with his quotes. When Serge had used 'Pikey' it had been thoughtless, ignorant perhaps, but not vindictive.

At the line 'We had some good times,' he paused. He saw the two of them passing popcorn in riveted silence, laughing too much at their own screenplays, engrossed in long dissections of films in Oxford's pubs. Serge was right – there had been real camaraderie, just as there had been with Rosie, and many other friends he had lost on moving to LA. Jessica Blackwell's view was just one side of a prism. His student years had not all been in a minor key.

And then the sting, 'I'm not going to pretend I can understand or forget the way you've acted this weekend.' Daniel knew that, yesterday, he would have read this as Serge 'lording it' over him. Now, he felt only fresh shame. He thought of his snide tweet, his spurious accusations about Serge and Rosie, the way he had homed in on Isla. In Serge's place, Daniel knew he would have been less generous.

He closed his eyes and saw the silver platter leaving his hands like a Frisbee, and wondered if he could stay in his childhood bedroom for ever.

Lucian & Marina's Airbnb

Rue de Vichy

11 a.m.

Serge found his parents' Airbnb, near Aix's university. It was in a surprisingly shabby modern block – but he remembered his parents booking accommodation late, having presumed they could stay at Villa des Pavots. When it had transpired that Caspar's parents were hosting JP's family – filling the whole house – Marina had been quietly piqued.

It was a shimmering day, their last in France. Serge had woken entwined with Isla, both of them a little surprised and almost bashful to find themselves this way. Then the twins had called, and they had jerked up like soldiers reporting for duty. Isla was waiting for him now, in Parc de la Torse, with Juno and Huck. He had left her sitting in the sun, looking hazy and relaxed, despite everything. The jibes on Twitter had stopped, at last, like a storm moving on.

His proposal to his parents ran in his head as he pressed their buzzer. The more he considered Isla's suggestion that he reframe their offer as an early inheritance, the more reasonable it seemed. Or – if not exactly reasonable – better than a handout. It was still a daunting prospect. Money had always been there, without him needing to ask.

The door opened into a communal hall, and he walked up four flights of stairs. Marina was standing on a landing that smelled of boiled vegetables and bleach. The flat was tiny, almost a studio. His parents looked out of place in its mid-century decor.

'This is cosy,' he said, diplomatically.

'Well, it's fine. The trouble is the kitchen's minute. We've been eating in the drawing room!'

His father said he would make coffee, and Serge followed his mother into the dim living area. They sat down on Ikea sofas.

'I really am sorry about yesterday,' said Serge, as soon as they were looking at one another. He felt that he needed to say it straight away, as if apologies were a new hobby. 'I know I must have seemed super ungrateful.'

'Darling, don't worry. You were tired,' said his mother. She looked at him with the same devoted expression she used to when he was a child.

'So Isla and I were talking,' he said, needing her to know that he and Isla were speaking again, 'and yeah, you're right, insolvency's a bit drastic. I just wanted to start over. But, if you're sure – obviously it's incredibly generous – I would massively appreciate some help. With the debts.'

His mother looked confused. He wondered if he had ever said sorry to her, so formally.

'But I was thinking,' he said, in a rush, 'God, this is weird to talk about, but – could we maybe, just, take it off Pa's will? Or your wills?'

'Our wills?'

He felt hot and awkward, referring to his parents' deaths.

'I just really don't want this help to be a handout,' he said. 'When this is my fault. So, yeah, I was hoping we could view it as, like, an early inheritance?'

His mother still looked confused and he saw that his suggestion sounded mercenary, even though he was technically asking for less – not more – than she had offered. This was why his parents never discussed family money, he thought. It was impossible to request anything without sounding insatiable or morbid.

'But darling, we didn't—' said Marina.

'Didn't what?' said Lucian, coming in with three cups.

'I was just saying, I'm sorry about yesterday,' said Serge. 'I was being an idiot.'

He looked his father in the eye. 'And we'd really appreciate your help, with the debts. I'd just prefer—'

'Serge, we didn't offer to pay off your debts,' said Marina.

She was looking at him as if she was concerned for his sanity.

'But you said—'

'I suggested you come and stay. At our house? So we could help you with the twins. And you could rent out the— Oh Christ, I'm sorry!'

She looked at Lucian, her eyes asking for support.

'Oh. Right, OK,' said Serge.

His mind was grappling to catch up. His father took a careful sip of coffee, staring at a Matisse reproduction hung too high on the wall.

'Serge, the trouble is, we're rather stretched ourselves,' he said. 'Various issues with the stock market. Investments. We had some hopeless advice. And La Brezza sold for so little. It may be that we need to think about selling Dorset. The roof cost a bomb.'

He tried to take in what they were saying. Nobody had ever mentioned problems with investments. He had noted the suddenness of the house sale in Italy, and his father's grumbling about the roof in Dorset, but not that either might carry high stakes.

'Well. All that, but also, Allegra's needed so much help, for years now,' said his mother. 'She's been, ah, she hasn't been well. At all. She had, well, she had a kind of breakdown.'

Marina sounded almost breathless.

'Last year. Just after the twins were born,' said Lucian.

'So we didn't want to worry you,' Marina added.

He remembered her jaded reference to 'therapy' in the car, and how she had said, after the twins' birth, that Allegra was at 'a sort-of health farm'. He had noticed his sister's emaciated limbs and empty eyes, but he had not registered a fresh crisis. He could not recall Allegra ever being in sound mental health as an adult, so that it had come to seem normal. It was a terrible thing to realise.

'And we've had to pay for everything. Because bloody Bupa had it all down as "pre-existing conditions", and the NHS – well, you'd be waiting ten years. The trouble is they have so many people who are completely loony. Schizophrenics or, which is the one we used to call manic depression?'

'Bipolar,' said Serge.

The refuge his mother took in semantics threatened to annoy him. Then he thought of Juno, and how his parents must feel seeing their daughter unable to bear daily life.

'You know we'd love to tide you over if we could,' she said, after Lucian had joked that the Priory cost more than a five-star hotel. They were aiming for black humour, as usual, but he could see they were desperate. He recalled his father taking the Francis Bacon etchings from the flat 'to be reframed'. They had never come back.

He thought back to the car journey, and how he had repeatedly heard the word 'help' as 'money'. It seemed incongruous that this small, bland room was to brand itself on his memory. This would be the place where he learned his life was not as he thought.

'No, no, I get it,' he said. 'I just, I had no idea she was so low. Or that you were, stretched,' he said, using his father's euphemism. 'You can tell me this stuff, you know.'

There was a pause as he thought how hypocritical this sounded – and then realised, like a punchline, that it was his parents who had taught him to keep any difficulty private.

'Oh, you mustn't worry about us!' said his mother, looking alarmed at this reversal in roles.

'Just not a huge amount of spare cash,' said his father, 'floating around.'

'Sure. Sure. How's Allegra now?' said Serge.

It was shameful that he needed to ask, he thought.

'Oh, up and down. Better than she was last year,' said Marina.

'Much better,' said Lucian, like a Greek chorus.

'Though she'll need, well, help, for a long time. So listen, we were talking it all over, last night, and of course you must sell the flat. Do that. We oughtn't to have put you off. We'd just been thinking—'

'We'll probably have to "downsize" ourselves,' said his father. 'If we want to keep Dorset. Or vice versa.'

Serge nodded and sipped his coffee, now tepid.

He wondered if his parents had been planning to "downsize" by moving into the flat, no doubt assuming Serge was planning to buy a house for his young family. He looked out of the grimy window, trying to absorb the fact that his parents could not save him.

'We'd still so love to have you to stay,' said his mother. 'All of you.'

'No plans to "downsize" yet!' said Lucian, the word apparently a joke.

'We were actually thinking of staying in Somerset, for a bit,' said Serge. 'Just while I sort stuff out. Saffron's away, and Isla's taking this zombie job. They're shooting in Devon. So it's easier from Isla's mum's than the flat.'

He had not expected to say any of this, the plan still being half-formed. There had been no chance to discuss it again, around the twins. But he realised, now, how badly he needed any plan with Isla, even if it involved squatting in Saffron's bungalow, while his life went into liquidation.

'Oh! Of course. Lovely for the twins,' said Marina. 'Well, anyhow, it would be so nice to see more of you, one way or the other. I don't really feel I've got to know Huckleberry and Juno, properly.'

'How d'you mean?' said Serge. His mother was rarely open this way.

'I suppose we've just been so preoccupied with Allegra. And Isla's always seemed so capable. But I hadn't realised, until this weekend, just how much she has on her plate. With twins. Far trickier than siblings.'

'Quite another proposition,' said Lucian.

Serge said he would tell Isla. He had never considered that his mother might feel tentative towards his children.

'And do let us know how you're getting on, won't you?' she said. It was typically opaque, but also uncharacteristically earnest. Serge promised and they began discussing a recent political scandal, for respite.

He opened the front door and stepped from the institutional-feeling hall into the brightness outside. Walking through Aix he found that he felt slightly floaty and unmoored, as if he had just received acupuncture rather than calamitous news. He would have to declare insolvency, after all. The luxury of creating his own films was over, probably for ever. Vanguard would cease to exist. And he would have to sell his home, if he was to do it right, the way he had pledged to.

He stopped outside one of Aix's art-house cinemas. After *Bursary* and *PLUR* he had imagined Vanguard growing and growing, like his godfather's company Reel. He had never even questioned the idea that he should keep doing what he loved. Now, he would either need to direct other people's ideas, or do something else entirely. He thought of Isla saying, 'You're going to teach your way out of it', jokingly, at the hotel bar.

After a while he turned away from the cinema, thinking of all the films he had hoped to make one day – all the situations and characters he wanted to bring to life. He passed the turning to the English bookshop, and recalled his attempts to get Daniel interested in *Beating Heart*. The idea of abandoning the whole project, all the people he would disappoint, was both overwhelming and a relief.

It was almost easier to focus on his parents' revelation. He was already anticipating Isla's shock and incomprehension. He knew that she had come to count on the Campbells' money. They had never discussed this, but he knew. He recalled the day when he had first confessed his inheritance, over Hugo's burgers. He had been craving absolution, having just slept with Rosie, and it had been easier to confess inherited wealth than infidelity. It was odd to think that this infidelity had actually accelerated his relationship with Isla, just as Isla's flirting with Daniel had brought their silent separation to a noisy close.

He turned onto the Cours Mirabeau, where so many people were busy pursuing their individual lives and dreams, thinking now of his sister and the years her mind had cost her. He paused at an ancient, imposing doorway, the entrance to Aix's commercial court. Two giant male stone torsos flanked the wooden doors, supporting a balcony on their heads with enormous, sinewy arms. They looked superhuman, and exhausted.

He stood staring at the statues, trying to visualise a different future. He pictured moving out of London, permanently, with Isla and the twins. He imagined spending so much time with his children that it stopped being special – every breakfast and bedtime and dentist appointment and school assembly. He saw Isla's talent and career taking precedence, and remembered what he had said himself the previous evening – about development hell, and the stress of independent film. He had been posturing, as usual. But he had to believe it now. He pictured daytime hours tutoring – perhaps teaching film at a college or university one day. It could all be so ordinary as to constitute a Campbell rebellion.

He considered this concept of ordinary rebellion as he walked on towards Parc de la Torse. It was not just the lifestyle that would be new. The imperative would be novel, too. He had chosen to do a lot – more than most people, and definitely more than most people with his privilege. But he had always had the choice.

He approached the street that led to Parc de la Torse. Isla had said she was in the playground at the bottom of the slope, and he quickened as he entered the park – the gradient forcing him into a jog. He spotted the playground across the grass, enclosed by a little red fence. It was full of noise and activity, and he strained to hear the twins' voices above the others.

He was almost running now, craning to see Isla and his children before he was even close.

Departures

Marseille Airport

3.30 p.m.

Serge had been in a strange, over-talkative state after seeing his parents. Isla could tell he was stunned, because at one point she thought he was about to laugh. Then he had begun to berate himself for not noticing his sister's crisis, and Isla had hugged him. For a moment, their bodies seemed to cheer and applaud at being against one another again.

They were approaching the airport now, Isla driving the hire car. Serge was quiet, so she joined him in his pensiveness. The clouds of money she had assumed were there, somewhere up above, did not exist. The conversations about his debt, whether or how he should accept funds from his parents, had been meaningless. And now, unexpectedly, Isla found she felt warmer towards Marina and Lucian. They wanted to know the twins, to help care for them, but their own adult daughter had absorbed everything.

'It's weird,' said Serge, as they stopped at a red light. 'Remember how last night you said it sounded "pretty great" to know my parents would always bail me out. I had this kind of epiphany after – nothing to do with money – that I've been so lucky. Just to have them, always there. Interested in me. And I was thinking, I really want the twins to feel that too. To just know we're there, wanting the best for them.'

Isla knew what he meant. He had grown up with consistent attention and it had helped to make him optimistic and curious – more so, perhaps, than his money. He was right to want the same for the twins. She wanted it for them too.

'But I haven't been that father. If I keep working like I have been, they won't ever have that feeling about me. So . . .'

'Maybe this could be the best thing that ever happened to you?'

He laughed, and she felt they were back in their old dance – one earnest, the other sarcastic, then switching round.

'Wouldn't go that far,' he said.

'I get it, though,' she said. 'And there's still time.'

She reached up to rub the back of his neck, a former habit of theirs at red lights. He leaned back like a cat being petted. They stayed that way until the lights turned green, and then drove on in easy silence.

As they parked at the airport, early, both their phones lit up with an initial round of wedding photos. For a while they sat, seat belts still fastened, scrolling through pictures of Caspar and JP looking besotted over the weekend – playing softball, at the opera, saying their vows and dancing. Serge looked up at her, his face cockier than she had seen for months, and said:

'So when are we doing all that?'

* * *

Their flight home was delayed. Ordinarily, Isla knew she would have felt this as a disaster. The hours in the lounge would have loomed, condemning her to a fractious journey and miserable homecoming. But now, it seemed surmountable. Serge was carrying Juno on his shoulders, Isla was restraining Huck with reins. They stood looking up at the departures board. She was about to suggest they each take a child, but Serge spoke first.

'OK, here's what we do. You go off, I'll stay with them here – watch planes, or whatever. And then come and find us at six, and we'll get dinner. There's a pizza place at the gate.'

His eyes were telling her to go, as Juno pulled his hair. She remembered the film set where they had met, and Serge's easy decisiveness from the first day of shooting. As she walked away the twins called, 'Mama!' but he distracted them, and they stopped. The lightness of wandering around Duty Free reminded her of how she had felt, briefly, dancing with strangers. But this was sanctioned solitude – she wasn't fleeing, or betraying, her real life. She hoped that work would feel this way, and not blighted with guilt.

She stood queuing for coffee, letting hurried people ahead of her. She thought how often she corrected Serge with the twins, but seethed when he asked for guidance. It had become an unkind joke with herself – asking him to dress Juno and Huck, knowing he would choose the wrong twin's clothes. And it had backfired. In declaring herself the sole authority she had rendered Serge incompetent, when his competence had first seduced her.

Across Departures she could see him with Juno and Huck, all pointing at something and then laughing. She knew, now, that she had wanted change – not severance. And change had come, or was coming, with all Serge's revelations. It was her turn to be candid. She still hadn't explained that she needed more help, every day. She hadn't wanted to hear herself say it.

From her café table she watched a plane taking off – enjoying the implausible lift, like a lorry launching into the air. She turned for a toddler to marvel with and realised, with a crackle of novelty, that she was alone. She thought how, just days earlier, she had seen herself as trapped in a three-man cell of love and demand. It seemed less accurate now.

A young man walked past, and made deliberate eye contact. She returned it for a single, flattering second, but then she looked past him and saw Serge across the lounge. He was reading aloud to the twins, one child under each elbow. Isla recognised the book by his gestures, though she had not expected him to know them.

She kept staring, her heart huge and unwieldy in her chest. She watched them for so long she expected them to feel her eyes, look up and wave. But they didn't, and in a way this was better.

Daniel's Bedroom

32 East Street

5 p.m. UK time

The landline was ringing, downstairs. Daniel heard his mother say, 'Coming, coming!' to nobody, as she hurried to pick it up. She sounded surprised as she said, 'Oh! OK. Yes, he's here. Let me get him for you.'

He sat very still, the way he used to listen to her phone calls from the stairs, hoping to hear something about himself. He tried to think who might have his childhood phone number.

'Dan,' she said, as he opened the door. 'Phone for you. Nate Kennedy?'

She pulled a helpless 'I didn't know what else to do!' face. He didn't want to take the handset, but she was almost pushing it into his hand.

'Y'all right?' he said, once Cheryl had closed the door.

Nate sounded tinny as he replied, speaking over the background noise of a public place. It made no sense that he knew Cheryl's landline, as if they were all in a dream. Nate moved somewhere quieter, and began again.

'Listen, I appreciate that this is out of the blue,' he said. 'But I wanted to talk with you. Today. I hope you can hear me out.'

Daniel knew what was coming. It was there, in the gentle but decisive tone.

'Go on,' he said.

'All right. So, listen, I'm here with Rosie. In Nice. At the train station. Sorry about the noise.'

Another miserable realisation groaned through him. Rosie and Nate. Daniel had seen him carrying a tray of breakfast things up to Rosie's turret, and still he had been convinced she was sleeping with Serge. He had misread the situation, like he misread everything.

'So here's the thing. We've been talking, a whole lot, about you,' said Nate. 'And Rosie wanted you to know that she has a lot of special memories of you guys goofing around together, at Oxford. With Caspar, and Serge. Like, I remember that, just from the sidelines. I used to envy you! But she was also saying how you two used to have these long phone calls, between semesters. How she used to call you on this number. Right here.'

Daniel waited for the inevitable 'but'. There was a rehearsed quality to Nate's voice, though he sounded very sincere too.

'But this weekend she saw, actually we both saw, that you were drinking quite a bit. And maybe using, because you didn't seem like yourself. The person she remembers.'

Daniel didn't answer. He wanted to ask why Rosie had enlisted Nate to speak for her, though he knew. He would not want to speak to himself, in Rosie's place. He had just accused her of sleeping with Serge, in public, in front of Isla. He was shocked Rosie was even deigning to contact him.

'And I'm just acting on her behalf, here, because, well, she wasn't sure you'd accept a call from her. After how you guys left it, at brunch. I mean, it sounded like things got a little heated. Plus, I'm in recovery myself. So, y'know, I get it.'

'Recovery?'

'Yeah. For alcohol,' said Nate. His voice was momentarily muffled by a station announcement, and then returned.

'I'm not—' Daniel began. 'I mean, I know I can—'

'Dan, chemical dependence is a disease,' said Nate, interrupting.

'It's not about stamina. Someone once said to me, and it really landed, you wouldn't try to heal a fracture with willpower.'

He was speaking slowly and calmly, as if to an animal that might bolt. The pressure was back in Daniel's chest and face, his eyes prickling.

'There's this place, the Lighthouse,' said Nate. 'It's a rehab facility. I basically owe them my life. They have one in LA. So, y'know, if you'd consider getting support, I would really recommend it.'

'Right,' said Daniel.

There was a pause. He heard Rosie say something, but not individual words.

'Can you, can you put me on speaker, mate?' he said. His voice was husky.

'Sure. You're loud and clear.'

'Rosie?' said Daniel.

'Hi, Dan.'

Her voice was tentative. He still couldn't believe she wasn't furious with him.

'How are you?' she said, after a second.

'OK. I mean, no. I'm not. Fucking hate myself.'

His voice shook, he sniffed as if he might inhale some self-control.

'Listen, we all respect you, buddy,' said Nate, intercepting again. 'None of us, nobody wants to see addiction stealing from you like this. You have so much to give.'

'We could send you the link. To the place Nate went?' said Rosie. 'I have your new email. From the wedding stuff.'

'Uh, yeah. Yeah, OK. So you remembered this number?' he said, trying to sound normal, his eyes brimming.

'Yeah. Somehow. I realised I don't actually have your mobile.'

'That's mental. That you remembered, I mean.'

He wanted to apologise for how he had behaved by the pool, but he couldn't seem to begin.

There was another booming station announcement.

'Listen, buddy, we need to go. We're gonna be on a train for the next few hours,' said Nate. 'We just wanted to catch you. Today. I'll send you that link.'

'Right. *Bon voyage*,' he said, and Rosie said '*Merci*!' as if she hadn't just staged an intervention via her new boyfriend.

He remembered suddenly how he and Rosie used to laugh at exactly this kind of social awkwardness, Rosie imploring him to act someone unsure whether to kiss on two cheeks or one, and Daniel berating her for laughing too much to act her part.

The link came through, minutes later. He lay down on his old bed and began scrolling through the Lighthouse website, looking at photos of empty beaches and rolling lawns alongside quizzes headed 'Do You Have A Problem?' The rooms looked like a Premier Inn at a glance, and then on inspection like a private hospital. He closed the tab, and turned his phone face down.

He thought back to the last time he and Rosie had spoken on the landline, their quietly disastrous final call. It had been another muggy August night, the same phone number, the same house. He recalled the first blow – Rosie silently taking Serge's side over *Bursary* – then their mutual mean-spirited accusations, then the news that Rosie was moving in with Caspar. Afterwards, he had stood in the garden in shock, as if a romance, or lifelong job, had ended without warning.

Looking back, Daniel wasn't sure why he had resented Rosie's siding with Serge so bitterly. Perhaps it had stung because he had understood. He had craved Serge's approval too. His own craving emerged in his bullish teasing and secret comparisons – where Rosie's showed in her blushing laughter – but it was the same impulse. Everyone had wanted to be close to Serge Campbell, perhaps even to be Serge. Loved, without having to try. Things were different, now. Even Serge had to try.

He thought of Nate looking so wholesome, so unlike an addict. But he had not seen Nate and Rosie as a couple, either. He had been so blind. Stupidly blind, again. And yet, Rosie still cared. Even after the way Daniel had spoken to her, by the pool, she had not given up on him. He could say sorry in reply to the email. That would work, he thought. He could say it in the right way, instead of trying to speak over a station announcement.

Rain began to flick the window – a British kind of rain, persistently feeble, different to Californian storms. He hadn't known he missed it. His old mattress was forgiving. He felt a deep fatigue, the closest he had come to peace for years. He needed help. But the help was there – out in the world, waiting for him. People were willing him to find it. He was not his father. It was not too late. As long as he was alive, it was not too late.

Hammersmith, June 2024

Fifty people are milling around a garden in west London. The late afternoon light is dim and watery. Caspar and JP move between their guests, handing round a magnum of Champagne and a baby. Allegra Campbell rings a Tibetan bell, and summons everyone to a pond, which is functioning as a kind of new-age font.

Allegra gives a short welcome address, explaining her role as a humanist ritual consultant, and offering her services for vow renewals, pet burials, sobriety anniversaries, the menarche and more. Rosie and Nate's four-year-old daughter asks loudly what the menarche is. Allegra's tone becomes conspiratorial as she replies that it is 'something magical' and promises to explain later. Lucian Campbell smiles valiantly through this exchange, avoiding anyone's eye.

Having named and blessed Silas Campbell Delahunt, and spoken at length about the beauty of adoption, and the way COVID delayed the process for Caspar and JP, Allegra asks the godparents to come forward.

Rosie, Nate, Serge and Daniel are among the line-up, looking pleased and dutiful. Isla stands back with Juno and Huck, who are eager to baptise their cousin with a water pistol. They are offhand with Marina and Lucian, almost rude, the way children are with very familiar adults.

After the ceremony JP cuts a cake and asks Daniel – jokingly – if he is planning to throw it in the pond. Daniel freezes, glancing anxiously at Caspar's mother.

'You aren't *still* beating yourself up about that, are you?' says Caspar, quickly. 'The Campbells love a food fight. Seriously!'

Behind Daniel's head, Caspar frowns furiously at his husband, who looks chastened.

Serge approaches, people standing aside to let him pass or stopping him to talk.

'Hey, man,' he says warmly to Daniel. 'We just binged *Freshers*. It's so good!'

He is referring to a BAFTA-winning TV drama, written and directed by Daniel. Serge begins analysing the final episode, and Daniel looks down humbly though his whole face has lit up. Caspar leaves to take the baby, but Serge and Daniel keep talking. They speak easily, with humour but without intimacy, as if they are accustomed to meeting at this kind of occasion.

Nate and Rosie appear, and conversation turns to their new home in upstate New York. Serge asks Rosie a question about renovations, revealing that they have spoken within the past year. After a while the four of them split into two pairs – Rosie and Daniel gossiping about Daniel's attempts to date, Nate asking about Serge's job teaching film at a local university.

The twins charge over and begin yanking Serge's wrists, which he doesn't seem to mind.

'So how'd you guys make it work?' says Nate, nodding at Isla. She is chatting to Marina, across the garden. 'Isla must be on location a lot, right?'

'My folks help out,' says Serge. 'They moved to Dorset, full time. So not too far from where we are, now. And obviously teaching fits round the kids' school. But, yeah, it's tough when she's shooting. The juggle is real!'

Nate laughs politely but catches Rosie's eye at this phrasing. Serge begins explaining his plan to make a documentary about twins. 'I've got so much footage on here,' he says, holding his phone.

'It's my little side project. One day. Not now. But some point.'

JP calls from the barbecue, and people begin moving in his direction. On his way, Serge intercepts Caspar. The Campbell cousins look less alike now, because Serge has lost nearly all his hair. He takes a small box out of his pocket, and hands it to Caspar.

'Christening present,' he says. 'Or, whatever – welcome present. For Silas.'

Inside is a pair of gold cufflinks, engraved 'S.C.'.

Allegra approaches Daniel, who is vaping alone by a magnolia tree. They are both holding non-alcoholic beers, and Allegra is eating a vegan burger. For a while they discuss her new career as a celebrant, and Daniel's move behind the camera. The conversation feels stilted with good manners.

'Thanks for your letter, by the way,' she says, after a pause. 'I always meant to reply.'

Daniel looks surprised, then nods and says, 'Of course.'

'I'm really sorry Serge gave you that impression,' she adds, in a rush. 'It was way more complex. Obviously. I explained that to him, too.'

'Right. Sure. He said the same, when he came to see me. In rehab.'

They make eye contact, and he adds, 'You look really well, by the way.'

'You too. I mean, no change there!'

There is another pause. In fact, Daniel looked glossier in 2019, when he had Botox and no beard. But he looks healthier now, too. Then he says: 'Well here's to quitting acting,' and they clink bottles.

The sky behind the chimney pots fades to violet. Someone puts on an early 2000s playlist, and people begin marvelling at the fact that their time at university was two decades ago.

Rosie approaches Daniel and Allegra. The two women smile, but then Allegra moves to kiss Rosie, who seems to instinctively withdraw – so that for a second Allegra is leaning into air. After a few banalities she excuses herself, and Daniel watches her walk away.

'She's actually all right, y'know,' he says.

Rosie pulls a sceptical face.

'She's changed,' says Daniel.

'Thank God.'

'So can I put Portaloo-gate in season two?' says Daniel, and Rosie laughs.

'Anyway, listen, we're going,' she says, looking at Nate who is hugging JP.

'But definitely come and stay. You can write in the cabin. Or not. Just come and see us.'

'I will. I'd love that. Any excuse.'

'OK, I'm going to send you dates,' says Rosie.

'Do that. Make me an itinerary.'

She hugs him, fondly, perhaps a little proudly.

'So lovely to see you,' she says.

'Likewise, babe. As always. So good to see you.'

Acknowledgements

I am extremely grateful to all the following people, for the many ways in which your encouragement, ideas, questions, answers, inside knowledge, attention to detail, loyalty, tolerance, wisdom, excitement, generosity, childcare and hospitality in Saint-Marc-Jaumegarde enabled me to write this book.

Tanisha Ali, Lucy Alder, Joe Barnes, Emma Beswetherick, Finlay Blackall, Laurence Blackall, Luke Blackall, Max Blackall, Oonagh Blackall, Pascoe Blackall, Anna Boatman, Jessica Case, Clementine Cecil, Stella Cecil, Sarah Chandler, Jill Cole, Caroline Collett, Bryony Cunningham, Gabriella Drinkald, Laura Cox-Watson, Ann Evans, Rachel Edwards-Stuart, Sandra Garcia, Charity Garnett, Olivia Guest, Claiborne Hancock, Mellis Haward, Angelo Hornak, Cosima Hornak, Laura Hornak, Leo Hornak, Michelle Hourihane, Jonathan Keates, Tatiana Kelly, Katherine Kingsley, Emma Knight, Tia Kulasuriya, Alan Mahar, Scarlett Mcpherson, Viva Mcpherson, Stephanie Morrison, Jessica Purdue, Lucy Punch, Lucie Sharpe, Cara Lee Simpson, Nina Rassaby-Lewis, Claire Rooney, Larry Ryan, Hannah Wann, Holly Watt and Hannah Wood. I would also like to thank all the friends and family whose weddings I may have unconsciously (or consciously!) drawn on.

I am especially grateful to three people. First, my mother Laura, for your confidence in me, your willingness to re-read nearly identical manuscripts and your infinite humour and sympathy. Second, my friend Laura Cox-Watson for your boundless enthusiasm, failsafe editorial judgement and eye for a dramatic scene. Lastly, my husband Luke, for all the above and more. This one, like everything, is for you.

Francesca Hornak is a writer and journalist, whose work has appeared in newspapers and magazines including the *Sunday Times*, the *Times*, the *Guardian*, the *Daily Mail*, the *FT*'s *HTSI* magazine, the *Economist*'s *1843* magazine, the *Evening Standard*'s *ES* magazine, *Marie Claire*, *Red* and *Elle*. Her fictional column History of the World in 100 Modern Objects first appeared in the *Sunday Times* Style magazine in 2013 and ran for two years, later becoming a book. Her first novel *Seven Days of Us* was a Radio 2 Book Club pick, and long listed for The Desmond Elliott Prize. She is also the author of the gift and humour book *Worry With Mother*. Francesca lives in London, with her husband and three children.